By Lewis Gannett

The Living One
Magazine Beach

MAGAZINE
BEACH

MAGAZINE BEACH

LEWIS GANNETT

HarperPrism

HarperPaperbacks *A Division of* HarperCollins*Publishers*
10 East 53rd Street, New York, N.Y. 10022

HarperPaperbacks may be purchased for educational, business, or sales promotional use. For information, please write:
Special Markets Department, HarperCollins*Publishers,*
10 East 53rd Street, New York, N.Y. 10022.

First printing: June 1996

Designed by Lili Schwartz

Printed in the United States of America

Library of Congress Cataloging-in-Publication Data

Gannett, Lewis.
    Magazine Beach/Lewis Gannett.
      p. cm.
    ISBN 0-06-105235-3 (hardcover)
    1. Terrorism—United States—Fiction. 2. Millennialism—Fiction.
  I. Title.
  PS3557. A517M3 1996
  813'.54--dc20   95-51567
                                        CIP

HarperPrism is an imprint of HarperPaperbacks. HarperPaperbacks, HarperPrism, and colophon are trademarks of HarperCollins*Publishers.*

96 97 98 99 ❖ 10 9 8 7 6 5 4 3 2 1

to Dad

Only those who have fled the world with pagan or Christian urgency, only those who have retreated into a fragment of soul whose origins lie elsewhere, in the beyond, only those who do not completely belong to this world are in a position to use the world and transform it with such efficiency and ruthlessness. And with that final transition to simply making use of the world we have arrived at an age that is neither pagan nor Christian, but that unknowingly continues to practice the same twin gesture of detachment and flight while sinking its claws into both earth and lunar dust.

The Marriage of Cadmus and Harmony,
Roberto Calasso
Tim Parks, translator

What is to be done? How is the race to be saved (I did not go into the more profound question of whether or not it *should* be saved)? My answer was simple enough: famine and war are now man's only hope. To survive, human population must be drastically reduced. Happily, our leaders are working instinctively toward that end . . .

Myra Breckinridge,
Gore Vidal

PROLOGUE

The icon came flying from space.

It penetrated the upper atmosphere, it dove further through howling wind and cloud. Then it hit the ice sheet.

The ice sheet didn't care. Vast, unfeeling, mute, it had been lying there, accumulating, for hundreds of thousands of years.

But on one of the higher plateaus, an instrument detected the icon. The instrument decoded. It processed. And in less than a millisecond of thorough cross-checking, it came to life.

A command, cable-borne, flashed vertically through the ice. Deep the command went, well over a mile, to a mountain that rose from the rock below. A volcano.

Millennia before, this volcano had erupted in open air. Now it slept in the sheet's stillness; the command flew down its cone, another three thousand feet to the bedrock, to the place where the device was waiting.

The device exploded.

On the surface, ice shuddered.

Two miles below, rock vaporized, ice vaporized, to a global diameter of several thousand feet. Beyond that, rock and ice melted more hundreds of feet, and the shape of the explosion began to change; for the rock, as the blast enlarged, yielded less willingly than did the ice.

This inferno—liquid rock, boiling water, and steam, cubic miles of it—looked for somewhere to go.

At the surface, ice bulged. Slowly it fashioned a gigantic dome. In the dome fissures appeared, from which vapor streamed.

Below, the explosion nudged a fault line in the continental crust. The fault slipped, releasing more energy, an earthquake. In all directions for hundreds of miles, the ice sheet shivered, its adhesion to the earth slightly undone.

The volcano's subterranean magma chute filled, and erupted. Lava smashed into the inferno, into the place where, moments before, a mountain had towered in an ocean of ice.

The dome on the surface disintegrated. A fiery cauldron, miles deep, miles wide, crammed vapor into the sky.

Gravity took hold. The inferno crept, downhill, toward the distant sea.

And so it began.

PART 1

FRIDAY

Toby was in the subway when he learned about the eruption.

He'd boarded the train at Central Square, one stop from his destination. Usually the trip took seventy seconds. Today, however, Toby was going nowhere fast. The train had slowed a few hundred feet out of Central. Then abruptly it ground to a halt.

Pagers bleeped. Telephones bleeped; soft voices answered. Not many people were riding at 3:48 in the afternoon. It was warm though, due to the heat wave that had delivered July three months early. Way ahead of the T's air-conditioning schedule.

Toby didn't mind the delay, at first. The trains of the Massachusetts Bay Transportation Authority often stopped midtunnel for no apparent reason. Most of the time they got going again after less than a minute.

But another minute passed. The quiet thickened. Toby and his fellow passengers studied the dark windows, the stilled murk of the tunnel beyond. They glanced at the policewoman at the far end of the car. Unconcerned, getting neither alarms nor bulletins from her comm unit, she yawned.

The passengers returned to their books, newspapers, computers, phones. A mild and prosperous bunch, Toby noted. Professionals, student professionals-to-be, some working poor, a few underclass types mixed in; cargo of a train come over the river from Boston, Cambridge-bound. Nearby, an elderly man in a slick suit watched TV on a laptop. His headset leaked audio: "From Singapore, this is Sun Business News."

Toby wondered what the man paid to get Singapore television via Net. Ironic, he thought. The "info-subway" had been wired to serve the masses. But the masses weren't availing themselves of its more wondrous capabilities. The Net's high-end bandwidth was just too expensive.

More minutes passed. Toby craved an activity besides staring at adscreens, or into space. Why didn't he have something to read?

He relaxed his grip on the overhead rail, dropped his backpack to the floor, and sat by the gent catching up with Asian business developments. Should have walked, he thought. He hadn't because the restaurant needed him in a hurry. Now it seemed walking might have been faster. Cooler too. His shirt was starting to stick.

That reminded him of the haste with which he'd ironed it. Which reminded him of the circumstances at his apartment. Dan and Selma, sleeping to midafternoon.

Toby's brother Dan had arrived for a visit three days before. Toby's roommate Selma, who'd never met Dan, instantly had proceeded to become his best friend; not a surprise, given Dan's charm, good looks, and unavailability. At any rate they'd bonded, and now were expending energy on two causes. The more important involved staying out late in tawdry nightclubs. The other was the question of what to do about Toby's birthday.

Which was today. Toby had turned twenty-six at 7:04 A.M., according to astrologically minded Dan. The significance eluded Toby. The whole birthday business, a reminder of Nadia and other unfortunate subjects, happened to be something he'd rather forget.

Dan and Selma didn't grasp this. Thus when a call came out of the blue from work, Toby hadn't hesitated. Sure, he'd go in.

The stalled train was delaying that plan. Above the windows, infomercials swirled on the adscreens. On most of them. Some weren't working, despite their supposed indestructibility. Toby wondered if loose wires were at fault, or vandals. Luddies, perhaps? He didn't see damage. A shame, in his opinion. He himself would have enjoyed taking a hammer to the relentlessly eye-catching things. Assuming he could evade the omnipresent police, and their sprays. Also assuming the T wouldn't ban him for life. Big assumptions on both counts.

The screen directly across featured a new organ flush procedure. It employed blood substitutes that purged toxins and lengthened life. Sick, Toby thought, watching molecules root through tissue, gobbling gunk. "It all comes out in 'The Wash,'" the caption proclaimed. "At approved facilities citywide."

The image shifted to the logo of the Mantis Corporation. Ovoid and brilliant, it rotated, radiating intricate energy waves. Toby knew "the orb" well, and found it creepy. So did practically everyone else on the planet. Still, Toby would take the orb over organ flush any day. Creepy or not, he had to admit, the computer animation was fascinating.

The way it mutated. Like lightning, like the surface of the sun, it never put out the same patterns twice, or so Mantis claimed. Toby had read about the viral ecology that generated the thing. The orb's software could be thought of as an artificial life-form, experts said. That was why it mutated. This corporate logo, in a sense, was "alive."

It also told stories. Or rather, it played roles in stories, the plots of which depended on what product Mantis was hyping. Toby realized he hadn't seen this episode before.

The orb shrank, as always when embarking on a sales pitch. Like a softball-size UFO, it floated through dark gardens. Through a large country estate . . .

The image vanished. Bold-face words appeared:

WE BRING YOU A PUBLIC SERVICE MOMENT

Toby glanced around. All the screens had switched. Cool, he thought. The T didn't mess with ad revenue lightly. So this had to be serious. Plague? Fresh atrocities in the Mexican civil war? More freak storms? Toby remembered the last Public Service Moment he'd had in the subway. The Orlando Hanta-3 outbreak. A notable catastrophe.

On the other hand, he considered, maybe they were announcing something mundane. The problem with the train, for instance. Was the T experiencing systemwide crash?

A manta-ray shape appeared on the screens. White, it sported a thick, bulbous tail. The headline scrolled:

SCIENTISTS REPORT EARTHQUAKE AND MAJOR VOLCANIC ERUPTION IN ANTARCTICA

Uh-oh, Toby thought. This could be quite good. Clearly it was, otherwise they wouldn't have made it a Moment.

However, the screens didn't elaborate. They were sticking with the manta-ray map and the headline. Then, to Toby's dismay, they reverted to infomercials.

A check revealed that the other passengers didn't share his curiosity. As before, they were busy being digital with powerful toys. Typical, Toby thought. Only one thing to do, he decided.

He nudged the man next to him, the well-dressed fellow watching TV, and said, "Excuse me. Did you notice the Moment?"

The man looked up from his laptop. Annoyance gleamed in red-rimmed eyes. "What?" he said, blinking.

Toby said more loudly, to get through the headset, "The screens flashed an eruption in Antarctica. An earthquake too."

"Yes?" the man said blankly.

"I was wondering if you'd mind accessing one of the newsnets. To see what's available."

The man smiled. "I'm on a newsnet already," he remarked, inspecting Toby's white shirt and black pants.

"Could you try CNN?" Toby didn't like the way the guy was looking at him. "They made it a Moment," he repeated. "It could be serious. Like, you know, Antarctica's instability? Implications for climate?"

The smile broadened, and broke into a dry chuckle. "Ah. The sky's falling, of course. Again." He lost the smile, eyes betraying contempt. Then he returned to Asian business.

Toby sighed. Idly, he fantasized standing up and yelling. Should he pull an eco-frenzy? Rave about climate shift, the wilting ecosphere, planetary doom? Or should he go totally nuts and pull an apoco-frenzy? Scream about God's great bloody Judgment?

No point, he thought. The people in the subway car had heard it before. They'd heard it for years now. On TV, in the streets, they'd seen frenzies of every variation on the crackpot spectrum. Fanatics declaring the End. In thrall to the End.

But the End hadn't come. The people here would tell themselves that, if Toby started raving. The End simply hasn't come. It's the new millennium, 2002, but the Apocalypse is a no-show, thank you very much. It just isn't happening. And if the weather's unusually warm, so what? Many climatologists say it has nothing to do with greenhouse effect. It's the natural cycle, they say; or they claim we don't have enough data. Meantime, life goes on. Life goes on.

So stop it with your catastrophe fixation.

Anyway, if Toby made a big enough scene, the policewoman would spray him. He'd go into paralytic shock. Eventually, a van would haul him off to the lock-up. Whenever the train reached Harvard.

Toby slid down the bench a foot, scratched a sweaty itch on his shoulder, and took a deep breath.

General Theodore Raffenelli, FATB, Boston, didn't consider himself a paranoid man. Suspicion was his game, quite true. But as befitted a lucid player, he despised the mentality, so prevalent in his line of work, that saw plots and schemes where none existed. Raffenelli stuck to the facts. He liked cold, demonstrable facts. Gross hypotheticals, trendy scenarios, conspiracies in the mist—for that kind of thinking he had no use whatsoever.

Unless mists solidified. And became facts.

He grimaced at the document his desk had printed twenty minutes before. The latest of many bulletins from Washington since 5:00 that morning, its contents were coldly factual. That gave Raffenelli little comfort. For the first time in his career, he wondered if fate might be his enemy. Was the grand scheme, via some stratagem he hadn't thought conceivable, out to get him?

Late afternoon sun played on the harbor beyond his windows. A lovely weekend was coming. Raffenelli's vantage point high above the waterfront should have evoked his sailboat, the beach and salt air of his Chatham cottage. He instead pondered a more primordial vista: the simple immensity of the Atlantic Ocean.

The day truly was beautiful, but for the general, it had been inauspicious from the start. Breakfast on the terrace of his Back Bay duplex had consisted of coffee, dry toast, and the *Globe*'s lead editorial: "DIET TIME FOR FATBOY."

Disrespect annoyed Raffenelli. After the Supreme Court massacre, hadn't all the media asked, the *Globe* conspicuous among them, how that tragedy could have happened? The same applied to the other attacks that had fanned the country's millennial Frenzy. The dud nuke that sent a plutonium plume over Chicago. The aerosol canisters on California's Bay Area Rapid Transit system, invisibly seeding anthrax spores. The literally garden-variety ammonium nitrate C4s. Why, the media had wondered loudly after each atrocity took us deeper into breakdown, wasn't the government prepared?

The Federal Anti-Terror Bureau had been created because of such questions, but the *Globe* was forgetting it had asked them, and saw fit to cast doubt not only on the FATB's worth, but its dignity: "FATBOY." Gutter language, Raffenelli thought bitterly.

They'll be singing a different tune, he reflected. All indications favored another crackdown. The nightmare on his desk, for instance. That might shove the country in the right direction.

When it came, could he deal with the maelstrom?

Raffenelli recalled how he'd dealt with the Frenzy. He brooded over painful memories; sealed, as if behind a firewall, far from his conscience. New England's underclass, crazed with AIDS, hunger, homicidal children. The ex-middle class, furious to find itself white trash. Hinterland extremists, obsessed with guns, "patriotism," government tyranny. Religion crazies, enraptured with Judgment Day; enviro nuts, despairing; Luddies, smashing; and at the fore of the madness, leading every variant of it, the demagogues, the preachers, the mini-Messiahs—howling, each out-howling the other, about the End.

The general had crushed them all. Could he do it again?

Maybe. Then again, maybe not. His chief of staff waited in the outer office. Yanked from a weekend departure, he knew something was up, but had no idea of the dimensions. Who did? Not many people, Raffenelli was sure. Of the twelve regional FATB directors around the country, he alone was authorized to share details with staff. The director general had emphasized containment. No FBI, no CIA, and no military, other than special units en route to Antarctica. Congress was off the map.

Elite company, Raffenelli mused. He reached for the intercom. To his secretary, Dworkin, he said, "Send him in."

Colonel Dalton Samaraweera came through the door. "Sit," Raffenelli commanded. Surprised, because he wasn't used to it—the general usually held meetings in the adjoining conference room—Samaraweera settled his trim frame on a straight-back Chippendale.

The Bureau's military roots involved some perks. Only an educated eye would know that the carpets, couches, and armchairs receding into the distance were reproductions; one reason Raffenelli seldom held meetings in the office, and never interviews with the press. He used plainer quarters when dealing with the press. Harsh lighting and linoleum didn't distract reporters. A shame, he often thought, they weren't accustomed to the ambience of the basement. There no distractions existed at all. That idea in mind, he held up the *Globe* editorial. "You've seen this?" he asked.

Samaraweera nodded. Satisfied he'd kicked things off with a dose of fear, Raffenelli tossed the paper into the bronze faux-Regency wastebasket. His chief of staff expected budget cuts. It would be a pleasure to disabuse him of that notion.

"Factions of the media," Raffenelli said quietly, "think the Bureau has grown too big. They think we don't know our limits. They also seem to think," he went on more quietly, watching disdain settle on the colonel's swarthy, clean-cut face, "that the dangers that brought us into being, have somehow . . . diminished. Do you suppose, Dalton, they've forgotten the Supreme Court attack?"

Raffenelli closed his eyes to indicate emotion, or rather to hide it. What he felt wasn't appropriate. Like many figures in law enforcement, he considered the justices mule-headed obstructionists, and would have shed few tears if they'd entered the hearing room forty seconds quicker, joining the litigants, clerks, and guards whom a nerve gas cartridge had sent into death throes on the shiny marble floor.

Those forty seconds had prevented a clean sweep. But the attack continued to reverberate; even if, in terms of body count, it ranked as bush league terror. Symbolism was what mattered at times like this. It put things in perspective.

Samaraweera wiped his palms on his trousers. He said, "Let me have it, General. Go ahead and spell it out."

Raffenelli examined his fingernails. "I'll give you a synopsis of the situation," he muttered. "Then you'll read the director general's overview." He pointed at the pale violet folder on his desk. "You'll commit it to memory, then destroy it, and will share what you've learned with no one. Security breaches will result in confinement at the Clinic, do I make myself clear?"

Samaraweera blushed. A sign, Raffenelli knew, of fury. And yes, his last remark was insulting, for Colonel Dalton Samaraweera many times had proved his trustworthiness. On the other hand, the general thought, nothing so concentrates the mind as the prospect of Clinic confinement. He leaned back, thrust his hands from crisply tailored cuffs, touched his fingertips together, and said, "Have you heard news reports about Antarctica?"

Samaraweera nodded. "About an eruption, sure. I saw something an hour ago. On Sun News."

Raffenelli said, "The so-called eruption. It wasn't an act of God. A nuclear device triggered it."

"Really," Samaraweera murmured, sitting straighter.

"Our scientists at the Pole," the general continued, "knew this immediately from seismic reads. They can distinguish, of course, between natural ground movements and manmade ones. Although natural phenomena quickly followed—the eruption, and an earthquake—this without question was a nuclear explosion.

"Confirmation came from a Russian research ship, the *Bellingshausen*. Scientists aboard it detected a signature—which experts in Moscow recognized. At a Kremlin meeting this morning, Defense Minister Pupov told our ambassador that the signature could only have come from a particular class of weaponry, one developed during the last stages of the Soviet empire, and never, until 12:11 A.M. today, used. Apart from tests in Siberia."

Raffenelli paused to take a sip of coffee. Fantastic though it was, what he'd said thus far didn't compare with what remained. "It was a Spezsevich, Dalton."

Samaraweera gasped. The Spezsevich devices were the Bureau's ultimate bête noire. Not just in concept, but for a very concrete reason; eleven had disappeared during the Russian Anarchy of '98, and still hadn't been found. No one in the world security community, including the Russians or so they claimed, knew who had stolen them. Or who might have black-marketed them, where they might have gone. To what use they might be put.

The public hadn't been told this. For good reason; the facts behind the theft were simply too frightening.

In the late '80s, the Soviet military was grappling with one of its most notorious problems: the unreliability of its ICBM missiles. It also was concerned about the American Star Wars program, then in full R&D swing. Two fundamental questions emerged. Could they hit the United States accurately? Even if they could, would the Americans blow their missiles out of the sky?

An analyst named Grigor Spezsevich came up with a solution. He figured, forget ICBMs. Forget missiles and anti-missile missiles, forget all forms of flying hardware, period. Drug lords, he reasoned, had armies smuggling tons of contraband across U.S. borders. Why not Soviet agents? Carrying much lighter loads?

Superiors liked the idea. Bomb designers went to work. Since miniaturization long had been a priority, to maximize payload on multiple-warhead missiles, they encountered little trouble reconfiguring a thermonuclear to fit inside a medium-size suitcase. One that packed almost half a megaton.

Spezsevich soon was inspecting a suitcase that looked exactly like a metal Halliburton. So far, so good. In theory, the two big problems, deliverability and accuracy, were solved. Agents could get bombs into the U.S.; they could put them close to ground zero of most any target. But another problem remained. How to set them off? On command, in a hair-trigger war situation?

It was then that Spezsevich came up with his most inspired flight of fancy. Why not, he suggested, plug the bombs into the telephone system? And if the time came, simply call them?

No problem, said the designers. To the suitcase prototype they added an answering machine. They installed a phone wire, tipped with a jack clip, that retracted like a vacuum cleaner's power cord. And voilà!

They had a bomb that plugged in and took calls. It could take calls in a Washington condo, in a New York hotel room, even at a roadside diner. Nuclear war suddenly seemed simple. The finger on the button would be pressing touchtones. Long distance.

Several dozen Spezseviches were manufactured. Fortunately for the United States, they never were deployed. Seasoned minds in the Kremlin pointed out the consequences of getting caught red-handed. Also, being so portable, the bombs could end up posing control difficulties. Suppose one fell into the wrong hands?

Wisdom prevailed. Spezsevich's suitcases, relegated to backup status, were warehoused at various secure locations.

Then came the Anarchy of '98. Eleven of them disappeared. Four years later, none had shown up. Until, it seemed, today.

Samaraweera thought it over. "I would venture to guess," he remarked, "we won't be going on a diet any time soon."

Raffenelli grunted his agreement.

"But why Antarctica?" Samaraweera wondered out loud. "Of all places to explode a suitcase—why there?"

"We'll get to that," the general said. "The first question is—why Boston?"

Samaraweera's face tightened. "What do you mean?" he asked.

"The Antarctica event has spooked our friends the Russians. So much so, they've started forking over new information, items they hadn't admitted they possessed. Pupov called the DG a couple hours ago. He told her that just last month, a source contacted PLU headquarters in Moscow—saying he had evidence that the missing Spezseviches may have come here."

"God damn," Samaraweera whispered.

"This source," the general continued, "requested a meeting. Right here in Boston. Apparently he wanted money for the info. The PLU obliged, they sent four agents right away. Which we detected. Didn't we, Dalton?"

"Not the 'trade representatives'?" Samaraweera asked.

"Indeed. What happened to them?"

"Dead," Samaraweera said, twitching. "Police found them on the Esplanade three weeks ago. Ran the names through the computer, turned the bodies over to us. Neurotoxin from some kind of pellet weapon. Professional job on the part of . . . whoever did it."

"Whoever did it," Raffenelli murmured. "The trillion-dollar question. Don't worry, I won't have you shot. Despite the fact that five megatons may have booked rooms at the Copley."

Samaraweera stammered, "I did my—damnedest . . . "

Raffenelli studied the shame the man's demeanor shielded. He said, "You handled it in terms of procedure. You handled it by the book. But you didn't find out that the PLU agents were meeting an informant. Or what they discovered in the informant's car—shortly before they were killed. Nor did you uncover the fact that the informant himself was murdered, at the Four Seasons Hotel. By pellet gun, Colonel."

Samaraweera gazed at striations in the veneer on the general's desk. Raffenelli muttered, "It's all in the director general's overview, courtesy of the suddenly cooperative Russians. You can read the details. Suffice it to say, the PLU agents found evidence that the devices were taken from Boston last year, not long after they arrived." Raffenelli smiled wanly. "Maybe they're lying low at the Ramada Inn in Worcester, gabbing on the phone with their girlfriends. Maybe they moved to San Francisco and started life over in telemarketing. Maybe, maybe, maybe—if you think you feel bad, how do you figure I've felt all day, dealing with the DG? How do you think she feels, dealing with the panicked President?"

"I'm sure," Samaraweera said gratefully, since the general was being kind, "it has been difficult."

Raffenelli glowered at the ceiling. "But just maybe the Spezseviches are in Antarctica. Which brings us to the question you raised. The most peculiar aspect of all. Why would somebody blow holes in that Godforsaken ice sheet?"

"The Russians must have some idea. Otherwise—why would they be cooperating?"

Raffenelli stared at him. Samaraweera possessed a certain edge. The general appreciated that. It helped to have an edge when serving with the Federal Anti-Terror Bureau. He said, "Sea level. And climate shift. Especially climate shift."

Samaraweera thought a moment. He asked, "Has anybody talked to Earnest Trefethen?"

Raffenelli snorted. "What do you think?" he said. "Yes, the director general conferred with Dr. Trefethen all day. But now the press is after him, so his lines are jammed—it's incredible, even I can't get through. And his staff is out, because he's retiring next week." Nervously, Raffenelli cracked knuckles. "They're both retiring—he and his wife, Dr. Helen Scarf. You know who *she* is. The dinner's tonight, actually. The DG won't make it."

"Press is on him? He's not saying anything that could . . . "

"Incite panic? Hardly, Colonel. Trefethen's all right." Raffenelli regarded his second-in-command with exasperation. "Besides being the foremost ice sheet expert, he and Helen go back with the DG. They're old friends, especially Helen—think of her work at the Clinic. In fact, the DG wanted to fly them down to Washington this morning. But Trefethen's pulling his database together. He has a mess of data from the last expedition to Antarctica. I'm told it's relevant, the data. Very relevant."

"How high is Trefethen talking?" Samaraweera inquired.

"Potentially, it's disastrous. New York, Washington, L.A., New Orleans, all of South Florida say good-bye. So do London, Holland, Bangladesh, the Nile Delta. Ports everywhere. Very few coastal cities would survive. Worst case, if East Antarctica gets in the act—Trefethen says it could—we're talking a hundred and seventy feet." Raffenelli stared at the harbor below his windows. "Boston wouldn't survive a best-case scenario. The lobby of this building? Full of water. Permanently. Then you get storm surges, and the city's gone." Raffenelli imagined a waterlogged Back Bay. Fish swimming in ground floors, the basements. Beacon Hill, a forlorn island. The North End, pathetically Venetian . . .

"But sea level," he continued, unwilling to dwell on those images, "isn't why the Russians are anxious. They could lose St. Petersburg, and numerous other ports—but they're Russians. They'd deal. What scares them is climate shift. And according to Trefethen, they're right. It could happen pretty damn . . ." Hearing his voice thin, Raffenelli stopped short.

Samaraweera tactfully averted his eyes. "I'm sure you have instructions," he said, looking at the violet folder on the desk.

Raffenelli re-examined his fingernails. "Our focus is the man who killed the PLU agents and their would-be informant. We assume he murdered them for reasons connected to the Spezseviches. So we assume he knows who has them. Therefore we must find him."

"Could the killer himself have them? Whoever this man is?"

"The Russians doubt it," Raffenelli said. "You see, they think they know who he is. The pellet-gun toxin, they say, has the m.o. of a particular individual written all over it. We don't have much about this gentleman in our files.

"But he's whom you're looking for. The name is Slotsky. A one-word name, that's it, the Russians tell us. Slotsky."

The train shuddered into Harvard Station at 4:19. Doors hissed open; Toby exited to the platform feeling as if he'd taken a sauna. He ran up the escalator into sunlight, and a sultry but welcome breeze. It carried the sound of sirens.

A convoy of FATBOY troop trucks was rumbling down Mass. Ave. Just out for show, Toby thought; of course they had sirens going, not only to make the usual statement, but because without sirens they'd never get by in one formation. Pedestrian swarms would snarl them. To people on foot in Harvard Square, vehicles didn't exist, not even FATBOY's behemoths. Toby watched office clerks scamper through the rolling thunder. Students followed, and spry businessmen dashed along behind. The convoy slowed. To an observer from Europe or Asia, this might have been taken as political defiance, a variation on the tank-stopping scene in Beijing. Nothing was farther from the truth. Here, stopping traffic, toying with it actually, was a civic entitlement, and a kind of sport.

Toby saw a deeper significance as the convoy regained momentum. It really was just another form of traffic. Not a threat, a symbol of decay, a harbinger of worse to come. The Federal Anti-Terror Bureau simply was a fact of life.

Crossing the street, he debated going into the Coop, a department store with a section full of on-line electronics. He wanted to scan a couple of newsnets to get some facts on happenings in Antarctica. Sometimes the clerks let people play with the machines if they thought you might be a real customer; unfortunately, most of them had learned Toby wasn't. He decided to skip the Coop. Not only was he running late. The radio at work, he reminded himself, probably would give him what he wanted.

He headed down Brattle Street past boutiques and bookstores, through throngs of suburban shoppers, Asian tourists, spaced-out kids, academic dignitaries, street musicians, reunioning classmates, and polite panhandlers; the impolite weren't allowed. Then he crossed to the walkway that led to a courtyard bounded by office buildings, and to Mifflin Place restaurant.

It was a quiet zone the establishment occupied, well off the street. Perhaps this contributed to its weirdly lengthy success. Fashionable eateries as a rule didn't last long in Harvard Square. But Mifflin Place, with its tree-shaded terrace that seemed like a secret garden, with decor that was a melange of '70s kitsch and quirky antiques, had been around for eons.

Toby had a theory about the restaurant. Thousands of scholars, lawyers, doctors, and scientists came to Cambridge every year, mostly to catch up with things at the Harvard and MIT professional schools. Many of these people were graduates of those schools. They had been students once, and young, in quaint old Cambridge. Nostalgia being what it was, they tended to gravitate, when hungry or in need of a drink, to their former haunts. Mifflin Place happened to be a prime former haunt. That, Toby surmised, explained its longevity, and its unchanging decor. The clientele didn't want it to change. They wanted it to evoke the ambience of distant, carefree times. Put simply, Mifflin Place was a memory lane for some of the world's most prominent technocrats.

The den of the enemy, as far as Toby was concerned.

Serving them, he felt like a spy. It was instructive to hear his customers talk about their firms, their cases, their labs; after some wine, they often would complain about spouses and children, about the toll their careers were taking on their personal lives. All of them, evidently, worked much, much too hard. Toby found this amusing. He also found it scary. These earnest careerists, with their holy grails of productivity, competitiveness, and profit, didn't see the big picture he saw. They thought they were forging a stable world economy. Toby viewed them as senior administrators of the End.

Not that he hated them. They were just another facet of the sleep everyone took to be everyday life.

He entered the restaurant lobby, loved its AC, and approached the podium where the reservation book lay, wanting to know what business so urgently required his coming in. An ordinary number of reservations, he saw. Then he noticed that the hostess's diagram didn't have his name in the dining room he usually worked. He'd been assigned to the private room. It was booked under the name Trefethen.

The evening looked simpler than he'd expected. He would be serving a single group of only twelve people. Something else occurred to him. As master of the private room, he could put the radio in there, and listen to it while he set up. Over his shoulder he heard, "Swett, you're late."

Toby turned to the manager, a fleshy fellow named Felice with a grandiose and watery stare. He said, "Trefethen?"

Twenty feet away, a young man swiveled from the bar. Dark eyes met Toby's for a moment; then dropped to the floor. The guy looked unremarkable in his gray raincoat and nondescript cap.

Felice said, "Don't know who it is. Somebody's retirement party. I have a feeling they'll be difficult—what the hell happened to your shirt?"

"The T broke down," Toby replied, watching the guy turn back to the bar. "Like a steam bath on the train. Did you hear about the eruption?"

"The T erupted?"

"No. In Antarctica."

"What are you talking about? Another disaster?"

"Forget it," Toby said, edging away.

A curt wave told him to stay put. "The Trefethens," Felice said, "are a 6:15, and the room is filthy. Sterling, who quit on Wednesday?" Toby nodded. "Somebody neglected to remember he was scheduled to work this party. Somebody also neglected to notice that he didn't do side work in the room. You'll need the vacuum and lots of Windex." He handed Toby a set of keys. "They want five DPs on ice. Big bucks, whoever they are—you'll have to iron that shirt." Toby nodded again. It was best to nod, with Felice in one of his moods. "One more thing. If anybody calls and asks about the Trefethens, you're to say the reservation was canceled."

"Really?" Toby said, intrigued. "Why?"

"I told you, they're difficult. For some reason that they didn't spell out, they don't want people to know they're here. So if we get calls, they're not here. They canceled."

"Fine," Toby said, noticing that the man at the bar seemed to be listening to this. "Kind of strange, isn't it?"

"They think they're celebrities," Felice said. "Maybe they are. If you need anything I'll be in the office . . . damn, would you look at her." He strode off toward the terrace, where a waitress was going nuts serving tea to a gang of people with name tags.

Toby went opposite, through the deserted cafe area to a set of double wood doors. He unlocked them. The private room always was locked when not open for business, mostly to prevent staff from using it as a clandestine lounge, but also to safeguard the old engravings that lined its walls. Thought to be priceless, they depicted various stages of banquet preparation in a cavernous medieval kitchen. Toby's favorite, a study of the slaughtering of a hog, inventoried saws, disembowelers, and brimming blood buckets. It was still there—safe and sound. However, Sterling had indeed been bad. Chairs weren't stacked on the big oak table. Breadcrumbs littered the sideboard. Toby shook his head sadly. How could a professional work in these conditions?

Something rustled behind him. He turned. The guy who'd been at the bar stood in the doorway. "Can I help you?" Toby asked.

"Just looking," the man said, hands thrust in the gray raincoat. True to his word, he glanced at every corner.

Toby shrugged. "Be my guest," he mumbled, going to a door with a round porthole-like window. He unlocked it and entered the rear kitchen corridor, specially installed to mute clattering cookware and screaming chefs. The door swung shut behind him. Toby walked through the kitchen to the locker room, deposited his backpack in a corner, and unplugged the beat-up radio. He wondered if he should take a sink bath. Later, he decided. He went back through the kitchen to the rear corridor. As he approached the door to the private room, he glimpsed something through its window that made him pause.

The guy in the raincoat. He'd entered the room; he was examining the hog-slaughter engraving. Uh-oh, thought Toby.

He was doing something to the frame. Vaguely thrilled to witness a possible larceny, Toby wondered if he should alert Felice. But suppose the guy made off with the engraving? Toby imagined running through the Square yelling, "Stop, thief!" No, he could never do that. He was about to burst into the room when the guy left, empty-handed.

Toby waited a moment. Then he went in. Through the cafe door he saw raincoat heading to the bar. A drunk, Toby concluded. He went to the engraving and checked the frame. Nothing seemed amiss. But wait a second . . . The frame wasn't quite flush with the wall. Toby poked it. A small silver object skittered down and rolled across the floor. Toby picked it up. The thing was the size and shape of a miniature battery.

He put it in a bowl of artificial sweetener packets sitting on the sideboard.

Then he plugged in the radio. None of the news stations was reporting an eruption. Toby started setting up.

Minutes later, getting soda water for the prep cooks, he saw the raincoat guy at the end of the bar, fiddling with a set of earphones. Toby had a hunch about that. He decided to experiment.

After delivering the soda water to the cooks, he swung through the rear corridor to the private room, put the bowl of artificial sweetener on his tray, and advanced slowly through the cafe until he could see the bar. Then he tapped the bowl with a spoon.

The man perked up. He adjusted a device connected to his earphones.

Toby retreated to his station. Gently, he put the bowl back on the sideboard. Wondering how he might entertain this fellow—should he sing songs, or whistle while he worked?—he plunged into vacuuming. He did it with vigor, playing bumper-car with the chairs. Having an audience made him want to perform.

That Felice should be told of his discovery didn't occur to him. He decided to leave the bug in the artificial sweetener bowl. It should work just as well there as behind the engraving. Plus, he could move it.

The Trefethens, apparently, had a fan.

4

At the bar, earphones off because the vacuum cleaner was roaring through them, Miles Malt listened to his fellow barflies. They were getting on his nerves. Three stools down, a couple of guys, young, his age anyway, argued about a "compensation package." Miles found this funny. Really, he did. What—like UPS? Comes in a box, tied with string? Wells Fargo delivers on Fridays?

"Package," Miles muttered, disgusted.

Accustomed to taverns in Southie and Everett, Miles felt out of his element here. The bartender seemed to think he should. She didn't love his draft being full an hour after she'd poured it. What the hell, Miles thought. Maybe order something steep?

Why not? He could have anything he wanted. Slotsky's bug was doing great. He'd get every word they said in there. Every chew they took, every sip of water. No question, Slotsky would be happy tonight; that meant Miles had a package coming.

Peanuts, though, compared to what might happen. Miles still couldn't believe he'd pulled it off. He couldn't believe the pure luck, making a deal with Brian Trefethen.

All he had to do was get the code.

Brian said he'd leave it under the table. Hidden in a pen. He was going to stick the pen to the bottom of the tabletop, like a piece of gum. Why do it that way, in a restaurant, with his parents right there? Miles didn't know. But Brian claimed this was the only way. Something about not having access any time except tonight, right before they left for the restaurant. Something else about maybe getting caught when they went home, his parents might see the code was missing. If that happened, forget it.

So he had to leave it tonight. In this dump with airs. Miles turned his thoughts to the question of what he'd do with the code when he got it. Well, that was obvious.

Or was it? Miles went over his options. Slotsky he knew to be a proven employer. The goon had paid him more over the last three weeks than Miles had made the last six months. It beat being Earnest Trefethen's janitor, that was most definite. Pushing brooms, fixing copiers—Miles got a much bigger kick out of bugging the copiers. And phones and computers, and private rooms in restaurants. Considering what Slotsky paid for those services.

But did Slotsky pay the best that was out there? Miles wasn't convinced he did. Information about Trefethen was hot, that was totally obvious; even if Miles didn't have any idea why.

But how hot? How could Miles even begin to know how much it really was worth? All he knew was what Slotsky told him.

Which meant he probably could get more. Maybe much more, if he went to the right people. For example, Agent Whipple at FATBOY.

Just thinking the word made Miles tremble. With fear, with excitement. Everybody knew FATBOY had money. Infinite money. And everybody knew they liked to spend it.

Miles felt a need for fresh air. Maybe he'd take a walk, to a park bench, and call Whipple—just to see what he'd say. If he gave him the cold shoulder, there was Slotsky for fallback, right?

As long as Brian came through. But Miles knew he would. The arrogant little fuck was crazy, but he would come through. No way the kid was feeding him a line of shit.

About the pen. That somehow held a code. Maybe, he thought, the code's rolled up on a piece of paper. Maybe the pen has a memory chip. Who could say?

It wasn't for him to say. Miles just wanted the pen, and a compensation package. He turned the earphones on. The vacuum shriek had stopped. Radio news came through again, loud and clear. Miles liked the expensive look of his little machine. Slotsky's toys; they were amazing.

He got up from his stool and walked out the door. He had to make that call. It might change his life.

Half a mile away, Slotsky dozed in his car. His earphone chimed. He woke and glanced at the tracker's message screen. Miles was moving.

Slotsky stretched his squat frame. Miles moving wasn't something that often interfered with naps. However, people like Miles didn't often make deals behind his back. Slotsky had listened to the tense negotiations with Brian Trefethen. He'd gathered that Brian intended to turn over some kind of code.

Miles didn't know Slotsky knew this. But then, there were many things Miles didn't know. Slotsky said, "Report."

The tracker blinked blue lights. Through the earphone it said in its breathy contralto, "Miles at Mifflin Place restaurant 1533 to 1644 hours. Four Miles speech events on file, total duration thirty-seven seconds. One remote activated at 1639 hours, on line, status good. Five remote speech events on file, sixth in progress, total duration to present one minute forty-three seconds. Miles now moving east on Brattle, filthy sucker, watch out or I'll step on you."

Slotsky said, "Remote on."

Sounds of metal hitting glass came through the earphone. Tableware, Slotsky judged. A male voice was saying, ". . . dee peas on ice?"

A younger male voice said, "You didn't give me the keys." The older voice said loudly, "I gave you the keys!" The clinking sound stopped. The younger voice said, "Not the ones to the wine room, Felice. Those aren't here." A busy metallic jangle came through the earphone. Keys, Slotsky judged. The younger voice continued, "Then you went to the office . . . "

Slotsky said, "Remote off." The earphone muted. He said, "Miles on. Location."

Breathily the tracker contralto said, "Miles location Brattle Square. Stationary since 1646 hours, filthy sucker, watch out or I'll step on you."

Motor traffic noise whooshed through the earphone. A horn honked. Passing voices, distant voices eddied. Slotsky was about to turn it off when the contralto said, "Miles initiating telephone transmission, filthy . . . "

Slotsky said, "Report number."

The contralto silenced. Two seconds went by. The contralto said, "655-4178, filthy . . . "

"ID number," Slotsky said.

The contralto silenced. Slotsky heard a telephone ring. He could hear Miles breathing; nervously, he judged. The contralto said, "Number shielded, fil . . . "

Slotsky snapped, "Stop slut."

The contralto said, "Slut stopped." Slotsky heard another ring. The contralto said, "ID shield down. Number reads Federal Anti-Terror Bureau, office Special Agent Lex Whipple."

Slotsky said, "Damn you, Miles."

A third ring cut short. Slotsky heard a voice say, "Whipple."

"Agent Whipple, this is Miles Malt." He's very nervous, Slotsky judged. But very eager. "I called yesterday about Trefethen?"

"Yes. You did." Ah, thought Slotsky. Miles must have used another phone. He hadn't called Whipple with the phone Slotsky had given him. For if Miles had used that phone, the tracker would have recorded the conversation.

"I—uh—mentioned a pen? That has a code in it?"

"Right." Then, with an edge of sarcasm, "Did you find out what this code is yet?"

"Yes. I mean no, not really—but I'm getting it tonight. See, Brian's leaving it for me. He swore he would, in a pen, at a restaurant . . . can we maybe talk? Later?"

"Find out what it is, Malt. I'll be happy to talk."

Slotsky heard a click. Then a sharp intake of breath. Whipple had hung up, and Miles didn't like it. Miles, Slotsky thought. You are being terribly foolish.

The room looked perfect. Toby looked perfect too; shirt, vest, and apron he'd freshly pressed. The only unperfect thing at 6:22 was being stuck at the restaurant while the media went crazy with an awesome story on Antarctica.

According to increasingly detailed radio reports, the volcano had erupted under more than a mile of solid ice. And it had blown right through! Right through the second-thickest ice sheet in the world. It actually was better than erupting under the thickest ice sheet, because that one covered East Antarctica. The second-thickest covered West Antarctica—the part that had been losing ice shelves in recent years. The area with a potential for "catastrophic collapse."

It put Toby in a terrific mood. Co-workers had noticed this, even Felice had, but Toby knew better than to reveal the reason. Not many people at Mifflin Place shared his fascination with megadisaster. Most of them, like most people Toby knew, including brother Dan and roommate Selma, considered the fascination just a little nuts. In fact, very nuts.

Toby didn't care. The way he saw it, his critics were sticking heads in sand while the world crumbled around them. One of these days they'd wake up and see he was right. Oh joyful day, he thought sardonically. A wake-up call loud enough to make people really pay attention was sure to come way too late.

Meantime, his customers were late. Toby hoped they wouldn't show up at all. That they might not show had received almost hypnotic reinforcement from visits to the podium, where the hostess, already crazed with the pre-theater rush, was having to tell very persistent people that they'd canceled. As predicted, the Trefethens were getting phone calls. Lots of them.

But they're not here, Toby told himself happily. Soon enough, he'd break the room down, rush home, wrest control of the TV from Dan and Selma—they'd be outraged, but it was, after all, his birthday—and immerse himself in eruption reportage.

Then a terrible thought crossed his mind. The cafe area, just beyond the closed doors of his empty private room, had filled up with the pre-theater crowd. The bar, the terrace, and the main dining room also were packed. What if Felice told him to let in the hordes? To open the room to burger-munching cafe customers?

He would be here till midnight. Unable to stand the thought, Toby moved to the sideboard. He'd hidden the radio there after Felice had told him to get rid of it. The artificial sweetener bowl caught his eye. Wondering if the raincoat spy appreciated the stream of news his bug was getting, he turned the radio up a notch.

The doors to the cafe burst open. Startled, Toby turned off the radio. Felice's florid face glided in. His eyes seemed less watery. As if they'd frozen over; it meant, Toby knew from experience, "I don't think you're up to this."

He immediately saw why. Close on Felice's heels came Barclay Piston, the talk-show magnate, Reheema Sampson, the movie star, and Al Molloy, the junior United States senator from Massachusetts.

In general, celebrities didn't tend to cause more than a passing stir at Mifflin Place. But these three reeked of bigness. Even Toby was impressed. It wasn't so much the bigness. It was Reheema Sampson's environmental activism, and the question of why she would be in the same room with a man like Piston.

Felice waved at Toby, then at the five sweating wine buckets, and declaimed, "If you care for champagne, we will pour it, or if you prefer something from the bar, please let us know. Thank you." He gave Toby a final admonitory glare and swept from the room.

"That's awful," Reheema Sampson said, staring at the hog-slaughter scene on the wall.

"You get used to it," Senator Molloy said. He advanced on the wine buckets, took out a bottle to inspect the label, and growled, "Dom Perignon. Superb. But how it sickens me." The bottle crashed back into its icy bath. "V.O. and water, tall."

Toby nodded, and looked at the others. Piston was watching Reheema—Toby couldn't help but think of her as Reheema—grimace at the engraving. She murmured, "Shoulda known it. Place like this. Harvard. No shame whatsoever—they have to rub it in, what ghouls they were two hundred years ago."

Piston said, "That's some castle in Europe, Reheema."

"Same difference," she replied. "The man needs to know if you want a drink." She glanced at Toby, rolled her eyes at the engraving, and winked. "Me," she added, "I'll have ginger ale."

Toby smiled, surprised that she seemed as charming in person as in her ubiquitous media appearances. She certainly looked as glamorous. Piston declared, "You know, I've stopped thinking of this as a social occasion. So I believe I'll stay sober. Grapefruit juice. Fresh-squeezed. Don't tell me you don't have it."

Toby nodded, left the room, and headed for the bar. Coming at him through the noisy cafe was Felice, in whose wake Martha Cliffcloud, billionaire chairwoman of the Mantis Corporation, and Lawrence Sforza, president of MIT, were attracting stares. Toby had served them before. Cliffcloud resembled a vertical anaconda that had swallowed something huge; tall, she wore her close-cropped black hair like a helmet, and sported an incongruously protruding stomach. Sforza, compact and suave, suggested the ferret she might consume for dessert. Toby considered stopping them to get drink orders. He decided against it. Felice was whisking them along with maximum finesse, and if disrupted by Toby in front of the oglers, easily could have a stroke.

The bar was getting very busy. Toby wrote out his order and put it beneath another order waiting to be filled. He should have pulled rank and put his on top, but he wanted to see if the man with the earphones had reappeared. The guy wasn't at the bar. Toby edged through a group of women, one of whom was hissing, "I came in behind her, of course it's Reheema." Earphones wasn't at the cocktail tables, either. Toby glimpsed a swatch of gray behind three hefty Australian executives in the early stages of letting it rip. Someone was sitting at the last table. One of the Aussies cracked a joke and as they erupted with laughter their paunches realigned, revealing the raincoat. The guy was sitting there. He was alone. He had the earphones on.

The paunches closed in. Toby went to get his drinks.

He bore them to the private room, theorizing that raincoat could be working for some tabloid, television, or print—or whatever. Probably all this amounted to was gossip. In the room, Felice was opening champagne. The guests stood around, chit-chatting; serving them, Toby absorbed snatches of talk. Reheema said to Martha Cliffcloud, "He hasn't been the same since the tragedy." A bell rang in Toby's mind; "tragedy" sounded familiar. Cliffcloud rumbled, "He was shattered." A vivacious woman Toby hadn't seen before was confiding to Senator Molloy, "I heard on the plane. It's just the eeriest coincidence." She took in the room and remarked, "Let's hope he doesn't tell us something dreadful." Toby realized he had seen this woman before. She was the American ambassador to the United Nations. Toby glimpsed a manic blur near the champagne. Felice was beckoning him. Toby went over.

"Open and pour," Felice said through clenched teeth. "I have to get up front." Toby nodded. It wasn't his fault only one waiter was working this event. On the other hand, it wasn't Felice's fault that the Trefethens, whoever they were, turned out to have the kind of friends whose most casual remarks, about the quality of service in a restaurant for example, could cause ripple effects. Toby later would rethink that idea in a different context. At this point, he mainly was intrigued by his customers' expectant mood. There was an air of anticipation, with an undertow of anxiety.

MIT president Sforza said, "I'll have champagne." Toby filled one of the tulip glasses lined up before him. He heard somebody somewhere say, "The terrible tragedy," and with an abrupt recollection of old headlines, he identified the name Trefethen. My God, he thought. Holy shit—the accident in the ice. In Antarctica.

Last winter, a scientist named Trefethen had led an expedition to a remote region of West Antarctica. It involved laser-drilling all the way through the ice sheet, over a mile down to the bedrock, to get geological samples. Returning to base camp, three of the four giant vehicles fell through a weak point that nobody had known existed, into a mysteriously vast crevasse that descended maybe a thousand feet below the surface. Everyone in those vehicles had to have died instantly. A blizzard was raging, and the Antarctic summer was coming to an end, so recovery proved impossible. Toby, always up on exotic disaster, had been interested to learn that the bodies might never be recovered, because Antarctic weather was by far the most brutal on earth, and the least predictable. It looked like a permanent burial; in ice that was hundreds of thousands of years old. However, the site happened to be in the middle of an "ice stream," something that flowed to the sea literally glacially, at the rate of a few feet a day, or slower. In the distant future, perhaps in a state of perfect preservation, the corpses would be delivered to the ocean, their ancient tomb suddenly an iceberg, drifting to the oblivion of warmer waters.

Toby didn't think humans would be around to spot a leg sticking out. But some kind of mutant squid might. He realized he'd gone into shock. The host is an expert on Antarctica . . .

The chit-chat buzz silenced. Toby looked up from the bottle he was opening and saw them coming through the doorway.

It was one of those moments when time seemed to swell and slow down, amplifying the details. Heightening the effect was the fact that everyone in the room was staring. No doubt they all had different reasons; but for Toby, in the seemingly long interval between the first glimpse and the applause that then broke the spell, an interval that in reality lasted two or three seconds, it wasn't the man, or the woman, or the boy, who transfixed him. It was the girl.

Dr. Trefethen he recognized from photos in the tragedy press accounts. Tall and thin, in his late fifties, he was bald, a feature that emphasized extravagant eyebrows and large, absolutely luminous blue eyes. Toby thought of the chasm in which this man's colleagues had perished. You could fall into eyes like that. It wouldn't be fun.

The woman beside him Toby also recognized, but not as Helen Trefethen. He knew the face from what had to be her professional name, Dr. Helen Scarf. Almost as tall as her husband, a bit younger and more ample, with regular features, honey-colored hair, gray eyes, austerely chic attire, and a rope-like pearl necklace coiled around her neck, she embodied what Toby thought of as a "handsome older woman." That didn't go far enough, he quickly perceived. She could only be described as a knockout. The sight made his palms film. Not in reaction to her looks; it was what she did. She was the psychiatrist who had founded, and continued to direct, the Center for the Study of Moral Reasoning, otherwise known as the Clinic; a research firm that supposedly was revolutionizing the science of criminal rehabilitation. She used radical techniques. She operated in near-secrecy. Her patients were limited to hardened convicts, preferably sociopaths and very young. Shadiest of all was the source of her money. As befitted a maximum-security facility where monsters checked in, but didn't check out, the Center for the Study of Moral Reasoning was FATBOY-funded.

Then there was the boy. Looking at him was painful. He so closely resembled the girl. It wasn't androgyny. He was a boy, she was a girl. Nonetheless they were duplicates, exact replicants of each other's beauty. And it was clear where they had gotten it. They were the offspring of Helen Scarf.

Help, thought Toby, drinking in that girl. About eighteen. Short strawberry-blond hair. Pale eyes. Shapely hot lips, defiantly set. Flawless skin that glowed. And a body that just shouted, finely knit. Every juncture was a perfect fit. Toby saw it as if with X-ray vision. His own bodily junctures, not worthy of contact with hers, not worthy even of imagining it but doing so anyway, seemed to disassemble and fly apart; he felt weak.

Then everyone was clapping, and the champagne cork exploded in his hand. The bottle gushed like a geyser. Toby shoved it under the table. He'd sprayed the ambassador's jacket, but she hadn't noticed, and once he had the bottle under control and was pouring, he actually caught a few approving glances being thrown his way, as if to commend his excellent timing. A genteel babble of greetings filled the room. The Drs. Trefethen, shaking hands and getting hugs, were metamorphosing into grandparents at a family reunion. Considering the grandchildren, Toby found this strange. Could Helen Scarf really have that much clout? The girl and the boy moved to the side. They looked bored, and a little annoyed. Something occurred to Toby. None of the dignitaries was with a spouse, or even a date. Was or wasn't this event social? He glanced at the girl, relieved that the kid with her so obviously was her brother. Probably her twin. No, definitely. If they weren't siblings at least, and were here on a date, they were psychotic narcissists. That seemed far-fetched. Martha Cliffcloud, Mantis chairwoman and orb impresario, approached. The square midriff of her serpentine form appeared bigger tonight. Perhaps, Toby speculated, she'd devoured a goat. She took a glass of champagne and offered it to Barclay Piston, who accepted. Toby noted the change of heart about staying sober. Cliffcloud took champagne for herself, tapped glasses with Piston, and said, "He gave me a C in bio-ethics." Piston laughed evilly. Then his eyes misted. He said, "He gave me a D, Martha." The two chortled at each other, and Toby suddenly understood.

The guests were former students.

But for most of them, the ages didn't add up. So they were former graduate students, or colleagues, or just plain old academic networkers. Toby glimpsed Helen Scarf air-kissing Senator Molloy. Maybe, he thought, they're former patients. Ex-inmates of the Center for the Study of Moral Reasoning?

That wasn't possible. Felice burst from the kitchen corridor carrying a tray of hors d'oeuvres. Toby gathered from his microwaving stare that this had nothing to do with Felice's job description. He abandoned his champagne post to take the tray.

Which was fine, because it provided a reason to approach that girl. She wouldn't swoon, he suspected. Even though he'd been told he was cute enough in his burning, demented way. Well, he wasn't Dan's brother for nothing. Dan, Toby thought, getting closer. He'd be as nervous as I am. He'd want the boy; Toby could understand that, dimly. He wished Dan were here to drag the kid out of his sight. Somehow, this twinship was a barrier. Toby paused and hovered. The way they were talking; it didn't offer admittance. The girl's face was flushed. Most becomingly. In fact she looked on the verge of tears. Toby lost nerve and swiveled the tray toward Reheema Sampson, who was passing. She plucked a canape and ate it. Then she turned to the young Trefethens and exclaimed, "Grace! Brian! How are you?"

I can't do it, Toby thought, slinking away with his tray. "Excuse me," a voice called out. Toby turned. The girl, Grace, was looking at him. She said, "Tea, please."

You hothead, Toby thought, gazing into smoldering gray eyes. He deposited the tray on the sideboard, rushed past the gabfest the elder Trefethens were conducting at the entrance, and exited into the cafe. Of course he hadn't set up for tea in the private room. So of course that girl would want it. The cafe was booming. Toby ransacked the cramped waiters' station, assembling cup, saucer, spoon, pot, bags, lemon, milk, and hot water, all the nightmare tea ingredients. A cafe waiter said behind him, "The queers at table six want Reheema's autograph, and so does Mr. Mannix." Then he heard Felice say, "What is he doing?"

Toby turned around, an empire of tea on his tray. Felice regarded him expressionlessly. He said, "You need help."

Toby said, "It's chaotic right now because they're standing up. When they sit down, I'll be fine. The menu's pretty simple. Excuse me." Toby pushed through and made for the room.

Felice snapped, "The senator wants V.O. and water, tall."

Toby called back, "Then go to the bar and get it." He didn't need this job. Who needed a job? There was the thrilling prospect of polite panhandling. He entered the room. Grace and Brian had seated themselves at the far end of the table, well away from the others, including Reheema. They were talking hushedly, heatedly. As Toby approached he heard Brian mutter, "No damn way." They shut up, not looking at him, as he started setting down tea items. He noticed Grace's long, nervous fingers. They were playing with something. With an artificial sweetener packet.

The bowl was on the table. She'd commandeered it from the side-board.

Toby reached for it. Grace clamped a hand on it. She looked at him and said, "I use a lot of this stuff." The tone of voice said, Get lost. Scram. Beat it.

Toby nodded. He walked away, thinking, Oh no, oh no, oh no—he's hearing every word.

Miles sat in the courtyard outside the restaurant, listening to the twins fight. Inside, the Australians had made it a case of dueling background noises—them versus the Trefethen dinner party. But now, out here, with just the birds singing, Miles was getting somewhere. Brian and Grace sounded like they were standing right in front of that picture. They came through so clearly.

There was only one problem. No, there were two. First, Grace was having a shitfit about the code. She didn't want Brian to leave it. Miles had been afraid of that. When they'd talked, she hadn't seemed to buy his story. And Miles couldn't deny it, the story had holes. Why would an undercover FATB agent be the custodian of her father's office building?

Still, he'd shown them the FATBOY ID. It was good. Slotsky had provided it, and he got the best of everything. Anyway it looked good to Miles. Most important, Brian had bought it. But now Miles wasn't so sure he'd stay persuaded.

Grace whispered through the earphones, "It's desperation."

Brian whispered, "Like it never was?" He was bitter. Yes, thought Miles. Stay bitter. Stay bitter.

Then there was problem number two. With them talking about the code, and Miles recording it, and Slotsky expecting the recording tonight—that meant Slotsky would find out about the code, which totally sucked. Because Whipple had sounded interested. Not like he'd fork over millions. But definitely interested.

And why not? Helen had a contract with FATBOY. Maybe she was a security risk. Because of whatever she and Dr. Trefethen were plotting, that Slotsky was so hot to find out.

Through the earphones, Miles heard a gravelly female voice say, "I bet you kids have better things to do than be cooped up with the likes of us."

Slotsky, sitting in his car and listening via tracker to the same conversation, took note of the voice. He'd heard it before. The voice he knew to be Grace's said with curious flatness, "Very funny."

"I suppose it isn't," said the gravel voice.

"ID voice," Slotsky said.

"Insufficient sample," the tracker replied.

"Are you ready?" the gravel voice said more clearly, and pitched lower; the source was closer to the bug, Slotsky judged. He'd already decided to instruct the tracker to run an acoustics analysis, to determine if the bug had been moved. Slotsky suspected it had. But at the moment, this woman interested him more. Her voice now conveyed a confidential attitude.

Brian muttered, "Ready for what?"

There was a sound of tense sighing. Grace, Slotsky judged.

"Come on," the gravel voice said, pitched even lower. "You're standing on the edge of history and you say for what?"

The tracker's contralto said, "Voice ID Martha Cliffcloud."

That electrified Slotsky. He hadn't thought Cliffcloud would be attending tonight.

Grace said, "You shouldn't be talking to us."

Brian whispered, "Father's looking, Martha."

Cliffcloud said very softly, "Relax, kids. We'll talk, Sunday, at my place." A moment passed. Then, sounding as if she'd moved away from the twins, she exclaimed, "Al Molloy!"

Brian said, "She's excited."

More moments passed. Grace said, "You can't do it. Father will see it." Again, that sigh. "Just mail it."

Brian said, "Stop talking about it."

More moments passed. Brian muttered, "The edge of history."

Grace said, "Ours. We're history."

The voices fell silent. Elated, Slotsky listened to the background chatter. He'd been looking into the enigmatic billionaire Martha Cliffcloud for three weeks now. His investigation had taken him to this dinner party at Mifflin Place restaurant. A dinner party that was being held—it so happened—on the day that a volcano had vaporized a chunk of the West Antarctic Ice Sheet.

A coincidence? Slotsky thought not.

Toby waited until he was serving the first course, game consommé, to make his move. Grace had been hunched over the table, exchanging occasional whispers with Brian, but mostly lost in stony-faced thought; from Toby's point of view, she'd been guarding the damn sweetener bowl like a dog guarding a bone. It lay directly below her chin. That wouldn't remain a problem for long. Toby knew well that when food lands, people react. A reflex born of the primordial fear of spillage.

His left hand thrust the steaming bowl in front of her face. Surprised, she sat back, watching his right hand make the snatch.

A quick fingering at the sideboard yielded the bug. Toby pocketed it. For good measure he agitated the contents of the pocket, which included his wine opener and loose change. This gave him a Captain Queeg-like thrill. Take that, he thought, you skulking, spying slob— ain't gonna get no more Grace tonight.

Toby served soup around the table, wondering how he might inform Grace of his good deed. He couldn't think of a way to do it that didn't involve self-implication. Even if his role had been unwitting, more or less.

He settled into making his rounds from kitchen to private room to bar, never before so conscious of the jangle produced by a pocket full of metal. Was the noise driving the spy out of his mind? Why, Toby wondered, do I enjoy that idea? The spy's presumptuousness, he guessed. His undeserved intimacy with Grace Trefethen.

Within an hour and a half Toby was clearing main course plates. Everybody seemed to have enjoyed the pasta with periwinkles and roasted shad roe. The mood in the room had drifted from convivial to subdued. Several times, with what seemed unnecessary brusqueness, Trefethen had deflected questions about the eruption. Conversation centered on past times when none of them had been famous; under the banter, Toby detected mounting impatience. The guests' curiosity, he could tell, almost matched his own.

No one wanted dessert. But they all wanted coffee, except Grace, who asked for more tea. After Toby delivered it, with an extra-full bowl of artificial sweetener, Trefethen stood up.

His guests settled back in their chairs with a collective attitude of, okay, shoot. Barclay Piston looked at his watch. Grace and Brian, model late adolescents, stared gloomily into their laps. Helen Scarf gave her husband a brittle smile; as if this phase of the evening promised both to amuse and pain her. Toby became aware of the silence. Would Trefethen's voice penetrate his pocket to the bug? Too late to worry, he decided. The scientist was starting.

"Thank you for being here," said the tall, bald man with blindingly blue eyes. Feet shuffled. Toby leaned against the wall near the kitchen corridor door, worried that Trefethen was going to ask for money. His tone had that fund-raising tang. Toby had heard it before. But he was wrong.

Trefethen said with a smile, "It's something of an irony that on the day of my retirement, a volcano has erupted in Antarctica. I suppose you're wondering if I arranged it—as a parting shot."

Laughter greeted the comment. Trefethen's smile faded. "We are honored that you are here. I should mention, Mary McMurtry sent regrets. It appears she is occupied with business."

What? Toby thought. Not *the* Mary McMurtry?

"Now, about the eruption. I realize you want to hear my professional opinion. I assure you, you're not alone. Barclay here can attest to the fact that the media have me under siege. His producers have been calling all day."

"You're on the show," Piston said flatly. "Tomorrow night."

"Barclay," Trefethen said, "as agreed, we'll discuss your show in the morning." He took a sip of water. "I confess, the attention has put me in an odd frame of mind. It has made me—how do I put this?— reflect. What do I tell people about the vast forces now at work in Antarctica?" He smiled again. "And what do I tell you, my friends?"

The interest level notched up to the boiling point.

"As it happens, I'm not at liberty to tell you much."

Piston was draining his coffee cup. He almost dropped it.

"The reasons will become apparent soon. Very soon, I fear." Trefethen grimaced at something invisible in the middle distance. "However, I would like to share a couple of related . . . reflections."

Toby couldn't believe he was listening to this.

"All of us here know," Trefethen declared, "that civilization has evolved into a self-destruct machine." Whoa, thought Toby. "And all of us have tried, in various ways, to stop that process. Let us admit something, my friends. We've failed. We have failed utterly. None of us has made a bit of difference."

"Now, now," Reheema said reprovingly.

"Hear me out!" Trefethen exclaimed. Everyone at the table seemed to cringe. God, Toby thought. Trefethen twirled a hand, as if to put his guests at ease. He said softly, but with conviction, "We also know what has made us a self-destruct machine. Overpopulation, and technology in the service of greed—those evils are the Beast. They're the Beast's two faces, and we know it."

Huh, Toby thought. The Beast. No one, he observed, appeared to disagree with that formulation.

"I offer you an idea," Trefethen continued. "Think about this. Might the planet have spoken today?"

What's he talking about? Toby wondered. The guests also seemed perplexed. Trefethen stared at them. "A fanciful notion, perhaps. But I tell you—I think the planet is putting us on a new road. I don't know where this road will lead. However, I suspect it will take us to frightening places."

Good lord, Toby thought.

"At the moment, I can say no more. But I hope you remember this evening, in the coming months. And I hope you will utilize the extraordinary talents and resources that each of you, in different ways, possesses." His voice rose. "To contribute! As you see fit, as you see fit!" The voice lowered. Into dead silence it intoned, "To the challenge that will unfold before you."

An irritated stir circled the table. Helen Scarf's brittle smile reappeared. Her children looked ready to explode. From boredom, maybe from disgust, Toby couldn't tell which. Barclay Piston said, "Earnest, what the hell are you talking about?"

Trefethen said, "I've not made myself clear?"

Reheema drawled, "Could you elaborate just a touch?" She smiled, trying to encourage him. "We've been through a lot together. I think we all agree you're the brainiest one here. I think we can agree you've provided the leadership when things got tough. So what's the story? Can't you let us in?"

Trefethen shook his head. "My dear former students," he said. "My esteemed co-activists and co-keepers of the faith, in so many futile, and frankly ridiculous—oh, what's a cheap enough word?" He frowned. "Causes, I suppose." He said it with true disdain.

Reheema recoiled as if she'd been slapped. The ambassador gasped. Senator Molloy cleared his throat. President Sforza rapidly recrossed his legs. Barclay Piston looked thunderstruck. Chairwoman Cliffcloud stared moodily at the ceiling. Wow, thought Toby—they're blown away. Trefethen continued coldly, "We have come to the end of the road. But ahead, the planet is opening a new one. That's all I'll say." As if to make this completely clear, he looked at Toby and snapped, "Bring me the bill."

It was like speaking into a vacuum, so extreme was the shock at the table. Toby said, "I understand you'll be billed by mail."

Trefethen nodded. "Helen, children. We will go."

Helen Scarf stood. The six guests, looking at Earnest, turned to look at her. It was then that Toby saw it. Brian and Grace were doing something. Something they didn't want the others to see; something the others couldn't see, because their faces were tilted up at Scarf and Trefethen. Those two meantime gazed at each other. Toby understood intuitively that the twins had chosen this moment to do what they were doing because they were below all lines of sight. Except, that is, his. No one at the table saw their shoulders press together. No one, except Toby, saw Brian use the joined shoulders for cover as he reached under the tablecloth. He seemed to touch the bottom of the tabletop. The action was what he would have done had he been sticking a piece of gum there; and wanted only his sister to know it. He pulled his arm back. The tablecloth fell over his knees.

He and Grace stood. Toby thought their faces had reddened. They looked like their hearts were pounding. But then, all of them looked like blood was flooding their heads.

Senator Molloy said, "Wait just a goddamn minute. Sit down. You can't do this."

Trefethen went to the coat tree and collected four umbrellas. With the air of a hunter carrying rifles, he motioned his family to the door. The twins walked swiftly toward it. Helen followed.

Her husband remarked, "It may rain tonight." He waggled his armful of umbrellas. "But I don't know why we brought these." He directed a contemplative stare at the guests, and Toby got an inkling of the power of the man. Force radiated. It was as if his mind could burn air. "Rain," he said quietly, "has its points, I think. Consider the cleansing effect of water."

How weird, Toby thought.

Trefethen opened the door. Cafe noise streamed from it. The twins and Helen walked out. Trefethen lingered, looking at his flabbergasted guests. He smiled frostily and said, "Remember, you have a role to play." Then he left.

Toby debated closing the door. A number of people stood outside, no doubt waiting for Reheema. He decided to leave it open. He wanted these customers out of here as fast as possible.

But the customers, studying each other with stunned disbelief, seemed immobilized. Piston said quietly, "He's cracked."

"Who would have thought it?" the ambassador asked.

President Sforza stood. "'The cleansing effect of water,'" he muttered. His eyes rolled. "Earnest is predicting the Great Flood?"

Molloy got up. He said dryly, "Our 'role,' whatever that is, is pointless." He strode to the door without a backward glance.

"This is quite upsetting," the ambassador said, standing. "But I have a plane to catch." She rummaged through her purse and found a compact. Inspecting her face, she added with a quaver, "If any of you feels like talking tomorrow, give me a call."

They're shaken, Toby thought.

"I will," Reheema said, pulling on her coat.

"Well, Barclay," Cliffcloud murmured. "It's you and me. Do we try to work it out?"

No, Toby thought. Just leave.

"He was a great man," Piston remarked. "Completely unknown to the public. Never sought recognition. But what a force for the good. All along he's been—tireless. You know what, Martha?"

"What?" she said.

Piston sighed. "I think he's fed up. Fed up with getting nowhere in the thankless business of doing good. Come. Let's go somewhere quiet and have a drink." They both stood.

Wonderful, thought Toby. He followed them to the door. Sforza and the ambassador already had left. Reheema stood with her back to the dozen or so autograph seekers outside the doorway. She said to Cliffcloud and Piston, "Can you play bodyguard?"

All three laughed. Funny, Toby thought. The billionaire and the TV magnate, bodyguarding the movie star. They went out. More fans appeared from the wings; the cafe was jammed. People were coming in from the bar. Among them Toby spotted a gray raincoat.

That didn't surprise him. It seemed the spy was just a Reheema hack. He was going to have to wait in line, though.

Toby closed the door and locked it. He went to where Brian had been sitting, and pulled the tablecloth up over the chair. Then he knelt to survey the many-legged netherworld.

Something was tacked to the bottom of the tabletop. A sealed envelope. Toby untacked it, stood, and debated opening it.

He opened it. Inside he found a round pin with yellowed lamination, and a typed note. The note read:

DO NOT REPRODUCE
IN ANY FORM WHATSOEVER.
USE IT TO FILTER THE MEDIA STREAMS.

Under the lamination, a childishly drawn animal decorated the pin. It appeared to be a rabbit. Toby thought, What?

He heard commotion in the cafe. Then he heard someone rattling the door. Felice, he thought. Toby shoved pin, envelope, and note into his apron. He went to the door and unlocked it.

The raincoat guy burst in. He slammed the door behind him.

Toby stepped back. The guy looked angry, and very determined.

The tablecloth was the first thing Miles saw. It wasn't hanging down. It was pulled up, like a woman exposing herself. Miles took this personally. He felt violated.

The waiter backed away, looking guilty as shit. Miles darted to the table and glared under it. Nothing but crumbs on the floor. He dropped to his knees and crawled in there, checking legs, the top, the joints of the legs with the top. Nothing but blobs of gum. He poked one to be sure, and knew beyond a shadow of a doubt that it was old, hard gum. Afraid the waiter might escape, he backed out rapidly. The waiter stood still, staring at him, amazed. But oh yeah, guilty all right. Miles jumped to his feet and grabbed him. The kid struggled. Miles snarled, "Don't mess with me—where is it?"

Slim but strong, the waiter broke away. They glared at each other. Miles reached for the razorwhip in his raincoat pocket. It didn't seem advisable to pull it. The kid looked like he'd fight. Maybe because he had backup. Cooks, busboys, the fucking Reheema Sampson fan club. He said, in a superior voice Miles wanted to squish, "Police get here very quickly." Miles thought about it. Then the waiter said, "What the fuck do you want?"

"The pen," Miles said. "You took it from under the table. Didn't you, Toby?"

The pin, Toby thought, looking at this lunatic who knew his name. He wondered what to tell him. That he'd found a pin under the table? In a sealed envelope with a bizarre note? Toby said, "You're nuts. What are you talking about?"

The guy said, "A pen. You know, Toby." He air-wrote, menacingly. "Something you write with."

"Huh," Toby said, feeling both outrage and relief. This guy had attacked him. On the other hand, the fellow was confused. What Toby had found wasn't something you write with. To Toby's way of thinking, that invalidated any claim the guy might make to it. An image of Grace's anguished face flashed through his mind. She hadn't seemed happy about leaving the pin. Both she and her brother had practically had heart attacks doing it. Maybe because this asshole could ruin their lives. Toby's duty seemed clear. He had to protect Grace. Maybe even Brian.

So he said, "Okay, okay. I did find it under the table." He reached in his apron and pulled out the pen he'd been using all night. An old beat-up ballpoint, it was almost out of ink anyway.

The spy snatched it from his hand. He examined it suspiciously. Then he said, "How do I know this is the right pen?"

Toby said, "Of course it's the right pen."

"You found it under the table?" the guy demanded.

"Uh-huh," Toby said.

"Was there anything else there?"

"Nothing but gum."

"How'd you know it was there?"

"When customers leave," Toby said, "the first thing we do is check under the table. We never know what we'll find."

"Smartass," the guy muttered. He carefully inserted the pen in his shirt pocket. As if it might explode, Toby thought. The guy then said, "You have any other pens, Toby?"

"Get the hell out," Toby said.

Fists balled, the guy took a step toward him. Toby heard someone coming down the kitchen corridor. In the nick of time, he thought. This looked like a fight. It was ludicrous.

Felice entered and went directly to the wine setup. The champagne was what interested him. Three bottles were empty, one was unopened, the fifth was half-full. He pulled it from its bucket and looked around for a glass. Toby said, "You should know something, Felice. Today is my birthday."

Felice said, "Oh, yeah? Tell you what—we'll split it." He turned, registered the stranger's scowling presence, and added, "Don't tell me it has to be three ways."

"He's not here to celebrate," Toby said. The idea of sharing champagne with the spy was almost funny. "He accused me of stealing his pen. And he won't get out."

Felice studied the guy. He said, "Did he? Steal your pen?" Tongue-tied, the guy gaped at him. Felice frowned and said, "You've been hanging around all night. What do you want?"

"The engravings, I think," Toby said, taking the bug from his pocket. He held it up between two fingers so the guy could get a good look. Then he dropped it in a creamer. It hit with a satisfying plop, sending shards of cream onto the table. Toby said, "When I was setting up I saw him fooling with one of the frames."

The guy made a guttural noise deep in his throat. Felice hadn't witnessed the bug-disposal. Preoccupied with thoughts of thievery, his eyes were bulging, and his complexion was taking on a faintly scarlet hue. Good, thought Toby, who knew what this meant. Felice extracted one of the champagne empties. He raised it to shoulder level. With quiet earnestness, he said to the guy, "Get out or I'll bash your brains in. I don't ever want to see you again." Toby admired the way Felice held the half-full bottle in reserve. He wouldn't spill a drop unless it were absolutely necessary. The man opened his mouth, then closed it. He stalked to the door, directed a seething look over his shoulder at Toby, then went out into the cafe, slamming the door behind him.

Felice and Toby eyed each other. "Glasses," Felice said. Toby got two from where he'd hidden them. It was necessary to hide them. Felice never brought enough over. If they weren't kept hidden, other waiters would take them. "Hiding again," Felice remarked as he poured.

"Your fault," Toby replied.

"I wish somebody would steal those things," Felice said, staring at the hog slaughter. "Vegetarians must be so disgusted."

"Blood buckets," Toby said. "Reheema couldn't believe it."

Felice raised his glass to Toby. Toby raised his in return. They grinned at each other. Felice said, "Happy birthday."

▬ ▬ ▬

Slotsky glared through his windshield at the busy villagers of Harvard Square. Damn Miles, he thought.

According to the tracker, the fool was loitering outside the restaurant. Undoubtedly waiting for Toby.

Slotsky instructed the tracker to replay portions of the evening's proceedings. He determined that Toby had discovered the bug moments after Miles activated it. Toby then placed it in a ceramic vessel, judging from resonance analysis; a bowl of sugar packets, judging from the rustles Grace generated. Slotsky replayed the sequence repeatedly. Grace herself apparently had brought the bowl to where she was sitting. How very helpful of her, Slotsky reflected. Without that move, the bug wouldn't have picked up Cliffcloud's sotto voce, and the twins' fevered whispers.

Other sequences of the recording interested Slotsky as well. One ended with Miles bursting into the private room. He accused Toby of having taken something from under the table. A careful study of various sounds in this sequence—furniture movements, tableware adjustments, a tintinnabulation in Toby's pocket as he perhaps knelt, a number of soft grunts, and other such sounds—led Slotsky to construct a scenario of Toby having done exactly that. Was what Toby found a pen? Quite possibly. Slotsky wasn't prepared to swear by it.

But he very much wanted to know.

He whiled away some time replaying Trefethen's dinner party address. The more Slotsky considered it, the more thought-provoking Earnest's words became. This wholesale, almost taunting break with the past—Slotsky knew it meant something extraordinary.

What, though? Beyond the fact that Trefethen expected a cataclysm of some kind in Antarctica? Could he truly be worried about the eruption? Or had he wanted to frighten his old friends and allies for another, more devious reason?

Slotsky suspected a great deal of thought had gone into Trefethen's postprandial remarks. They struck him as having been crafted to achieve a particular effect.

What effect?

Because Slotsky lacked answers, the elusive code took on increasing significance. He considered calling Miles to ascertain his plans. No, he decided. Stepping in at this juncture would rattle Miles. Slotsky sat back, lit a cigar, and considered the events that had brought him here.

His investigation of Martha Cliffcloud began shortly after he'd run into Raymond Pandoleon, an acquaintance dating to Slotsky's Kiev days. Pandoleon and he had worked the black market there in the late '80s. As state controls unraveled, and the military establishment fragmented, both had been among the first to recognize the profit potential of the new era.

They'd parted ways since then, drifting into different sectors of the byzantine economy that Eurasia rapidly developed. Time passed. They lost touch. But almost a year ago, a mutual associate—the fraternal nature of their activities guaranteed many mutual associates—informed Slotsky that Pandoleon had engineered a stunning coup.

It involved the theft of the Spezsevich weapons.

Slotsky by this time was educated in the difficulties of unloading such merchandise. Customers for it tended to be untrustworthy, since they themselves, by definition, were outlaws of the most serious magnitude. Terror organizations, rogue governments, even "respectable" governments—they all were obliged to cover their tracks when seeking nukes, especially advanced nukes in good working condition. That made them tricky trading partners. Their representatives would just as soon kill you as give you money for your trouble, simply to clean up the acquisition process. Slotsky personally knew of several dealers who had met terrible fates. He knew of others who had been forced to sell at absurdly low prices, simply to find buyers who wouldn't murder them. This saddened Slotsky. It also interested him. How could anyone conduct business in so adverse an environment?

Apparently Pandoleon could.

Thus Slotsky had been intrigued when, not a month before and quite by chance, he encountered Pandoleon in the lobby of Boston's Four Seasons Hotel. Dismayed that Slotsky saw through his disguise and expensive plastic surgery, Pandoleon at first resisted an invitation to have drinks in Slotsky's suite. He relented when Slotsky pulled his pellet gun. In the suite's jacuzzi—well removed from doors through which others might hear voices, or any loud sound—Slotsky asked for pointers on negotiating technique. Pandoleon knew that his host often got what he wanted. Genially, he provided advice. He became more helpful when Slotsky opened his nerve kit, an assembly of drugs, needles, and inhalants.

Two days later, having eschewed maid service and relying on room service for meals, Slotsky learned that Pandoleon was conducting research on the client to whom he'd sold the Spezsevich weapons. He hadn't been told the client's identity, naturally. But if Pandoleon was to realize the deal's maximum value, he needed to know that. And once again, he'd scored a major coup.

Not only had he established the weapons' recipient. Much to Slotsky's admiration, Pandoleon had gone a step further. He was negotiating with the Russian PLU, offering to provide it, for a fee: information on the weapons he himself had stolen.

Slotsky understood why Pandoleon had contacted the PLU and not, say, the FATB. It was preferable to be far removed from the interrogation facilities of one's client; particularly if one had something to hide. In Boston, PLU agents couldn't use home-turf resources to extract the whole story behind the weapons' theft. Making a sale, not a confession, was what motivated Pandoleon.

But he hadn't reckoned on running into Slotsky, who prided himself on traveling with every resource he might need. Slotsky didn't really have a home. Wherever he went, that was turf.

Pandoleon died peacefully the third day of his stay. At four in the morning, using a requisitioned wheelchair, Slotsky took him through empty corridors to his room, and put him to bed. Neither fingerprints nor witnesses could tell the tale, as none existed. But to be on the safe side, Slotsky checked out.

At the desk, four PLU agents, posing as trade representatives, happened to be checking in. They recognized Slotsky. That created an awkward situation. The agents were there to see Pandoleon, of course, and if allowed to learn of his unavailability, would associate Slotsky with it. The prospect of appearing in a report to Moscow discomfited Slotsky. He didn't want interference; a lot of money was at stake. Besides which, the PLU held him in low enough esteem already.

So he told the Russians that his old friend Ray Pandoleon was sleeping off the effects of too much drink. With a wink, he proposed comparing notes on Ray's state of mind, and suggested walking down the Esplanade, a scenic stretch of green along the river where they could talk with no fear of being overheard. Unlike the hotel, Slotsky stressed. He assured them it was heavily bugged.

In a copse of trees, at that hour of the morning inhabited by birds, squirrels, and soiled condoms, Slotsky dispatched the Russians with pellet-borne neurotoxin.

He then wasted no time making use of the facts he'd gleaned from Pandoleon.

Three weeks later, Slotsky waited for a dimwitted employee to deal with a meddling waiter. "The edge of history," he mused. Whatever could Cliffcloud mean?

He reached into the box at his feet. The nap of the suede made him catch his breath. He felt the tightening in his liver; it was always in his liver that he felt it. As he stroked the suede, his heart rate mounted. Oh, the pressure. The softness. Slotsky licked his lips. He was sweating. He had to stop. Willing it, forcing it, he released the shoe.

Something would come from tonight's misadventure. Of that Slotsky was sure. He said, "Slut on."

Breathily the tracker said, "Filthy sucker, watch out or I'll step on you."

He squirmed in the bucket seat. "Yes," he muttered. "Step."

But the tracker wasn't programmed to respond to that. His thoughts drifted to Miles, and to Special Agent Whipple. To the issue of a code. The twins hadn't told Miles what it was, or what it did. Therefore, Slotsky also hadn't been told. But judging from what little the twins had told Miles, and therefore Slotsky, this code was important, and extremely dangerous.

Slotsky suspected he might be on the verge of a career-defining moment. A moment that could rival even Ray Pandoleon's triumph. And unlike poor Ray, he wouldn't get his hands dirty trafficking dangerous devices.

Cleanliness was Slotsky's hallmark. The commodities he sold couldn't have been more sanitary, or easy to handle. They traveled, when he wished it, at the speed of light; and if the need arose, he could make them disappear just as fast, for Slotsky, white-glove gangster that he was, dealt exclusively with information.

8

Toby finished breaking down the room. He went through the kitchen to the locker room, where he stripped off apron and vest. What a night, he thought. The evening's events throbbed with scary disorder behind that mental picture of Grace Trefethen. Toby kept seeing the anguish on her lovely face.

No woman had affected him this strongly since he'd stopped seeing Nadia. Since she'd dumped him.

He fished the pin out of his apron. The thing was about two and a half inches in diameter, about twice the size of a political campaign button. The drawing under the lamination—a rabbit? A lapdog with tall ears? It had been rendered two-dimensionally, in profile, with very little shading. Pen and ink—a line drawing. Yet it had personality. The single staring eye, the set of the ears, the stance of its legs, suggested eagerness—a willingness, Toby thought, to pounce. He'd never seen anything like it.

Impulsively, he attached it to his shirt, and checked it out in the mirror over the sink. The reverse image seemed to glare at him. With sinister intent, he thought. "DO NOT REPRODUCE IN ANY FORM WHATSOEVER. USE IT TO FILTER THE MEDIA STREAMS." Toby shivered. Those words made no sense. But they creeped him out.

It's not, he told himself for the twentieth time, a pen.

He put his stuff in his backpack and went up front to get somebody to sign his time card.

Dan sat at the bar. He'd done something to his hair. Or Selma had, Toby remembered. The last he'd seen them they were sprawled on the porch at home, sunbathing. Dan was undergoing one of Selma's henna treatments. She'd achieved a turquoise effect, Toby observed. Peter the bartender seemed taken with it. He was listening to Dan say, "It'll go late. Maybe all night."

"Look at you," Toby said.

"Hi," Dan said with a guilty smile. What's he up to? Toby wondered. Dan remarked, "You waited on Reheema. Was she great?"

"Indescribably glamorous," Toby said glumly. "How'd you know I'm getting out of here?"

"I called," Dan replied. "Cute," he said, looking at Toby's shirt. Toby realized he meant the pin. "What is it?"

"I can't even begin to tell you," Toby said. Should he inform Dan that a leading Antarctic scientist had announced the coming of the Great Flood? That there's serious trouble with the media streams too? So serious, nobody even knows what they are? "You called," he said meditatively, checking out highlights in Dan's wavy brown hair. "Old ladies dye their hair that color."

"The spinster look," Peter said with approval.

"What?" Toby said.

Dan said, "Don't worry. It's not a granny cult or anything."

"Yes it is," Peter said. "Of course it is."

"Okay, it is," Dan said. He grinned. "And I have to admit, I love feeling seventy-five."

Toby didn't understand this. He said, "Peter, pour Dan a drink. Don't bother with ID—he's my kid brother and I know for a fact he'll be twelve next month. Dan, if Peter asks you for a date, or makes comments about your physique, remember what Mom says about older men. Excuse me. I have to make a call."

He went to the public phone and got directory assistance. The operator didn't have any listings under Trefethen or Scarf. But she did have a listing for the Center for the Study of Moral Reasoning. Toby called it. He expected to get a machine. But a male voice answered with, "Clinic."

Toby said, "May I leave a message for Grace Trefethen?"

Silence came over the line. Toby started to repeat the question. The voice said, "Who is calling?"

"Mifflin Place restaurant," Toby replied. "I'm the waiter who served the Trefethens tonight. Grace left something here. I'm wondering how to return it."

Another silence. Then the voice said, "Dr. Scarf is moving, so she might not get a message. What did Grace leave?"

Toby had thought about this. "A piece of jewelry," he said.

"Your name?"

Toby gave the man his name and home number. That wasn't standard procedure. He should have given the number for the restaurant's office, since lost items went there. However, the pin wasn't going there. Toby wanted to talk to Grace personally.

He headed back to the bar. Dan was sipping a margarita. Toby said to him, "Let me guess. You're taking me out?"

"Nah," Dan said. "You're too feeble for that."

"Then we have a quiet evening at home. Until you go out with Selma to some bar with naked go-go boys. Sorry. I'm grumpy."

"Toby," Dan said, eyes radiating brotherly concern. "You're always grumpy. It's because you think everything's coming to an end." He put a hand on Toby's arm and said in a lower voice, "Look at these guys." Toby glanced around. He saw what Dan meant. The queers working that night were pretending to be busy. But what they really were doing was watching Dan.

"You're safe with me," Toby said. "Those rapists don't stand a chance."

Dan snorted. "What do you notice about them?" he asked.

"They're waiters. Who have the hots for you."

"What's their average age?"

Toby thought a moment. "Early twenties," he said. "Why?"

Dan said, "Do you know what it's like to be trapped in a social life where almost everybody is under thirty?"

Shit, Toby thought. Dan said, "You mentioned older men. There aren't that many of them. Not in my life. They're either dead or sick or they're completely freaked out because a lot of their friends have come to an . . ."

Toby said, "Yeah."

"Anyway," Dan continued, "I can't spend all my time being grumpy about the world coming to an end. Even if it seems like it already has." Toby didn't know what to say. Dan stared at him. Then he laughed. "I shouldn't discuss this with you," he remarked. "You look like I kicked you in the stomach. Hey—I have an idea."

"Great," Toby said.

"Let's go have a really quiet evening at home."

"Okay," Toby said.

Miles stood in courtyard shadows watching Toby walk to Brattle. Somebody walked with him. That was too bad. Bringing Toby down and searching him would have taken less than a minute if he'd been alone. But he wasn't, and his friend looked athletic.

They reached the street. Toby hailed a passing taxi. It had a fare and didn't stop. They started talking. Miles slipped behind them up to the street and hurried to his car. With any luck they wouldn't get a cab for another minute.

Toby was going to be sorry by the time Miles was done. It was bad enough to be in his pants, listening to the jangle. Bad enough to hear the hand there, too. Bad enough to get muffled voices, coming through cloth and who knew what junk. Then, seeing what he'd done to the table, that was a kick in the ass. But on top of it all, to have this worthless, stupid pen—Miles was enraged.

But maybe it was the right pen. How could he be sure it wasn't? What should he do, break it in half? What if he ruined it? He was afraid even to see if it wrote—could the code be a microdot? Would it come out in the ink and be lost forever?

Worst of all, how would Miles explain this to Whipple?

He didn't know. But he wasn't going to take any chances. He was
going to corner the kid and collect his pens. All of them. Every single
one. Then Miles would see what was what with the code. And as for
Toby the waiter, he'd wish he'd minded his business.

The tracker gave Slotsky directions.
Right from Mt. Auburn Street onto Putnam Avenue, left from Putnam
onto Magazine Street. "Stop," the contralto said, indicating Miles had
slowed, or stopped. The tracker was keeping Slotsky out of Miles'
rearview mirror. The young man possessed a degree of streetwise cun-
ning; Slotsky didn't want it squandered on himself.

He wanted Miles to concentrate on Toby.

Slotsky parked. He waited for the tracker to tell him Miles was
leaving his car. Minutes passed. Miles evidently saw no need to hurry.

Trees lined the street. Damp brick sidewalks glowed under the
lamps. The buildings, a mixture of apartment houses and single-family
homes, had a modest, well-tended look. Very nice, thought Slotsky. A
nice night indeed here in Cambridgeport. According to the tracker,
that was where Miles had led him. Slotsky found the placename a tri-
fle grand. What the devil was Miles doing?

He put the tracker in his coat, firmed the earphone in his ear,
selected an umbrella from the backseat—he kept several bumber-
shoots in the car, of different makes and styles to cope with a spectrum of weather—and got out. Miles, he knew, remained in his car, or
near it. The tracker would have told him if he'd moved more than a
few feet.

Thus it was Miles' car Slotsky sought as he waddled slowly up Magazine Street. Within three blocks he saw it, and, leaning against it,
Miles, smoking a cigarette, and studying a three-story building. It
looked like the lone survivor of a once-elegant townhouse block.
Probably it wouldn't survive much longer; the structure seemed
skewed. Slotsky sidled into the shadow of a hedge. He heard music.
Boisterous and raw, it came from that building. A group of young people, approaching down Magazine, turned into the front walk, atti-

tudes expectant. Slotsky's gaze settled on a ramshackle third-floor porch at the rear. He squinted through the moist darkness. The porch held numerous people.

He sighed. Toby, apparently, was attending a party.

Words Slotsky had heard earlier, moments before the bug suddenly had ceased functioning, came back to him: "You should know something, Felice. Today is my birthday."

Two taxis pulled up and disgorged more youngsters. They carried full paper bags. Beer, Slotsky judged. How, he wondered, is Miles going to handle this?

The answer came soon. Miles got in his car and slammed the door. The window rolled down. From it the cigarette sailed to the pavement. Within the car a lighter flared. Slotsky deduced that Miles would smoke a good deal, and wait.

If he was prepared to do that, Slotsky was too. He hurried to his car. In its air-conditioned comfort he lit a cigar. It became a stub that he hurled to the sidewalk. Still no move from Miles. Slotsky pulled up a block. Through night-vision binoculars he watched a flow of arrivals and departures outside the building; the latter category, judging from Miles' inertia, didn't include Toby.

Slotsky found himself thinking of rear exits, of various means by which Toby might leave the building undetected. Could he trust Miles with a mission of this importance? The tracker held telephone listings for the metropolitan area. Slotsky ordered a search for Tobys on Magazine Street. The tracker came up with a Swett at Number 94; Slotsky was parked by Number 176; he counted buildings and satisfied himself that Miles indeed was targeting Number 94. Slotsky called the Swett phone number. Someone answered; deafening music came through. Slotsky hung up. This Toby, at least, was having a party. That was something. But only something. Worrying tired Slotsky. He found it disagreeable, even alien.

He calmed himself by performing a ritual, the transmission of the day's data to his computer in Zurich. Slotsky didn't like to keep important information near his person. Experience had taught him that the potential for accident or theft could never be overestimated. He in particular wanted to safeguard the dinner party recording. It might bring a tidy sum. What with Cliffcloud et al. nearing "the edge of history."

Slotsky had reason to believe that Cliffcloud could take whomever she wished right over the edge of history, if she were so inclined. For it was she, according to Ray Pandoleon, who had acquired the Spezse-vich weapons. At rock-bottom rates, at that. Her emissaries had paid only three hundred million dollars.

Poor Ray, Slotsky reflected. He'd held onto the bombs for more than three years after stealing them; so apprehensive had he been that a buyer would kill him. Then he'd sold them for a tiny fraction of their worth. He'd then established some facts concerning the identity of the buyer. But then he'd died. A shame.

Slotsky stared through his windshield at 94 Magazine Street. What ignominy, he thought, if his investigation were to stall there. At that dilapidated building.

His thoughts meandered, back to the beginning of his scrutiny of Martha Cliffcloud's affairs.

A remarkable woman, he'd quickly discovered. Despite her disap-pointing penchant for moccasins and sandals. Flat soles did nothing for Slotsky. In fact, they unnerved him.

Everything else about Cliffcloud impressed him deeply. Half Native American, half old-line WASP, she'd received a Ph.D. in applied physics from MIT. She then landed a job doing laser research at the Sublime Corporation, a high-tech holding company. Her work, by all accounts brilliant, attracted the attention of Sublime's founder, owner, and chief executive, the legendary entrepreneur Julius Roth. The two married after Roth's wife died in 1989. When Roth himself died, childless, in 1998, Cliffcloud inherited the immense fortune that Sub-lime by that time had come to be worth—lock, stock, and barrel.

She immediately renamed Sublime the Mantis Corporation. Despite doubts in the business community, she in due course proved her management skills equal to her scientific expertise. Among other strokes of genius, she created a new logo for Mantis, the computer animation known as "the orb." As Mantis grew, finding ever more lucrative niches in the information technology boom, the orb came to be an emblem of the new age.

Its eerie radiance now emanated from advertisements on every tele-vision screen in the world. Many people considered Cliffcloud the most canny entrepreneur in corporate America. With holdings in biotech, laser applications, defense technology, software, and telecom-munications, Mantis had made her a multibillionaire.

Almost as beguiling, she was ruthless. The name "Mantis," she once told an interviewer, symbolized her business style: "Corporately speaking, I mate. And then I devour." Slotsky found such an attitude bracing. Finally, her recorded thoughts on politics, public service, and morality exhibited the most profound cynicism Slotsky ever had come across. Compared to her, the Eurasian mafia seemed like a charitable organization run by nuns.

But none of this explained what she intended to do with eleven nuclear bombs. Did the woman consider them toys? With all her wealth and power and lack of faith in the human spirit, had her ennui reached the point of nihilism? And could she think of nothing better than to go out with a bang, taking whatever with her?

That didn't make sense. Slotsky dug deeper. He looked into the Mantis subsidiary, ColdCut Holdings, which Pandoleon had identified as the bombs' recipient. It occupied a building in the downscale community of Chelsea. Not surprisingly, ColdCut turned out to be defunct. No one worked there. Its phone lines were disconnected. No business went through its locked doors.

Slotsky doubted the building now harbored the bombs. Even an eccentric billionaire wouldn't store them in a semi-residential location, a place children might break into just for the hell of it. But even if the bombs weren't there, someone had to be monitoring the building's security, due to trace radioactivity that eleven powerful devices would leave behind, no matter how well fabricated they might be. A sensitive sensor—one like those the FATB used to screen airports and border crossings—could pick up such traces from the street, perhaps even from several blocks away.

Who, Slotsky wondered, kept an eye on the place?

He scouted the building's rear. A window proved easy to smash. That done, he retreated to his car, which he'd parked in an alley across the way.

Twenty minutes later—a rather leisurely response time, in Slotsky's opinion—a windowless van cruised by. It cruised by once more, and parked several blocks down. From it three burly men emerged. They ambled past the building to a sub shop a block and a half in the other direction. Fifteen minutes later, they ambled back to the building. There they paused, munching grinders. Without quite appearing to do so, they studied the faux-brick facade and the small, shuttered windows.

Then they went to the rear. A half hour passed. The men reappeared, got in the van, and left.

Slotsky didn't follow. That he judged too blatant. But he noted the plate number; and soon determined, via some hacking with the tracker, that the van was registered to an institution called the Center for the Study of Moral Reasoning.

He investigated, and learned that "the Clinic," as those familiar with the Center for the Study of Moral Reasoning referred to it, had been founded to address the problem of overflowing prisons. Due to the drearily ongoing drug war, the mutinous underclass, the fact that American children ranked as the world's most murderous by far, and the criminalization of a large segment of the population following the FATB's crackdown on the Frenzy, the U.S. penitentiary system exceeded the housing stock of most small countries. New facilities literally couldn't be built quickly enough.

This had made the science of rehabilitation very much in vogue. The Clinic was riding that wave. Slotsky, always attentive to crime-control innovation, discovered that the Clinic performed other services as well.

For example, it did contract work for the FATB in the cutting-edge field of "psychosecurity."

The more Slotsky learned about that field, the more intrigued he became. Dr. Helen Scarf, the Clinic's founder and director, struck him as being the kind of FATB associate he should avoid at all costs. Most of her activities were classified. But Slotsky was able to access enough information to speculate about what she conceivably could be doing, and getting away with, almost wholly shielded from public scrutiny. He marveled at the possibilities. "Psychosecurity" would be rather useful to someone hatching a nuclear plot. Among other things, it could help tie up the traditional loose ends of motivation, discretion, and obedience.

But Slotsky still had no proof of a plot. If anything, the mystery had deepened. Why would an FATB psychiatrist ally herself with a billionaire in a scheme involving weapons of mass destruction? Slotsky found himself wondering if the FATB could be setting up a crisis for purposes of self-promotion. A couple of incinerated cities, the threat of more on the way, would work wonders with the American political system. A military dictatorship, overnight.

Slotsky doubted Americans had that much imagination. Let alone the nerve. He delved further into Dr. Scarf's life, and soon discovered the world of her husband, Dr. Earnest Trefethen. Several facts stood out in that rather odd place.

A distinguished professor at both Harvard and MIT, now retired, Trefethen ran a nonprofit foundation that used a sizable ship, the

Pelagic, to conduct scientific research in various parts of the world. About ten months before, the *Pelagic* had completed a climatological survey of the Baltic Sea. It docked for a week at Koenigsberg, Lithuania. Then it returned to its home port at Woods Hole, Massachusetts.

Three months later, the *Pelagic* set sail for Antarctica, where Trefethen continued a long-term study of volcanism, ice streams, and ice shelves associated with the West Antarctic Ice Sheet. Toward the end of the research phase of this mission, almost all of Trefethen's fellow expeditionists died in an accident. Trefethen survived. So did his two children, Brian and Grace, budding scientists following their father's footsteps. The only other survivor, apart from crew on the ship, was a man named Charles Fladgate. Slotsky was interested to learn that Fladgate's primary occupation had nothing to do with Antarctic science. When not at sea in the Baltic or the South Pacific, he served as security chief for the Clinic. He policed the Center for the Study of Moral Reasoning.

Did Fladgate also police Trefethen's outfit, the Ecologic Foundation? The question took on added resonance when, with the help of Miles Malt, Slotsky discovered that the Clinic provided "counseling services" to Trefethen's people; to those still alive, that is. At this point, more than a dozen lay in the deep freezer of an Antarctic crevasse.

Slotsky had an odd feeling about the accident. According to Miles, the mood at Ecologic wasn't one of grief. People seemed more "spaced out" than bereaved. Perhaps they were working things through. Then again, perhaps they needed more counseling.

Dr. Scarf, Slotsky was confident, could provide it.

Miles had been working for Slotsky just over two weeks now. Due to being the janitor at Ecologic's Plympton Street building, he'd come up with a variety of intriguing trivia. But nothing to indicate that the *Pelagic* had picked up the Spezsevich bombs in Lithuania. Nothing to indicate that it then had delivered one or more of them to Antarctica. And nothing to support Slotsky's most recent, and most astonishing, hypothesis—that one or more of the bombs had caused the Antarctic eruption.

On the surface, all of those hypotheses couldn't have been more preposterous. Earnest Trefethen, nuclear eco-terrorist? The idea seemed oxymoronic in more ways than one. But that was its beauty. Who would suspect a "tireless" environmentalist? A respected scholar whose friends included FATB chieftains both national and local? Whose wife ran the Clinic? Whose eco-radicalism always had been couched in reason, not in inflammatory, attention-getting tactics? A man who, on paper, would be the last person in the world to violate one of science's most sacred commandments: *Thou shalt not despoil the pristine environment of Antarctica.*

Of course, Trefethen's expertise made him perhaps the single most qualified person in the world to do just that. In a way that could inflict almost unimaginable planetary destruction.

But who would suspect?

Slotsky would. He not only would, he did. Unfortunately, his employee Miles Malt thus far hadn't delivered definitive proof. And without proof, Slotsky couldn't cash in.

How much was it worth, this information he believed to be true? Only one word described it: Incalculable.

The party at 94 Magazine showed no signs of abating. On the contrary, it was just getting started; Slotsky had been watching a steady flow of new arrivals. This, he thought, could be messy.

10

"Few new facts are in," the CNN anchor said, "but what we know is sufficiently compelling that we will continue to provide updates throughout the night. An earthquake has occurred in Antarctica. The epicenter was six hundred miles from the Pole, deep in the western part of the continent, with a magnitude estimated at six point nine on the Richter scale. That's a record for Antarctica. But the more worrisome part of this story concerns fire in the coldest part of the world. The quake has triggered a major volcanic eruption."

Toby practically had to sit on the TV to hear it. His room was a madhouse. People he'd never seen before were shouting at the tops of their lungs—and still not hearing each other over the music blasting from the next room.

"Eruptions are always dramatic," the anchor continued. "What makes this one particularly so is its location—underneath the West

Antarctic Ice Sheet, which is to say, under more than a mile of solid ice." The anchor smiled faintly. "That ice is solid no longer. The eruption appears to have vaporized everything around it. In short, a vast crater, perhaps two miles deep, now roils in the West Antarctic Ice Sheet.

"Evidence for this is indirect due to steam the eruption is producing. Mammoth banks of clouds already have developed into a storm system, cloaking the area and hindering aerial and satellite surveillance. But seismological and infrared data, coupled with the quantity of vapor thrown into the atmosphere, leave scientists with little doubt as to the fundamentals of what is happening.

"Glaciologists, volcanologists and climatologists around the world say the event is unique in the history of such phenomena. They assert that it was, and I quote, 'extraordinarily explosive.' Never before have they known of an ice-submerged volcano erupting in this fashion. The consequences are sure to become the subject of an intense debate in the scientific community, especially regarding the stability of the West Antarctic Ice Sheet, or WAIS.

"With us to discuss the eruption is Dr. Stanley Vole of the University of Texas at Austin. Dr. Vole, what is the history of volcanoes under the ice sheet?"

Vole, a chubby man, smiled tensely. He said, "The first evidence of volcanism below the WAIS came to light in late 1992. Since then, we've established the presence of dozens of volcanoes there, many buried more than a mile deep. Geologically, the area is a 'rift zone'— the lithospheric crust is thin, permitting the upward flow of the magma that creates volcanoes. It's relevant to point out that the continental plate underlying West Antarctica actually belongs to the South American crustal plate, not to the Antarctic plate proper. So you have stresses associated with plate collision. Such conditions can favor volcano formation."

"I see. I think I see. You're saying there's a system of volcanic activity under the ice sheet?"

"Yes, I am."

"What's the chance of the entire system exploding?"

Vole chortled. "Very, very slight," he said.

"But if more volcanoes do erupt—what effect would that have on the sheet?"

"Not a good one. The sheet's adhesion to the bedrock would deteriorate, because basal ice would melt. However, that's not . . . "

"We've heard reports since the mid-nineties of substantial melting in Antarctica. Will the eruption speed that process?"

"No. We're talking about geophysical processes playing out over thousands of years. A long time from now, the WAIS might collapse, which in turn could trigger ice discharge from East Antarctica—bringing true disaster. If East Antarctica lost only a third of its ice following a WAIS collapse, sea level would rise a hundred and seventy feet. But again, it's unlikely to happen for a very, very long time."

CNN wasn't reporting anything Toby hadn't heard before. Nor were newsnets he'd accessed through his computer.

Strangely, he found it a relief. What he'd witnessed at the restaurant seemed enough for one day. Besides which, he felt an obligation to try to enjoy this party. His birthday party, he reminded himself. Dan and Selma had gone all out. There was enough liquor in the kitchen to float an aircraft carrier.

He wended his way through the middle room, gasping from the cigarette smoke and nodding at the occasional person he recognized. The crowd's so young, he thought. And stylish. Not a care in the world. No concern, for example, about Antarctica. But that was normal. Nobody cared about catastrophe. Catastrophe had become ordinary, even banal. Toby watched a ruggedly beautiful black kid enter from the kitchen. The boy approached a Latino guy and two girls who were arguing over the disc collection by the stereo; he greeted the guy with a passionate kiss, then launched enthusiastically into a story about something or another. The girls laughed. They entwined arms around each other's waists.

Toby remembered Dan's comments about "older men." With full-blown AIDS long having passed the million-case mark in the U.S., with more than ninety million cases worldwide, the crisis applied to everyone, of course. But in the U.S., it remained very bad for gay men. And completely disastrous for men and women of color.

Toby wondered how many older queers carried on at parties in the fashion of these young ones, with such abandon. He knew plenty who did. Then again, maybe what Dan said was true. Maybe a lot of others were too freaked for social effervescence.

Freaked, Toby considered, is a mild way to put it. So many people were dealing with post-trauma stress. Tons of it was out there. Millions of nervous ills, afflicting all kinds of people. The trendy term at the moment was "occluded." People who couldn't take it any more burned out and shut down. They'd occluded.

That brought them little sympathy. To the rest of the world, they hadn't learned the lesson of what Toby considered the three scariest words in the English language: Life goes on.

A euphemism for compassion fizzle, Toby thought. One can care about only so much suffering. After a while, you stop feeling it. The same with catastrophe. You stop thinking about it after a while, and life goes on.

Which meant, in Toby's view, that the entire culture had occluded. Post-trauma stress from the Frenzy had done it. After the country's millennarian nervous breakdown—race wars and class wars and hate wars and holy wars and terror wars, during which so many people had just plain lost it—everyone seemed in a state of aftershock daze. A kind of tranked-out, numbed-out, denialed-out sleep.

But life goes on. Two kids necked in a corner. The girl looked seventeen, the boy fifteen; both were lost in bliss. A lot of life going on, Toby thought. How come I can't get into it?

Because I'm occluded, he decided. He went through the kitchen to the porch. At the rail, he stared into the night. I'll make myself have fun, he vowed. Too bad Grace Trefethen isn't around to liven things up . . .

The screen door opened. Toby turned. Dan and Selma were following Nadia through the door. "Happy birthday," she said.

No, Toby thought. Why? Why are you here?

"I think it's time you met James," she said, her voice soft, her body a slim blot in the kitchen's backlighting glare. A heftier blot materialized beside her, extending a hand. Toby shook it. It felt meaty. And strong. A paw, Toby thought with shock. This thing paws Nadia.

"Hi," the blot said. "I've heard a lot about you."

"Something to drink, anyone?" Selma asked.

"Yeah," Toby said.

"I'll get punch," Dan said, disappearing into the bright din of the kitchen. Like Selma, he was shaken.

"Have a seat," Toby said.

They sat. The blots resolved. Nadia looked a little pinched. James looked bland and rich. "Happy birthday," he said.

"Thanks," Toby said.

"Quite a crowd," Nadia remarked. "Who are they?"

"No idea," Toby replied. "I didn't invite them. I just got here myself, from work."

"A lot of them are people I know," Selma said tactfully.

"Downstairs people better be invited," James said. "The music's as loud at the front door as it is on this porch."

Nadia said, "I think those apartments are vacant. Or they used to be. Toby?"

"Yeah," Toby said.

"The building inspector," Selma explained to James, "is going to uncondemn us next month. We think."

James laughed. "Are you bribing him?" he said. Nobody replied. They listened to the music for a moment. Waves of laughter crashed from the kitchen. Someone opened the screen door, took one look at them, and disappeared. The door slammed shut. "Big cleanup tomorrow," James said. "Do you recycle?"

"Why do you ask?" Toby asked, knowing why. James was in the business. A recycling industrialist, he'd attained a degree of fame. Local media profiled him, making much of his blunt good looks, his vintage car collection, his company's profits. The government subsidized those profits, critics noted. Few held that against him. Most everyone considered James a "pathbreaker," "a visionary entrepreneur," and, most magical of all, a "job creator."

Toby despised him. Not just because of Nadia. More damning still, James had enriched himself by persuading people that things would be okay. Toby had nothing but contempt for opportunists like James. They preyed on the public's irrational hope that civilization might survive. No better than money-grubbing evangelists, they sold fake salvation. Worst of all, they made realists, such as Toby, look bad. Staring at James, Toby recalled something Nadia often had said. "If the situation is so terrible, Toby, why don't you do something about it?"

Now she sat on his porch, on his birthday, with a new boyfriend who was—from Nadia's point of view, Toby had to concede, James was indeed doing something. "About it." He furthermore had the gall to ask if Toby recycles. Dan arrived clutching a quintet of punch-filled plastic cups. Toby took his and gulped it straight down. Then he said, "No. I don't."

"What?" James said.

"He does," Nadia said.

"No more," Toby said. "Recycling's a fraud, in my opinion."

"How so?" James asked.

"It's a religion," Toby declared. "Like all religions, it deals with guilt. And denies reality."

"Let's talk about something else," Nadia said.

"Smile, Toby," Dan said, aiming Selma's Polaroid.

Toby winced at the flash. He put up a hand to ward off three more that followed. It wouldn't work. Now that he'd started, he wasn't going to be derailed. To James he explained why recycling is an exercise in self-delusion. The real problems, the real trashings, are something recycling can't touch. Isn't it obvious that the exportation of American life is proceeding relentlessly? That everybody on the planet wants to live like we do? That consumerism rules, and there's no way to stop it? That we're implicated up to our necks, because our economy's growth depends on its aggressive exportation? That basically, we're killing the biosphere with carbon and literally hundreds of millions of tons of toxic gunk? That therefore the human race is fucked? Isn't it obvious, he summed up, borrowing Earnest Trefethen's formulation, that we've evolved into a self-destruct machine?

Pity oozed from James's eyes. "Don't know what to say, Toby. Except that I think it's better to be constructive and do something— instead of just sitting here. Talking like a frenzie."

Toby grimaced at him. "You think I'm nuts?" he asked.

James shrugged. "You're harping on the negative," he said. "And forgetting the positive. Take the environment. We've made progress— amazing, comprehensive progress. But listening to you, no one would know it. What about the way we've cleaned up air and water? Stopped making chlorofluorocarbons? What about the forest recanopy in the northern hemisphere?"

Toby waved a hand with disgust. "Pat-ourselves-on-the-back propaganda. Easter Eggbook said those things years ago. Look—all that stuff is semi-true. It's also irrelevant. Those environmental success stories apply to the first world only, and even there in a limited way. Don't tell me you don't know this?"

"You really are a frenzie," James remarked.

"Who is Easter Eggbook?" Nadia said.

"One of the mid-nineties aren't-we-great prosperity cheerleaders," Toby replied. "People like him paved the way for the Republican gutting of the enviro laws. There was this sudden discovery that the biosphere is fine, pollution is vanquished, the world is saved. But it wasn't, and isn't. Biodiversity is shriveling, and everybody knows it. Carbon is even worse. And everybody knows that too. Everybody knows that to stop runaway greenhouse, we not only have to cap carbon emissions—we have to roll them back, drastically. But heaven forbid!" Nadia shrank as Toby started waving an arm to emphasize his points. He yelled, "That would cap economic growth! Not possible, not possible! It's treasonous to even *suggest* messing with economic growth! So do we roll back carbon? No. Do we even cap it? *No!*"

"You have a problem with prosperity," James observed. "But economic dislocation helped fuel the Frenzy, didn't it? We need jobs, don't we? For social peace, we *need* an expanding economy."

"Yeah," Toby said. "People want economic boom. But a boom based on carbon emissions equals ecological and climate doom. The equation is simple: boom equals doom. And everybody knows it."

James sipped punch. He murmured, "The facts are far from clear. We don't have the data."

"We do!" Toby snapped. "The data are there, they have been for quite a while. The trouble is, they make us look like pigs. They expose the fact that we sit on top of the carbon food chain. They do an excellent job of proving that the current first world is the greediest and most selfish culture in the history of the human race. So how do we handle this unpleasant truth? We make it go away. We listen to hack scientists who talk about lack of data. That solves the problem—'We don't have data, we don't have data.'"

James said, "Okay, Toby. What are you going to do about it?"

Toby muttered, "I wish I knew."

Nadia sighed. As if saying, Toby thought, You see how he is? She leaned across to peer at his shirt. "What's that?" she asked.

Toby looked down. He'd forgotten he was wearing the pin. "I found it at the restaurant. Attractive, wouldn't you agree?"

Nadia stared levelly at him. He debated telling her and James about what had happened. That in the opinion of a major scientist, Antarctica was speaking out on behalf of the planet. And that what it had to say wasn't reassuring. He said instead, "Nadia, I can't believe you're here with him."

If there had been any possibility he and Nadia might have had a little birthday chat somewhere in private, it now was out of the question, and she knew it. Dan and Selma were nowhere to be seen. They'd bolted for cheerier company, which kept arriving in droves.

Toby excused himself. He found a bottle of bourbon, and in fine isolation swigged it on the roof. From this aerie he witnessed Nadia's exit, half an hour later. She and James drove off in an antique, resplendently restored Cadillac. Six miles to the gallon, Toby thought. Convinced he's saving the world.

If only there was a way to save it. But that was the problem. What could Toby, or anyone, do to stop the self-destruct machine?

Meantime, he thought disconsolately, Nadia's in that car. Probably he's pawing her. Later they'll make jokes about me, about my loser fixations. And then they'll fuck.

Toby hurled the bottle into the vacant lot next door. Damn, he thought. Why can't I find something constructive to do?

At 4:05 in the morning on Magazine Street, Slotsky's phone buzzed.

Slotsky expected it to be Miles, lying about delays he'd encountered delivering the recording. He instead heard the plangent voice of his old chum Yvonne Delors. "You answer, thank God!" she cried. "You are not asleep?"

"No, Yvonne," Slotsky replied. "I do not sleep. You know this." Voices swirled in the background. Surely she wasn't entertaining; it was 6:05 A.M. in Buenos Aires. Slotsky said, "To what do I owe the privilege of hearing from you?"

She replied in a rush, "I have been trying to reach Dr. Earnest Trefethen, and cannot do it, which drives me to fury, Slotsky! You know where he is?"

Slotsky pondered the question. He asked, "Why would I know where Dr. Trefethen is?"

"You called about him one week ago!" she shouted. That was true. He had. Yvonne sat on the board of the Antarktiploit Condominium, the minerals concern that was trying to get around the 1991 treaty that banned prospecting in Antarctica. She thus was familiar with politics and personalities associated with the continent. However, she knew disappointingly little about Earnest Trefethen. Much, Slotsky had learned, like the rest of the world. She exclaimed, "I must talk with him now! Where is he?"

"I'm not sure, Yvonne. But I will try to find out. If you would be so kind as to tell me what has got you in this turmoil."

She hissed, "I take it you have not heard the news."

"About the eruption, I presume? Of course I've heard."

"And the rumors?" she inquired. "You have heard those?"

"Ah. Perhaps I haven't. What rumors?"

"That the eruption wasn't entirely a . . . natural event, Slotsky. You have Trefethen's home phone number? You have it, if I know you, and oh! I do! Do not lie, Slotsky!"

Slotsky felt sudden and fervent appreciation for Yvonne. He said, "Many people are trying to reach Dr. Trefethen. It may be difficult to get through."

"This is why I call *you!* I will pay, you can be sure."

"Yes. Who is spreading these rumors?"

"They come from McMurdo." That was the American base on the seaward fringe of Antarctica's Ross Ice Shelf. "Nobody is confirming, they have it under very tight security, of course. But I've heard now from three different sources. A bomb, Slotsky. A nuke."

"You cannot be serious?" Slotsky said.

"But I am."

"Are you certain the sources are correct?"

"How can anyone be certain! About something like this!" She seemed to pant for a moment. "Why," she then inquired with more reasonable volume, "do you think I must talk with Trefethen?"

"He is the foremost expert, quite true," Slotsky murmured, heart racing. Events were moving a bit too quickly. How soon would the media report nuclear rumors?

"Slotsky!" Delors screamed. "You are there?"

"Yes, dear," Slotsky replied. "I was just—ah—thinking. Oh yes, I will attempt to ascertain the Trefethen home number, and as soon as I do, if I do, I will call you. I wish you a good night."

"You are holding back! A time like this, you hold back!"

Slotsky smiled. He enjoyed the fiery side of Yvonne Delors. He was quite fond of the way she sometimes stamped her feet; which she always kept ever so bewitchingly shod. Pumps, heels, jackboots, Yvonne had a flair for footwear. Slotsky admired this in a woman. In a stamper like Yvonne, he found it entrancing. "Nonsense," he lied. Of course he had that very unlisted number.

He also was getting the chime in his earphone. A glance through the binoculars revealed Miles crossing the street toward the building that both of them for so many hours had been hoping would empty. He said to Yvonne, "You are upset, and forget yourself. Good-bye."

He hung up and watched Miles climb the front steps and try the door. It swung open. Not locked, Slotsky noted. Miles entered.

Slotsky strategized a moment. Then he started his car, drove to the building, and parked directly in front. Miles' voice came through the earphone: "Where's Toby? Where's Toby?"

A discussion ensued with a voluble young woman. She did not seem cooperative. Slotsky debated intervening. He decided against it; background noise indicated the presence of a number of people. Ah well, thought Slotsky. This indeed will be messy.

Three minutes later a stream of drunken youths emerged. One of them said, "Who does the fuckin' weirdo think he is?"

"Weird shit, man," mumbled another one, who was having trouble standing.

"Weird," a third agreed.

Slotsky found this eloquence amusing. They wobbled away. A taxi arrived and honked its horn. A second wave of indignant bon vivants, three girls and a boy, soon exited the building. They jammed themselves into the taxi, which took off. Slotsky began to feel somewhat impressed. Miles was creating a stir. In the process clearing the place of witnesses.

But another minute went by. On hearing the young woman threaten to call police, Slotsky's confidence began to wane. He reached for the umbrella, opened the car door, clambered out, and stretched his short hulk, waving the umbrella at sky. A lovely dawn was coming. Yvonne's news made it so, he thought; yes, there was a good chance today would be quite significant indeed.

That in mind, Slotsky mounted the stoop and pushed through the door. He scaled the stairs rapidly. The musty silence of the first two floors suggested vacancy. Very good, thought Slotsky. Neighbors would be a nuisance. Off the third-floor landing, a door stood ajar. Bright light poured from it. He heard Miles and the girl unaided now. She urged him to leave. Miles mumbled something. She again mentioned police. Slotsky pulled out his phone and punched Miles' number.

Miles answered with a surprised, "Hello."

"Come downstairs, Miles," Slotsky whispered. "I am here now."

"Oh—Mr. Slotsky," Miles mumbled. He appeared in the doorway. Behind him, obscured from Slotsky's view, stood a girl with a big head of black hair. Slotsky studied her, assessing what kind of struggle she might put up. Miles stepped out onto the landing, revealing her fully, and for Slotsky, time stopped.

They were hip-length. They were purple suede. Small yellow lightning bolts, exquisitely stitched, electrified the purple; the heels and soles gleamed blackly. Slotsky's liver writhed. Bells seemed to clang. He sensed an envelopment of orange fog, drifting and burning in the peripheries. The girl towered. Her feet, huge, were goddess feet. But those boots—wearing them, she was, without question, a major wonder of the world.

The door swung shut, terminating the vision. Slotsky blinked. Slowly, very slowly, the fog lifted. He recalled his business here, and said, "Hello, Miles."

Miles made an attempt to smile. He failed. He put his phone in his raincoat. The hand, Slotsky noted, stayed there. Miles said, "Keeping track of me, Mr. Slotsky?"

"Why, yes. I am. Where is the code, Miles?"

Miles' eyes slitted. He said, "What?"

"The code. Brian's code. The one you promised to give to Agent Whipple, Miles. You believe Toby has it?"

Miles' face palsied. He couldn't speak. But Slotsky doubted he had much of value to say. "Come," he whispered.

"Try something—I'll yell," Miles said, choking on the words.

"Oh, do. Yell. It might inspire that astonishing girl to open the door, and I would very much like that. Miles, I asked you to come down the stairs."

"Wh-What you gonna do?" Miles stuttered. He hadn't failed to notice the way Slotsky held his umbrella.

Slotsky hadn't failed to notice the way Miles kept his hand in the raincoat pocket. "Come to me," he said, smiling wistfully.

"You go down first!" Miles exclaimed.

Slotsky took a step up the stairs. Miles' eyes widened. His hand jerked from the raincoat; a blade flashed from the sleeve. He raised it protectively, almost, Slotsky reflected, incantatorily, as if he thought the razor were magic, capable of casting spells. But nothing could hex the umbrella. Slotsky trained it on the abdomen. Miles lurched forward, blade extended. The umbrella spat. Slotsky watched the shirt shimmy at the puncture site, the soft spot just below the breastbone. Miles gasped. He fell at Slotsky, shivering, toxin jellying his lungs. Slotsky calculated the trajectory. He seized Miles' lapels, took four rapid steps up the stairs, and used his weight to execute a powerful swivel, both lifting the body and turning it. The razor arm drooped now, posing no threat. The twitching legs slipped forward onto the steps. Slotsky grunted from the strain. How he hated that. In his youth, he'd done this with perfect soundlessness.

He set the body down. The eyes were glazing. The razor hand slackened. Slotsky stared at the blade. Surprisingly, it appeared high-quality. Swedish, perhaps, he thought, looking closer; as Miles, gurgling, entered the tunnel of light.

It was so cold. But awesome, all right. It faded Miles' view of Slotsky's head. It bleached the black of the hair, and put a halo around Slotsky's face. Miles studied the nose. The light became brighter, and opened wider, but as Miles drifted into it, farther, farther, away from the nose, he felt the onset of a spasm, his very last spasm, it had to be, he knew it. He wondered if he could use it. He didn't really care. But maybe he should try. It was coming, he could feel it coming, that last dying twitch. And it came.

And he used it. With gauzy, careless joy. And he saw—over his shoulder, so to speak, as the light took him—a sight that made him smile.

Slotsky stood up, face on fire. Blood spurted as if from a hydrant. He clawed open his coat, then his shirt, groping for the patches in a pouch in his armpit. He opened the pouch, selected a Number 20, and unpeeled it with shaking, sticky fingers. His shirt hindered access to the shaved spot on his left shoulder. The patch folded; for a moment he thought it had adhered to itself. This wasn't easy with the blinding pain, the shock.

But he did it. The patch hit the shaved spot, and the amphendorph rush came instantly. Shock subsided. He could think, at least.

In his coat he carried a silk handkerchief. He plastered it on the wound. Blood shot right through. He kicked Miles' raincoat, seeking the pocket with the surveillance electronics. He was obliged to do this, to retain sole possession of the Trefethen recording. His foot found the machine. He dragged it out and shoved it in his coat.

I must leave, he thought. A shame.

The code. The boots. A really quite dreadful shame.

PART 2

SATURDAY

12

Toby dreamed he was voyaging through the stars. He wanted to continue with it forever. He didn't want the dream to end.

His ship churned steadily along. At the helm, free to roam where he wished, Toby prowled byways of the cosmos. He sought wonder, and found it. He witnessed war, he saw piracy, he met all manner of drama. This involved risk, needless to say. But Toby thrived on risk, and fortunately for him and his crew, the ship moved like lightning, with precision stealth.

What a crew, too. Down corridors and between decks they glided with guileless eyes, the noblest, cleverest specimens of a noble and clever tribe. Souls pure, physiques sturdy, they were splendid lovers, of course—with names like Marsh and Biff, Herculise and Swifty, Jed and Dirk. They knew what they were doing, these venturesome youths. And boy, were they doing it.

Such a ship. Such a crew. Toby felt so lucky.

Still, he knew disaster might strike. In the far reaches of space, surprise ever was lurking—like right now, for example. What caused that gong? Why the sudden clamor in the gangways?

Herculise screamed, "Wake up! *Wake up!*"

Toby woke and the roar began, a rasp of pressure and pain. He felt bound and gagged. In fact he felt dead, noxious with bloat. Toby tasted evil textures. Thirst and his bladder were twin emergencies, equally dire. Through slitted eyes he saw the blue wash of TV, silent, still on. The flickering light mocked him. Get up, get up, it seemed to say. Drink water. Take a pee.

Toby sat up, and moaned. Before crashing, he'd nailed blankets over the windows of his room. He'd wanted a barricade against the coming day. Day was here now, had been long since; it X-rayed the blankets, creating with the TV a restless gloom. Toby moaned again. He squinted. Everywhere, he saw a monstrous mess.

Liquids glinted. Fluid-filled things covered the floor. Vessels lay askew—glasses, bottles, ashtrays, wallowing in their own filth. The drunken hordes, Toby thought. The bastards.

He'd slept in his clothes. Carefully, he stood on his bed. A floor-level futon, stable as pavement, it seemed afloat in the glints; drifting, liable to capsize. Toby swayed. The TV caught his eye. A beacon, he thought, staring at it. A reality fix, giving him bearings. A woman held a mop. Her floor seemed so clean. Now proffering a miracle foam, she looked on top of things, and reminded Toby of Nadia. Why was she so ecstatic about being clean?

Foam lady yielded to news, to grinning newspeople in a clean news-room. Toby blinked. No, he thought; please, no news. The grins switched off. A man filled the screen, silently mouthing. He looked serious. Above him, Toby noticed a map. Of a manta ray thing, white, with a thick, bulbous tail.

Huh, thought Toby. He reached in his pocket. It was still there, his memento of the night before.

And it still wasn't a pen.

The newsman's mouthings looked more serious. Wanting audio, Toby scanned his desk, then his dresser, for the remote control. He saw nothing but more of last night's leavings. He'd never find the remote. So forget it.

For the moment, forget Antarctica.

He took the first step from the futon, then a second, finding it easier than he'd expected. His socks stuck to the floor, giving him traction. Anyway, what difference would it make if he slipped and fell and spilled more shit? He approached the curtain that shielded his room from the middle room. A Guatemalan weaving dotted with duck creatures on a field of red, he'd hung it three years before in lieu of a door, when, upon moving in, he concluded that no normal door would ever fit. The entire apartment sagged. Floors sloped, walls listed. Newcomers often remarked on these anomalies, which Toby attributed to "Cambridge architecture." Usually that explanation sufficed; except for the diehard incredulous, who would insist on experiments with rolling marbles, or proclaim that the place tilted like a boat at sea. Toby had learned to ignore the infirmities of his home. But now, at the curtain's dim thresh-old, he felt something of a deck's incline, and steadied himself for the coming pitch. He knew what lay beyond wouldn't be a pretty sight.

It was awe-inspiring.

Under daylight's full force the party's aftermath reposed with hideous tranquility. The middle room, the kitchen beyond, had the look of a ruined civilization. There had been upheaval and pillage; but everything was still now, as if it had happened long ago. Toby felt humbled. He felt like the first of the simple-minded folk to wander through remnants of a grander race.

The place was in worse shape than he'd thought. But it somehow seemed splendid. Endless rows of beer bottles suggested monumental design, as if aliens had come to bury the dead. Hundreds of plastic cups were druidically huddled, things floating in them the product of ritual, slaughter perhaps. Empties lay crashed like failed escape-craft. Objects sprawled in tragic final throes. From ashtrays, butts mounded imposingly, like volcanic cones.

A sudden roar reminded Toby he was looking at his apartment. The air conditioner had come to life. A big closet opened off the middle room, spacious enough to do lots of things in besides store junk. Taking advantage of this, a previous tenant had installed an air conditioner. It poked incongruously through the wall opposite the window. Old, the machine didn't cool, but it ventilated. It also made privacy. No sound could penetrate the grinding, rattling wheeze. Accordingly, the closet had been dubbed the "orgy room." Toby stared at the closed door. He wondered if Dan slept inside. Or if he was alone.

Meditative now, and melancholy, Toby ventured into the kitchen. The table was an altar to disintegration, fettuccine writhed from the sink, the stove bristled with yet more bottles.

In the bathroom, vomit stank. Toby, peeing quarts, didn't care. This was overload. It just seemed way beyond. He drank water, quarts of it, using cupped hands. The available glasses looked risky.

Back in the kitchen, he debated launching into cleanup. Out loud he said, "No," and headed for a window.

The afternoon radiated springtime loveliness. Everything was so warm, bright, airy. How dismal, Toby thought. Birds sang. Bugs buzzed. Trees waggled branches, the shocking-lime buds almost painfully pert. Squirrels scampered, dogs barked, pedestrians roamed the street three stories below; their movements were puzzling, and vaguely idiotic.

Where do they think they're going? Toby wondered.

The view from the window became a screen for reverie. He remembered finding a lot of people jammed in the kitchen, in the middle room, even on his bed, partying as if there were no tomorrow. What's the point? he thought. Why bother? If there's no tomorrow?

But it seemed to have come. Somehow, despite everything, tomorrows never failed to happen. There was no stopping them.

Last night's talk with James came back. The accusation came back, too: "You really are a frenzie."

Of course I am, Toby thought dully. But then, so is everybody else. We're all artifacts of this crazy millennarian era, whether or not we want to admit it. The Frenzy scarred everyone.

In Toby's case, the craziness, or perhaps the insight, had been integral to his thinking for years. Since early adolescence he'd seen the world coming to an end; and had annoyed family and friends alike with his pessimistic views. No one had wanted to hear it. For good reason. It was so depressing.

Then as the '90s dragged on, it became increasingly clear that Toby's dire predictions weren't so nuts after all. In fact, they fell short of the mark. Far short. As things fell apart, as fundamentalists of every stripe started megaphoning louder, as economic injustice fostered ever more desperate underclass revolt, as terrorists, cultists, and crazies started unleashing their sickness, many people not only came to believe that the End was nigh—in various ways, they started trying to hasten it.

But of course, the End didn't come. Which hadn't surprised Toby, because he'd never envisioned a literal stop. He'd never, for example, bought into religious Endism. He'd never had any interest in Judgment Day, the prophecies of Nostradamus, the coming of the Messiah. "Endists" and "apocalypticists" left him cold; he couldn't understand the allure of junk superstition when reality itself offered so much more terror. Why camouflage the truth with supernatural doom, supernatural saviors? Anyway, unlike the nuts who believed such things, to Toby the idea of the world itself ending was completely absurd.

The planet would continue to spin for millions of years. Meantime, life would go on. Some kind of life would. The question was, what kind? For humans, and for the many flora and fauna who were their victims, Toby did see an end.

He saw the end of life as they knew it.

This outlook Toby called "catastrophism." He considered himself a catastrophist. He studied, he in a sense curated catastrophes, with the ardor of a serious collector. Not that he delighted in them. What he found fascinating about catastrophe was the way it proved the human race's ability to become accustomed to—even bored with—almost anything that threatened a decent way of life.

Since his earliest awareness, the list had grown more menacing every day: Nukes, AIDS, toxic disposal, greenhouse, ozone depletion, mutant viruses, refugee floodtides, the Pope, fundamentalists, the NRA, race wars, Islamic avengers, terror nukes, climate shift, tribal wars, ethnic holocaust, holy wars, the worldwide triumph of consumerism, Singapore-lovers, larcenous elites keeping whole populations in penury, information elites who didn't care, killer youths, toxins going amok, unknown toxins that had to be out there, bacteria gobbling human flesh, the world's addiction to fossil fuels, China's vast coal reserves going up in smoke, El Niño, freakishly violent weather, fishless oceans, chlorofluorocarbon smugglers, UV radiation zapping plankton and everything else, food chain breakdown, global immune breakdown, the ex-middle class gone mean due to its unemployability in the knowledge economy, sadistic underclass-bashers, unsustainable development, hungry people with guns, angry people with machine guns, plague-ridden machete-wielders, famine, mad dog cultists who would destroy whole cities to fulfill stupid prophecies, "patriots" full of hate, Jew-haters, the general gamut of authoritarian personality, bio-weapon fermenters, water wars, food wars, holy nukes, holy viruses, holier-than-thou viruses, vicious smash-the-machine Luddies, third world hatred of first world hogs, police state enthusiasts, the transformation of life into low-grade terror, the increasing frequency of high-grade terror, millennarian Frenzy, the Federal Anti-Terror Bureau, near-fascism in the U.S., the innate murderousness of the human race, the greed, myopia, and savagery of the human race, and above all else, the crowning evil, the absolute guarantee of doom, population explosion.

Such diagnoses weren't original, of course. Everybody knew them. Many people still discussed them with dread; Luddies still tried to smash the machine, and frenzies still paraded, screaming about the end of the world.

Toby felt, however, that almost all such activities weren't quite serious. People talked about the End, sure. It was still fashionable in a perverse, taken-for-granted way. But did these amateurs, mostly drugged to the gills with antidepressants, actually feel the reality breathing down their necks? More to the point, did the controlling majority care?

Toby knew they did not. They were too busy making life go on. In a kind of trance, Toby thought. A kind of sleep, that enabled adjustment to the escalating horror of modern life—bit by bit, day by day, until people had tuned it out, until they'd buried the grossness under thickening scar tissue, leaving, way down, a kind of quiet, frozen terror.

Hence Toby's catastrophism. On the Toby scale, a catastrophe was "good" if it was big enough that people actually noticed.

His friends found this obsession unhealthy. They were sick of it. Deep down, so was he. He turned from the window, unable to stomach the day, the neighborhood, all the blithe spirits. His destroyed kitchen better suited him; from the bathroom, puke fumes eddied, currents of bile that came and went. Toby imagined tendrils coursing through the air to his nose, delicately, like nerve gas. Fresh proof the world would end?

What if, he wondered, it doesn't?

He'd be ruined.

That idea used to make him smile. Today it didn't. Why, he wondered, did I have to drop out of Tufts? Why did I spurn the advantages of an expensive education? Why couldn't I have become a crusading doctor or lawyer or information specialist—somebody with the training to actually *do* something?

Maybe, with training, he could help stop civilization's metamorphosis into a self-destruct machine. Help thwart "the Beast." Earnest Trefethen's Beast—overpopulation, technology in the service of greed.

Those two evils just about summed it up. If enough people were to agree, Toby reflected, maybe things could turn around.

Then again, maybe it really was hopeless. Trefethen seemed to think so. There was somebody who'd gotten training. But who, last night, issued one of the most scathing denunciations of hopeful dogooderism that Toby had ever heard.

A corner of the porch caught his eye. Lamps and a tangle of wires lay exposed to the elements. Last night there'd been drizzle. No electrocution, though, as far as he could remember. He unlatched the door and went out. Hot tarpaper roasted his socks. Squirrels, feeding, inspected him beadily, then beat it for home, a tree branching to the rail. Sorry guys, Toby thought. So sorry to spoil your party. Paper plates reflected the sky. Liquefied cake, spent candles—more evidence of Dan and Selma's stab at festivity.

They'd done it more for their benefit, Toby thought, than for mine. But they'd tried. He mulled it over. Mostly the party had been for Dan, he decided. Selma's arty friends had loved him, practically had eaten him alive, of course. But was it Dan's fault that, unlike Toby, he knew how to have fun? And whose fault was it that Nadia had shown up, for the express purpose, Toby was sure, to humiliate her ex-boyfriend, not so long ago dumped?

"Morning," Dan said behind him.

Toby jumped. The party, Nadia, James, all of Friday night evaporated into blazing daylight. Toby turned to face his brother. Shirtless, he seemed too alert. He looked too fit. The lean waist, the solid chest, the bright eyes, and the turquoise glimmers in his hair—Toby suppressed a shudder. This, he remarked to himself for at least the seventh time since Dan had come to visit, isn't what you expect in a kid brother. You expect scrawniness, sickliness, and squalling fights. All the things that used to be. But almost overnight, Dan seemed to have become—Toby searched for the right word—grown? A disturbing thought bloomed in his mind. Dan, he realized, was the type who would crew that ship. The spaceship in his dream; the crash of which had delivered this hideous day. He pondered the dream. It seemed so dumb. He, Toby, risk-defying leader of space cadets? He muttered, "Hi."

"Nice," Dan said, grinning at Toby's dishevelment. "You slept in your clothes?"

"Yes, yes," Toby replied. "You didn't?"

Shiftily, Dan said, "Uh." Then he added, "No."

Toby raised his eyebrows. Dan appeared pleased. "You picked somebody up," Toby accused.

"The other way around."

"I bet," Toby said. Sun spangled off liquid cake. He sighed, and said, "The orgy room."

Dan laughed.

"He's still here," Toby said. "Selma will want to cook him breakfast. Then when he leaves she'll want to know what you did. You'll tell her . . . "

"He left," Dan interjected, "last night. I was glad, to tell the truth. Kind of drunk, that boy. But fun."

Toby shook his head. Dan's blasé attitude about sex he'd always found freakish. It seemed so dangerous. But every now and then, such as right now, he envied the fact that Dan didn't have to work on getting laid. Somehow, it just happened. "So," he said. "Right in the middle of the party."

Dan nodded. Toby imagined the air conditioner turned up full-blast. Dan walked to the rail and looked down. "This is like a treehouse," he remarked. "Falling off would be really easy." Toby didn't reply. Dan then said, "Hey. I'm sorry about what happened. With Nadia. Her warthog friend and everything."

"It's okay," Toby said.

Dan turned around. "There's a big deal going on in Antarctica," he said cheerfully.

He's trying to raise my spirits, Toby thought.

"I went in your room to find you, and the TV . . . "

"What is it?" Toby asked.

"Lava flows. Giant lava flows."

"Really?" Toby said. That sounded good. Very disastrous.

"You can't see anything because of the steam. But a lot of ice is melting, I guess. Cool, right?"

Toby remembered Dr. Earnest Trefethen's blazing blue eyes. That man knew about lava at the bottom of the world. Loud thrashing noises came from the kitchen. Selma, bagging garbage. "Love her," Dan said.

"It's mutual," Toby said.

"We should help," Dan said.

Neither one moved. Toby lost himself in clouds scudding through ponds of cake. He heard Selma dragging garbage to the stairs: Clump of feet, hiss of plastic, clank of bottles. "You help her," he said. "I'm meditating. The first day of the rest of my life . . . "

Selma screamed. They looked at each other, then banged through the screen door into the kitchen. The stairwell door was open. Selma backed up from it.

Toby lunged by to check out the stairwell. Somebody lay on the steps. Somebody in a gray raincoat, spattered with blood.

13

Head kitchenward, the body rested on its side. The eyes, wide open, had a strangled look. Redness filmed the whites; the pupils, big and black, seemed to stare at the banister. Toby didn't see any wounds. Wondering where the blood had come from, he touched the raincoat. It felt cheap, slightly greasy, normal. Toby prodded it. The arm inside was rigid.

"Dead?" Dan asked from the kitchen doorway.

Toby stood, nodded, and backed up the stairs. Dan slid around for a better look. Toby blocked him. "Go back," he said. "We have to talk."

"Wait," Dan protested, squirming by. "What's that?" He pointed. Toby hadn't noticed the thing. Pale, resembling a scrap of raw chicken, it lay four steps beneath the dead man, in a pool of dark wet. "Give me room," Dan murmured. He flexed for a jump.

"No," Toby said, grabbing Dan's belt. It jerked from his hand as Dan jumped anyway. He sailed over the corpse and thudded onto the landing below. The building shook; Toby winced. Dan squatted to examine the object. "Don't touch it!" Toby yelled. A few seconds went by. Dan seemed mystified. Toby barked, "What?"

"I think it's a nose," Dan said.

Toby said thinly, "A nose."

"Really gross," Dan muttered. "Damn, there's blood. Lots."

"Come back," Toby said. He rushed into the kitchen to find Selma, and stepped on her bag of garbage. The plastic burst. His foot plunged through a frantic logroll of bottles. He went down, thinking, as the floor came at him, That's not recycling. Pretzels pulverized as he hit. For a moment he lay still, stupid with shock. The garbage bag spewed bottles, generating a rollathon to the stove; a loopy, rustic downhill sport. One of his feet felt wet. Red stuff clung to the sock. Appalled, Toby wiggled toes, and realized the red was pizza. He got up. Dead, he kept thinking. Dead on the stairs, oh shit. He went through the screen door to the porch. Selma wasn't there, either. The tarpaper fried his gunky sock. Birds flew through the sky. Squirrels watched from their branches. He flung open the screen door and bellowed, "Selma, where are you?"

"Here," came a croak from the bathroom. Toby went in. She was kneeling over the toilet, her long black hair obscuring her face, brushing the bowl. Pukier and pukier, Toby thought with detachment. Bare legs poked from her robe. The outsize feet were spazzing. Her shoulders shuddered; she threw up, gagging.

"Jesus," Toby said. Dan came in. He put a hand on Toby's arm, and squeezed. Wants to say something, Toby thought. But it can wait. "Get water," he said. "Paper towels."

Dan didn't move. He was watching Selma snort into the toilet. God, Toby thought—not from her nose. She turned a pasty face toward them and bleated fiercely, "No paper towels!" Toby stared at her. "No towels!" she shouted. Spittle laced the air. A phobia, Toby thought. She's afraid of the towels. "Last night," she then gasped, "we used them all up."

"Would you get water at least?" Toby snapped at Dan.

"Yes," Dan said, departing.

"Toby," Selma moaned, her brown eyes wide and sad, "I am so pissed off."

"Talk when you feel okay," he replied.

"That dork," she moaned.

"Yeah," Toby said with sudden conviction.

"Green chartreuse . . . "

"Huh?" Toby said.

"He kept pouring it. Shot after shot. While you were on the roof . . ." She glared into the toilet bowl. "I'm never drinking chartreuse again."

"What are you talking about?" Toby asked.

"James of course. The creep who came with Nadia."

"Selma, there's a dead man on the stairs. Unfortunately, he isn't James!"

She blinked at him. Gathering her robe, she stood, and shivered. "Yeah. Yeah, he crashed the party too." Dan scooted in with a glass of water. Selma seized it and drank.

"He crashed the party?" Toby asked with disbelief.

"Yes," Selma said. "Give me a minute and I'll tell you." She peered in the mirror. "Out. I'm a mess."

"Selma!" Toby yelled.

"Be done soon!" she called as Toby exited, slamming the door.

"Relax," Dan said. "What's the matter with your hand?"

Toby had a hand jammed in his pants pocket. It clutched something. He released the thing, and pulled out the hand; revealing on the palm a crescent-shaped welt. "I think I need to sit down," Toby said.

The closest chair held a bowl full of chips, ice cream containers, beer cans. Dan tilted the chair; bowl and contents cartwheeled across the room. Toby sat. "Should I call the police?" Dan asked.

"Have to think," Toby muttered. "Have to find out what happened with Selma."

"Do you know who he is?"

"No. He made a big scene at the restaurant last night. That's all I know."

"He caused trouble?"

"Sort of. Well—yeah, he did."

"Enough to get murdered for?"

Toby glanced nervously at him. "Why murder?"

Dan shrugged. "The nose. The blood. And the razor." He looked away and said, "There's a razor under his arm. I think he used it to defend himself. But it didn't work."

"You're saying he cut off the killer's nose?"

"Wouldn't you? If somebody was murdering you?"

"Wait a second!" Toby exclaimed. "If it was murder, and the killer was wounded, what if he . . . "

"I checked," Dan said. "There's no more bodies. A trail of blood goes to the first floor and out the front door."

"Unbelievable," Toby said. "Why didn't we hear anything?"

The bathroom door flew open. Selma charged from it. "You were passed out drunk, Dan was in the orgy room, and I was on the porch on the phone yakking with Dolores about what a great party we had. Or I should say, some of us had. Too bad Nadia came, huh?" Her eyes darted around the room. "We're out of cigarettes. We're even out of coffee." She gave up looking, waved at the stairwell and yelled, "Why did that happen?"

Toby said, "Sit down. Anywhere. Just stop moving, okay?"

Selma was a big girl. Tall, she had big arms and legs, big black hair, and a big, voluptuous mouth. In fact she was voluptuous all over. But she wasn't fat. Apart from the hair, she mostly was bone and muscle, and although her stature sometimes made her seem a little clumsy, she projected, when disturbed, danger. "There's instant coffee in the pantry," she growled. "It's ancient. All glued together. But it probably melts."

Dan went to a chair, shook pizza off it, offered it to Selma, and said, "Toby will have a psychotic break if you don't tell him what happened with the stiff."

Selma sat. She examined a plateful of cigarette butts on the table, and said, "He's got the explaining to do."

Toby said, "True."

Dan and Selma studied him. He was staring at finely crushed pretzels on the floor. "Late," Selma said, "really late, he came in. Almost everybody had gone. You were in your room, Toby, snoring, which I know because Dolores wanted to say hi, and I looked for you. I even tried to wake you up. But, no way. So I came back. He was standing right there." She waved at the door to the porch. "He looked—I don't know. Mad. Annoyed. I thought he was from FATBOY. For a second I was sure they'd line us up outside while they tore the place apart." She surveyed the kitchen. "Can't you see them on the rampage, destroying everything?"

"Yes," Toby said.

"Did you call them?" Selma asked, lighting a longish butt. "Police, I mean."

"No," Toby replied. "Go on."

"He said, 'Where is Toby?' I said, 'Who?' He said, 'Does Toby live here?' I said, 'Who are you and why are you in my apartment?' I should point out, he didn't seem very bright. He kept squinting at me. . . ."

"Your outfit," Dan said, clearing bottles from the stove.

Selma shrugged. "Not that outrageous. Anyway, none of his business." She frowned. "Huh. My outfit—that reminds me—something happened as he was leaving. . . ."

"No shit," Toby said. "He's squinting at you and asking for me. Then what?"

"Suddenly he seemed mean. When I asked what he was doing. He said, 'I have to talk with him right away.' I said, 'How come?' And he said, 'He's in danger.' How interesting, I thought. I wondered if I should wake you up. Then I decided not to."

"Why?" Toby asked.

"Because it wasn't possible," Dan suggested, putting water on to boil.

"Exactly," Selma said. "Also, it crossed my mind that he might be the danger he was talking about. He went on the porch, rudely asked where you were, everybody stared at him but didn't say a word. It was getting kind of tense. People started to leave. It was time for them to leave, so I didn't mind, but you'd think somebody could have volunteered to escort him out. Nobody did. They just left, all of them. So I had an inspiration. I said, 'That's right—Toby took off hours ago.' He said, 'Oh, yeah? Why didn't you say so?' And I said, 'I was distracted by the fact that you're behaving like a complete asshole. If you don't get out, I'm calling the police, who happen to be close associates, and they're right up the street.' That seemed to upset him."

"So—he left?" Toby asked.

"No. He got a phone call."

"You're kidding," Toby said.

"Not on our phone. He had one with him. A fancy one, too. He took it out of his coat and answered. And all of a sudden—he looked scared. I'm getting scared now, remembering it."

Dan said, "Did Toby tell you about the nose?"

"Shut up," Toby said. "What did he say?"

Selma stubbed out the cigarette. "He said, 'Okay, Mr. Slatsky.'" She frowned. "Maybe it was Mr. Slosty. It could have been Slutsky. Anyway, he went to the top of the stairs. I followed. A man stood at the bottom, waiting. He also had a phone. I guess he was Slatsky, the one who was calling. Short, big in the middle, he wore dark clothes. What's this about a nose?"

"We'll get to it," Toby said.

"Look," she said. "I'm sure you have an explanation, and I know you're out of your mind, so I will do my best to not make things worse, but—this man, I noticed, had a fairly large nose."

"We think it's on the stairs," Dan said.

"Fascinating," Selma said, rummaging for a viable butt. "He also seemed obsessed with my boots."

"Those things," Dan said.

"What things?" Toby asked. He hadn't been paying attention.

"The ones I wore last night. You know—my party boots."

"Oh," Toby said. "Those things. Are you making this up?"

"I swear to God!" Selma exclaimed. "This short, fat guy couldn't take his eyes off my boots!"

"Was he brandishing a weapon?" Dan asked.

"No," she said. "He was just standing there. With his phone, and an umbrella, I think. Staring, like he was hypnotized, at my boots. And if you must know, the light was gleaming on his nose. Don't tell me . . . "

"The light," Dan affirmed, "is still gleaming on it."

"Maybe," Toby said. "Could be somebody else's nose."

"Oh my God," Selma whispered, scandalized. "Really?"

"Selma," Toby said, "there is something that looks like raw chicken on the stairs, and Dan, who's an expert, thinks it's a nose. But we don't know whose nose it is."

"Maybe Selma can identify it," Dan said.

"Shitheads," she said. "I don't believe you."

"It even has hairs," Dan said. "Even . . ." He shuddered. "It's too disgusting. Anyway you can't tell because of the blood."

"Selma," Toby said, "the man's staring at your boots. You're staring at his nose. What happened then?"

"I said, 'Good night,' and slammed the door. It seemed like he wanted to come back in here. I don't think he was glad to see Slatsky. Guess we can't blame him, huh? Excuse me. I have to look at the nose." She stomped to the stairwell.

The water on the stove began to boil. Dan said, "You're really freaked out, right?"

"Yeah," Toby said. He shivered. "Dan, find out if the instant shit melts."

Dan moved to the pantry. Toby tried to make sense of what Selma had said. From the stairwell she shouted, "Holy shit!" Toby and Dan glanced at each other; wondering if she'd recognized the nose. She yelled loudly, "Come here!"

They ran to the stairs. Selma wasn't looking at the nose. She sat on a step above the dead guy, pointing at his raincoat.

"What?" Toby asked.

Then he heard the faint buzz. It came from the raincoat. Selma said, "That's his phone. He's getting a call."

The raincoat buzzed again. Selma said, "It has to be the phone—it made the same sound last night."

In the kitchen, the kettle Dan had put on the stove started to shriek. Again the raincoat buzzed.

Toby said, "I'm going to answer it. Selma, move."

"I'll get it," she said, grimacing at the blood-speckled fabric. She reached in the pocket whence the buzzes were coming, took out a sleek cellular, and extended it to Toby.

Toby had second thoughts. What could he say to the caller? Selma shook the thing at him and exclaimed, "I said I'd get it, not answer it!" The phone buzzed again. She shuddered.

Toby took it from her. Why, he wondered, are we putting finger-prints on this?

Slotsky was adjusting his bandage and watching Antarctica news in his hotel room when the tracker, on the bedside table, chimed. He glanced at it. The screen blinked blue lights.

He said, "Report." The tracker didn't react to the command. Slotsky realized the bandage was muffling his voice. Then it occurred to him that his voice itself had been mangled. He said, as distinctly as he could, "Report."

Breathily the contralto said, "Miles receiving telephone transmission. Bootlick craves the stomp?"

"Slut off!" Slotsky rasped through the bandage.

"Slut off," the tracker said.

Slotsky said, "Miles phone on." From the tracker came the sound of ringing. He wondered where the phone was, and who, if anyone, would answer it. Not Miles, he was confident. Not himself, an answer could be traced. Police, perhaps?

He listened to a succession of buzzes. No one, it seemed, would answer. But then a voice, oddly familiar, quavered, "Hello?"

"Miles?" said a voice Slotsky recognized right away.

"No," said the answerer's voice. "Who is calling?"

Slotsky identified the voice. As always, he enjoyed the way amphendorph sped the workings of his mind. Cognitive tasks like recognizing a seldom-heard voice, or a face not seen for years—the drug made it effortless. Slotsky wasn't able to smile. Those muscles weren't working at the moment. He started humming instead.

"Who are you?" Brian said sharply into the phone. He sat on the bunk in his tiny stateroom. Grace, in the armchair, watched him with dread. Something terrible has happened, she thought. She'd known it would be this way. She'd expected it.

Toby said into the dead man's phone, "The circumstances are . . . unusual. I'm sorry, but I need to know who I'm talking to." He glanced at Selma. Her eyes were bugging out of her head. Behind him, he heard Dan exhaling.

The young phone-voice, in a tone that struck Toby as arrogant, said, "How unusual?"

Toby replied, "Do you mean, 'How is it unusual?' Or do you mean, 'How unusual is it?'" He took a deep breath. Losing his temper seemed a bad idea. "Put it this way, unusual enough that I should talk to police, not you. How do you know—um—Miles?"

The voice said, "Something happened to him?" Toby heard another voice in the background. It sounded familiar. Then he heard the first voice mutter, "No damn way." The tone suggested the caller was about to hang up; the words themselves told Toby that he knew this voice too. He'd heard it say those words.

"Wait," he said. "Don't hang up—I'm probably more freaked out than you are."

The voice said, "Who are you?"

Again Toby heard the background voice. A girl, murmuring. Now he was positive he'd heard these two before. He said, "All right. But first I have bad news. Miles is dead."

"Good-bye!" the voice snarled.

"The pin!" Toby yelled.

Absolute silence came from the phone. A pin could be dropping, Toby thought. He felt sudden conviction that it had.

"What did you say?" the voice asked.

Toby said, "I'm a waiter at Mifflin Place. I found a pin there. That's how I got—uh—involved with Miles."

"Oh, no."

Toby heard confusion and shock in the voice, and knew he was right. He said, "You're Brian Trefethen." More absolute silence. "If it matters to you, I still have the pin. I wish I didn't. In fact I wish I'd never waited on you to begin with, Brian. But I did. And as long as we're talking, maybe you can tell me why somebody killed this Miles guy."

Three more seconds of silence ticked by. Brian said, "You have the pin?"

In the hotel room, Slotsky heard Toby say from the tracker, "That's what I said. Right here in my pocket." Slotsky's humming took on a livelier rhythm. "Why is Miles dead?"

Because, Slotsky thought, he was disloyal, and a fool.

"I don't know," he heard Brian say. "Excuse me, I have to confer." Slotsky pictured him pressing his hand over the mouthpiece. Ten seconds went by.

From the tracker came briskly, "This is Grace Trefethen. What is your name, please?"

"Toby Swett," Toby said, feeling sweat running down his rib cage and into his pants.

"You were the waiter last night?" Grace asked.

"Yes," Toby said.

"And you have the pin?"

Toby wanted to shout, I've said it twice. But he wasn't talking with Brian now. He said, "Yes. I also have a corpse in my apartment building. And—a severed nose. They've been on the stairs for hours, since sometime early this morning. Shortly I'll be calling the police to report . . . "

"You haven't reported it?" Grace asked.

"We just found it. Half an hour ago."

"Who is 'we'?" Grace asked.

Again Toby quelled an urge to shout. "Me and the other members of my fearless adventure team," he said. "Look. This Miles, he wanted the pin. Badly. And he accused me of taking it from under the table—which I denied untruthfully because I thought he might be bad news for you. He seemed like a real creep."

"You also found a nose?" Grace said.

"Yeah," Toby said. "We think it belonged to the killer. A short, heavyset man wearing dark clothes."

"My God. Have you done anything with the pin?"

"Done something?" Toby said.

"Have you reproduced it?"

The question baffled Toby. "What do you mean?" he asked.

Slotsky wished to know the same. But Grace wasn't replying. From the tracker, Toby's puzzled voice inquired, "You're asking if we sat around making copies of that little animal?"

"Uh-huh," Grace said. "For example, photos. Have you taken pictures of it?"

A photographable animal? Slotsky thought.

"You must be kidding," Toby said. "No. We haven't."

Grace said, "Please listen carefully."

No problem, thought Toby. Something bothered him. Had somebody taken pictures last night? He couldn't remember.

"You have a right to be upset," she said. "But you're in a more crazy situation than you realize. Uh—you mentioned the police. Of course you have to call them. But please—I'm begging you—don't tell them about the, ah, pin."

"Why?" Toby asked.

"You wouldn't believe me if I told you."

"Try me," Toby said.

"I will. I'll gladly tell you everything. Can you hold off on the police for a few more minutes?"

Toby thought a moment. He said, "Yeah."

"Can I call you back?"

"Uh. Well. I guess."

"I remember you from last night. You are a very good—waiter." Gee, he thought. "Toby," she then asked, "are you interested in getting to know me?"

"I think," he said, trying not to blush, "we have a problem to take care of. If that means getting to know you, then . . . "

"You won't call the police until we've talked again?"

"Sure. No. I mean, I can hold off for a little while."

"Thank you. Sit tight. Bye." The phone went dead.

Toby glanced at Selma, then at Dan. He gestured at the body and muttered, "Let's get away from that."

They shuffled into the kitchen. Toby brought the phone with him. "If somebody makes coffee," he said, taking a seat, "I'll spill my guts. That girl I just talked to—she was there last night. When all of this started." He pulled the pin from his pocket. "Believe it or not, it seems to revolve around somebody's kindergarten project."

Dan and Selma silently collaborated in making coffee. For once they were speechless. They knew this would be good.

Grace and Brian looked at each other. Sometimes they could communicate quite a lot without saying a word.

Right now wasn't such a time. Grace said, "Miles didn't work for the FATB. We have to think fast."

The confined and windowless space suddenly felt smaller. Brian stared at the new carpet. He slumped onto his bunk, an elbow in the embroidered pillow Mother made when they'd been three. She'd made one for Grace too, of course. It adorned her bunk in the state-room that connected through the compact metal bathroom. The built-in closets and dressers of all three rooms were crammed with clothes, belongings, memorabilia, the selection of which Mother had super-vised carefully. It was their little suite in the tractor trailer's cargo bay; the rest of which likewise had been subdivided into living spaces, to accommodate the Trefethen family comfortably and efficiently as it departed Cambridge and headed for parts unknown, for the future.

The truck seemed prison-like to Brian. It symbolized the prison their entire lives had been. That it was mobile, and would end up tak-ing them who knew where, did nothing to diminish its oppressive-ness. On the contrary; the ingenuity and taste with which Mother had compressed the big house on Francis Avenue into this rectangu-lar box, made it worse than a prison. It was more like a mobile family crypt. Brian said, "Just because he's dead? That means Miles didn't work for FATBOY?"

Grace said, "Miles has been there, dead, for hours. Don't you think, if he was an FATB agent, his superiors would have known what he was doing, and would have found him by now?"

Brian chewed his lower lip. "You never thought he was one," he muttered.

She said, "I wanted to. But not as much as you did." Trying to keep panic from her voice, she added, "We really screwed up."

"You mean I did. I know, I know—'Reckless. Desperate.'" He couldn't look her in the eyes. "Grace, it was our only chance."

"Bullshit!" she snapped. "Why can't you face it—giving FATBOY the pin wasn't the only option! It never was, and still isn't. But what-ever we do now—Brian, we have to get it back."

Brian glowered at the embroidered pillow. "Maybe we should run away," he said.

They'd been over this so many times. In concept, running away had seemed a wondrous solution. But faced with doing it, especially now that they'd moved into the truck, which itself was an elaborate run-away—it just seemed futile. Run where? And do what?

The fact of the matter was, they couldn't imagine life apart from their parents. They had even more trouble imagining life without each other. "No," Grace said. "Running away is worse than staying—listen to me!"

Brian forced his eyes at hers.

Grace declared, "The pin can't be out there like this. I have to call him, the waiter. Remember how he looked at me last night?" Brian scowled. "He'll cooperate. Think. How do we do it?"

Brian muttered, "It's time to run Mother-check." He pulled the Gutzymes from his pocket and offered one to Grace. She took a piece of the candy-like ulcer medication. Together sucking, they considered the drama of their current situation. Much of it stemmed from the fact that Mother didn't know they'd stolen the pin, but at any moment could find out. She could have found out literally within seconds after last night's return from the nervewracking retirement dinner. That she still hadn't, at 2:43 the next afternoon, seemed a miracle.

Brian hopped from the bunk and opened the metal door to the narrow corridor that ran the length of the truck. From the other end, where the "salon" was—Mother insisted on using Pullman railway car terminology to refer to this mobile home—came echoes of television crisis news. Brian suspected Mother couldn't quite believe it was happening, now that it really *was* happening. Unlike Father, Brian thought, who had no trouble at all believing it. Right then he was using his last day at the office to orchestrate a series of media hits, milking the idiots at last night's dinner for all they were worth.

Grace followed him into the corridor. They walked quietly to their parents' room. Brian opened the door. The room was larger than their rooms put together. It had to be, to hold the stuff. Mother's safe, for example. There it loomed, taking up a corner. The door was locked. On top, however—still in the heap she'd left it in last night, when removing her party things—lay the pearl necklace.

They were all right, with the necklace out. It meant she hadn't opened the safe. Which meant she hadn't had an opportunity to notice a certain item was missing.

Party things, Brian thought, gazing at the pearls. Mother was so in love with her jewels. They were heirlooms. Old, heavy, beautiful pieces. From infancy onward he and Grace had watched her, and had advised her—inarticulately, to be sure, at first—as she got ready to go out. When she and Father were going somewhere fancy—mostly long ago, since evenings like that were rare now—she would open the safe, not letting them see the combination. Father disallowed that. She'd take out the jewelry box and spread dozens of items on her table. Then she'd get clothes, dresses and suits and gowns, and the three of them would play the matching game. What goes with what? Then she'd have her bath, leaving the safe open, jewelry on the table. So the twins could deliberate about what she should wear with what.

Last night, on the eve of their old life's end, the three of them, one last time, had played the matching game.

Father had been wrapping things up at the office. If he'd been in the truck, the game probably wouldn't have happened. Brian closed the door. They went back to his room. Grace said, "She might not put them away for a while."

Brian said, "The truck's like a giant safe anyway."

She said, "So how do we get out of it?"

"We go to Mother and tell her we want to take a drive around the city we grew up in, just to see the sights. Since we never will have a chance to do that again."

"She won't let us. Father would be so angry."

The truck hid from the world behind the steel doors of a warehouse in a seedy East Cambridge industrial park. For the last month, the warehouse had been the site of a lot of work. The truck bore no external insignia or markings, except rust here and there; carefully cultivated rust, because the enormous eighteen-wheeler was brand new. Every precaution had been taken to make it anonymous, as exactly like a thousand other trucks as possible. Yesterday, Clinic zombies had made super-discreet runs with the vans, moving things in. Mother and the twins had taken up residence in the midafternoon. After the dinner party they returned with Father, and stayed overnight for the first time.

That would be the truck's last night in the warehouse. Tonight, after Father's appearance on Barclay Piston's show, it was evacuating them to somewhere far from the Boston area.

Until then the twins were under orders to stay put. Father had been very clear about it. He'd forbidden them to leave the warehouse, even to open a door for fresh air. They weren't to risk the slightest chance that someone might see them, and later, post-Barclay, associate them with either warehouse or truck.

Thus the twins had a problem. Brian said, "Father's busy now. And he will be till—9:30? 9:45? So it's simple. He just doesn't have to know."

"I don't think Mother will agree," Grace said.

"Everything's going so smoothly," Brian remarked. "Mother's in a daze—'a quartz contentment, like a stone.' She'll agree."

Grace looked doubtful. Permission was mandatory. Three vans were parked in the warehouse, full of Clinic zombies.

"I'll talk to her," Brian said. "It just hit me, how to get her to go along. She won't be able to say no."

■ ■ ■

Slotsky, waiting for the tracker to resume giving him the twins and Toby, sipped his third jumbo protein shake of the day. He wasn't feeling up to par. Not having been able to arrange for a transfusion until early afternoon, he'd bled virtually to the point of coma, according to the doctor who'd finally arrived. Slotsky avoided hospitals. He disliked the measures they took to identify patients. They also tended to medicate trauma victims, and medication, the kind dispensed in ER rooms at any rate, Slotsky was obliged to avoid. It would interact badly with the amphendorph. In general terms he had explained this to the doctor, who had required other explanations as well. For example, why wasn't Slotsky anxious to have the nose reattached?

Slotsky was losing patience by then. Tersely he'd replied, "The attacker ate it, I'm afraid, on the spot. While I watched."

The doctor required a few moments to recover from the shock that gave him. But once recovered, he couldn't understand how Slotsky was tolerating the pain, or how a man in his condition had managed to return to his hotel at all. In fact, that had taken some doing on Slotsky's part; getting through the garage and up to the room unnoticed had been ticklish, to say the least. But it was something else the doctor didn't need to know. So Slotsky finally pulled a gun and said, "Fix my face and shut up."

The doctor had done as he was told. He now lay on the spare bed, dead to the world, not destined to wake any time soon.

Slotsky finished the shake. He opened the 'dorph pouch, selected a Number 7, unpeeled it, and applied it to the shaved spot on his shoulder. Then, energetically, he started packing. He would be leaving soon. Very soon, he hoped. The media still weren't connecting a nuclear bomb to the eruption. At any moment, however . . .

Slotsky heard the tracker's chime on the bedside table. "Report," he said.

"Miles receiving telephone transmission," the contralto said.

"Miles phone on," Slotsky said. He heard a pickup click.

"Hello," Toby Swett said from the tracker.

Grace Trefethen said from the tracker, "Hi. Did you call the police?"

■ ■ ■

"Not yet," Toby said into the phone, uncomfortably aware of the eye-balling he was getting from Dan and Selma. They seemed to think he'd invented the story about the pin.

"This is the situation," Grace said. "We're stuck where we are. But we think we can get out later. Can you meet us?"

"You could come here," Toby said. He looked at the ruined kitchen and reconsidered the idea.

But Grace was saying, "We'd rather avoid police." That's a little alarming, Toby thought. "Don't jump to conclusions," Grace went on. "We're at your mercy, see. I'm not exaggerating. You hold the key to our survival."

"Really?" Toby said.

"Yes!" she said. "Unless we get the pin back, we won't make it. It's not just my brother and me. It's—bigger than that."

Grace's fervor impressed Toby. Her survival was at stake; she was at his mercy. She probably was manipulating the hell out of him, but also was the most gorgeous girl he'd ever laid eyes on. He said, "What do you want me to do?"

"Think of a place we can meet. It doesn't make any difference where. As long as you can get there by—seven? And can hang out for a while if we're late?"

"Just a second," Toby said. He turned to Selma and asked, "Where's a good place to meet somebody at seven if they might be late, and I have to hang out?"

Without hesitation Selma replied, "Dick's. In Harvard Square. At seven on a Saturday, it'll be empty but fun. What kind of deal are you making, Toby?"

Toby said into the phone, "Dick's in Harvard Square."

"Fine," Grace said. "You'll bring the pin?"

"Uh," Toby said. "Sure."

"I'll never be able to repay you," she said, and hung up.

Toby turned off the phone, wondering what spin he could put on this that wouldn't prove to Dan and Selma he'd lost his mind.

Slotsky regarded himself in the mirror above the beds, feeling mild dismay. He didn't mind the bandage making him look like a B-movie bogeyman. But he did mind the prospect of a lengthy wait. It was 3:34, and the hotel room, with its unconscious guest, was losing its charm.

Then there was the issue of the parking garage attendant. He'd suffered the misfortune of seeing Slotsky drive in just before dawn. Slotsky's face had upset him. He'd wanted to help. Now he hid behind the basement dumpster, not breathing, and likely to be discovered shortly. If he hadn't been already.

And then there was the bellhop in the closet. What duty had compelled him to prowl the corridor at five in the morning?

"Damn Miles," Slotsky muttered.

Something else bothered him as well. Why hadn't he taken his nose from the Magazine Street stairwell? Not for the sake of reattachment; for the simpler sake of keeping his disfigurement secret? Within an hour or so, police would be looking for a killer without a nose. The bandage made him a walking target.

Slotsky wondered if he was losing his touch.

"Controversy is mounting," the CNN anchor said, "over the implications of recent developments in Antarctica. Two schools of thought have emerged among scientists with expertise on the subject. The first view, so far the more widespread, holds that both the earthquake and the eruption are isolated events, ones that will not affect the long-term stability of the West Antarctic Ice Sheet. The minority position holds that such optimism is, at best, premature. While not going so far as to issue public warnings about possible destabilization of the ice sheet, advocates of the second view reportedly are airing their concerns in private settings.

"Joining the program by videolink from his office in Cambridge, Massachusetts, is Dr. Earnest Trefethen, a leading expert in the fields of Antarctic volcanology and glaciology. Dr. Trefethen, thank you for joining us."

"A pleasure," Earnest said in his most distinguished voice.

Helen could suppress herself no longer. "Children! He's on again!"

The anchor asked, "What is your assessment of the situation? Where do you put yourself, in terms of the camps that are dividing your colleagues? Or would you say there is more of a consensus than my opening remarks suggest?"

"I would not say so," Earnest replied. "Let me first say, all the data are preliminary. We don't yet have answers to numerous questions about either the earthquake or the eruption; and as you pointed out in earlier coverage, the circumstances are unique. However, I have been in touch with colleagues in Antarctica, and with colleagues elsewhere, and a general picture is emerging among these individuals, based on what they know. I am afraid that picture will change."

"Tell us why, Dr. Trefethen," the anchor said.

Helen suppressed herself. She couldn't expect the twins to feel the same giddiness she was experiencing. After all, they were going through a difficult time.

Earnest said, "The quake and the eruption are rather serious developments. The long-term effects could well be—ah—significant. As you know, I've spent the last five years conducting a survey of volcanism beneath the ice sheet. My findings, I should mention, have yet to be published, and my colleagues are largely unfamiliar with them, unfortunately. Thus they may be somewhat surprised by what I will have to say tonight."

"Tonight? What can you say now, Dr. Trefethen?"

"If you will forgive me, I won't say much more just now. You see, the eruption has put me in an awkward position. I possess a large body of data that is germane to the eruption in particular, and to the ice sheet in general. However, the data are not organized in a fashion suitable for simple presentation. At the moment I am rather hurriedly whipping the material into shape. That task will take several more hours."

"I understand you'll appear on tonight's Barclay Piston Show?"

"Yes, indeed. And I plan to make a statement at that time."

"Have you heard," the anchor asked, "the rumors that are circling, to the effect that you very recently painted, in a private setting, a potentially disastrous scenario? Are those rumors true, Dr. Trefethen? If so, may I ask why you haven't been more public about the possible dangers?"

"For some time now, my data have indicated that volcanic activity in Antarctica could be on the near-horizon. But frankly, this event has stunned me. It's all I can do to catch my breath."

"We've received reports that the Pentagon has taken an interest in the eruption. One source suggests there may be some kind of cover-up involving the event. Any comments?"

"I've no idea what that's about."

"Thank you, Dr. Trefethen, for interrupting your work to join us. You clearly are busy. Good luck with that data, sir. I'm sure a great many of us look forward to seeing you on Barclay."

"Thank you."

Helen turned off the TV. This was the third such appearance Earnest had made on network news. Isn't he, she wondered, undermining the idea that he's madly organizing data?

Not her department, she reflected. Earnest knew what he was doing. She hoped he could manage tonight's endgame without complications. How soon might well-informed people, among them Barclay and other attendees of last night's dinner, become suspicious?

Her thoughts turned to the twins. They'd been behaving oddly the last few days. That didn't surprise her. She would have been surprised if they weren't. She'd done her best to make things cozy and snug for the darlings; could she be doing more? She picked up the intercom and keyed both staterooms. "Twins? Are you sulking? Why won't you come out and be with Mother?"

Brian said, voice tinny over the speakerphone, "Actually, I need to talk to you. Is Father still on TV?"

"No, dear. I turned it off. Would you like me to visit? Or will you come to the salon?"

"I'll come down," he said. "But I want your undivided attention, okay? This is important."

"Of course," Helen said soothingly. "You come right on down, and we'll talk." She clicked off, hoping it wasn't serious. A very long day still stretched ahead. She would have to devote all her energy to Earnest, later. And goodness, the drive to Martha's. They wouldn't get there until three or so in the morning.

Brian appeared, footfalls soft on the carpet. My princeling, thought Helen. She'd always been certain that hers were the most beautiful children in the world. "Sit down," she said, patting the divan that had come from Grandmother Scarf's in Cleveland Heights. The roomy house on Francis Avenue had made it minuscule. But here in the truck, the divan seemed baronial. "Tell me," she said as he sat, "what's on your mind."

He regarded her gravely, the gray eyes troubled, the ash-blond lashes fluttering. "Mother, we've been thinking. Tonight's the end of an era."

"It is," she replied. "And the beginning of a new one."

"Yes," he said. "The . . . new one. It's exciting. We're completely psyched. It's so great everything's going so well."

"Father and I have worked hard, Brian," she said, relieved she didn't confront some kind of last-minute resistance. At the same time, she wondered what he really was saying. "We've made sure things would go well, you know that."

"There are some things, though, in the new era," he continued, "that we won't be able to do. We know that too. But since the serious stuff won't happen until later on, we were thinking—well, that the next few hours are the last chance Grace and I will have. To do those things . . . "

"What in particular are you talking about?"

"Simple things. Regular, normal things. Like going out to eat in a restaurant."

"Sweetie, we did that last night."

"That doesn't count, Mother. Last night was work."

"But still. It was a restaurant. A normal restaurant."

"We were with those people—and that wasn't normal. Maybe it was, but not, you know, in terms of regular life. Of what ordinary people get to do every day of their lives. Which Grace and I probably will never get to do, after tonight. So we were thinking . . . "

"Out of the question," Helen said, astonished at the direction Brian seemed to be taking.

"Think about it," he said. "Grace could wear her nicest dress. I could wear my nicest suit. We could go out to a fine place somewhere, with candles and soft music in the background. Like, you know, a date type thing."

Helen cleared her throat and said, "We have candles and music. And a lovely little dining room we haven't even used yet. I could make a fancy . . . something . . . right here."

"But it wouldn't be just Grace and me."

"What's wrong with the three of us?"

"Mother," Brian said, eyes turning stormy, "it'll be 'just the five of us,' including Martha. For the rest of our lives."

Helen thought about that. "You mean to tell me," she said slowly, "you actually want to get—dressed up? You didn't feel like it yesterday."

"Mother. I told you, and you know it, so admit it. That wasn't the same thing at all."

"I suppose not," she said.

"We really do. We want to get dressed up and go out on a formal-type date. You and Father did that for years and years. Think about all the times Grace and I watched you get ready, dreaming of when we'd do the same ourselves. Now, all that, boom! Gone!"

Brina was getting a touch heated. Helen's heart then skipped a beat, because he smiled. Such an angelic smile . . . he said, voice softer, "Grace even wants to wear your pearls."

"Heavens," Helen said, her vision blurring. "Grace, wearing my pearls . . ." She felt on the verge of bursting into tears; and was thankful Earnest couldn't see it. The strain, she thought. Getting to me. There's been so much . . .

The steely part of her mind told her, This is all very, very foolish. She picked up the intercom and keyed Grace's room. "Am I hearing correctly?" she demanded. "You want to play dress-up, pretend to go on a date, and wear my pearls?"

"Yes, Mother," Grace's disembodied voice replied. "Not only do I want to do it. I insist on doing it. You have no right to hog that kind of experience to yourself."

Helen protested, "I never . . . "

"You will be if you don't let us go out!"

Helen said, "But Father would . . . "

Brian exclaimed, "Father will not know! He's too busy bamboozling the world!" Helen stared at him. "This," he declared, "will be our secret. If you say yes, Mother—you have no idea how much this means."

Helen said to the intercom, "Grace, join us."

A few moments passed. Is she being obstinate? Helen wondered. But then came the padding of feet in the corridor. Firming her resolve, about to lay down the law, Helen took one look at the divine princess entering the salon, and felt her heart melt utterly.

Grace already was wearing the pearls.

Otherwise, she wore only a translucent silk slip. "Oh!" Helen gasped. "You look stunning!"

"Thank you, Mother," Grace said. She turned to show off the opalescent globes against her bare back. Striking a sophisticate's stance, she said languidly to Brian, "Would you be ever so kind and ask the maitre d' to bring me a little something from the bar . . . "

"You're not old enough!" Helen snapped. "Furthermore, it would provoke your ulcers." She sighed, and said, "I completely forgot about putting those away."

"But you're not going to, Mother," said the slinky Grace, fondling the pearls. "You are going to let me to wear these into the starry night."

"Think again," Helen said.

"You can't say no," Brian said. "You know you can't."

"The starry night," Helen said with mounting irritation, "is fantasy, children. You know Father's on Barclay at nine. And not very long after that, we're on the road to Martha's . . ."

Helen stopped. She'd just violated a direct order; Earnest hadn't wanted the twins to learn tonight's destination. The mistake distracted her. "You don't know that," she said. "About going to Martha's." The twins nodded. It wasn't the first time Mother had let something slip. Angry with herself, Helen thought a moment. "What about security?" she said plaintively.

"We stay in the back of a van," Brian replied. "Guards drive. They drop us off, and then later, they pick us up. Nobody gets even a glimpse of us anywhere near the truck."

"The guards might talk to Father," Helen said.

"The guards do what you tell them to do," Grace remarked.

Helen felt slippage, somewhere, in her steely resolve. The two of them were being very persuasive. And they did have a point. Never would they be able to indulge in such an escapade again. She put her face in her hands and thought. Through her hands she said hollowly, "Father would kill me."

"He won't know," Brian whispered.

"It's our secret," Grace said.

"All right," Helen said. "All right, all right. But if you're having an evening of glamor on the town, I think we should do a role reversal. I think it would be appropriate, as you attire yourselves in your finery, for us to play the matching game—except that I, for once, will be audience and adviser." She stood, adding, "I'll get the things from the safe right now."

"Don't bother," Grace said. "Pearls for me, tonight." She directed a sidelong glance at Brian and said, "Don't you think?"

"Absolutely, my sweet," said Brian.

"Oh, come on," Helen muttered, moving toward the corridor. "Let's do it right if we're going to be jackass-stupid enough to actually do it."

"Mother," Grace said, "I don't want to even look at the stuff. I have made up my mind, it's the pearls, only the pearls, nothing but the pearls. Seeing the rest of that junk would make me sick to my stomach. Really. It would." She pressed a glistening strand against her cheek. "You know these have always been my favorite. And more than these—bad taste, for a maiden like me."

Helen reseated herself. "Can't I at least advise on the wardrobe?" she asked.

"Perhaps," Grace said. "We'll see." She beckoned Brian.

Helen watched them slip away down the corridor. How sweet, she thought. She heard a door open, then slam shut. It seemed they were serious. Helen realized she'd be lucky if this proved to be the kind of coping strategy they adopted, to deal with the stress. Absently, she turned on the TV.

In Grace's room, they didn't look at each other for a few moments. Grace then muttered, "I almost died."

"Yeah," Brian said. He directed a searching stare at his sister. "You know what really would convince her? Make it hard for her to change her mind? And she will, you know."

Grace's eyes clouded. "I . . . um . . . Brian. No. Not now."

"It would put us in the mood. For the starry date. She'd get mushy and guilty, you know she would. And besides . . . "

"You want to," Grace observed. "Okay," she said.

He shrugged out of his shirt. She shrugged off the slip, then watched him dance around pulling off jeans. They gazed at their nakedness. She at his body, he at hers. She at his chest, arms, and thighs; he at her breasts, waist, and knees. What they saw enraptured them. Despite years of intimacy, they found each other perhaps more enrapturing than ever. They didn't know that their beauty, by objective standards, was extraordinary. Neither one had seen another human being naked. Neither had seen another vagina or penis, not even in pornography, for they had grown up in a protected zone, away from other children, away from the dangerous world, away from virtually anyone except their parents. Thus they didn't have a means to comparatively evaluate what they saw. But they didn't need to, or want to, because they didn't care what the bodies of strangers were like. For each, the other was more than enough. For each, the other completed existence. They were mates, essentially, and had been all their lives.

Both still standing, his boything nuzzled her girlthing. He pushed into her and they pressed together, shuddering, squirming, hands gripping the other's butts. Loving it, loving the goose pimples and the tiny hairs standing on end all over, they grinned their febrile flesh-grins, and moaned.

Mother knocked on the door.

"Busy," Grace called.

"Very," Brian called.

"Sorry," Mother called.

"No change of heart now," Brian whispered in Grace's ear.

Helen walked back to the salon thinking she should have known. It seemed perfect that they were *busy*. What with the evening they'd planned, and the larger evening she and Earnest had planned, stretching ahead.

How could she deny them their fantasy?

She sat on the divan and looked at the TV. More news of Antarctica. More news of fire and ice . . . Helen watched without seeing, her mind occupied with her poor darlings. At least they have each other, she thought. It was fortunate they did, for it meant they didn't need outsiders. This family had no room, literally, for outsiders.

Helen's only regret about the arrangement concerned the impossibility of grandchildren. Brian and Grace should never, and would never, have children.

Anyhow, that issue was moot. When it had become clear that the twins were destined for each other, when she and Earnest had concluded that all four of them were destined to stay together, forever, until death did them part, she had dealt decisively with the issue of children.

She'd sterilized Brian, six years before. He and Grace had been twelve.

Helen turned her attention to the news.

The Magazine Street apartment teemed with activity. In the stairwell and kitchen, officers, forensic experts, a photographer, and medical technicians bustled about, accompanied by the crackle of high-powered radios. Partly because so many people in the kitchen made it easy to stumble on party debris, partly because they didn't feel welcome there, and partly because they thought Toby had gone insane, Selma and Dan were camped out on his futon, watching him. Toby in turn was watching television news with almost religious devotion.

"Just incredible," he muttered.

Distractions had slowed Toby's learning curve about events in Antarctica. Ordinarily, with a catastrophe of this magnitude unfolding, he would have risen early to watch the day's breaking developments. But today he'd woken in circumstances that had overshadowed the news: Hangover, the condition of the apartment, heartsickness about Nadia, heartsickness about his aimless—clinically depressed?—life, his general gloom about doom, and most distracting of all, the corpse on the stairs.

Now, though, waiting for the detective to arrive, he'd had a little hiatus, and was catching up. The folks in the kitchen had asked some questions, but it seemed the real face-to-face couldn't proceed without the detective. That was just as well, for two reasons. One, Toby intended to lie to this person. He wasn't looking forward to it; nor were Dan and Selma. Two, the Antarctica story was clobbering Toby. With every passing hour it had been getting bigger, scarier, and more mysterious.

A high point had come a few minutes before, when on CNN the anchor asked Earnest Trefethen about rumors that he recently "painted, in a private setting, a potentially disastrous scenario." This had made Toby sit up in his chair, turn to Dan and Selma, and yell, "I told you, this Trefethen practically announced the Great Flood! Cleansing effects of water, cleansing effects of water! And who better than him to know, the man spent the last five years X-raying the fucking ice sheet and finding the fucking volcanoes!" Then muttering, "Oh my God, oh my God, oh my God," and ignoring the pitying stares from both brother and roommate, he'd reglued himself to the TV screen.

"Was he always like that?" Selma asked Dan as she brushed out her hair, frowning at dried flecks of something flying from it.

"One way or another," Dan replied, flat on his back, arms crossed behind his head. "He always thought he was the only person who comprehended the terrible beauty of any given situation. When the rest of us just wanted to get past the car crash and the blood, and go on with our day."

"I see," Selma said darkly, half in reaction to what she'd just found in her brush. "Toby, do you realize that the detective is going to have you locked up on grounds that your psychosis makes you a menace not just to yourself, but to society? Damn. What the hell happened to my hair?"

"Party damage," Dan said. "Don't worry about it. Take a shower and think of the cleansing effects of water."

"With those guys standing around? Undressing me with their eyes? They'd decide crucial evidence is in the bathroom just as I'm getting wet. From the shower, I mean. You know what I mean."

Dan said, "Do any of them? Make you?"

"You must be joking," Selma replied. She looked at him with narrowed eyes. "Any of them make you?"

"I like the big one with the sad face and the quivery love handles. Such a daddy. A bear. He'd have to work on getting me wet, though." Dan sighed. "We could go out dancing . . . "

"Those nicknames are so tired," Selma remarked. "'Swear Engine. Dance Wet.' Last night, I wanted to slap that kid."

Oh, Toby thought. Dan Swett is Dance Wet. Selma Swearingen is Swear Engine. What kind of goofballs are they hanging out with?

"Toby," Selma said, "before the detective gets here, shouldn't we discuss obstruction of justice—and decide it's a bad idea?"

Dan said, "I'd hate to get to Grand Cayman tomorrow and tell Mom and Dad what it felt like to see you driven away to prison."

"In a funny white jacket," Selma added.

Toby didn't reply. "I wish you weren't leaving," Selma said to Dan. "Why not finish your vacation here?"

"What a vacationland," he said. "How can I leave this tranquility? And subject myself to tropical beaches?"

Toby said, "Better subject yourself while you can." He gestured at the TV. "If this keeps up, there won't be any beaches."

"You've got to stay," Selma said to Dan. She glanced at Toby. "To protect me from him. And whoever the noseless murderer is who wants the pin."

Eyes not wavering from the TV, Toby said, "We have no idea if the noseless one wants the pin." It didn't seem farfetched that he might, but Toby was disinclined to give Selma and Dan more leverage. Determined to make him be responsible, they'd analyzed, in detail, the similar pronunciation of the words "pen" and "pin." They'd frowned and squinted at the pin, unable to believe the rabbit drawing could be anything more than some child's idea of a fashion accessory. However, they'd made much of the emergency the pin seemed to be causing for the Trefethen twins; and had pointed out, over and over, that murder most foul had been committed while all three of them, in different ways, were helpless with party afterglow. At one stage they'd even shouted, "We could be dead in our beds! Dead in our beds!"

They'd also puzzled over the meaning of the note Toby had found with the pin: "DO NOT REPRODUCE IN ANY FORM WHATSOEVER. USE IT TO FILTER THE MEDIA STREAMS."

Dan then remembered he'd taken Polaroids of Toby wearing the pin. Did that qualify as reproduction?

Selma looked for them, and found four, unscathed, under a plate on the porch. In three, the pin appeared pretty well reproduced. In one of them, it almost seemed the focus of the composition; the rabbit was boldly clear against Toby's white shirt. Would that, Dan had asked, wreak havoc with the "media streams"?

Toby didn't know. But his curiosity about the Trefethens had become quite keen. Last night's private party at Mifflin Place, considering who'd been there, seemed the likely source of the "rumor" reported by CNN. The mad-seer remarks Trefethen had inflicted on his guests must have made an impact. And why not? He'd suggested that the planet was telling the human race something with the eruption. He'd also talked about traveling a new road to the future, a road he wouldn't specify, but which he'd said would be "frightening." It just seemed—what?

Was "apocalyptic" going too far? What could be more apocalyptic than a volcano that might trigger a big rise in sea level? And what was the stuff about a Pentagon cover-up?

Of course, all of this could be putting two and two together and getting thirteen. Dan and Selma thought so. But Toby wanted to find out if others who'd been at the restaurant last night were having similar thoughts. For example, Grace.

He couldn't wait to get to Dick's and talk with that girl. And maybe buy her a drink. Or two. Unfortunately, there was the problem of Brian. Toby wondered if he should ask Selma and Dan to come along. For a moment he considered possibilities. Selma and Brian? Dan and Brian? He turned from the TV, which was doing a Mantis orb commercial, and said, "Something I didn't mention."

Dan and Selma regarded him suspiciously. "Yes?" Selma said.

"This girl Grace. You know how you can be walking down the street, and get a glimpse of someone so beautiful that you're afraid to take a second look? Because you don't want to find out it's an illusion? But also because you don't want to find out it's true, since then you'd have to deal with the beauty's unavailability, and the torment of that?"

The suspicion in their stares deepened. "Ohhhhh," Selma said. "Now we know why you've flipped. Of course—that girl."

"Wait a second," Dan said. "Her brother's her twin?"

Toby nodded, and just looked at them.

"Ohhhhh," Dan and Selma said in unison. Dan then said, "So you mean . . . ?"

Again Toby nodded, pleased with the bull's eye in their sweet spots. "Both of you," he said, "would be like dogs in heat. One look and you'd be humping the nearest telephone pole."

Their eyes widened.

"Excuse me," said a strange baritone voice. They looked at the curtain shutting off the middle room and saw a middle-aged African American man peering in. He came through, glanced around, and asked, "Who is Toby?"

"Me," Toby replied.

"I am Detective Potts," the man said.

Toby stood and extended his hand. Potts shook it. "Glad you're here," Toby said. "Over there are Selma and Dan." They nodded at the detective. Registering, Toby thought, that he isn't bad-looking himself.

"Is your apartment always like this?" Potts asked. "Or only when you have parties?"

"Only when people die on the stairs," Toby said, attempting light-heartedness. "Sorry," he added quickly, "that's not funny. Yeah, we had a party last night." Potts gazed at him. Toby indicated the chair in which he'd been sitting and said, "Have a seat."

"Thank you," said the detective, sinking into it. Well-dressed, Toby noted. An air of calm about the man; unfazed by blood, mayhem, and squalid living conditions. Toby instinctively liked the guy. He wished his heart weren't pounding.

"Now then," Potts said, eyes settling on Dan and Selma, who were sitting up straight on the futon. "What do you party animals have to tell me?"

Dan and Selma turned heads to Toby, who coughed. It felt odd to be the only one standing. There was no good place to sit, though. He asked Potts, "Want us to run through what happened?"

Potts said, "I've been here half an hour. So I know a bit about what happened. Tell me—did Mr. Miles Malt identify himself as an FATB agent?"

"What?" Toby said, shocked.

"I take it he didn't," Potts said. "Well. He had undercover certification. No reason for him to advertise it."

"Uh-oh," said Selma, looking worriedly at Toby.

"A big uh-oh," Potts said. "But not for the reasons you might be thinking." He pulled out a notebook, found a page, and added, "To be candid, it's worse than what you're thinking."

Shit, thought Toby. He said, "I thought Miles was nuts."

"I didn't say he wasn't," Potts murmured. He looked up with a dazzling smile. "But don't get me wrong. Far be it from me to imply mental instability in the FATB."

"I guess I'm confused," Toby said.

"For your sake you better be," Potts said. He lost the smile, reconsulted his notes, snapped shut the notebook, put it away, settled back into the chair, and hit Toby with a puncturing look. "You told the sergeant that Malt invaded the private dining room after the party left and accused you of stealing his—pen. You denied stealing it, but Malt insisted you had, and a brief struggle ensued. The manager came by and threw Malt out. Malt later came here looking for you but you were passed out drunk, which," he said sending eyes around the room, "I don't have trouble thinking likely. Selma here got Malt to leave after threatening to call the police. Next thing you know, today he's cold on the stairs. Do I have the gist down correctly?"

"The short, fat guy at the bottom of the stairs?" Toby said.

Potts nodded. "Slatsky, Slutsky, or Slasty. The man who's got a bandage on his face—if he's alive, maybe even if he isn't. That cut went deep, by the way, Malt got cartilage and bone. A real clean chop. Anything else? Toby?"

Toby frowned, wondering if he could do it. That is, not mention the phone calls. He'd wiped the phone off and put it back in the raincoat.

"Never mind," Potts said. "Don't waste your fibs on me."

"Excuse me?" Toby said.

"Don't bother making up something about this pen, Toby. I'm not the one gonna dry clean your ass cause you're lying."

If you aren't, Toby wondered, who will?

Potts declared, "This case is going to the FATB."

"Great," Selma muttered.

"What makes you think," Toby asked with all the affrontedness he could summon, "that I . . . "

"ESP, Toby. I'm a mind reader." He raised a hand and shimmied long fingers. "I pick up on vibes, see." He smiled at Toby's consternation. "Don't shit your pants, boy. Wish I did but I don't. Do voodoo, I mean. What I know is, this Malt, though he may have been nuts like you say, wasn't fooling around with his FATB ID. Why, he had the best damn ID I ever saw. People like that, they don't go on dumb chases after pens. No, they go on chases after other kinds of stuff." He paused, studying Toby. "You want to tell me," he inquired, "what it is?"

Toby said, "You mean his ID is, like, really high-clearance or something? What do you mean?"

Potts sighed. He looked at the floor's impressive overlay of filth, and said, "Guess I can tell you. The ID's fake. I didn't know it was, I thought it was real as day. Until I called it in." He glanced at Selma and Dan, who sat like motionless Buddhas on the futon, mouths open. "FATB headquarters says no Agent Malt exists, real or alias, and the ID numbers match nothing. Don't take comfort, though. That just makes it worse."

"What's going to happen?" Selma asked.

"Well," Potts said, "we'll just have to see. When the FATB boys get here." He looked at Toby. "Notice, I didn't say 'fatboys,' did I? You better not either. Contrary to popular opinion, they don't like it."

"When will they get here?" Toby asked. It was quarter of five already.

"You got something better to do?" Potts said. "Look. I don't want to scare you. No, I guess I do. It's just this—if there's more to the story on the pen, and I am pretty damn sure there is, you better be upfront with them. As you may have heard, they can get rough. Real rough, in lots of ways, like making life hell for a long, long time, for instance. Tell you the truth, I don't even want to know what you planned to not tell me. I am curious, yes; this case is more interesting than the usual of what I do. But it's not worth it, because FATB people get bothered when police like me mess with their jurisdiction. If you know what I mean."

"Thanks for the advice," Toby said.

"You're welcome," Potts said. He stood up. "Now, I go."

"That's it?" Toby asked, amazed.

"That's it for now," Potts replied. "Special Agent Whipple and I will be here sometime between eight and ten tonight. You better be here too."

"Huh," said Toby. "Detective Potts, one last thing. Have you been following the Antarctica crisis?"

"Not really. Why?"

"Did you know that the ice in Antarctica has a water volume equal to the North Atlantic Ocean? And that there are rumors of a cover-up about where it might be going?"

"No shit," Potts said. "You giving me lip, kid?"

"No, no!" Toby said hastily. "They reported it on the news, and . . . sorry, I've got water on my mind. On my brain, I guess."

Potts rubbed his chin. He pulled the curtain open, glanced back at Selma, and said, "Watch out for those telephone poles, young lady." He smiled at her and left.

Dan and Selma stared stonily at Toby. "See?" Selma said.

"I know," Toby said. He sighed. "Nobody thinks it's important. I'm just cuckoo, I guess."

"Cuckoo, cuckoo!" Dan and Selma chirped in unison. They'd gotten a kick out of doing that at the height of the argument, earlier. When they'd tired of the "Dead in our beds!" routine.

Toby pushed between them and knelt on the futon to look out the window. It provided a view of the street in front. Dan and Selma pressed against his shoulders.

"Think of it," Toby said reflectively.

"Of what?" Selma inquired.

"The ocean, rising. This neighborhood could be like Venice. Water right up to this window."

"And no beaches," Dan commented. "That's so horrible, I can't even imagine it. A world without—*beaches?*"

"God won't allow that," Selma said.

"He'd make new beaches," Toby said. "In a hundred years."

They watched a parade of police people leave the building. It broke up at the sidewalk as the cops headed to a variety of official vehicles. A covered stretcher slid unceremoniously into an ambulance. One by one, the vehicles sped down Magazine Street.

"I don't know, Toby," Dan said.

"I don't know," Selma echoed.

"Are you coming to Dick's?" Toby asked. He glanced left, then right, to gauge their thinking.

"I," Selma said, standing up, "need the cleansing effects of water." She tromped across the futon to the curtain.

Toby looked at Dan. "You," Dan said, "have let disaster mania go to your head."

Special Agent Lex Whipple, Federal Anti-Terror Bureau, Boston, stared gloomily at his computer screen. He'd performed many data-pulls during his three years with the Bureau. The current job, compared to most, didn't pose much of a challenge. His machine was combing the records of several telecommunications carriers, and soon would produce a list of recent phone calls to Antarctica. Automated search programs made it simple as pie.

However, Whipple had better things to do. A nice Saturday afternoon was wasting, and the nice evening it promised to become would go to waste too, because of the crisis that was driving the top floor nuts—a crisis that somehow involved the Antarctic eruption. And, evidently, people who called Antarctica.

No one had explained the Bureau's interest in this. Officially, the Bureau's interest didn't exist. But something big had prompted the general and his staff to seal themselves off. The Bureau's more mundane business, which included a corpse named Miles Malt, meantime had piled up on Whipple's desk. When would he get out of here and back to his weekend?

He wouldn't. This weekend, Whipple suspected, he could kiss good-bye. Tomorrow they'd have him checking calls to the North Pole. Tonight looked just as bad, involving as it did the Cambridge police. Detective Potts, with whom Whipple had just talked, thought the Malt case deserved priority attention. What did the local constabulary know about Bureau priorities?

At the moment, about as much as Whipple knew, truth be told. Furthermore, the detective was right. Counterfeit Bureau ID required action. In ordinary circumstances, Colonel Samaraweera would have been all over this case. Same with Colonel Angelides, chief of Overt Ops and Whipple's immediate superior. But with the chiefs tending to more important affairs, and procedure leaving little doubt about responsibility, Whipple had no choice but to pick up the slack.

In a few minutes he'd possess electronic addresses in Maine, New Hampshire, Vermont, Massachusetts, Rhode Island, and Connecticut; those addresses that had initiated datalinks with Antarctic addresses over the last two months. Whipple wondered what Angelides would do with the information. It occurred to him that the Bureau might be preparing to pull the plug on telecommunications with Antarctica. Possibly to put a cap on news of the crisis?

But how could a volcanic eruption—or whatever it was—be so important?

Whipple's salary didn't cover that kind of speculation. He left the search program to its own devices, and opened the Malt file he'd created the day before: "pen," "code," a custodial job at Earnest Trefethen's office. To those lackluster facts he added what Potts had explained. Malt found dead, carrying fake Bureau ID, the victim of a sophisticated pellet weapon. A killer—likely professional, despite separation from his nose—named "Slutsky," "Slatsky," or "Slosty."

Two floors above Whipple's cubbyhole, General Raffenelli brooded about the limitations of power, the politics of his job, and the shadowy freelance operator named Slotsky. Where did this man come from? How could the Russians know so much about him, and not the Bureau? Did Moscow have more than it was admitting?

Of course the Russians were hoarding. They'd been dribbling out bits and pieces on Slotsky all day. According to liaison people in Washington, they were worried about "compromising intelligence sources." In other words, "Sharing secrets makes us crazy."

But they'd come across with a few facts, from which Raffenelli gathered that Slotsky could be described as a kind of information gangster. An obscure Orthodox Christian sect constituted his only known credo. Politics didn't motivate him. Apparently he did what he did for the money. His modus operandi involved buying and selling "attack data"—the kind that brought top dollar. Until recently he'd preyed on billionaires who didn't need publicity. Now he was branching into the geopolitical arena, trafficking dirt with governments instead of individuals.

The profile of a nuclear profiteer, Raffenelli reflected. Not necessarily one with weapons. He could extort as much money, or issue almost as many demands, using intelligence about others who did have weapons. Today's world of plundered armories and renegade bomb-makers made that kind of information the coin of the realm. Literally, it was priceless. For a player like Slotsky—no scruples, limitless greed—it had to be irresistible.

In the twenty-four hours since the general had briefed Colonel Samaraweera, the Covert Ops department had been working the Slot-sky angle exclusively. Covert was ransacking files and grilling sources about a squat, heavy, dark-haired man who used neurotoxin pellet weapons, who displayed impeccable manners even when killing, and who, if the Russians weren't cloddishly being funny, had a predilec-tion for women with muscular feet.

Such a person could be in Boston that very minute. But if he was, Samaraweera didn't know it. Raffenelli wondered if Covert needed help. Had it been a mistake to confine the Slotsky search to that one division? Should he expand the net?

No, the general decided. Overt Ops couldn't keep secrets; too much overlap with police and press. Overt didn't deliver anyway, their agents mostly were for show, for putting out fresh-faced zeal as they harassed subversives and rode around on tanks. It boiled down to one question: When was the last time Overt hit gold?

Raffenelli couldn't remember such a time. His intercom buzzed. Dworkin said, "Dr. Trefethen on line two, line is secure."

At last, thought the general. He'd been waiting for this all day. Tre-fethen's phones were impenetrable, and not just because of calls from the press. Heavyweights in Washington wanted his advice, a fact Raf-fenelli had learned with humbling certainty when he'd ordered an override of Trefethen's busy signal, only to hear a crisp artificial voice say, "Override blocked." It meant somebody with higher priority had control of the line.

Who—the DG? The President?

I'm not, he reminded himself, a paranoid man.

He picked up his phone and said, "Earnest, you're in demand."

"Hello," the familiar voice replied. They'd met socially at Clinic functions. Trefethen somewhat intimidated the general. Apart from his academic reputation and powerful connections, he was married to Helen Scarf. What kind of fellow could endure that? "I would guess," Trefethen remarked, "you're getting calls too."

"Not enough," Raffenelli said equably. "How's Helen?"

"Annoyed. She was looking forward to a post-retirement vacation.

I'd like to get away too, but can't at the moment, of course. Well I suppose I will—Mary has a plane at Logan. To take me to Washington after Barclay. Perhaps I should mention, Ted—I've been briefed." He paused, then added, "If you're calling to get an update on the eruption, I'm afraid . . . "

"I'll have to wait for Barclay?" As silence descended, the general wondered if Trefethen realized he was joking. Along with just about everyone else with a brain and a television set, Raffenelli intended to catch Earnest at nine. The Barclay promo had been relentless all day. Hundreds of millions would be watching, and for that reason alone the general was obliged to watch as well, just to keep up with media spin. Raffenelli didn't expect Trefethen to say much of substance. How could he? Revealing substance would amount to high treason.

"I take it you plan to tune in?" Trefethen inquired.

"I shouldn't bother?" Raffenelli asked. "Oh, come on. The whole world will be watching. If I didn't know better, I'd suspect you of masterminding one of the most ingenious hypes in broadcast history. People are expecting some kind of bombshell—I'm sure you've been over this with the DG."

Trefethen chuckled. "Exhaustively," he said. "We considered canceling the appearance. But Mary feels that would fan the flames. Charges of cover-up, and so on. The media snowball took me by surprise, you know. The business of 'making a statement' on Barclay's program—that simply was a way of buying time. Then it developed a life of its own. At this point, if I don't appear and say something, they'll suspect the worst. Goodness knows what rumors might start flying."

"That's right, I think. The 'prediction,' for example?"

"I'm the Oracle of Delphi, Ted. It pains me to say it, but we live in a deeply superstitious world. People look for excuses to believe the silliest things. Mary was just telling me that Senator Molloy called her this morning with that bit about 'cleansing water.' Absolute foolishness. I was referring to rain. A perfect example of how people lose their heads."

Raffenelli sighed; partly to indicate agreement, partly out of relief that he needn't pursue the "prediction" issue. The general didn't quite know what to make of that. But if Earnest had discussed it with the DG, he happily could leave it alone. "Let's get real," he said. "A lot of people will be losing their heads."

"Yes," Trefethen said softly. "The potential for mass irrationality, and worse—I can't begin to fathom it. Has Mary kept you informed?"

Raffenelli grimaced. To hear a private citizen ask if Mary

McMurtry, director general of the Federal Anti-Terror Bureau, was keeping one of her regional directors "informed"—aside from the obvious slight, it raised the question of whether she in fact was. Raffenelli couldn't be sure of that. He said, "I understand from the last bulletin there is 'increased activity'?"

"I'm afraid so. Seismic sensors indicate a possible activation of the entire rift system. You're aware that this system underlies a very large portion of the ice sheet?"

"That's what the bulletin said. It's serious?"

"Potentially, very. We're talking about heat, Ted. About a thin lithospheric crust that's in flux, which could mean more eruptions, and extensive venting of gases. That would melt a lot of ice at the sheet's bed. The more melt, the less stable the sheet becomes, because wet subglacial sediment creates a kind of lubricant, mud essentially, that— think of it as slipperiness, Ted. Think of a giant banana peel. I mean a truly gargantuan banana peel. Many, many thousands of square miles."

"You're saying the ice sheet might slip? Into the ocean, I assume."

"That's the danger. But it's not likely to happen, if the ice shelves stay put. The Ross and Ronne Shelves. Do you know about the shelves? Never mind, you'll find out on Barclay, it's my ace in the hole for—reassuring people. Excuse me." Raffenelli went on hold. Who's calling now? he wondered irritably. "Ted, I've just learned that the Dutch prime minister is on hold. Before I tend to his anxieties, is there anything I may help you with?"

"I'll make it brief. If somebody's tampering with the ice sheet— somebody is, obviously—who would know how to do it?"

"I would. At least, I'd have enough insight to try."

Raffenelli snickered. The idea of Trefethen, a longtime champion of Antarctica's pristine environment, exploding a nuke there—nothing could be more outlandish. Dryly he asked, "Are you confessing, Earnest?"

"Arrest me, Ted, before I do more damage. But first let me speak to the prime minister, will you?"

"Seriously. Who would have the expertise?"

"That's a good question, and I've thought about it. Not more than two hundred people. If I were you I'd start with glaciologists and volcanologists who've put in time on the Ice. Who've spent time in Antarctica, that is. Good-bye. And best of luck."

Raffenelli hung up feeling deflated. Five minutes with the great scientist, that's what he rated. He couldn't even override the busy signal;

Mary, Mary, Mary—Trefethen was so damn cozy with Mary. And how could the general compete with the prime minister of a country half below sea level already?

By sticking, Raffenelli supposed, to a couple hundred glaciologists and volcanologists. But Mary had to be working that angle. The approach exceeded his jurisdiction, since only a fraction of those scientists could be based in New England. That reminded Raffenelli of something. He wondered if Angelides had come up with a list of Antarctica phone callers.

The general doubted they'd include someone named Slotsky. But why not make sure?

"Surely," said the accented voice, "you can give some indication. At least, your professional opinion."

"Mr. Prime Minister," Earnest Trefethen said into his phone, "I am not at liberty to speak for my government, and cannot comment on evidence for a nuclear explosion. From a scientific standpoint, however, I can say that if such an explosion occurred, it is a crime of the greatest magnitude—in terms of ice sheet destabilization, and in terms of fouling the unique purity of Antarctica. If I may, I urge you to facilitate the broadcast of tonight's Barclay Piston program in Holland—I then will have more of a perspective, one that I think you, and your people, will find absorbing."

"Your perspective is optimistic, I hope?"

"Very," Earnest replied cordially.

"Good. Thank you. Perhaps we shall speak again."

"Perhaps. Good-bye, sir."

"Yes. Good-bye."

Earnest put down the phone, doubting he ever would talk with him again. After today, he didn't expect to be talking with much of anyone. That suited him perfectly. Talking with people fatigued Earnest. Not because he'd run out of things to say; he had much to say. What he'd run out of was the capacity to listen.

After today, he would do the talking, and others, a great many others,

would do the listening. He looked at the phone console. Its five buttons, including the one the prime minister had just vacated, blinked
beseechingly. Earnest yawned.

He'd been taking calls since early morning. Having told the same
half-truths over and over, and being a man who disliked repeating
himself, he now, at 6:13, was feeling edgy. He also was pushing his
luck. The chat with Raffenelli, for example. Why, Earnest wondered,
point directly at myself? What purpose does that serve? Other than to
make Ted, in due course, feel very stupid?

A good enough purpose right there, Earnest supposed. However, he
should stop this. He buzzed Darlene in reception and said, "Tell the
people on hold I can't talk at the moment. Tell them . . . I am . . . tell
them the usual. I'm busy with data."

"The White House is on line three," Darlene reminded him.

"Tell them I'm very busy with data."

"Reheema Sampson is on line one. She's been there an hour."

"She can stay there. Keep her on hold."

"Yes, sir. More people are outside. With cameras."

"Don't let them in."

"Dr. Trefethen."

"Yes?"

"I ordered pizza."

"If you have any trouble with those reporters, Darlene—simply call
the police. All right?"

"Yes, sir. Do you want some pizza?"

"No. But thank you." Earnest cut the intercom. Darlene was one of
the few people he knew with whom he effortlessly could be polite. Her
simplicity he found soothing. In fact, he liked her. He also needed her,
as only she buffered him from the clamorous world. Everyone else he'd
sent home. The staff's primary function, keeping up appearances,
didn't have much relevance to this most abnormal of days, a day that in
any case was the last day of the Ecologic Foundation's existence.

Just he and Darlene remained. Earnest pondered the irony. He
leaned back, swung his feet on his desk, and folded his hands over his
bony chest. The clock read 6:15 now. Two hours and forty-five minutes to go. Then, he thought impatiently, it begins.

The office felt oppressive. Plaques, awards, and citations lined the
opposite wall. Relics of his crusading past, they amounted, in
Earnest's opinion, to so much bric-a-brac. Something about them
caught his eye.

The early honors testified to hopeful diligence. The more recent, to calculated deceit. Intermingled, Earnest realized, they presented a kind of comedy. The peculiar farce of his career. He glanced around the room, aware that the many personal objects, the souvenirs and gifts, the decorative touches supplied by Helen, had been all but invisible for a very long time. Why should they now draw his attention?

Because, he thought, I soon part with them.

He wondered who would claim custody. He'd never considered that issue. What kind of exhibit might the room make?

On his desk stood a silver-framed photograph taken fifteen years before, of Helen, himself, and the twins. We look so much younger, he thought. Happier, too; Papa and Mama, smiling, proud of our delightful tykes. In the glass Earnest saw a bald visage, gaunt and lined, reflecting from that distant past. He frowned. The self-scrutiny, joined with the gaze of a cheerier self, pained him. He set the photo down.

Taken in 1987, he thought. Just fifteen years ago. But a different era.

Actually, they'd reached the turning point three years earlier, in '84. Reagan's reelection had been the final straw; that landslide endorsement of a culture of ruin. Of corruption, hypocrisy, selfishness, waste. For those with the wit to see it, 1984 had put the writing on the wall. And they had seen it, he and Helen.

That year too, the twins were born. For another family, the arrival of two perfect babies might have had a softening effect. Not for them. If anything, Earnest remembered, the twins had firmed their ambition to do something about it all, to try to make a difference. They were the Brave New Family. Hiding their rage, covering up their plans. Thinking long-range.

He'd wanted to name the babies Winston and Julia. Helen vetoed that. No Orwellian sarcasm for us—we must maintain, she'd reminded him, unimpeachable cover. They were obliged to pretend that they, like so many of their colleagues, were joining, guiltlessly and even gleefully, the national swing to the right. Otherwise they wouldn't get anywhere.

We've gotten there, Earnest thought. It's astounding we have. Given that we started as a couple of grad school lefties, hippies really. That's what we were at the beginning.

But we're there. Having paid a price, he reflected. We've paid all along, and will pay more, no doubt the ultimate price. Poor Helen—

she has so perverted her science. The uses to which she put it! The poor twins—raised in an airless bubble of deception. And poor me. Poor, poor me. A merciless monster.

He considered Martha, too. Of the five of us, he thought, the only one who hasn't suffered is Martha. But she will. She will . . .

Earnest pulled from his suit jacket pocket an object resembling an old-style Zippo cigarette lighter. He flipped the silver lid. The device didn't ignite tobacco. It ignited something else. Earnest inspected a safety catch that prevented the accidental depression of a shiny metal button.

A computer in a sealed Kansas City office awaited the push of that button. The Zippo was a pager. From anywhere in the info-wired world, it could page the computer. Telling it to flood the Net with a photograph of the icon.

A simple photo. Which would transform everything . . .

The intercom buzzed. "Yes," Earnest said.

"Mr. Piston is here. With people." Darlene sounded awed.

"Good. Show them to the conference room. Darlene—the rest room off the conference room?"

"I know. It's not working."

"In fact, it is."

"Dr. Trefethen. You always keep it locked."

"But it's unlocked now. Please let Mr. Piston and his people know it's available."

"Not the second floor one?"

"No. The conference room one. Darlene, I'm counting on you. Are you going to forget what we talked about?"

"No!" she exclaimed.

"Wonderful. Please tell Mr. Piston to come up here."

"Okay," Darlene said, voice tinged with hurt.

"Thank you," Earnest said. "Thank you very much."

He stood, slipped the Zippo-like device in a pocket, and went to the windows. Two stories below an enormous truck filled Plympton Street. Earlier, police had closed the street off. They did that for Barclay Piston. Police made way for Barclay all over the world, wherever he and his entourage rolled into town. Earnest studied the truck's rounded contours, the warship-like transceivers. Fancier than our truck, he thought. At least on the outside. And the inside? He sighed. Helen's sentimentality, at this juncture, seemed not just a waste of brainpower. It bordered on the pathetic.

He concentrated on the truck in the street. My megaphone to a listening world, he thought. Along with the support flotilla of trucks, vans, and limousines, it would hinder access to Plympton Street, later. Earnest imagined the pandemonium. Gridlock and sirens in Harvard Square, that's what he wanted. Barclay's cameras would feed on that.

Someone thumped the door. "Come in," he called.

Piston entered, all business with a bulging leather valise and an electronics carryall. He appeared annoyed. "Long wait outside," he remarked, closing the door. "Nobody answered the bell."

"I'm under siege, Barclay. The portcullis is down."

"I couldn't even call you. Couldn't get through."

"Join the family of man, my friend. No one gets through."

"Excuse me for saying this, but that's some receptionist you have downstairs."

"Darlene is a valued employee."

"She's retarded, Earnest."

"She is mentally challenged, yes."

"She's fucking retarded! How do you do business? I swear to God, everything they say about Cambridge is true!"

"Yet you're here. With your trusty truck. Barclay, perhaps you should sit down."

He remained standing. "Can we speak freely?" he asked.

Earnest smiled. "You're asking," he replied, "if I'm bugged?"

"Yes," Barclay said seriously.

"Not to my knowledge," Earnest murmured, noting worry in the man's eyes. "What have you heard?"

"I think you know."

"Perhaps I do. But I'm not a telepath. Spit it out."

Barclay said deliberately, "I've heard from several different sources that the eruption wasn't an eruption."

"What was it?"

"Don't play dumb."

"You're boring me, Barclay."

"This is off the record. I won't cite you."

"You are interviewing me in a couple of hours."

"So? That means we can't talk?"

Earnest went to the desk, sat, and assumed the meditative stare he knew to be inscrutable even to rabid newshounds like Barclay, who did in fact look rabid. As well he should. "Of course we can talk," Earnest said.

Barclay muttered, "Headline: 'PLANET'S COASTS HELD HOSTAGE.'"

"My," Earnest said airily.

"Who do you think's doing it?" Barclay snapped.

"I think you may be jumping to conclusions."

Barclay snorted. "You of all people! If you weren't in bed with Mary McMurtry and the rest, you'd be screaming about this. Earnest—it's a nightmare."

"You do seem quite upset."

"Upset? You know how much coastal property I own? On the Cape, on the Vineyard, on St. Thomas? Not to mention Florida, where my wife's family would be . . . wiped out, old man. Of course I'm upset." He paused for breath. Then he said quietly, "So I'm asking you. Could it happen? Could a madman blow the ice sheet?"

"Yes," Earnest said.

"Holy Mary, Mother of God," Barclay moaned.

Earnest said, "You're behaving like a textbook hysteric."

"All right, you just answer one question. What did you mean last night about 'the cleansing effects of water'? The FATB tipped you off, right? The madman made threats, obviously, and Mary called you to find out if it's possible—you're the first person she'd call, if they got a credible threat. And you bet it was credible, because the madman went and exploded the thing! And now you're saying it's possible he could go all the way! Blow the ice sheet into the ocean! So you tell me this—what if this terrorist really does it? Damn you—don't call me an hysteric!"

As he watched Barclay deliver his tirade, Earnest felt justified in having risked "cleansing water." The world's top tabloid television personality stood before him, quaking with panic. Panic seemed like a virus to Earnest. It was contagious; and in terms of transmission, Barclay couldn't have been a mightier vector. The many influential people with whom he talked, not to mention those with whom Reheema, and Al Molloy, and Sforza, and the rest of them talked—they too had to be extremely worried.

Earnest decided against taking more calls. He'd achieved critical mass. To the glowering Barclay he said, "I wish I could guarantee your coastal property is safe. But I can't."

"So it's true," Barclay said, paling.

Earnest nodded. He said, "Keep in mind that the 'terrorist' might not know what he's doing. It would take great ingenuity to, as you say, 'blow the ice sheet.' And we don't even know if that's the intention behind the—eruption."

"We don't?" Barclay asked.

"No. We don't. Now, about tonight."

"Hold it!" Barclay barked. "I have a few . . . "

"Quiet!" Earnest shouted. "Behave like the professional you think you are!"

Barclay blinked. Then, unpleasantly, he laughed. "Mary is leaning on you," he said. "She wants you to rig the show. And you're about to specify how I do it—am I right?"

"You're wrong," Earnest said.

"The genie is out of the bottle, Earnest. New Zealand TV's reporting fallout. A research boat picked it up in the Ross Sea. Just twenty minutes ago, I got a fax from somebody at the *Sydney Times*—a banner headline in the morning, do you hear what I'm saying? I'm saying I can go without you tonight."

"Barclay, you're going with me, of course. I will give you the story of a lifetime. That I assure you."

"All right," Barclay said with sudden reasonableness. "I like it. I'll even be professional. Whatever it takes to make you happy. What were you going to ask?"

"Visuals, Barclay. I was wondering if we can find a way to convey the reality—the brute vastness—of Antarctica. People don't know about Antarctica. They think it's a frozen puddle at the bottom of the map . . . "

"Done!" Barclay exclaimed. Earnest raised his eyebrows. Barclay smiled. "We have a live remote," he said. "Canadian crew doing a documentary—'The Onset of Antarctic Winter'—it's a nature thing, they happened to be there, so we bought them. Booked them indefinitely. They have 'copters, by the way. Equipped for satellite feed. What do you think?"

Earnest thought it was marvelous. But it didn't come as a surprise. He'd arranged, indirectly, for the funding that had sent the Canadians to Antarctica. He'd also arranged for the phone call offering their services to the relevant producers. Now he wanted to confirm those services would be put to good use. "Where are they?" he asked, beaming at Barclay's legerdemain.

"McMurdo Base," Barclay replied. "Not near the eruption, which is too bad." He shrugged. "It's cloudy there anyway."

"McMurdo," Earnest said, "is nine hundred miles from the eruption, on the other side of the Ross Ice Shelf. But Barclay, that's ideal."

"No kidding. Why?"

"If there's continued volcanic activity in the rift zone, Ross Shelf could be the only thing stopping collapse. Ross is crucial. If it weren't for Ross, the ice sheet probably would have collapsed long ago. With or without volcanoes."

"So? The McMurdo location gets that across?"

"Absolutely. McMurdo's on Ross Island, at the edge of Ross Shelf. Barclay, do you know what ice shelves are?"

"They float. That's all I know."

"They form when glaciers and ice streams flow from the interior into protected ocean bays along the coast. So yes, they float. And they're dynamic. Basically, they're floating glaciers delivering ice to the sea. Icebergs, that is—chunks of ice break off a shelf and drift into the ocean, that's what creates icebergs. But meantime the ice streams and glaciers continue to feed the shelf, so its size stays stable.

"And Ross is enormous. The size of France. Two hundred thousand square miles—it covers half the huge Ross Embayment. You get a 'copter over Ross, people will see what's holding the ice sheet back. That shelf is a key feature of Antarctica's ice system."

"I'll be damned," Barclay said.

Right, Earnest thought. He said, pensively, "The first European sailors to approach Ross Shelf saw a towering cliff of ice, in places over a hundred feet high, that went on for hundreds of miles. They couldn't seem to find a way around this wall, so they called it the 'Great Ice Barrier.' It's interesting, Barclay. If there was a reason to call it that then, there's another one now."

"Ah. It acts as a barrier to the ice sheet?"

Earnest nodded. "First, it moderates the sheet's ice stream velocity. In other words, it puts a damper on how fast the streams can conduct interior ice to the ocean. Second, it protects the interior from the ocean's ravaging effect. That's very important with the western sheet. Unlike the east sheet, the western one is almost entirely submarine. The bedrock it sits on is well below sea level, that is. Which is why it's unstable, why it periodically undergoes collapse. It's not high and dry, you see—it's glued to the ocean floor. And if conditions get rough, it becomes unglued."

Barclay thought a moment. "Ross Shelf keeps it glued?"

"It's more complicated than that. But essentially, yes."

"The size of France," Barclay said appreciatively. "McMurdo, if one wants to be geographically imaginative, is what? Cannes?"

"No. More like Nice."

"This has possibilities," Barclay declared. Earnest nodded. "The twist is," Barclay went on, "we get to scare people—but then have a way to maintain hope. Ross Ice Shelf spells hope."

"Exactly. Ross spells hope. I'm pleased you have helicopters there. It will make everything so much more vivid."

"Television loves vivid, Earnest."

"Yes," Earnest said. "It does."

At 6:29, Slotsky drove into Harvard Square.

He'd left the hotel peppily and without incident, his head shrouded in a burnoose he'd scissored from a bedsheet. Not one of the sheets he'd napped on; Slotsky was finicky about linen. The burnoose had come from the spare bed. The doctor he'd made comfortable on the floor.

His head remained shrouded as he progressed down Massachusetts Avenue, approaching, at the Plympton Street intersection on the left, the Ecologic Foundation. The building comprised three stories of solid and vaguely pompous design, with a fourth floor hidden behind the roofline. It once housed a Harvard club. Ecologic had bought it two years before, Slotsky's research had established. A retail store fronting Mass. Ave. occupied much of the first floor. Ecologic's entrance, around the corner on Plympton, lay within a massive stone stoop. Thus the foundation's offices had almost no ground-level exposure to the street; the arrangement struck Slotsky as quite secure. He'd learned from Miles, however, that Trefethen recently had put a good deal of money into renovating doors, windows, and locks. Did the president of the Ecologic Foundation expect a mob attack? Or perhaps some other kind of attack?

Slotsky pulled over on Mass. Ave. opposite the building. A police barricade closed Plympton off. Slotsky espied a broadcast truck behind it. Ah yes, he thought; the puissant chariot of Barclay Piston, airwave magnate. As if unrolling a gigantic carpet, technicians were unfurling a silverish video display over the building's Plympton Street facade. Such screens, Slotsky knew, were a Barclay trademark. They often drew quite a street crowd. Aside from lending the Barclay show an air of public-spiritedness, they attracted local television news teams interested in reactions to whatever topic Barclay happened to be doing. Good business for local TV. Even better business for Barclay, who didn't shrink from the carnival aspects of his trade.

Slotsky suspected he would deliver a blockbuster tonight. He eased back into traffic, continued down Mass. Ave. to Dunster Street, where, following the tracker's instructions, he made a left. He made another left, then a right. The tracker told him to make another right on Winthrop Street. He cruised down Winthrop to JFK Street, crossed it, and had continued on Winthrop but twenty feet when the tracker's contralto said breathily, "Park."

Winthrop Street, narrow and one-way, Slotsky found to be more alley than street. Slender sidewalks bordered it. To the right lay a small open green, after which buildings hemmed the street in. On the left, an arcade of shops trafficked food and ice cream; beyond which stood three older structures, wood-frame and handsome, that formerly must have been private homes. One sold curios. Another housed a "Class Report" Office. The closest and largest housed the nightclub called Dick's.

Slotsky cruised a hundred feet or so to Winthrop's terminus, Eliot Street. Also one-way, Eliot looked to be a major thoroughfare; traffic swarmed from right to left. Slotsky waited for an opening and made the left. From there he could go right toward a hotel, or make a curving left past the red-brick ziggurats of the Harvard School of Government. He went left and came to JFK Street. A right would take him to the nearby Charles River, a left back into the Square. Slotsky went left. He made another left onto Winthrop, completing the circle, and halted in front of Dick's.

It was 6:40 now. Slotsky pondered the evident fact that Eliot and JFK conducted traffic from Harvard Square to the fast-moving arteries bordering the river, Memorial Drive on the Cambridge side, and, over the bridge, Storrow Drive. This he found satisfactory. What with the maze of one-ways, dead-ends, and traffic lights that ruled the Square's vehicular flow, Dick's hardly could have been better situated for a quick exit.

He pulled onto the sidewalk opposite the nightclub. In the vanity mirror he checked the fit of his burnoose. It didn't conceal the bandage completely. But with the car's windows set at maximum tint, it would do.

He knew the Arab-style headdress made him the Hollywood conception of a terrorist. That he preferred, however, to the Hollywood conception of a horrorist. Seepage had stained the bandage, and the eye and mouth slits leered unappealingly.

Slotsky thought about turning this to his advantage. The shock element might help him achieve his goal; he wanted the code, and at least one of the twins. Everybody and everything else in Harvard Square, from his point of view, simply were in the way.

He left the car and entered Dick's. A dim cocktail lounge filled the first floor. Above the bar, a television set played Antarctica news. Slotsky eyed it. More talk of strange military goings-on on the icy continent. But no hint, still, of a nuclear aspect. He studied the lounge. But for two men playing chess by a window overlooking the street, it was devoid of people. He walked to the room's middle. The chess players ignored him. Very good, thought Slotsky, as he wandered around planting bugs. At this stage in his career, he liked a free ride.

Mission accomplished, he left, and saw a station wagon coming down Winthrop. It barely cleared his car. But it wasn't passing through. The driver, a woman, turned onto the sidewalk and parked directly in front of his car. She and a female companion got out.

Slotsky watched them unload things from the wagon's rear. Photographic equipment, he noted as he crossed the street, holding the burnoose to his eyes. Tripods, film cameras, advanced digital cameras, flashes, a professional assortment. He entered his car, closed the door, and lowered the window an inch. The women carried the equipment to the bar's entrance. In their thirties and sportively dressed, perhaps too sportively, they seemed harried. One of them looked at her watch. She exclaimed, "Half an hour!"

Ah, thought Slotsky. A photo shoot at Dick's. That could be bad. On the other hand, it could be good. If police were to come by and order him to move off the sidewalk, he would adopt his most liquid Tunisian accent and explain, with earnest volubility, that "I'm with the shoot." He hoped this wouldn't be necessary. If the officer turned out to have been instructed to detain short, rotund men with bandages on their faces, Slotsky would invite him into the rear of his car. He could accommodate at least three officers, he was sure; room enough on the back seat, a tarpaulin to cover them. The fresh Number 11 on his shoulder would make it child's play.

A "shoot," Slotsky mused. Remembering he hadn't yet done so, he checked his weapons.

━ ━ ━

In East Cambridge, the warehouse door rattled up. A van rolled into the slanting sunlight. The warehouse door rattled down.

Seated in the van's windowless rear, Grace and Brian exchanged fervid glances. They were on a survival mission. It was either get the pin or bail out.

Fladgate drove. Searles rode shotgun. To the twins, neither man was a presence. Mother's security employees didn't have a whole lot to say, in general. That was because they couldn't think, in general. They could understand orders, they could perform basic tasks like drive, eat, and sleep, and they were very good with guns. Other than that they didn't do much, and didn't particularly want to, on account of having been through one of the Clinic's more innovative programs.

Six minutes later, Fladgate pulled into the parking lot of a defunct electronics retailer. Two sedans waited there, each holding two men, security zombies from the Clinic.

The men in the cars got out. One carried a satchel containing Mother's mail and messages. There was no telephone contact between the warehouse and the Clinic; couriers ferried communications back and forth, using a minimum of two vehicles, randomly switched, to make the run.

The mail courier entered the van. He and Searles would return to the warehouse. Fladgate issued orders to the others. Then he opened the van's back door. "Come," he said to the twins. They hurried to the sedan Fladgate indicated.

Fladgate put his hefty frame behind the wheel, turned to his charges, and said, "Where we going?"

At 6:50, Selma ran around the apartment getting her things together. Toby and Dan waited downstairs in a taxi. The three of them were going to Harvard Square.

What is it, Selma asked herself, that I'm forgetting?

She remembered. Jeremy, of course. Selma didn't know where he was, and the machine at his place was broken. She couldn't leave a message there.

Jeremy had been making himself scarce the last couple of days. Selma suspected he felt uncomfortable about Dan. But it wasn't her fault, and she resented the way he'd shunned last night's party. She did want to see him, though, because of everything that had happened, and the way Toby was handling it. Jeremy was good with emergencies. Also, tonight Selma had off, rare for a Saturday. Tomorrow night she'd be back tending bar in the hellhole club.

Why did that boy have to be so hard to get hold of? Selma went to the answering machine, pressed the outgoing message button, and said, "Hi, Jeremy, wherever you are. We'll be at Dick's from seven until—I don't know, for a while, but not all night. If you're around, come by—I want to get together. Stuff has happened. Very strange stuff. If anybody else calls and sees Jeremy, tell him, please. Thank you. Bye."

She grabbed her bag and keys. The bag, she confirmed, held the can of mace. She'd never used the stuff. But you never knew.

The plan was for her and Dan to precede Toby into Dick's, to "case the joint," as Dan melodramatically had put it. They wanted to be sure that the drop-dead twins, who wouldn't know who Dan and Selma were, hadn't planned something funny. If it seemed okay, she'd go to the front window and wave at Toby, who'd be watching from the sidewalk. Then they'd grill the twins about the pin. And point out that she and Toby had a date later on with the FATB, that the detective had said would go badly if Toby didn't come clean.

Selma and Dan had discussed the subject. Toby most certainly was going to come clean.

Through his side window Slotsky watched two sedans slide by, inches away due to the narrow clearance on Winthrop. Clinic cars, he noted. The men in them he also recognized; Clinic guards, among them Fladgate, chief of security. The twins, elegantly dressed, emerged from his car. They headed for Dick's.

Both cars pulled onto the sidewalk in front of the station wagon. That annoyed Slotsky. He disliked being the rearmost of a four-car lineup. Especially in such close quarters. But he couldn't move to the front, the sidewalk ended there.

Slotsky meditated. Fladgate et al. would pose a challenge.

In the cocktail lounge at Dick's, Sylvia Porter, art director of Szene Magazene, despondently sized up the premises. A TV set over the bar played stock footage of volcanic eruptions, providing the sole enlivenment to an atmosphere that could be summed up in three words: Dark and scruffy.

Sylvia didn't care about that. Dark and scruffy suited a Simone shoot. But the clientele here didn't. It amounted to two middle-aged men. Balding and bedraggled, playing chess by the front window, they failed to provide the atmospheric zing Sylvia had expected, considering the promo she'd paid for. She wanted *louche* foreign students, skeptical fashion critics, generic club brats, and of course, faithful Simone cultists. Instead she had sedentary geezers. Sylvia knew this wasn't New York. However, it was Harvard Square. Where were all the fabulous people?

"Don't panic," Doris said. The photographer, Doris came from Boston. Not only had she suggested Dick's, she'd also organized the promo. Sylvia was readying a sarcastic reply when Doris added, "Check out these two."

Sylvia turned. A couple of kids entered the room. She sized them up and realized they were twins—breathtaking, eye-popping, mouthwatering twins. Sylvia felt sudden hope. "Who are they?" she asked Doris under her breath. Doris shook her head. "You've never seen them anywhere?" Sylvia whispered with disbelief.

Doris said, "They don't look like club types, Sylvia."

Sylvia agreed. They looked more like cotillion types. The correctitude with which they were dressed and coiffed was European. Young Americans didn't have that conservative, at the same time stylish, knack. They glanced around, as if unfamiliar with this obscure *boite* they'd come across. As if uncertain, Sylvia thought, the place is quite appropriate. But they moved to the lounge's gloomiest corner. The boy seated the girl formally. He then seated himself with self-assuredness bordering on the foppish. Magnificent, Sylvia thought. Doris muttered something. Sylvia poked her to get a repeat. "I heard," Doris whispered, "that members of the Danish royal family are studying at Harvard. Under fake names. Nobody knows what they look like."

"Doris," Sylvia said, "I want pictures."

Doris nodded.

In the office in the truck, Helen finished sorting mail, and turned to the phone log. An item caught her eye. A message for Grace. From, of all places, Mifflin Place restaurant. Grace had left a "piece of jewelry" there.

Helen didn't recall Grace wearing jewelry. She was sure Grace hadn't. Helen frowned at the phone number. Apparently it was the waiter's. This Toby was attempting to romance her daughter?

Helen sensed a problem. A bigger one than a Grace-struck waiter. Something about it made her acutely uncomfortable.

She punched the waiter's number. After two rings she got a machine. The message, spoken by a youthful female voice, rambled on about "Jeremy," "Dick's," and "stuff" that had happened. "Very strange stuff." Helen's psychiatric antennae detected anxiety in this voice. It wasn't garden variety. The girl sounded shaken.

Helen hung up at the beep, and sat back, thinking. Grace never wore jewelry. That was what had been so surprising about the pearls. To Helen's knowledge, Grace didn't even possess any jewelry. Of course, Helen did; Grace had looked at it last night, when it came out of the safe. Had she taken something? And then, bizarrely, lost it at the restaurant?

A foreboding entered Helen's mind. She didn't want to check the safe. What difference would it make if, because of some kind of child-ish acting-out, Grace had purloined one of those clunky brooches? But now, thinking about it more, Helen realized that the twins' "date" smacked of artifice; of pretext, with something going on under the surface; of, in fact, desperation. . . .

Helen stood, and hurried to the safe.

At 6:58, Toby watched Selma and Dan walk toward Dick's. The business of casing the joint seemed overcautious. What kind of threat could the twins pose?

He stood in the small park on the corner of JFK and Winthrop, not far from the club, but sufficiently far to blend in with the bustle that always filled the Square on Saturdays. Dan and Selma he'd parted with on Mt. Auburn Street. What if, Dan had asked, the twins were keeping a vigilant eye from Dick's? What if they were staking the place out from a car? A true casing, according to Dan, meant that he, Selma and Toby shouldn't arrive as a threesome. That might blow his and Selma's anonymity.

Dan had a point, Toby supposed. Four cars were parked opposite the club on Winthrop's sidewalk. Burly men sat in the front two. The third car, a station wagon, appeared empty. Tinted glass veiled the rearmost car's interior. Behind the wheel of that car, Toby glimpsed a bulky shape that suggested an Arab-style hood.

He moved closer. The hooded person seemed to be watching Selma and Dan approach the nightclub. Toby crossed Winthrop. He followed a group of German-speaking tourists down the street. Coming abreast of the car with tinted glass, he glanced at it casually; and glimpsed the face under the cloth.

A filthy bandage covered it. Toby continued walking behind the Germans. Saying to himself, Holy shit.

Thirty feet down he stopped and leaned against a wrought-iron fence. The bandaged man, if the killer, might have recognized Selma. But not necessarily himself. Toby studied the lineup of cars. It struck him as sinister. Four cars bumper-to-bumper on the sidewalk, right across the street from Dick's? He noticed something. A man in the lead car held a phone to his head.

The sight clarified Toby's thinking. Only one thing to do, he realized. Go straight to Dick's and call the cops.

He walked swiftly up the street toward the nightclub.

Dan and Selma had paused in the vestibule to check out the lounge. No one seemed to be there.

They entered. A voice exclaimed, "Selma!" It was Doris. Uh-oh, thought Selma. Somebody like her would have to be here. Doing a completely dumb event. Why hadn't she realized that?

"Hi," she said, glancing around and seeing two young blond look-alikes in the corner. Yes, they were gorgeous. "Doris," she said quietly, "this is Dan."

Doris smiled and said, "I heard about the party last night. Sorry I couldn't make it." Too loudly she added, "You're Toby's brother?" Dan nodded. He also had espied the blonds in the corner. Like Selma, he was trying not to make it obvious. Doris said, "You're just in time for Simone, she'll be here any minute—Simone, the performance artist? This is Sylvia from Szene Magazene, you've heard of Szene, right?"

Sylvia's eyes ate them alive. Selma led Doris a few feet away and whispered, "We're here for reasons I can't explain now, except that they're serious, and I'd appreciate it if you'd . . . "

Toby's sudden arrival interrupted her. "Selma, Dan, you have to see this!" he exclaimed. Ignoring Doris, he took them to the window. The chess players, crowded, looked up with annoyance. "That car with dark windows," Toby blurted, pointing. "There's a man in it with a bandage on his face, the grossest bandage you ever saw." He looked back at the twins and yelled, "It's call-the-cops-time—I think the guy who got Malt is right out front!"

The twins rushed to the window, their sedate poise gone. Toby couldn't help but stare at the way Grace's pearls flapped on her chest. Even more riveting, as she gazed through the window, was the fear in her eyes. The man who'd been on the phone in the car now stood in the street. He still had the phone pressed to his head. Grace didn't seem to like the look of that.

She muttered to Brian, "Fladgate's talking with Mother."

Toby watched Brian shudder. He glanced at Selma and Dan. They also had picked up on the twins' alarm.

"What's happening?" Sylvia inquired, approaching the window. A white limousine crept down Winthrop, its left wheels on the sidewalk to get by the line of parked cars. "Simone!" Sylvia exclaimed. "Doris, Simone's here!"

The limousine slowed. Fladgate was waving it back. His car and the one behind it lurched into the street. Blocked, the limousine halted.

"Would you get out of our fuckin' faces," one of the chess players growled.

"Sorry," Selma said. "This is a crisis."

"Doris, shoot!" Sylvia shouted, backing away from the window. Rapid-fire flashes emanated from Doris. Sylvia already knew the caption: SIMONE'S ARRIVAL THRILLS CAMBRIDGE SZENE-MAKERS.

Both twins stared at the cars blocking the limo. The men in them got out. They followed Fladgate, who was coming toward Dick's. "Where's the icon?" Brian nervously asked Toby. "I mean, the pin?"

"You mean," Toby said, pulling it from his pocket, "this, the killer-attracter?" More flashes went off.

"Damn!" Brian shouted. He tried to grab it. Toby brought his hand back. Brian missed, but Grace came at him.

"Give it to me," she hissed, punching him viciously in the stomach. Toby gasped. She snatched the pin. Brian meantime bolted toward Doris and tried to grab the camera. Doris howled in protest. Brian flipped her to the floor. The players stood up fast, upending the table they'd been wedged against; chess pieces flew across the room. Brian was wrestling Doris for the camera. She clutched it tightly. Grace darted over and kicked her hard in the butt.

"How dare you!" cried Sylvia. "Even if you are—royalty!"

"Zipper it," snarled Grace.

"Cunt!" Sylvia yelled, seizing Grace by the shoulders. Doris, wailing, released the camera. Brian got up. Aghast, Sylvia watched him rip out film. Wriggling in Sylvia's iron grip, Grace stomped one of her feet. Sylvia screamed, seized the necklace, and yanked. A spume of pearls filled the air.

Toby sat down, clutching his stomach. Dan and Selma stood frozen with fascinated shock. Grace covered her face with her hands. Brian put the camera on a table and gravely crossed his arms over his chest. Pearls rolled madly across the floor.

"Listen, assholes," roared the bigger of the chess players, "I own this place and I'm calling the cops!" The other chess player ran behind the bar. He emerged from it holding a jackiron.

"Good idea," croaked Toby. He winced at his stomach, looked at the twins, and said, "No reproduction, huh? Guess what—we have pictures. Party pictures, of me wearing it last night. Does that drive you out of your minds?"

Brian and Grace glowered. Toby glowered back. An air of puzzled violence filled the room as footfalls echoed from the front steps. Dan said, "I'll call the cops. Where's the . . . "

"Don't bother," said Fladgate as he came through the doorway. He listened a moment to his phone. Then he looked around and asked, "Anybody waiting to hear from Jeremy?"

Selma cleared her throat. "Why do you ask?" she said.

"Your name?" Fladgate asked her.

"Selma," she said. "How do you know Jeremy?"

Fladgate asked the room, "Who is Toby?"

"Me," Toby said weakly.

"Anybody else with Selma and Toby?" Fladgate asked.

No one replied. The owner said, "Who are you?"

"Security," Fladgate informed him.

The owner frowned. He said, "Private?"

Fladgate turned to the twins and said, "Do you have it?"

In a strangled voice Grace said, "Yes! I have it!"

Fladgate asked the phone, "You heard her?" He listened a moment. Then he said to Grace, "Come here."

She went over, snow pale. Fladgate opened his hand. Trembling,

Grace dropped the pin in it. Fladgate turned his back on the others. He studied the pin; into the phone he said, "Yeah."

"I gave it to him, Mother," Grace quavered at the phone.

Fladgate nodded at one of his men, pointed at Selma, and said, "Her." He pointed at Toby and said, "Him." He glanced at Grace, then at Brian, and said, "Separate cars for the twins, Jenkins. Selma, Toby. Let's go."

Brian walked docilely to his sister. Dan looked at Toby and Selma. Neither was moving. Fladgate barked, "I said, let's go!"

Face darkening, Toby said, "Why is Helen Scarf telling you to kidnap us? That is Dr. Scarf on the phone? Isn't it?"

Fladgate said, "You're under arrest. Jenkins, take him out."

With increasing volume as Jenkins approached him, then seized him, Toby said, "There's a murderer outside and you're arresting me? Where's your badge, big shot? Would somebody call the police? God damn it! Keep your hands off of . . ."

Jenkins pulled a gun and said, "Shut your piss-ant mouth."

"Hey!" the owner exclaimed. "You can't do this!"

"Oh, yeah?" Jenkins said. "Watch."

Toby cast a desperate look at Selma and Dan. The guy coming at Selma was absorbing her attention. Dan mouthed almost imperceptibly, but to Toby as if he were talking aloud, "Fucked up."

Brian and one of the men suddenly were leading the way. Behind them, with the gun in his back, Toby followed. Dan listened to footsteps clatter down the front steps. Selma said to the guy whose fingers had sunk into her arm, "Wait a second."

He pulled a gun and grunted, "Move."

Dan watched Selma move. Nobody, himself included, seemed prepared to do shit about this. The owner just stood there, gaping. Dan saw Selma's hand go in her purse. At the doorway, she looked back at him. Dan could tell she wanted to say something, but wouldn't—the only reason he hadn't been seized was because he hadn't been identified as being "with Selma and Toby." Dan thought of the mace Selma had in her purse. Would she use it?

Fladgate followed Grace, Selma, and the gunman through the door. More clatter came from the steps.

"What the hell?" the owner said to his friend.

The man shrugged. He tossed the jackiron on a table and said, "They're leaving."

From the street came a volley of car honks. Sylvia looked out the window. She said distractedly to Doris, "Simone's trapped. The cars are blocking the limo." In a daze, Doris blinked. Sylvia shouted, "Get to work—I'm paying you, aren't I?"

Doris picked up a digital camera. She went to the window and aimed. The camera buzzed as it took exposures; the sound galvanized Dan. He grabbed the jackiron, then ran out, paying no heed to the shouts behind him.

Winthrop Street was an ear-splitting honking mess. Dan didn't see Toby or Brian. But he noticed the men's lead car at the end of the street. It turned left, and disappeared into traffic.

The other car still blocked the limo. Selma sat shuddering in the back seat. Grace got in beside her. Fladgate, talking into his phone, motioned Grace over so he could get in too. The car was running. Its front door also was open.

The goon who apparently would get in and drive it was fending off the enraged limousine driver. The parked station wagon blocked the limo's right rear door; the left rear door banged against Dick's fence. The banger, an enormous and irate creature, couldn't squeeze through the foot-wide clearance. Dan recognized the massive bald head of Simone, Hawaii's sex-change sumo superstar.

Directly behind the limo, preventing it from backing up even an inch, was the car with dark glass. Its horn made a steady, unrelenting blast. The driver, Dan saw, appeared swathed with gauze.

Slotsky glared at the limousine blocking his view. He'd seen enough to know that Brian and a young man—almost certainly Toby—had been abducted by Clinic guards. Worse, Fladgate was poised to make off with the code in the second Clinic car. Slotsky knew this beyond doubt; via bugs, he'd heard the proceedings in Dick's.

Fladgate also would make off with Grace, and with Selma—she of the wondrous boots. Slotsky considered getting out and using weapons. No, he decided. Even if he made major mess, he still would be stuck here, cut off from his prey, behind the limo. It, and the station wagon parked beside it, made the street impassable. Slotsky continued to lean on his horn.

A youth stood on the sidewalk, brandishing a jackiron. Slotsky studied him. What did this boy think he was doing?

Dan was trying to get Selma's attention. Through the car's rear window, she saw him. With one hand, Dan simulated pressing the nozzle of a spray can. Fladgate, shoving in next to Grace, had his back to this. Dan turned to the other gunman—the one telling the limo guy to get lost—and bonked the jackiron on his head.

The man collapsed noiselessly in the din of the horn. Shocked, fight draining from his face, the limo guy stepped back.

Selma watched this through the rear window. Now sitting next to Grace, Fladgate didn't have a clue. Selma heard a woman on his phone, talking loudly. Say good-bye, she thought, leaning across to give Fladgate a blast of mace.

He went berserk. The phone flew from his hand, a flailing arm bashed Grace, the car rocked as he seemed to explode. Dan appeared, leaning over the front seat with the jackiron. He thunked Fladgate hard. Shuddering, the man slumped onto Grace, who screamed the most piercing scream, Selma and Dan later agreed, that either of them had ever heard.

On the floor, the phone emitted a flood of angry shouts. Dan dropped behind the wheel, put the car in gear, and gunned it. They shot down Winthrop. The doors flapped shut of their own accord.

At Eliot, the one-way sign failed to make an impression on Dan. All he knew was that the other car had gone left. He went right without pause at the stop sign.

Forty feet away, a wave of traffic rolled at him.

In Cambridge, thought Dan, do as they do. He mashed the horn and kept going. Magically, the oncoming wave began to part.

"Grace!" the phone screamed from the floor. "Grace!"

22

The limo could move now. Its driver had gotten in, and the way was clear. But it didn't move. Driver confusion, Slotsky judged. He backed up, shifted, and rammed the limo's rear.

It heaved forward and to the right; not far enough to let Slotsky by, but enough that the fence-banging door could open. With a weighty flop it did open, complicating matters.

That didn't stop Slotsky. Horns echoing from Eliot Street suggested the car he wanted was fighting traffic. Music to Slotsky's ears.

Again he backed up and again he rammed, this time slamming the limo against the station wagon. An incredulous face, heavily made-up, peered from the open doorway. It saw Slotsky readying for another bash and ducked back in. Slotsky bashed, then forced his car along the white whale's flank. Metal scraped loudly. Chrome curled into the air. The limo driver panicked. He turned sharply right, onto the side-walk in front of the wagon. Slotsky's car, unimpeded, shot forward into the limo's open door.

It snapped off and careened into something on the street. A body? The guard, Jenkins, Slotsky thought; the one the boy had knocked unconscious. His car hit door and body simultaneously.

A violent grinding shuddered from the pavement. The door caught a crack and cartwheeled up, flinging a melon-like object onto Slot-sky's hood. It slid frontward into the limo-mangled grillwork; jagged chrome impaled it, snaring it securely, making the thing a kind of hood ornament. Slotsky ignored the bobbing, bloody hair. Nothing could distract him. Not even Jenkins' head.

He turned right on Eliot into a sea of honking cars. The alignment of spectators' stares, and the lack of alternatives, told him the Clinic sedan had turned right on Mt. Auburn. That was a legal direction, even if access to it wasn't; a bus drifted through with eerie serenity, cutting Slotsky off. He jumped a sidewalk. Bystanders didn't flee. He grazed them, sending three through a bank's plate glass. Slotsky zoomed up Mt. Auburn.

The woman kept shouting from the phone on the floor. Her angry voice seemed canned, like a sound track. Everything seemed canned. Nothing seemed real; Dan wondered how he'd gotten through that melee of cars.

A red light at Mt. Auburn and JFK had stopped him. The intersec-tion, full of pedestrians, looked like an outdoor festival. In the rearview mirror he saw a car bearing down. The car with dark glass—something vibrated on its hood. Dan blinked. No, he thought. Not possible. Yet there it was, trailing gore—it came closer. Dan wondered dazedly, Where are the police?

Straight ahead, milling middle-aged gentry choked Mt. Auburn. Delivery trucks prevented a left turn. Right was another wrong-way one-way; a few blocks down, Dan saw, it became a two-way. Could he get there? In two seconds the head on the hood would kiss his ass. "Company," he said.

Selma and Grace looked out the rear window. The approaching head nodded with manic fervor, as if saying, "Yes, yes, that's right, yes!" Selma squealed. Grace gulped, closed her eyes, and pressed her face to the seatback. Hand on the horn, Dan edged right. A bicyclist cursed, somebody kicked the car, shouts welled up among passers-by, then screams as they glimpsed the head on the car behind. The foot traffic froze. A ghastly stillness settled. All around, with slow-motion shock, people stared. A woman fainted; suddenly the crowd recoiled, and a gap appeared. Dan pushed through.

He sped wrong-way down JFK. Cars coming at him swerved and slowed, horns thinning to banshee wails as he hurtled past. The darkening sky seemed jaundiced. Trees whipped by jerkily, a newsreel from some distant and appalling time. From the floor the phone screamed, "Grace, talk to me!"

"Holy cow!" Selma shouted. She'd watched the pursuing car plow through the crosswalk. People and shopping bags flew, some slowly, others quickly. Grace raised her head, took a look, and promptly threw up on the man slumped against her.

"Where do I go!" Dan yelled. He had a feeling that the farther they got from the Square, the sparser police would be.

"Away!" Selma yelled. "The maniac's committing mass murder!"

Right, thought Dan. JFK now was two-way, thank God. Ahead, the color of old aluminum, the river glimmered. At Memorial Drive the light was green. To the right and left people strolled the crosswalks, sitting ducks for the psychopath. Dan kept straight, toward the bridge, and saw what he'd been praying for, a cop car.

It idled at the light on Memorial Drive. Dan whizzed by at ninety miles an hour. He braked hard on the bridge, laying rubber; then pulled over, thinking, Save us, Officer.

Four seconds passed. The pursuing car skidded up behind them. Slack-jawed, glittery-eyed, the head shuddered, as if suggesting that it too was very excited. Cop car, Dan thought with rising panic. What's the matter? Where are you?

Winking lights appeared. The siren wailed. From the floor the phone snapped peevishly, "What has happened?"

Selma said, "Dan, the cops might not save us. That guy—he's crazy."

She's right, Dan realized.

The circumstances, Slotsky thought as he stepped onto the bridge, are ideal. He and his prey had escaped the Square's confinement. The only difficulty, before getting into the Clinic sedan and disappearing across the river, was these policemen.

One stayed in the car. The other got out from behind the wheel.

Slotsky shot him. A hole bloomed in the man's forehead. Slotsky fired on the windshield. Glass milkened, but didn't break. Bullet-proof, Slotsky noted, hearing the Clinic car move. He fired several rounds with both guns. The windshield sagged. He fired more rounds and it caved in, revealing death spasms on the front seat. Slotsky turned.

The Clinic car was rushing at him.

He hopped onto the trunk of his car, guns seeking a target. The boy was wide-eyed and pale behind the glass. Fladgate sat in the rear; Slotsky didn't care about him, apart from the code he carried. Grace and the boot goddess he cared about, but that would be moot if he were crushed. He slid farther, reducing exposure to the sedan, and squeezed triggers—a fraction of a second late. The sedan hit, upsetting his aim. His bullets went high.

Then he too was going high. That boy, he thought as his legs flew up, is of my school of ramming. Oh, dear. Propelled into a reverse somersault, he rolled onto—into—into what?

Thin air, he realized. He'd rolled from the trunk onto the guard-wall, and from there sailed through space. The wall, the bridge itself, receded from his view.

Below, the river shimmered vastly. Slotsky fell toward it at very high speed. As best he could, he aligned himself for the dive.

The phone screamed, "Grace, answer!"

Dan looked at Selma. Selma looked at Dan. Grace was leaning on the unconscious guy. She almost was holding him.

Cars and people on the bridge seemed frozen. Sirens howled in the distance. Dan stared at the cop car's shattered windshield, and said, "I hope they don't blame us for this."

Selma said, "I hope they have boats. With harpoons."

"I hope," Grace said, pulling a gun from the man's jacket, "I don't have to kill you."

Dan and Selma flinched.

"Grace?" the phone said hopefully.

"Drive," Grace said. "Drive fast, that way." She pointed at the far side of the bridge, the direction away from Harvard. Not taking her eyes from Dan, she sat forward, put the gun to his head, and added, "Use the mace, Selma, and I'll blow his head off. Drop it by my feet."

"Okay, okay," Selma said. She tossed the can at Grace's feet.

"Pick up the phone," Grace said.

"At last!" the phone cried. Selma picked it up. "Hello?" the phone said. "Are you all right?"

"Mother," Grace said throatily, "go to hell."

"Grace!" the phone shouted.

"Throw it out the window," Grace ordered Selma. "Into the river—now!"

"Nooooo . . ." screamed the phone as Selma complied.

"Drive," Grace said.

Dan pulled the car back, and floored it. In the mirror, Grace looked at him. Their eyes connected. He saw where she pointed the gun now. At Selma.

"Faster," Grace said. "Or she's dead, and I mean it."

No one on the bridge tried to stop them. No one honked, or even shouted. It was as if everybody watching had turned to stone.

Sirens in the distance getting louder, they raced away.

23

The impact tore off his bandage. Slotsky flailed in the cold murk, unwilling to lose consciousness. At the back of his mind, something struggled for air; it was something he had to do. What, besides breathe?

Ah yes, he knew. He had to get out of sight.

Feebly, he breaststroked toward the bridge. His first line of defense would be under it, away from eyes that already, he suspected, were looking his way. Did he hear voices far above? Yes. Did he hear sirens, loud ones, coming closer? He did.

The sun was setting, luckily. He reached a piling. Kicking the concrete, he thrashed into dimness. A ledge gave him support. One arm clutched it as the other shed his coat, then vice-versa and the coat was off. The weapon-stuffed garment sank.

Slotsky's 'dorph pouch came next. Would the adhesive work when wet? He had no idea.

The Number 11 already on him empowered his legs. Churning them, he seemed to rise an inch or two, as if with speedboat thrust. Both hands free, he unpeeled a Number 20 and slapped it over the obvious place, the place that needed it, the gash in his face. Distantly, it stung. He raised his eyebrows and wiggled his mouth. The patch tugged at the movement. Marvelous, he thought, savoring the rush. A perfect stick.

Oh, it felt good. So very good.

Was it enough? He ran fingers across his face. The wound still was exposed. Unacceptable, Slotsky thought. The Charles River, he knew, wasn't noted for the cleansing effect of its water. Treading without effort now, he unpeeled a Number 11, probed for raw flesh, and plastered it.

That was better. Much better.

Extraordinarily better. Slotsky never had done this much in one dose. The drug became psychotropic beyond certain levels, he knew. But those levels varied from person to person, from situation to situation, pharmacologists said. Slotsky had heard tales of 'dorph-laced exploits. The stories of braggarts, mostly.

Perhaps he'd taken too much. However, situations did vary, of course. His happened to be extreme just now. He needed all the help he could get.

The tracker was gone, sunk in his coat. No great loss. Most of its data he'd sent to Zurich. What he hadn't sent was the audio from Dick's. But the key data there, Toby's remark about "party pictures," Slotsky wouldn't forget.

Shouts fell from above. They caromed off the water and echoed, excitedly, in his grotto. Slotsky discovered that the frigid river was acquiring the texture of lukewarm chocolate. He enjoyed the slap of its wavelets. His hand on the ledge tingling with almost erotic pleasure, he felt at the center of things, suddenly. The goo inside a cosmic candy.

He would have to swing by the depot to replenish supplies. A car, weapons, more 'dorphs. So much to do, he thought.

But for the moment, like something out of Scandinavian myth, he would lurk under the arch of this bridge. Waiting for dusk to settle. Waiting for the right moment to emerge, dripping. And prowl the land.

Slotsky meditated. At Dick's, a word Brian had used surfaced in his mind. Had he referred to the code as "the icon"?

"Go right," Grace said.

Dan turned down the side street. They'd driven into a mangy section of town, not far from the bridge. The sky had darkened.

Selma, watching Grace, saw simple fright in her eyes. It reminded Selma of a scared rabbit. Which in turn reminded her of something else.

She herself was terrified. This kid seemed crazy. So did a lot of other people. The world had gone psychotic.

Grace said, "Over there." She waved the gun, indicating the parking area of a boarded-up laundry. Dan drove into it. "Behind that," she said. The wall she indicated screened a dumpster. Dan parked beside it. How appropriate, he thought. Moments passed.

"Now what?" said Selma.

"Execution style," Dan said. "In the back of my head."

"Don't talk like a jerk," Grace said.

"How should we talk?" Selma asked faintly.

"Don't say anything," Grace said. "I have to—think."

Is it possible? Selma wondered.

Dan wondered the same. He saw no signs, nor heard any, of nearby people. After a minute he cleared his throat. His eyes sought Grace's in the rearview mirror. He said, "Grace?"

She raised her chin. "Yeah?"

"Maybe we can help you. Think."

"You're idiots," she said. "Ignorant idiots."

Dan studied her. He said, "Maybe. But ignorant only if you don't tell us. What is it . . . you need to do?"

Grace's eyes met his in the mirror. "He's your brother?" she asked. "Toby?"

Dan nodded.

"My mother has him now. You know what that means?"

Dan shook his head.

"You don't know what she does?" Grace said it tonelessly.

"Toby mentioned something," Selma said. "She studies 'moral reasoning,' but it's—I'm not sure. She does research."

"She used to," Grace said. "Forget what you heard. Basically, she works for my father."

"He was on the news," Dan remarked.

"You don't know anything about him," Grace said. "But you will—if you live. Listen to what I have to say."

Dan and Selma nodded.

"Right now, my mother is worried. Worried about a lot of things." Grace rummaged in the unconscious man's pocket. The pocket, Selma knew, where he'd put the pin. Grace pulled it out. "One of the things worrying her," she said, "is this."

"The 'icon,'" Dan said. "That's what Brian called it."

Grace nodded. "Mother will ask Toby what he did with it." She frowned. "He said he has pictures. Does he?"

"Well," Dan said. "Uh—I took pictures. Of Toby wearing it, I mean. Polaroids. Four of them, last night."

"Where are they?" Grace asked.

"At home," Selma said. "On top of the refrigerator."

"We have to get them," Grace said. "Now."

Dan and Selma pondered. "Somebody from the FATB," Selma said, "is supposed to be there. Between eight and ten tonight."

Grace's eyes hardened. "What time is it?" she asked.

"Seven thirty-four," Dan read from the car's clock.

"Drive to your house," Grace said. "Quickly."

Selma said, "Maybe we should know what's going on."

"What's going on," Grace muttered. "Wait till you get a load of what's going on." She held up the pin. "This is a bargaining chip. It'll be worth a lot less if it—gets loose. It will be worthless if my father thinks the FATB has photos of it."

Her baffled prisoners stared at her.

"It's not just Mother," Grace whispered. "If it were, I'd be the bargaining chip. A better one than this thing." She shook the pin at them. "But it's not just her."

Dan and Selma looked at the rabbity animal. Selma realized what Grace's pale face and scared eyes evoked. The image on the pin was like handwriting. It conveyed a personality. Before she could stop herself she was saying, "You made it. You drew it, a long time ago."

"Shut up," Grace said, eyes going glassy. "And drive."

Dan turned to the wheel. He said, "What are you bargaining for?"

"My brother," Grace said. "If you cooperate, maybe yours." She waved the gun and said in a rush, "I'm sorry about this, but if you don't want FATBOY to kill you, and you want Toby alive, do what I say."

"Him?" Dan said, jerking a thumb at the quiet passenger.

"Get rid of him," Grace ordered, gun trained on Selma.

Dan jumped out, opened the rear door, and pulled the man to the ground. He got back in and said, "Directions, Selma."

Selma gave them.

"Avoid the police," Grace said. "They're looking for us."

From the car's speakerphone, Helen Scarf delivered a steadily angrier harangue. Something had happened to the other car. She couldn't get hold of Fladgate or Jenkins, and was upset about it. More than upset. The tone of her voice said heads would roll.

Toby sat in the rear. Brian shivered to his right. A thug loomed to his left. For five minutes or so, they'd been parked off Central Square while Scarf tried to find the others.

She'd failed. Now they cruised the outback of Kendall Square, a district of rehabbed warehouses and gleaming new construction that housed high-tech facilities, MIT spinoffs mostly. The streets were empty. Few cars, no people. Industrial lamps glared in the rapidly falling night.

To Toby it was like entering the bowels of hell. Scarf was en route to the Clinic, and would meet them there, she'd said. They were going to the Center for the Study of Moral Reasoning.

Protest was futile. The man next to him had a gun. He looked capable of using it for any reason at all, including stupidity.

A tall cement wall went to the end of the block. The car turned. The wall went to the end of that block too. Halfway down a heavy-gauge steel gate blocked an entry. The car stopped at it. The gate swung open. Armed guards waved them in.

They drove across a dark court, passing the front entrance of a big, windowless building. At the far corner, more guards waved them through another gate into a service alley. They went down it to the building's rear, where they passed through a third guarded gate into a smaller courtyard. A loading dock ran the building's width. Bright klieg lights made it hard to look at. A van idled there. They parked.

The door locks clicked up. Somebody opened Brian's door and hauled him out. The man next to Toby got out, dragging Toby with him. A white-gowned man pushed a wheelchair at them. No, thought Toby, as he was made to sit with stunning speed. Straps snaked around him, clinking. Seconds later he was rolling up a ramp.

Brian, likewise chaired and trussed, rolled up just ahead, yelling, "No! No! No!" Suddenly he went quiet. Toby saw the reason. Helen Scarf, almost invisible in a white coat under the loading dock's blinding light, stood with hands in her pockets and murder on her face.

She said to Brian, "How could you?"

"Please," he muttered.

Dr. Scarf sneered, eyes an emulsion of rage, disgust, and despair. "Take them," she ordered the attendants, "to Arena D."

Toby's chair rushed at a large steel door. He thought he'd hit it when a vertical crack halved it. One half zapped leftward, the other rightward, and the chair burst through an empty lobby toward a hospital-size elevator.

He whizzed in, Brian right behind him. The elevator sank. Arena D, Toby thought, is in the basement.

The elevator opened on a white corridor, dazzlingly bright. They rolled down it, then down another, past a series of heavy double doors marked A, B, and C. Indicator lights protruded from the ceiling. None was on, but Toby could see the legend they lit. Over door after door, it read: PROCEDURE IN PROGRESS.

Toby shouted, "Stop this! You can't do this! Stop, stop, stop!" Double doors marked "D" came at him. They hissed open and Toby rolled into an overwhelming display of applied science.

Electronic consoles lined the walls. On a raised dais in the middle, four surgical couches reclined uninvitingly. Equipment hung from cantilevered booms. Six attendants, wearing medical gowns and masks, stood on the dais. A disinfectant tang in the air spoke of fear, bodily fluids, intrusion. We take people apart, the smell seemed to confide. We make sure they don't like it.

Toby howled with panic.

The attendants weren't moved. With the practiced ease of having done this countless times before, they unstrapped and literally flipped the prisoners onto adjacent couches. In two teams of three, one working Toby, the other Brian, they picked up power scissors and started cutting off clothes. Buttons, buckles, zippers didn't interest them; Toby yelled and writhed to no avail as they sheared through his shirt from collar to waist, used a heavier implement to snip his belt, guided coldly snicking blades down his pants, got his briefs at the pelvis, cut into his shoes, and suddenly everything was off, the remnants jerking away under him.

In less than thirty seconds, the attendants had rendered Toby and Brian stark naked.

Straps came next, clinking, cinching. Sun-bright lights ignited above, robbing Toby of his breath; midshout, his voice went still, and so did his body, for he now was too scared to resist. In the silence he heard Brian moaning. An attendant clamped steel around Toby's skull, neck, and jaw, immobilizing his head. More steel clamped his shoulders and chest, then his waist, legs, and feet. He realized he couldn't move. Not a centimeter.

A small video camera glided at him, snakily inquisitive on a flexible stalk. As if sensing food, it inspected his eyes.

The camera withdrew. A device with a round and furry brush that resembled a car polisher came at his head. The furry stuff glistened. It started rotating, splattering Toby with warm liquid, and before he could blink, it covered his face, scouring every recess, drowning new-found screams.

I'm an American citizen, a voice wailed deep within Toby's mind. This is Cambridge, Massachusetts, where a lot of people would riot, lay waste to the streets, if they knew that you do this. They probably would, I hope they would, and even if they wouldn't, I've done no wrong—why, why, why?

Watching Toby get the prep, Brian resigned himself to the same. He wanted this finished. He wanted to die.

Nothing ever had separated him and his sister. Nothing on the scale of tonight's events; never before had he not known what she was doing, how she was feeling, what she was thinking. If only she were on the couch beside him. It would have brought comfort to both of them, to confront this together.

Instead he beheld an alien man, Toby, lying there shockingly, repulsively naked. His howls and shouts Brian couldn't feel. He wasn't Grace.

The couch's camera undulated at him, looking him over. She's deciding, Brian thought, how to torture me.

One of the zombies put a plug in Brian's ear. Through it Mother said, "I will perform a procedure. You will watch. I want you to imagine you're undergoing the experience. Keep in mind, I haven't decided if you need it." Her voice didn't waver. She went on, "Your sister is missing. I am extremely angry about that. Can you begin to estimate Father's reaction?" Brian couldn't. "And the icon. Today of all days, I simply can't comprehend . . . "

Brian thought he heard a sniffle. Mother? Sniffling? Unable to hold it in, he bawled like a baby.

"You!" she shouted. "Treacherous child—you get a grip! And watch what I might do to you—watch, do you hear me?"

Brian nodded frantically.

She said with no trace of emotion, "I will find out what this man knows. I will listen to what you have to say. I will evaluate the situation. And then, I will decide how to proceed."

The earphone fell silent. A zombie pressed buttons on his couch. It swiveled, giving him a direct view of Toby.

Brian hadn't witnessed this live before. But two years before, Mother had showed him and Grace a video the staff had prepared for the government funders—who, of course, had been quite impressed. So had Brian and Grace. To them, the video constituted a threat. It made graphically real what Mother could do to them if she so chose.

She'd always seemed a kind of mind reader. Until they entered puberty, she'd known exactly what they did, felt, thought. Much as they knew those things of each other.

Midway between ages eleven and twelve, when they discovered sex, that changed. They became even more aware of each other, telepathically it seemed. But Mother, not part of their new world, took a step back. She knew what they were doing. They didn't go to great lengths to hide it. However, to the same degree Mother was tactful, they were discreet.

When they turned twelve she sat them down for a talk on the topics of "boundaries" and "biology." Mother made it seem natural. The twins knew that her views differed from those of the rest of the world. But as she often explained, the rest of the world was a flawed place, full of blindness, selfishness, and cowardice.

She convinced them that their feelings for each other not only were natural, but also very special, extremely so in fact. With Father never saying a word about it, or even indicating he had any idea they were lovers, Mother's support reassured them. It was important to hear. They needed it.

142 — LEWIS GANNETT

As they got older they discovered that Mother's understanding and approval allowed them to expand the private zone. They began using it to shield things other than sex.

At first they were silly things. It seemed a game. They enjoyed being sneaky. Mother, they figured, knew all about it.

But more recently, over the last year, they'd begun to find serious things to hide. For example, their doubts about Father's plans. Doubts that a few months before had turned bleaker and more desperate, in the wake of the "tragedy."

They'd been with him in Antarctica when it happened. When Father had made it happen.

He'd forced them to participate. And they had started to come apart. The private zone became more important. It became crucial, for Mother and Father couldn't know how they felt about the murders. Indeed, about the whole project.

Most particularly, Mother and Father couldn't know about the sabotage fantasies. Halfhearted, half-baked, ill-conceived fantasies; Brian knew them for what they were. That insight didn't help. Their culmination, the Malt blunder, was entirely his fault.

Now he faced the music. Brian was sure she'd invade, and find all the shameful things he hid. The doubts, the fear, the horror.

Toby's scrub phase ended. The brush retracted, and the spray series began. A nozzle snaked forth and delivered a hissing puff into his face. Two more hissing nozzles followed. Toby's eyes opened widely, pupils dilating to the irises. They appeared to relax. Brian knew that was a misleading impression. The sprays had paralyzed several suites of musculature controlling the upper portion of his face, especially those controlling the eyes.

Next came the mechanical arm bearing the puncture array. It hovered over the left eye, sensors reading the topology. With a tiny whine the first needle extruded. Laser-guided, it found its target, the corner by the nose. It sank in; and seemed to stay in for a very long time.

Out came the needle. It retracted into the array, the head of which rotated. A second needle extruded.

Brian felt ill. Involuntarily, he closed his eyes. The earplug barked, "You will watch!" His eyes flew open. With bile rising in his gorge, he saw the array finish its job.

Then came the temple work. A heavier mechanical arm took over. Its needle was longer, it bored harder, and it was multisectional, for not only did it penetrate directly to the brain, it telescoped into finer and finer filaments that navigated very precisely around it.

The needle pricked the right temple. It buzzed; and slid in, evading the artery that throbbed there. Toby's wide-open eyes didn't flicker.

Within moments his neural stem received a series of chemical prompts, preparing him for the next phase, optic nerve conductivity. The glowing screen, a foot square, swung six inches from his eyes. Free and clear tunnels now, they would take whatever Mother wished to send down them. What she sent depended on how far she wanted to go. And what she wanted Toby to do.

The screen's pulsing light washed over Toby's face. He might get off easy, Brian thought. Mother didn't have time to rewire the neurology. Please, Brian thought, feeling a sudden wave of compassion for this pitiful guy. Don't make him a zombie . . .

Toby felt wonderful, traveling the light. It was so relaxing. So comforting. His new friend, Wanda, had such a nice voice, too. It stroked him like a hand on a purring cat.

Wanda asked a lot of questions, though. Question after question, on and on, it seemed. He had to think hard, to tell her all he knew. But that didn't matter. Toby wanted to tell her every detail—because Wanda was adorable.

"I love you," he said.

"I know," Wanda said tenderly. "I love you too. Let's see. You're at Dick's, and Brian just ripped film from the camera. Now Grace is giving the pin to the man with the phone. He's putting it in his pocket. Toby, are cameras taking pictures of that?"

"No, Wanda," Toby said.

"Does Dick's have a video security system? I want you to concentrate, Toby. You can remember more than you think you can—just relax, and look around. Any security cameras?"

"Not that I see. Wait. There is one, Wanda. On the ceiling behind the bar."

The young man's voice issued from a monitor in Helen's control console, two floors above Arena D. Another monitor displayed Brian's sweat-filmed bondage. As ordered, he was paying attention. Helen knew from the readouts—heart and breath rates, brain waves—that the probe terrified him.

She'd extracted relevant portions of Toby Swett's recent history, in the process performing a kind of vivisection of Brian's guilt. His crimes still twitched in her pincers; for example, the furtive tablework at the restaurant when he and Grace gave away not only the icon, but directions as well— "Use it to filter the media streams." Other discoveries included Miles Malt's mysterious quest, not to mention his bug, fake ID, and murder.

The debacle seemed without end. For more than half an hour Toby had yielded a portrait of bungled betrayal, the continuing complications of which, most especially Grace's defection, couldn't have come at a worse time.

Helen's state of mind transcended rage. But she needed to be careful. The question of punishment she couldn't decide now. For the moment, she would take comfort from the fact that Brian already was suffering. The most choice of his many humiliations involved Grace. In response to leading questions, Toby had described feelings for her. His physiology also had responded. With a vigor that sent Brian's vital signs right off the charts.

Even if punishment waited, she was working her son over on multiple fronts. Meantime the top priority concerned four Polaroid photographs. All of them featured Toby wearing the rabbit badge—the artifact from which Earnest had fashioned the icon.

In one of the Polaroids, according to Toby, the rabbit occupied the very center of the composition. It was clearly discernible against his white shirt, he'd said.

Despite that, Helen thought she might be able to salvage the situation. It depended on how bad the news was, and if Grace came to her senses. Very bad news Helen would be obliged to tell Earnest. The not-so-bad she might be able to cover up. As for Grace—Helen could only hope the child would appear, and beg forgiveness. Unthinkable things would happen if she didn't.

Into the mike Helen said sharply, "Does the security camera have a view of the pin?" An algorithm sweetened her voice. No matter how harsh Helen's tone, Wanda's mellifluence wouldn't waver.

"I don't think so. No, it isn't."

"Good. Let's move along. The man is taking you outside?"

"Yes, Wanda."

The console's telephone beeped. Helen grimaced. She'd told the staff not to disturb her. That they were doing it anyway meant the call was important. She said, "Toby, Wanda has to leave for a minute. What will you think about while I'm gone?"

"Cameras," he said devoutly.

"Thank you," Helen snarled. She killed the mike, picked up the phone, and snapped, "Yes?"

"Sorry to bother you," said Dr. Oliver Wang, the Clinic's acting director. Just in from Amarillo, and nominally in charge until someone of sufficient stature took Helen's place, Wang didn't know that later tonight the FATB almost certainly would invade his new domain. And put its staff, himself included, behind bars. He happened to be thoroughly innocent. Only two days on the job, he had no inkling of the Clinic's secret purpose. The FATB wouldn't take that for granted, however. Not after Earnest was done with them. Helen bit her lip. Earnest would be done with them all too soon.

"What's the problem, Wang?" she said.

"An agent from the Bureau is on line four. As instructed, I told him you aren't here." Wang's tone suggested he disliked lying. "His name is Whipple. He said, and I quote, 'The matter is very grave.' It concerns two cars from the Clinic's fleet. Something happened in Harvard Square. The plate numbers . . . "

"Did he say," Helen asked, "if he knows where the cars are?"

"No," Wang replied.

Helen massaged her forehead. With Earnest going on Barclay at 9:00, forty-three minutes away, Whipple could become a major nuisance. The idea maddened her. However, he might help find Grace. She mashed line four's blinking button.

Special Agent Whipple sat in his car on the night-shrouded street, wondering what kind of deep shit had engulfed him. Why was he dealing with this? The phone barked, "Helen Scarf."

Surprised, Whipple said, "Dr. Scarf, you're there."

"Yes," said the woman everyone at the Bureau hoped never to meet. Stories about Helen Scarf circulated often. Officially, Bureau employees revered her. Personally, she scared them witless; unlike the public, they knew about the things she did to people, including Bureau people whom the brass deemed untrustworthy. "I am aware of the Harvard Square incident," she said. "Do you have any information on my daughter, Grace?"

Whipple said, "A person matching her description, and someone matching your son's, were at the scene. Other than that, no information. I got the call from headquarters just a minute ago."

"Why are you, and not someone more senior, telling me this?"

"The information," he replied, wondering which angle would best cover his ass, "came to me because I'm working a related case, and headquarters is busy, you see." Whipple prayed she wouldn't ask why it was busy. He'd been ordered not to discuss the matter.

"I see. What is the related case?"

"A corpse with forged Bureau ID," Whipple said.

"Miles Malt, I presume?"

"Yeah," said Whipple, relieved she knew.

"Where are you now," Scarf asked, "and what are you doing?"

Technically, Scarf lacked the authority to ask those questions. Given the circumstances, Whipple wouldn't say so. "Magazine Street, off Central Square. We're . . . "

"Investigating Toby Swett. Have you gone into the apartment?"

She's omniscient, Whipple thought. "Not yet," he replied. "The occupants are supposed to be here, but aren't. We have indications they played a part in the Harvard Square incident. So we wait a few more minutes. Then we go in."

"Agent Whipple, I appreciate the call. If you learn anything about my daughter, will you get in touch with me immediately?"

"Of course, Dr. Scarf."

"Please don't contact my husband about this. He's busy at the moment, and it would—damage his concentration."

"No problem," Whipple said.

She hung up, somewhat to his puzzlement, but much to his relief. He got out of the car. Detective Potts was parked behind him. Pesta and Gloss were straight ahead. They'd go in soon. Swett and friends, Whipple thought, are in a hell of a jam.

Helen gnawed her lip. She had to do something right away. I'm having a heart attack, she thought.

She'd been so stupid. For example, how could she have told the twins about going to Martha's tonight? Grace wouldn't forget that. Was she capable of . . . ?

Helen couldn't finish thinking the idea.

She'd been fool enough already to have told them that Earnest was using the badge for the icon. Earnest had asked her not to tell them, why had she? To please them? To flatter them with the thought that the rabbit badge, something they'd made at age five, now serves a grand purpose?

Helen fought a desperate urge to slap herself. Earnest, she thought feverishly, cannot know. She pressed buttons, altering the Arena D procedure, aborting its more invasive aspects. Into the mike she spat, "Wanda's back!"

"Hi," Toby replied from the monitor.

"We're doing something new. I want you to listen very, very carefully." Helen was almost screaming.

She didn't have time to erase Toby's memory. Too bad. Because eventually, he'd remember what had happened here.

That she would deal with later. Helen instructed the surgical robot to administer a radically different drug regime.

Selma, Dan, and Grace crouched on the third-floor fire escape of the building behind 94 Magazine Street. Darkness and a line of laundry concealed them.

They'd been there about twenty minutes, but the chilly iron bars, the cramped space, and most of all, the tension, made it seem like hours. Five blocks away, they'd ditched the car. Grace, expecting undesirables, had ordered a cautious approach. From her standpoint she'd turned out to be right. A police car and two late-model sedans idled on Magazine. The latter she'd identified as "probable FATB."

The fire escape, Selma's idea, gave a view of her and Toby's apartment. Trees shrouded much of the building. The moon, rising fatly, lit the back porch. With the door to the kitchen closed and the lights in there off, they couldn't see the refrigerator. But the door's window enabled them to make out the area next to it. So far, they'd seen no one rummage through the junk on the refrigerator's top.

Selma tried to keep her screaming fantasies under control. Her strangling fantasies too. She'd had several opportunities to take Grace by surprise, and Dan had as well, but neither was willing to make a move. Why? It was as if they wanted to go along with the quest for the "icon reproductions."

Both had done some thinking about the way Grace told her mother to fuck off, an hour before. They'd also thought about her obviously genuine panic concerning Brian. Somehow, it legitimized her urgency. It also called into question Toby's fate. Selma was having anxiety attacks about him. So, she could tell, was Dan. Five minutes ago, in response to a question about the police presence in front of the building, Grace had said, "Cops won't save your brother. Trust me. Right now, cops are your enemy."

Dan said, "If they find the Polaroids, will they know they are . . . whatever they are? Pictures of a icon?"

"I doubt it," Grace replied. "But they might decide to seize everything in there. They do that."

Dan imagined policemen passing endless bags of trash, carefully labeled "evidence," down the stairs. That would clean up the apartment. Crickets throbbed in the murk below them. Somewhere a TV set spewed news. Amid the gibberish, Dan caught the words "Antarctica," "eruption," and "Barclay Piston."

"All right," he muttered. "Spill it, Grace. How do the Polaroids save Toby and Brian?"

Grace grimaced at the gently swaying laundry that was keeping them hidden. She said, "The icon's valuable, okay? It's vital to something that Father's been working on . . . for a long, long time."

"What's that?" Selma demanded.

"Boobytrapping the datasphere," Grace said.

Dan and Selma considered the statement. It didn't make sense; worse, the feverish way Grace delivered it didn't enhance her credibility. Dan said, "What does the icon—do?"

"If it's used," Grace replied, "and it's easy to use—very easy—we think it ends the world as we know it."

"You 'think'?" Dan inquired.

Grace shrugged. She had no more to say on the subject.

"Toby would find this fascinating," Selma commented.

"Why?" Grace asked.

"He's a doomsday nut," Dan told her.

"Then he's in good company," Grace said. She pointed the gun through a slew of camisoles. "What's that?"

Across the way, a tree rose over Toby and Selma's porch. It had started to shake. Something big, like a gorilla, seemed to be climbing it. Selma saw the thick shape. With peculiar agility, the thing climbed higher and higher. Soon a man came into view—walking a branch like a tightrope, using overhead branches for balance. The moonlit face looked strange. Somehow deformed. And familiar.

"Bandage," Dan whispered.

It is, Selma thought with shock. He headed with acrobatic skill straight for her porch. Nearing it, he stepped from the branch onto a post that anchored the railing. The branch waggled as his weight left it. Arms outstretched, one foot on the post and the other midair, he suggested a fanciful statue, a grotesquerie poised on a pedestal.

The impression vanished as he dropped to the porch and scuttled to the kitchen door. "Wow," Dan said softly.

"Shoot him," Selma whispered to Grace.

A faint snapping noise floated through the darkness. Bandage slipped into the kitchen. He'd forced the door.

Slotsky felt splendid. Everything happened so very slowly. It put exactitude in his movements; he had a great deal of room, so to speak, to think. At any given moment, numerous alternatives presented themselves for his leisurely inspection, allowing him to winnow all possible mistakes. He knew that in real time, this unfolded in split-second intervals. That just made it more fun.

He also couldn't escape an extraordinarily vivid feeling that he was underwater. Perhaps the sensation came from his swim in the Charles. By the time he'd hit the shore, on the Allston side—police were gathering on the Cambridge side—and had slithered up the bank and across Storrow Drive, he'd become so acclimated to the river's wetness that it was as if he hadn't left it.

The effect had persisted as he journeyed to the depot, a garage near Fenway Park that held a fresh car and various supplies. The young couple whose Jeep he'd carjacked seemed to pilot a bathysphere through Kenmore Square. The Citgo sign and the nightclub marquees glimmered gaudily, suggesting a Vegas-like Atlantis beneath the waves. Slotsky knew the 'dorph patches had a lot to do with that.

But maybe the effect also sprang from his ongoing consideration of what the collapse of the West Antarctic Ice Sheet might do to this part of the world, to this particular neighborhood in Cambridge, for example. How far above street level would the sea rise? Fifteen feet, Slotsky judged. High enough that he couldn't help but entertain postdiluvian scenarios. He imagined the effects of all of Antarctica's ice falling into the ocean. Were that to happen, every building in sight would be underwater—by several hundred feet. Much the way he felt himself to be right now.

And a nasty wreck it was that he'd penetrated. The *Titanic*'s sculleries couldn't be fouler than this kitchen. His flashlight played across the phosphorescent tableau. Small fish seemed to flicker, as if fleeing his visit. Slotsky blinked; the flashlight sought party pictures, not denizens of the deep, entertaining though those hallucinations were. Party pictures, he reflected. Pictures of Toby Swett wearing a pin. A code. An "icon."

He hoped to find the pictures quickly, for enemies lurked without. They too, he suspected, would be diving this wreck. However, he'd gotten here first . . .

Slotsky heard feet stamping up stairs. There they are, he thought. He debated killing them right away. No need, he decided. Let them do the looking. If they found what he wanted, well. So much labor saved.

Stealthily he retreated through his entry point. The inner door he left open. The screen door he shut.

Potts, Pesta, and Gloss followed Whipple to the top landing. Whipple tried the door. It was locked. "Do it," he said to Pesta.

Gloss could pick most any lock he came across. Pesta, a more physical sort, liked to smash those he encountered. Whipple had no patience tonight. Smash was quicker than pick.

Pesta produced his hammer and iron. Two hits did it; the door banged open. "Jeez," Pesta said, smelling stale beer and watching Whipple's flashlight outline the chaos within.

"Big party last night," Potts said as he followed them through the doorway. He flipped a wall switch. The room filled with light.

Pesta's tiny eyes darted around. "Pigs," he declared, midriff aflutter with indignation. "Fuckin' animals. No self-respect!"

Potts said, "Guess they didn't have time to clean up."

"Too busy getting in trouble," Whipple said.

"What're we looking for?" Gloss asked, going to the screen door. He glared at the dark porch.

"The usual," Whipple replied.

Potts wondered what that was. He still couldn't get over the FATB's right to punch computer codes for automatic warrants. In a real emergency, with bona fide terrorists and the like, Potts favored drastic measures; and the Harvard Square thing was an emergency, no question. But this was the place to pursue it?

If he were calling the shots he wouldn't be wasting time here. He'd have every patrol car available scouring the streets of Cambridge and environs, looking for a couple of cars registered to the Center for the Study of Moral Reasoning. But, as his wife liked to say when they argued domestic issues, he was getting, not calling, the pottshots now. "What's 'the usual'?" he asked Whipple as Pesta and Gloss began tearing the place apart.

"Guns, drugs, explosives, cash," Whipple replied. "Items of a seditious nature." Everything that wasn't already on the floor started flying to it. "People like this," Whipple went on, gesturing at his men but not, Potts hoped, referring to them, "you know they have tendencies. Drugs, at least. And probably guns."

"Uh-huh," Potts murmured, wondering if Pesta and Gloss were indeed on drugs. Pesta rooted around in the bathroom. Face knotting with concentration, he ripped open a box of tampons, and sniffed it. Apparently satisfied it contained nothing seditious, he threw it over his shoulder. Tampons sped at the bathtub like a swarm of ballistic missiles.

Gloss, still in the kitchen and stripping it of objects above floor level, stood on a chair to get at cookware over the sink. Pans hit the floor and stayed intact. A collection of old plates didn't. Cobalt bowls and glasses followed. The floor began to look very much like a municipal dump. Gloss moved the chair. Miscellaneous objects crowned the refrigerator. A sweep of his arm decrowned it. Potts noticed photos in the cascade. One of them landed near his feet. He stooped to pick it up. A familiar face, as if aware of his home's dismantlement, stared unhappily at him.

Whipple moved into the next room. Gloss, finished with the kitchen, followed. The sound of things breaking indicated he hadn't paused for rest. "Agent Whipple," Potts called, "I found you something useful!"

"Yeah, what?" Whipple yelled back.

"A picture of the guy you're looking for!"

"What?" Whipple shouted.

Potts bellowed, "A picture of Toby Swett!"

The screen door, ablaze with the kitchen's light, framed the detective. From the point of view of the fire escape spectators, he looked to be examining a small piece of paper. His voice had carried through the darkness. The words still rang in their ears.

Bandage they couldn't see. Dan guessed he'd hunkered down in a corner, away from the door's brightness. His manner of leaving the kitchen suggested he didn't want attention from the men inside. So far, he'd avoided it.

"That African-American guy found a Polaroid," Grace said, dismayed.

"The detective," Selma muttered. "It fell down when the asshole . . ." Everyone knew how FATBOY did business. Like a lot of depressing things, you tried not to think about it. That was hard though, when watching them do it to your apartment.

The detective moved out of view. From the side street next door came sounds of a vehicle slowing, then parking. The motor's throb reminded Grace of something. She glanced over there, recognized the van, and moaned.

"What?" Selma whispered.

"They're here," Grace said. "The zombies."

"Who?" Dan asked, looking. The van's rear door opened. Three men jumped to the street. Somebody else needed help getting out. Nervously, Dan said to Selma, "Is that who I think it is?"

Selma peered through the gloom. "What's wrong with him?"

"He's wearing," Dan observed incredulously, "*pajamas.*"

Toby wasn't sure he could stand. But he could. Gradually, he realized where the van had taken him. His building reared up in the buzzing night. Bernie and the other guys had brought him home.

Light poured from the third-floor windows. Dan and Selma, he thought, must be here. He hoped they were okay. Last he'd seen them—where was that? Something huge vibrated in his head. Something that affected his mind. The sensation didn't hurt. Toby felt fine, actually. But it all seemed very strange—and extremely fuzzy. For example, he had no idea why he was wearing pajamas. He couldn't recall having worn pajamas since he was eleven years old.

Then he remembered what they were doing. The Polaroids. Wanda wanted him to find those Polaroids. Bernie, the driver, hadn't discussed it on the way over. As for the other three, they hadn't talked at all. Toby didn't even know their names. They were supposed to help him, though. He did know that.

Bernie stayed behind the wheel. One of the others took Toby's hand. They walked to the front door. Not locked, Toby saw. A good thing, since he didn't have keys. Where were his keys? And his clothes? He started to ask, but the man snapped, "Quiet!"

"Okay," Toby said.

They entered. "Stay here," the man said.

Toby nodded. Silently, the men climbed the stairs.

In Swett's bedroom, Whipple studied the photo. What does Potts expect, he wondered. A commendation? He turned on the TV. Cola-drinking youths scampered across the screen. He switched channels. The Mantis orb spun slowly, giving off its spooky rays. Bored, Whipple sat. Barclay Piston would start in a few minutes. "You been following the news?" he asked the detective.

"Don't have time," Potts replied. So this, he thought, is how FAT-BOY stays busy. While troops crash and smash, agents catch up on television. The commercial's sound track suddenly seemed louder. After a couple of moments, Potts realized why. Gloss, in the next room, must have decided to take a break, because the crashing and smashing had stopped.

Gloss scanned the kitchen. Pesta seemed to be spending a lot of time on the bathroom. Had he found something good? Conscious of the crunch of his feet, wanting to take Pesta by surprise, Gloss walked over there. He burst into the bathroom, hoping to find his partner putting evidence to personal use.

Pesta lay in the tub, in a swirling flood of red.

Coldness entered Gloss's neck. His body disappeared. Then his head evaporated, leaving only his mind, his scalding mind.

Slotsky guided him to the tub. He sat him on the rim, and pushed him, gently, onto the fat one. The bodies settled into a clumsy embrace. They seemed to sigh. As if appreciative, Slotsky thought, of their nice, warm bloodbath.

He yanked his knife from the neck and wiped spinal fluid off it. The apartment no longer seemed underwater. Harsh light had dispelled that illusion. Nonetheless, Slotsky felt akin to a giant squid. His awareness undulated. Like far-flung tentacles, it read subtle vibrations for news of prey.

Whoever was creeping up the stairs didn't stand a chance.

Slotsky would deal with them and the remaining police quickly, for he had something else to attend to. Not the photos. He'd already found two Polaroids on the kitchen floor. Safe from his dampness in a plastic pouch, they featured a pin on which a pictograph of an animal was starkly outlined against Toby Swett's shirt.

That issue Slotsky had well in hand. His current priority concerned a pair of hip boots. Purple majesties of suede, monuments to the indomitability of the female foot, they occupied a corner of the bathroom. Slotsky toyed with the idea of wearing them. Did he deserve such glory?

Of course he did. Three men entered the kitchen, guns drawn. Slotsky stepped through the bathroom door and shot them each in the face. His silencer reduced the reports to hollow pops. However, his victims' collapse—they fell virtually in unison, so rapidly had he fired—made a terrific commotion on the glass-littered floor.

26

The building vibrated. Potts and Whipple stared at the cloth that curtained the doorway. What they'd just heard didn't suggest a resumption of work. It suggested bodies hitting the floor.

Both men drew guns. Whipple pulled the curtain aside. They went through to the next room. Except for beer bottles rolling in from the kitchen, nothing moved.

"Gloss?" Whipple called. "Pesta?" Neither replied. Potts watched Whipple advance on the kitchen door. He'd almost reached it when something the size of an ice cube came at him. The room exploded.

Whipple took the brunt. His body shattered, plastering Potts with flesh; the detective flew through the curtain, hit the futon, and slammed against the wall.

Slotsky walked into pinkish mist. Very little remained of the first man. The second man, in the bedroom, appeared thoroughly flayed. The television had suffered no damage. "Stay tuned," it was shouting, "for Barclay! Right after these messages."

He fully intended to see the show, but not here. He'd watch it in the car he'd taken from the depot. For the sake of his remaining minute or two in this morgue-like apartment, he turned up the television's volume. A Polaroid on the set's top caught his attention.

That made three. Slotsky put it with the others in the plastic pouch.

He went back to the bathroom, where he collected the boots. In the kitchen, sitting down to put them on, his roving eyes located yet another Polaroid. Right by the door to the porch.

Could there be more? He'd have to move bodies and check.

"What are you doing," said a curiously flat voice, "with Selma's boots?"

Slotsky turned. Toby Swett had a gun trained on him. One of the downed guards' guns, Slotsky saw. The boy's vacant demeanor suggested serious drugs; the eyes were extremely bloodshot. Slotsky smiled. He said, "A pleasure to meet you, Toby."

Toby took in the matted hair, the wet and filthy clothes, the stained patchwork on the face. No nose, he noticed. That nudged a memory. He was looking at a killer. A multiple killer . . . blood flowing from their heads, the men from the van lay still on the floor.

Everything, Toby saw, lay on the floor. The walls and shelves were bare, the place had been stripped, the contents broken. How could anyone commit such atrocities? Toby scowled at the monster, outrage mounting. He said slowly, "If you move, I'll shoot you."

"In that case," said the noseless one, "I will not move."

"Take the boots off," Toby muttered. Too big, they looked ridiculous on the killer. They made him a dwarf musketeer.

The man sighed. "Must I?" he asked.

"Yes!" shouted Toby, not sure why he felt indignant about this issue. Then he knew why. Having destroyed the apartment, the killer wasn't finished. He was stealing the only apparent survivors.

"Very well," said the killer. Eyes unnaturally bright, he stood. The boots sagged and flopped. But they gave him grandeur as he swashbuckled over the bodies, avoiding rivers of blood.

Toby said, "What are you doing?"

"You will help me," the man replied, approaching.

"I don't think so," Toby said.

"Yes, yes, you will," the killer insisted, frowning at the boots. As if to suggest they posed a problem. "You see, these mean a lot to me. They mean a great deal."

"What?" Toby said. "What do they mean?"

Swampy odors wafted as the pirate shuffled closer. "I," he confided, "am in love with Selma."

"Liar," Toby said.

"I adore her," he said, smiling dreamily. Then, with confusing speed, he knocked the gun from Toby's hand.

Damn, Toby thought. The killer pulled a knife. Fascinated, and surprised that he didn't care—how could it be that he didn't care?—Toby watched the knife flash at him.

Something boomed. The knife froze; then clattered to the floor. With a thrash of the boots, the killer collapsed.

A man pointed a gun from the middle room doorway. Covered with gore, he didn't look so hot. In fact, he looked like he should be dead. But he wasn't, because he said, "Toby, back off."

"Detective Potts?" Toby said, recognizing his friend from that distant era, the late afternoon. What did he mean, back off? Toby gazed at the man on the floor. Knifeless now, he clutched his shoulder. "Detective," Toby said as calmly as he could, "I have to find the Polaroids. First, though," he went on, voice rising, "I have to kick this bastard's butt."

"Back off!" the detective shouted.

But a door had opened in Toby's mind, and it led to rage. "Take that!" he howled, stomping the killer's chest. It crunched satisfyingly. Toby jumped, landing like a pile driver on the stomach. The killer's eyes screwed shut, the mouth flew open. Toby grabbed the head by the hair and banged it on the floor as hard as he could, yelling, "That's for Malt!" He banged it again, shrieking, "That's for these guys here!"

The killer tried to get up. Toby pulled the wet jacket over his head, immobilizing his arms. A plastic bag, fastened to a chain around the neck, slipped to the floor. Toby saw Polaroids in it. Pleased to be doing something constructive, he ripped the bag free and tossed it on the table.

Again the killer tried to get up. Toby stepped on him. The killer started wriggling toward the door to the porch. A body blocked the way; unstoppable, he crawled right over it. The detective should handle this, Toby decided. The detective should shoot him.

Potts, he saw, had passed out. Toby went to him and knelt. Potts was dead. Oh no, Toby thought, feeling more wretched, more foul, than he'd ever imagined he could feel. He glanced around the charnel house his kitchen had become. Not real, he thought. It's an illusion. Obviously.

He looked at the killer. Still down, jacket tangled over his head, the man was picking up something by the door to the porch. He can't stop stealing things, Toby thought.

No doubt about it. The asshole had something in his hand. What? Toby wondered, watching him push through the screen door and roll out on the porch. Toby grabbed Potts's gun. He went to the door and through it. The killer was wriggling to the edge. Toby debated shooting him. The idea made him sick. So much blood already. So much death. He dropped the gun and seized a boot.

The killer crawled on, leaving the boot behind. Toby seized the other boot. The killer crawled out of that one too. In moments he'd pass under the rail and over the edge. Should Toby allow him to do it? Was suicide an appropriate fate?

The issue left Toby's jurisdiction as the man fell away. A loud thump announced his landing. Toby leaned over the rail. He heard rolling trash bins; but couldn't see anything in the dark yard. Trees and the building blocked the moon's rays.

Something occurred to him. The trash bins. They were plastic. Maybe the killer hit them? And survived the fall?

"Toby!" a voice called. Sounds like Dan, Toby thought dully. He remembered standing here with Dan in the afternoon sun. Then Selma had found a corpse. That made their day.

"Toby!" another voice called, and now he knew he'd gone crazy, because this one sounded like Selma. But neither she nor Dan was here, only dead people were. Toby felt guilty about it. The carnage inside was his fault. He was sure he'd made it happen.

"Over here!" Dan's voice hooted.

Toby's mind seemed to break. I'm a madman, he thought, hearing voices in the night. He bellowed at the spirits or the ghouls, whatever it was that sought to torment him, "Can't you see it's the end? Can't you see this is doom? Go away! Please, go away!"

Someone came out on the porch. Dizzy, Toby turned. The doorway backlit the van driver, Bernie. Behind him, in the kitchen, a blond woman stood near the table. She was examining the killer's plastic bag.

Bernie beckoned. Toby stooped to pick up the boots. The only survivors, he thought mournfully—can't leave without them. Bernie grabbed his arm and dragged him in the kitchen, where, with a mysterious sensation of dread, Toby recognized Dr. Helen Scarf.

She gave him a haggard stare. "Did you find these?" she asked, shaking the Polaroids from the bag onto the table.

Toby didn't know how to reply. He had found them, yes. Then again, the killer had found them first. To keep things simple, because he had a headache now, Toby nodded.

"There are three here," she said. "Do you have the fourth?"

"No," Toby said. "No, I don't."

Dr. Scarf said, "Is the missing one the close-up of the pin?" Toby stared at the photos. He nodded. She said, "Do you know where it is?" Toby wondered. Did he know? It occurred to him that the killer could have stolen it while crawling to the porch. That might have been the thing he'd picked up. Unsure, Toby shook his head. Far-off sirens wailed in the night. "Go," Dr. Scarf ordered Bernie. She flicked a hand at Toby and added, "You too."

Boots clutched to his chest, Toby ran down the stairs.

"Fools!" Grace whispered. She was furious that Dan and Selma had tried to get Toby's attention.

"Fuck off," Dan said.

Selma said, "We didn't know anybody was coming."

"'Anybody,'" Grace hissed. "That was Mother! She almost heard you!"

"Maybe she did," Dan snarled. "But didn't care."

"I think," said the middle-aged gentleman who'd leaned from his window to see what was going on, only to find Grace pointing the gun at him, "I'm going to throw up."

"Join the club," Selma said. She'd thrown up twice herself. Their view of the kitchen, although limited to the open screen door, left no doubt about the scope of the slaughter. They'd seen bodies fall. They'd heard the explosion, they'd even felt it. The sole good thing about this was the apparent suicide of the noseless man. Selma worried about Dan. He seemed in shock. So did Grace; however, she continued to train her gun on the fellow leaning from the window. The man looked paralyzed.

They saw Toby hurry down the street to the van, crazily holding the boots. A zombie followed. Mother must have parked out front, Grace thought. "Stay quiet," she whispered to Dan.

"Or you'll shoot me?" Dan stood up, knuckles white on the fire escape's iron bars.

"No," she said, trembling. "But do you want to become like your brother?" She jerked her chin at the street.

Toby entered the van's rear door. The zombie climbed in after him. For some reason, the van started rocking.

Dan exclaimed, "Toby's fighting him!"

"Get down," Grace whispered desperately.

The boots flew from the van to the pavement. The door slammed shut. Moments later, the van took off.

"What is it with my boots?" Selma muttered.

"He's fucked up," Dan snapped.

"Treatment," Grace said. "Mother's treatment." She met Dan's bewildered stare, and added, "It might not be bad. Some of the stuff she does isn't—permanent." Sirens seemed to be coming closer. "You get on the floor," Grace said to the man in the window. He complied. "Go inside," Grace told Dan and Selma. They clambered through the window. Grace followed.

"What do you want from me?" the apartment-dweller asked. Selma studied the paunchy guy with frizzy hair and steel-framed glasses. She could see him writing software all day. And now this. "Sedatives," she said.

"Okay," the man said. "I have some."

"Don't go anywhere," Grace muttered. "Don't move." In the next room a TV was on. Grace heard Barclay Piston's voice. That meant Father would be talking soon. The thought made her feel like she was about to join Selma's club. Their near-encounter with Mother had been such a close call.

Dan walked toward the TV sound. He paused at the doorway and glanced back at Grace. "Barclay looks psyched," he commented.

"Yeah," Grace said. "In about twenty minutes, he'll know what psyched is."

"Anything," the man said. "I'll give you whatever you want."

"Do you," Grace asked, "have a car?"

The helicopter thundered through autumnal light, the wan twilight presaging Antarctica's winter darkness.

Clouds massed on the western horizon. Ahead and to the east rose the Transantarctic Mountains, the continental divide that separated East and West Antarctica, walling off from the lower-lying West the titanic East Antarctic Ice Sheet. Straight ahead, seven hundred miles over the horizon, lay the Pole. And a thousand feet below, the endlessly flat, blue-white terrain of the Ross Ice Shelf stretched westward as far as the eye could see.

Nigel piloted. Bertrand operated camera one. Louise operated camera two. A third camera stood ready to take commentary from the crew, should the producers want it.

Marcel tended the satellite uplink at the cabin's rear. In his console, monitors showed him what the cameras saw. Another monitor played the opening graphics and musical fanfare of the *Barclay Piston Show,* downlinking from Cambridge, Massachusetts, where the time was exactly 9:00 P.M.

The musical theme swelled to a crescendo in Marcel's headset. Lights on the console blinked, indicating that the cameras' feeds were being broadcast. An announcer's voice boomed, "Tonight! We bring you: 'FIRE AND ICE!' This! Is! BARCLAY!"

Titles dervished on the downlink screen, forming an arabesque around three inset images; two of which, Marcel saw with a frisson of pride, came from the cameras up front. The third showed a volcano, bejungled in a tropical setting, blowing its top.

"*Mes copains!*" Marcel shouted over his intercom mike. "We are on the air!" Bertrand and Louise already knew this from indicator lights in their camera sightscreens. Furthermore, producers were telling them via headset what to shoot. Bertrand zoomed into the distant storm clouds, Ross Shelf conspicuously gigantic from foreground to infinity. Louise panned the towering eastward mountains.

She wondered if the audience took those mountains to be active volcanoes. It wouldn't surprise her if the far-off producers, via digital trickery, were making them convulsively erupt. Louise had trouble focusing on this job. She didn't want to be doing a fluff piece on fire and ice.

Louise wanted to know the truth about the talk swirling around McMurdo Base. What she'd heard was too ghastly, too sickening to comprehend. But she had a feeling that it was true; a nuclear bomb had triggered the eruption.

Something horrible was happening to Antarctica. Would Barclay Piston report it? Louise didn't think so. She feared she was participating in a slick coverup.

— — —

In Plympton Street outside the Ecologic Foundation, onlookers pressed against police barricades, claiming front-row spots from which to view the huge videoscreen on the building's facade. The crowd steadily grew larger as Harvard Square's Saturday night population of youthful revelers, strolling tourists, suburban theater-goers, and miscellaneous wanderers encountered the excitement.

Four policemen stood guard at the foundation's closed front door. From the broadcast truck parked before it, cables snaked across the sidewalk and penetrated the steel grillwork barring a small window. Additional policemen guarded both truck and cables. *The Barclay Show*'s producers weren't skimping on security tonight. Along with routine precautions that attended a field location, they were making extra efforts to keep things under control; for the program's subject, even by Barclay's standards, was sensational. Television teasers had been promising a shocker all day.

In the foundation's lobby, fifteen feet from the front door, Darlene sat at her desk munching Doritos and watching a monitor tuned to Barclay. She thought about her responsibilities. In part, they concerned a metal box screwed to the underside of the desk. She hoped she could do what Dr. Trefethen expected of her. It was very important, he'd said. She didn't want to let him down.

The front door flew open. A young man in a fancy suit burst in, looking worried. Darlene bellowed at the top of her lungs, "Close that door, mister!"

Startled, the young man stopped short. Darlene glared imperiously at him. He went back to the door and closed it.

"You people!" Darlene exclaimed with disgust.

The man followed cables past Darlene's desk down the hall to the rear, where a security guard stood by the conference room's locked door. They began a whispered conversation.

Darlene returned her attention to the front door. Dr. Trefethen wanted it closed at all times, she reminded herself anxiously. A smile settled on her face as she remembered why.

In the conference room, Barclay Piston sat at an elegant antique table on the makeshift set, the Ecologic Foundation's logo prominent behind him. He'd just delivered a forty-second introduction, short on specifics, long on ominous insinuation; a pre-taped recap of the day's developments now was rolling, giving himself, the crew, and Earnest almost a minute of downtime.

Lights floodlit the conference room. Cameras were poised to resume the broadcast. Sound people, technicians, Marvin the executive producer and his assistant occupied their various stations, ready to get back on the air. Earnest, having felt a need to "look at this damned itching makeup," was in the nearby rest room.

Barclay saw the door to the hallway open. Why? he wondered. They were supposed to be sealed off. One of the interns leaned through and beckoned Marvin, who, shaking his head, crossed the room. He read something the intern gave him. Then he looked at his watch, glanced at Barclay, and strode to the set.

"We have twenty seconds," Marvin said, showing Barclay a piece of paper. "Where's Dr. Trefethen?"

"Here," Earnest said, taking his seat at the table. He peered at the fax Barclay was reading. It read:

TO: BARCLAY PISTON & EARNEST TREFETHEN
FROM: MARY MCMURTRY,
  DIRECTOR GENERAL, FATB
JUST SAW THE TOP OF THE SHOW, AND I'M
CONCERNED.
DON'T BE STUPID.
DON'T EVEN THINK ABOUT IT.
CONSIDER THIS A THREAT.

Barclay balled it up. "We go as planned," he said to Marvin.

Marvin scurried away. "Five!" yelled the assistant producer. "Four! Three! Two! ON AIR!"

Barclay Piston's sharp-featured face filled the television screen in General Raffenelli's penthouse office.

"It gives me great pleasure," Piston said, "to introduce the president of the Ecologic Foundation, Dr. Earnest Trefethen. As many of you now know, Dr. Trefethen is widely considered one of world's leading authorities on the West Antarctic Ice Sheet—or, as he refers to it, the 'WAIS.'" The image pulled back to include Trefethen. "Thank you for allowing us to visit, Dr. Trefethen."

Trefethen said, "I am happy to be of service."

Better keep your mouth shut, thought the general.

Piston said smoothly, "We saw from the introductory piece that there seems to be quite a bit of mystery surrounding the eruption in Antarctica. Do you wish to comment on that?"

"The forces of nature, Barclay, like those of God, often are mysterious." Trefethen smiled. Raffenelli noted an odd gleam in his eyes. "But before I comment on the eruption, I would like to point out that Antarctica's mysteries are perhaps deeper than those elsewhere on earth. This is important to keep in mind, because Antarctica affects many things important to all of us—sea level, for instance." Raffenelli again noted the gleam. "However, sea level is only one everyday reality that Antarctica affects. The wind currents of the atmosphere are another example. It controls ocean currents as well. Put simply, Antarctica is an engine that creates much of the planet's climate. Changes there, you see, affect climate everywhere."

"By changes," Piston said, "I assume you're referring to the possibility we've heard so much about today, namely the 'catastrophic collapse' of the West Antarctic Ice Sheet?"

"Indeed. If the WAIS slides into the ocean, sea level rises a full twenty feet. And that would be just the beginning."

"Twenty feet doesn't seem very high," Piston remarked.

"It's a monster rise, Barclay. Furthermore, as I said, it's just the beginning. Look at this." Trefethen pressed a button. A screen descended behind him. The American eastern seaboard appeared on it. "There," Trefethen said, "is our east coast." He pressed another button; the coast veered inland, and Florida shrank considerably. "There's the seaboard after a twenty-foot rise. As you see, most major metropolitan areas are under water." He again pressed a button. Florida disappeared altogether. The rest of the seaboard altered beyond recognition. "And there," Trefethen said, "we see the effects of a hundred-seventy-foot rise."

"A hundred and seventy feet," Piston said. "Could sea level really go that high?"

General Raffenelli tried to imagine Boston Harbor lapping at the windows of his twentieth-floor office. It seemed impossible.

But Trefethen was saying, "It certainly could. If the WAIS slips, the consequent twenty-foot rise would subject the East Antarctic Ice Sheet, and its subglacial basins in particular, to radically different conditions. We know that if East Antarctica were to shed the ice it holds in those basins—the ice is up to three miles thick there—sea level rises by another one hundred and fifty feet." Trefethen gazed thoughtfully at the camera. "And that ice is only one-third of the East Antarctic total. So you see, we're talking about extremely large quantities of ice."

"Yes," Piston murmured. "But it would take a long time to melt, wouldn't it? To raise sea level?"

"It doesn't have to melt. Take the famous example of an iceberg. A small fraction is above water. The rest is underwater. Thus with a WAIS collapse, and an East Antarctic discharge, the sheer volume of displaced ocean would raise sea level. Think of dropping an ice cube in a glass of water. The water in the glass goes up, does it not?"

Huh, thought Raffenelli.

"One must remember," Trefethen went on, "the magnitudes with which we're dealing. Are you aware that Antarctica holds more than ninety percent of the world's ice, and eighty-six percent of its fresh water?"

Piston shook his head.

"Back to the climate issue," Trefethen said. "Some experts have contended that a WAIS collapse might trigger another ice age. You may know that the last ice age ended only ten thousand years ago. But the glaciers of that ice age scraped off the face of North America. Literally scraped the earth bare. The soil and rock that the glaciers shoved along created Cape Cod, Nantucket, Martha's Vineyard, and Long Island— simply because it was at those places that the glaciers happened to stop."

"You're claiming," Piston said, "that if Antarctica discharges ice, glaciers will scrape civilization off North America? And dump it on Martha's Vineyard?"

"It's possible," Trefethen replied evenly. "Many outcomes are possible, even probable. We would confront . . . a huge climate flux."

What the hell, Raffenelli wondered, is Trefethen trying to do? Scare the public to death? The idea of North America's shopping malls and whatnot obliterating his beloved Chatham on Cape Cod—it made his heart pound.

Piston said, "Then let us hope that Antarctica doesn't discharge. Which brings us to the meat of the matter. What could cause a catastrophic collapse of the WAIS?"

Trefethen said, "At the opening of the program, we saw that you have a helicopter over Antarctica's Ross Ice Shelf, transmitting video to us live. May we take another look?"

The television image shifted to a featureless flat plain, stretching bluishly white as far as the eye could see. "There," Trefethen voice-overed, "is the Ross Ice Shelf, a floating slab of ice that covers the enormous Ross Embayment. At two hundred thousand square miles, Ross Shelf is roughly the size of France, or of Spain. A bit smaller than Texas. A bit larger than California. Its surface averages two hundred feet above sea level. But the shelf is fairly thick. On average, two thousand feet; like an ice cube or an iceberg, most of it's underwater.

"Keep in mind that, gargantuan though Ross is, it's quite small compared to the WAIS. I'll describe what creates the shelf—if we can pull up, and pan east . . ." A majestic range of mountains came into view, rising from the shelf's distant edge like the Rockies rising from the prairie of the American West. "Those are the Transantarctic Mountains. Glaciers flow down through their valleys from the East Antarctic Ice Sheet, giving the shelf ice. If we can have a westward shot . . . "

The image shifted to a cloud bank covering a flat and far-off horizon. "Four hundred miles in that direction," Trefethen continued, "too far for us to see, is the WAIS. It too feeds the shelf ice. But the WAIS's ice doesn't arrive via valley glaciers. The reason is important—mountains don't bound that edge of the WAIS."

"Earnest, the clouds in the distance there—are they vapor from the volcano's eruption?"

"Indeed," Trefethen said. "The vapor the eruption threw in the atmosphere is a large storm now. We see it approaching."

"As to how the WAIS feeds the shelf—ice from the western sheet comes in via something called 'ice streams.' Like glaciers, ice streams are slow-moving rivers of ice. But instead of flowing through mountain valleys, they flow through areas of stationary ice—ice that is glued to the bedrock."

"I'm not sure why that's important," Piston interjected.

"It's extremely important. Mountains buttress much of the eastern sheet. Mountains also happen to buttress much of the WAIS. But in the direction we're looking, a several-hundred-mile-long flank of the WAIS slopes directly to Ross Shelf, with nothing to hold it back. Except, that is, for two things."

Raffenelli sighed. Trefethen's drift was making him uneasy.

"All right," Piston said. "What are those things?"

"First, under normal conditions, most of the WAIS's ice is firmly glued to the bedrock. That tends to keep it stable. Again, under normal conditions. The second thing keeping the WAIS stable, you're looking at—Ross Ice Shelf."

The image shifted to Piston and Trefethen. "What do you mean by 'normal conditions'?" Piston asked.

"At the moment, conditions beneath the WAIS aren't normal. A large volcanic rift zone is in flux there. Not only did it play a role in the eruption; it's venting gases, and may spawn more eruptions. The net effect, Barclay, is heat. That heat is melting ice at the WAIS's base—and I don't think one needs much imagination to realize that such a process could unglue the WAIS's grip on the land. In fact, basal melt is what permits ice streams and glaciers to move—it's what makes them ice rivers, as opposed to stationary ice. The meltwater mixes with sediment, producing a mud-like mixture called 'till,' which is a potent lubricant. It reduces friction between the ice and the supporting bedrock; it causes, you might say, slipperiness, enabling ice movement. And right now, the rift zone underneath the WAIS may be becoming quite slippery indeed. One could liken it to a titanic banana peel."

"Do you mean," Barclay asked dutifully—the deal he'd made with Earnest required that he play along with this exposition—"that the entire WAIS might become an ice stream?"

"That's not far off the mark. Now, about Ross Shelf. I've mentioned that it covers the Ross Embayment. In effect, it's wedged into that embayment, and when you consider the fact that it's two hundred thousand square miles in area, with an average thickness of two thousand feet, we're talking about quite a wedge. And so by virtue of sheer mass, it acts as a barrier to WAIS movement. However, it does something else as well—it protects the WAIS from the open ocean. Remember, the WAIS's border with Ross Shelf isn't buttressed by mountains. The WAIS simply rolls into the shelf, and from the air, it's hard to see where the WAIS ends and where the shelf begins. The two entities, so to speak, are fused.

"But let us imagine that the shelf disappeared, making the Ross Embayment a large body of open water. The ocean then would pound against the WAIS itself. That brings me to my final point.

"One must take into account, to consider how the WAIS might become unglued, the fact that it's a submarine ice sheet. Its base is below sea level—which means it's glued not to high and dry land, but, in fact, to the ocean floor.

"This makes the WAIS inherently unstable. It is why it periodically has collapsed in the course of its history. And it is why Ross Shelf is crucial. Without the shelf—if the open ocean were to pound the WAIS's unprotected flank—we would have, what with the banana peel, as it were, the potential for a colossal disaster.

"We'd be looking at the possibility that the WAIS could simply slide into the South Pacific."

Barclay cleared his throat. He said, "I suppose it would cause tidal waves?"

"Perhaps. Just as alarming would be the slow inward creep."

"Slow inward creep?"

"Of the sea, Barclay. All over the world. A slow but steady migration of the coastlines, inland, as the WAIS slides." Trefethen gave Barclay a pensive stare. "Actually, it wouldn't necessarily be all that slow. You might be able to stand on your favorite beach, and watch it." He chuckled. "Rather like watching the tide come in. Except it wouldn't stop. It would keep on coming."

"The idea seems to amuse you. Is that because the Ross Shelf, God bless it, will save the day?"

"I wouldn't be so sure," Earnest declared. "The shelf is due for a shock. A very powerful shock."

Barclay frowned with surprise. This wasn't scripted; they were supposed to be getting into the eruption now. He said, "You just explained that Ross Shelf is the size of France. What could shock it?"

Earnest smiled his most brilliant smile. "Consider this," he said. "The shelf covers a very large area, yes. And yes, it is two thousand feet thick. But think of the thickness in relation to the surface area. What you have is something akin more to a thin membrane than, say, a thick block. Now imagine that glaciers and ice streams continually flow into this membrane, creating a complex system of stresses, pressure points, shear vectors, and so on. You still have an entity of enormous mass. But it holds a great deal of internal tension. Tension that could break. What I'm talking about, Barclay, are the dynamics of fracture."

Barclay's face betrayed puzzlement giving way to suspicion. "Okay. But—what could deliver the fracturing shock?"

Earnest looked directly into the camera taking his close-up, and said, "Nuclear explosions could."

He pulled a cell-phone from his jacket pocket.

28

On her monitor, Darlene saw Dr. Trefethen pull out the phone. That was her cue. She looked at the front door. It was closed, the way it had to be for her to do her job.

She reached under the desk. Her hand found the metal box, flipped the cover, and pressed the button inside.

Power bolts slammed into doors all around the building.

General Raffenelli stared at his television set with disbelief. He picked up his phone and punched a number. On the TV, Piston looked at a loss for words. But after a moment he said, "Earnest, why would nuclear weapons explode in Ross Shelf?"

"Barclay," Trefethen said from a TV in the sitting room of a sumptuous townhouse in the Georgetown district of Washington, D.C., "you know perfectly well that a nuclear explosion triggered the eruption in the ice sheet. Yes, a nuclear explosion—let's say it out loud, nuclear." He paused, giving the word time to linger. "Now then," he continued, "if such an explosion can make a volcano erupt, why couldn't a few more take care of Ross?"

Piston said, "You have proof a nuclear bomb made the volcano erupt?"

"Oh, yes," Trefethen replied. "You see, I put it there. And I set it off."

Mary McMurtry rose from the sitting room's sofa. Patting smooth the pleats of her cocktail dress, she said to her slack-jawed guests, who included several senior national security officials, "I'm going to my office. You'll be going to yours, I'd think. Sorry I can't offer a lift." She headed for the door.

From the television Piston muttered, "Surely—you jest."

Earnest smiled at the dismay covering Barclay's face. Beyond the glare of the lights, he thought he saw signs that the crew, professionals that they were, had kept their grip. "I could not be more serious," he said.

"Well—if you did blow up the volcano—why did you do it?"

"To join Mother Earth in giving this miserable, corrupt world a kick in the butt. That just might save it."

"You're saving the world?" Barclay asked incredulously.

Earnest shrugged. "We'll see," he replied. "It's quite possible, Barclay, that it's beyond saving."

"Let me be sure I understand you. You are taking responsibility for the explosion of a nuclear bomb that caused Antarctica's volcanic eruption? You confess this on worldwide television?"

"Precisely," Earnest said.

"And now you threaten to damage the Ross Ice Shelf?"

"I intend to destroy it."

"I see. Earnest, I'm obliged to make a brief statement to the authorities who are watching. Can you deal with that?"

"Absolutely, old boy."

Barclay turned to the camera. "Dr. Trefethen may have suffered a psychotic break," he said solemnly. "On the other hand, given the faint possibility that what he says is true, I want to assure all concerned parties that this man isn't going anywhere." Barclay turned back to Earnest, who smiled quizzically. "You heard me. So—how are you going to destroy Ross Shelf?"

Earnest held up his phone. "By making a telephone call."

"By making a phone call. To whom?"

"To the nuclear devices I placed in Ross Shelf."

Barclay blinked at him.

"These bombs take calls, Barclay."

Once again, Barclay blinked. "I find that hard to believe," he said.

"Do you? In this day and age of magic telephony?"

Barclay thought a moment. And then said, "Give me the phone."

"Shortly, I will. But I can't give it to you now. I haven't called the bombs yet."

Sweat beaded in Barclay's temples. "Then I'll have to take it from you by force," he said.

Earnest pulled a gun from his jacket and trained it on Barclay's abdomen. "Get the guard," Barclay called to the crew. Marvin strode to the door. He tried to open it. It wouldn't budge.

"That door," Earnest announced, "and various other doors in this building are quite securely locked."

Marvin tugged furiously on the door. He started pounding it.

"Ladies and gentlemen," Barclay said owlishly into the camera, "it would appear that I and my crew are trapped in this room with a madman. We will do our best to stay calm. I urge everyone who is watching to do the same. I also," he added pointedly, "want the FATB here right away." He gave Earnest a scathing stare. "I'm sure they'll arrive soon."

"Yes," Earnest murmured. "Barclay, I will now call the bombs. It's an automatic dial; the number is programmed into the phone, so I need press only one button." He mashed a button on the phone, which he held near the mike concealed under his jacket. The mike caught a rapid sequence of tones.

Barclay studied the gun pointed at his stomach.

Earnest said, "I suspect you will attempt to subdue me, Barclay. I can see it in your body language, my friend. Don't try it. If you do, I'll put a bullet in your intestines . . . ah, there it is. The answer tone. Barclay, the bombs have answered. All three of them have. This is a conference call, of sorts."

"Now, really—come to your senses."

Earnest gazed at the world's highest-paid television personality. "All I have to do now," he said, "is press the pound key."

"Don't!" Barclay cried.

"But first, I have a message for the 'copter over Ross Shelf."

"You do?" Barclay asked, blinking again. "Well—talk to them, Earnest. They're listening. Talk to them as much as you want."

"Barclay, you are transparent. You think that if you can distract me, somehow delay me, FATBOY will get here in time. But my message for the 'copter is brief, you see."

"Go ahead, then. Say it."

"Climb," Earnest said.

Marcel lurched from his console at the helicopter cabin's rear. "Climb!" he bellowed at Nigel. "Climb!"

Everyone on board was listening to the *Barclay Show*, for Marcel had alerted the others to the developments in Cambridge. But what they'd heard hadn't sunk in. Until now.

Nigel climbed.

In Plympton Street outside the foundation, the watching crowd stood riveted. The video format had shifted to split-image. One half showed Piston and Trefethen continuing their face-off inside. The other half showed the interior of the helicopter. A French-Canadian voice, backgrounded by the chopper's roar, hung electrifyingly in the air: "Climb! Climb!"

━ ━ ━

"While they climb," Earnest said, watching the helicopter action on a monitor facing the set, "I'll explain what is about to happen to the shelf. My calculations indicate that three explosions will demolish it. If the bombs are correctly placed, and go off at properly staggered intervals, they should create interpenetrating shock waves—the cross-shear of which should fracture the shelf into millions of icebergs. I expect that the prevailing katabatic winds coming down from the polar plateau will take those bergs out to sea . . . a vast armada, setting sail for the South Pacific. Helicopter, can you hear me? Hello! Helicopter, this is Earnest Trefethen! Can you hear me?"

Static squawked from the monitor. "Nigel Ditchley here, pilot of this rapidly climbing helicopter. What in God's name are you doing, man? I beg you—in the name of Antarctic science—in the name of this unique part of the world! Don't do it!"

Another voice, hard with fury, came through the monitor. "This is Louise Lemieux, operator of camera two aboard the 'copter. If you so much as lay a hand on that shelf, I personally will track you down! And garrote you! Is that clear?"

"Yes," Earnest replied. "But you know as well as I that the Antarctica we love is doomed . . . what is your precise location?"

"We're at 170—79!" Nigel shouted.

"You're all right, then. Hold tight, though." Earnest held up his phone. "Cameraman, may I have a close-up of this?"

"No," Barclay said, shoving his chair closer.

"Stay back," Earnest said. "You've reached the high point of your career, Barclay. Don't ruin it with shattered intestines—there, I see everyone has a view of my finger on the pound key. After I press it, approximately four minutes will pass before the first shock wave approaches the 'copter; and then a minute or so more for the following shock waves. I trust the audience will be patient. We're talking less than six minutes of waiting. Presumably you all have at least that much patience. Although, of course, in this day and age, one never knows—Barclay, are we ready?"

"May God have mercy on your soul," Barclay whispered.

"God is delighted, you fool," Earnest replied.

He pressed the pound key. Many millions watched him do it.

And they heard the tone.

━ ━ ━

In the climbing 'copter, no one said a word. They waited.

Earnest slid the phone across the table to Barclay. "Hold on to that," he said, winking. "I suspect it's rather valuable now." Ashen-faced, Barclay stared back.

"I would like to announce to the viewing public," Earnest informed the camera, "that I have seven more bombs in Antarctica. They're strategically placed, these bombs. And like the ones with which I just communicated, they take phone calls." He gazed contemplatively at the camera. "But they do more than that," he went on. "For example, they receive E-mail. They get everything—these bombs, you see, are plugged into the Net. They're fully integrated with the datasphere." He glanced at Barclay. "It should warm your heart, old fellow. They get television too, of course. They're watching this program right now."

Barclay swallowed. He said, "Nukes are watching TV?"

"Indeed they are. Avidly! Much like the rest of the world."

"Do you care to explain why?"

"Because they're looking for something, Barclay." Earnest stood. He stared into the camera and said, "Think about that. In Antarctica, seven more nuclear bombs are watching television. Everything you see, they also see. However, they happen to see more—much, much more. And I stress to you, all of you out there—you, the bombs' fellow viewers—they're looking for something." Earnest raised shaggy eyebrows. "What could that be?"

Barclay muttered, "I'm sure we're all dying to know."

"Well, I'll tell you," Earnest said, drawing himself to his full height. "They're looking for the Beast," he declared.

"What?" Barclay said.

"For the Beast," Earnest repeated. "For its two faces, in point of fact. That's what the bombs want."

"Ah . . . Earnest . . . why? What are . . . the faces . . . of . . . ?"

With professorial authority Earnest said, "Barclay, the Beast is abroad in the world. And it deals in signs, particular signs, two particular images, actually—that show its face. As to what those images are . . . I won't say much. All I'll say, one is primitive. Very primitive—even primordial. As to the other—why, it's technological. A thing of science, you see."

"But I don't see. And I doubt many people do."

"Oh, you will. When the bombs see them. When the bombs see the Beast, all of us will know. We won't be able to avoid it."

"Of course, Earnest. Perhaps you can put down your gun?"

"You doubt me?" Earnest said.

Barclay blinked with staccato rapidity. He said, "I don't think nuclear bombs are capable of watching television."

"These bombs are," Earnest replied. "They're plugged into all kinds of networks. Into every network—including planetwide TV." He smiled frigidly. "By satellite, of course. Which brings me to my final remarks." Again he stared at the camera. "The bombs enjoy watching TV. They're hooked, to be honest—just like you. And like you, they hate reception interruption." As if with regret, he sighed. "I don't advise meddling with the satellites. Or with the programming that goes through them—the bombs must remain integrated with the datasphere. Any hint of a disconnection . . ." Earnest's eyes drilled the lens. "They'll explode."

Barclay exclaimed, "This is science fiction!"

Earnest said, "So is everyday life. As we all are aware." He glanced at the camera and remarked, "Don't bother sending marines across the ice sheet. They'll vaporize if they so much as touch the dish receivers." To Barclay he said, "I must make a trip to the rest room now." He waved the gun at his head. "Who knows? I may feel compelled to end it all. But I know people are curious as to why I would take such extreme measures." Walking backward, he moved to the rest room, gun held steadily on Barclay. "I have comments about that. A message will be going out on the Net in a few minutes, its dispersal aided by a flooding algorithm. I hope you find it interesting." He groped behind himself for the rest room doorknob. "One last thought," he said, opening the door. "Consider, if you will, the cleansing effects of water."

He backed in and closed the door. A camera zoomed to the doorknob. Amid complete silence, the lock clicked sharply.

Earnest removed the microphone from his shirt, tossed it in the sink, and turned on tapwater. He then unlocked a cabinet beneath the sink. From it he took a flashlight and a digital audioplayer. He put the player on a counter near the door, and keyed a control.

He went to the rearmost of three toilet stalls. His finger found a concealed button near the ceiling. He pressed it. A portion of the tiled wall slid silently into darkness. Earnest probed with the flashlight.

The beam illuminated steel rungs set into the damp brickwork of a vertical shaft. Earnest put a foot on a rung, grasped another with his free hand, and eased himself in. His finger found a second button. He pressed it. The access hatch swung back to the rest room wall.

Earnest descended the rungs. The shaft dropped to a moldering and unlit concrete tunnel. He jumped the last few feet, a certain springiness in his knees. The flashlight beam brushed something shiny leaning against the tunnel wall. An electric motorbike.

He mounted the bike, and started it. The motor hummed softly. He switched the headlight on. A waggle of the handles swept the beam down the tunnel, revealing it to be long and fairly clear of obstructions. His mouth curled in a tight smile, Earnest set off.

Generations of students, faculty, and employees associated with Harvard University had heard stories about the labyrinthine and largely unused network of service tunnels connecting the basements of the university's buildings. Earnest was no exception. He'd been planning to make use of the tunnels for a while.

Now that he was using them, now that he was riding away through the catacombs below Harvard Square on his virtually silent motorbike—riding away from his past, away from the lies and the frustrations, from the stymied outrage of his career, indeed of his entire life—he experienced a mixture of feelings.

He felt nausea, mingled with exhilaration.

29

Louise first saw the disturbance on the southern horizon. She zoomed it with her camera. The magnification showed a haze cloud, slowly growing denser.

She next noticed a change in the light. The air seemed to brighten. The shelf's surface milkened. A curtain of snow hurtled across it.

The shock wave hit. The 'copter went into a sidelong swerve, rotors struggling to keep a grip on the hammer-like airstream. Nigel fought for control. As long seconds passed, it didn't seem he'd succeed.

But the shock wave passed. The 'copter clawed through gale-force winds. "*Fourré*," Bertrand whispered, staring south.

Something in the shelf was coming at them. A dark line snaked through the vibrating whiteness. As it came closer, it seemed to widen. In Louise's photozoom it looked like the supernatural construction of a highway. God was laying asphalt at seven hundred miles an hour; paving, for some reason, a route to the 'copter. A rumbling roar grew louder. The thing in the ice came closer, and closer, then it flashed by three hundred yards to the east, the roar crescendoing with a monumental *THWACK!*

Again the 'copter swerved. Clumsily, Nigel brought it around. Louise and Bertrand struggled with their cameras, trying to follow the crack. Like a lightning bolt it raced north through the ice, toward the sea, its velocity undiminished. The roar receded slowly, deliberately—train-like—into the distance.

"*Chalice!*" Marcel exclaimed.

The second shock wave hit. Rotors screaming, the 'copter danced feverishly, fighting the new wave's brawl with the first one's residue. The air itself seemed to snap, buckle, and shatter into a multitude of warring elements. Marcel hit the uplink console, gashing his scalp. Bertrand slapped his hands over his eyes. Louise gripped a balance bar with ivory knuckles, stomach molten with rage and terror.

A violent minute passed. Nigel regained control as the turbulence subsided. Blood poured down Marcel's face. Panting, Louise ripped a sleeve from her shirt, and passed it to him. Unable to speak, nodding thanks, he pressed the cloth to the wound.

"*Non!*" Bertrand exclaimed, staring southwest.

Three new highways rushed from the cloudy horizon. The most southerly intersected the first crack; spokes radiated from the juncture point. Rapidly, they fanned southeast.

The other two fissures sped north. The easterly one seemed wider than a highway. When it passed them, fifty or so miles away, it looked more like an eight-lane interstate.

"I'll garrote him!" Louise shouted. "And then chop off his criminal head! And then . . . "

The third shock wave hit, bringing a maelstrom that sucked the shouts right out of her throat.

The crowd in Plympton Street stood still and silent, watching the 'copter's ordeal on the videoscreen. The images veered wildly now, too blurry and violent to read; but most everyone had an idea of what was happening. They'd seen the fractures scoring the shelf. They still heard the bone-deep booms of splitting ice, the tortured thrash of the rotors. And Louise's furious shouts still rang in their ears.

The question was: Would the 'copter survive?

It seemed to plunge into spastic whiteness. The videoscreen blanked out.

In the conference room's rest room, the audioplayer continued to play. Nothing had issued from its speakers. Nothing would for several more minutes.

Barclay stared at the monitor's blank screen. He inhaled raggedly. Marvin said, "Can you go?"

Out of reflex, Barclay said, "Yes."

A camera pulled in. The on-air signal lit. Barclay muttered, "Please join me in a moment of silence. To pray for the safety of the brave people in that helicopter . . . "

He closed his eyes.

Six seconds later, he opened them, for he'd come up with something to say. "What we just saw," he whispered, "suggests that humanity is under attack. Yes, ladies and gentlemen—we are, all of us, under attack. Nuclear bombs appear to be destroying the Ross Ice Shelf. The size of France, it now lies broken—smashed into—into thousands of pathetic little . . . *arrondissements*."

Barclay's head was reeling. The words "high point" and "shattered" syncopated insistently at the bottom of his mind; he could not think. What was that he'd just said about *arrondissements*?

Words swam at him. "If we are to believe the man who sat here, at this table, but minutes ago—he detonated those bombs by telephone." Pointing, he exclaimed, "With that telephone right there!" He frowned, and said with a catch in his throat, "Incredible. But if we are to believe our eyes—true."

Barclay stood, hands flat on the table. Softly he continued, "And where is the monster now? Where is the coward capable of this horrendous crime?" Barclay pointed at the rest room door. The camera panned with him. "He hides, alone, in there. With the gun he used to hijack this program before your very eyes."

Marvin signaled to wrap it up. But Barclay wasn't quite finished. He said more softly, "I happened to be in that rest room an hour ago. I didn't see any way out except for that door. This is Barclay Piston—standing guard. Standing guard over the most heinous terrorist in the history of mankind.

"Stay with us. I'll be back."

Darlene ignored the bangs on the front door. Too many people were outside. Causing trouble. Anyway, what could she do? The button under her desk didn't unlock. All it did was lock.

The man who'd been guarding the conference room came running downstairs. "Every last God-damned door!" he yelled. "Locked! Can't even get to the windows!"

"Yeah," Darlene said. "I know."

"Are there windows on the ground floor," he asked, "that don't have bars? Even one?"

"No," Darlene said, opening a bag of popcorn.

"What about the basement?" he demanded.

"Locked," Darlene said.

"You're upset, huh?" the guard observed angrily.

Darlene shrugged. "Want some popcorn?" she asked.

The motorbike's headlight lit the heavy wood door. Earnest used the key Fladgate had given him. He pushed the door open, went back for the bike, and wheeled it into a storage area beneath Harvard's Peabody Museum complex.

Old packing crates filled the room. They didn't contain glass flowers, butterflies, or bones, or any of the Peabody's fabled treasures. This was a low-security area, with access to the street. Earnest combed shadows with his flashlight.

"Dr. Trefethen?" someone called from stairs in the next room.

Earnest went through. His flash found the pale face of Hugh Searles. He said, "Don't use that name. Where is Fladgate?"

"I don't know," Searles replied timidly.

"Has something gone wrong?" Earnest asked.

"No," Searles said.

"Do you have my helmet and my coat?"

"Uh—no. I don't."

"Do you have a motorcycle parked outside?"

"A van, Dr. Trefeth—"

"What the hell has gone wrong?" Earnest shouted. His voice reverberated through the high-ceilinged basement. "Forget it, Hugh. Just tell me—how bad is the traffic?"

"Pretty bad."

"Let's go," Earnest ordered. He ran up the stairs with manic energy. Searles shrank to the wall to let him by, then followed.

The traffic jam curled around Harvard Square like the coils of an anaconda steadily squeezing tighter. Mass. Ave. had backed up to Central and Porter Squares. JFK, Brattle, and Mt. Auburn were gridlocked. Kirkland, Cambridge, Garden, and Concord were filling up, and Memorial Drive had simply congealed, bumper-to-bumper.

Radio news and carphones were responsible for this. Along with television. People near the Square were learning, from a multitude of sources, that they occupied history's ground zero.

The rumors weren't plausible, but that didn't prevent their rapid circulation. Someone had blown up Antarctica. The tidal waves alone would kill billions. Somehow, the end of the world had just been called in by telephone. France already lay in ruins, mysteriously but gruesomely smashed. The Beast was berserking—laying waste to the planet before the horrified eyes of a vast television audience.

And the mastermind in charge, the man who'd set the Beast loose—who'd somehow conjured it directly from the datasphere—now made his last stand in Harvard Square.

Everybody wanted to be there when he was taken out.

General Raffenelli, approaching by helicopter, was especially eager to be present. Unfortunately, it was an executive helicopter. Only three troopers could fit in back. Ground forces were on the way, of course. But what Raffenelli saw in the streets said they'd experience delays.

His 'copter approached Plympton, and hovered over it. The videoscreen on the building cast flickering light over a canyon densely packed with human heads. The crowd had broken through the police barricade; several dozen people sat on the broadcast truck's roof. Amazingly, the videoscreen seemed to be commanding the crowd's rapt, even respectful attention.

What, he wondered, is Barclay telling them now?

To Colonel Jeannette Gwathmey, the pilot and head of FATB New England's aerial forces, he said, "Put down on the roof." The general figured it would take seconds to force an entry, given the flimsiness typical of rooftop doors.

He looked forward to his guest appearance on Barclay. With the world's eyes trained on the incomparable enormity of Trefethen's crimes, with those crimes having been perpetrated under his nose, the general felt a surge of resolve.

Not only did civilization cry out for his steadying hand. His career was on the line. Raffenelli watched the roof rise toward him.

Barclay stood by the door to the rest room, ears straining. A camera captured the scene. This was going out live.

Again he heard it. An agonized moan. "Earnest!" he called. "Earnest—are you feeling remorse?"

Silence greeted the question. But then again, Barclay heard a moan. He turned to the camera and said, "Dr. Earnest Trefethen, the once-respected scientist and environmentalist who tonight so nonchalantly inflicted disaster on us all, now seems overcome with—dare we guess?—what could it be? Guilt?"

Barclay faced the door. "Earnest! Will you surrender? And face the consequences of your actions? Or will you . . . "

A gunshot rang out. Barclay cringed. Then, satisfied that the bullet had penetrated neither himself nor the door, he listened intently. Did he hear the thud of a body's collapse?

Barclay was sure he had. Shoulders bowed, he walked to the table and sat. The camera pulled in; to it he said, "As I mentioned a few moments ago, the FATB has instructed me by telephone to under no circumstances try to force that door. Thus we must wait for General Raffenelli's arrival to learn if Earnest Trefethen, by his own hand, lies dead in that rest room.

"I confess to feeling a rather eerie sensation, trapped as I am with a monster beyond that door. I feel somewhat the way Allied soldiers must have felt at the close of World War II—as they stood outside Hitler's bunker, wondering if the madman still lived.

"Whether Trefethen is dead, or wounded, or merely is playing some twisted game, I think we now know he hasn't used the rest room to conceal an escape. For those of you who may fear he somehow is at large, perhaps the sound of that gunshot will provide some solace.

This crisis isn't over. In many ways, it's just beginning. But I, for one, feel safer. I hope you do, too."

Darlene, watching her monitor, wiped tears from her face.

"*Enfin!*" cried Marcel. "We have the uplink back!"

"Fabulous," Louise muttered, gazing at the chaos six thousand feet below. Ross Shelf had ceased to be a featureless plain. Cracks criss-crossed it to every horizon, creating a puzzle of countless individual pieces, most huge, some not. Turbulence agitated them in undulating waves, grinding city-size slabs against each other. Here and there, pressure propelled whole bergs high in the air. Steam, steadily thicker, poured from the interstices. The spectacle awed the 'copter's crew. And it deafened them.

After riding out the final cataclysm, they'd been too shaken to do much, or say much, for almost half an hour. They'd simply stared at the dying shelf.

"I think we should head back to base," Bertrand said.

"The steam probably is radioactive," Marcel remarked.

"Hold on," Nigel said, listening to his headset. "We're getting orders."

"Orders?" Louise inquired sarcastically. "We are on a military mission?"

Nigel continued to listen. He looked up and announced, "The television man says he'll pay five million if we get more video."

"Not enough," Louise declared. "I'll talk with him."

She patched the television executive into her headset, and commenced negotiations.

Raffenelli tried to keep his voice steady. He asked Colonel Gwathmey, "Are there explosives on board?"

"I'll check," Gwathmey replied. She went to the 'copter.

The general was having trouble with the Ecologic Foundation's rooftop door. He couldn't make it open. He, Gwathmey, and the troopers had tried everything, including a lengthy spray of bullets from the 'copter's machine gun. The door seemed impregnable.

Loud cheers suddenly emanated from the crowd four stories below. Hoots, howls, and what sounded suspiciously like screams of joy— Raffenelli didn't like it. Gwathmey approached, lugging a metal box. "Blow the thing," he said.

The videoscreen on the building had brought the Canadians back to life, and Plympton Street was thrilled. The crowd couldn't hear what the red-faced woman was saying. But the simple sight was enough. There she talked, alive with her crewmates, in that cramped, equipment-filled cabin.

The image shifted to a shot of what lay below. The crowd silenced; it stared at the shattered icescape beneath the 'copter. Five seconds passed. Then everyone, simultaneously, understood.

And the crowd erupted again, with the frenzy of a stadium full of triumphant soccer zealots. The cheers blasted through Harvard Square like seismic force.

To the police on Mt. Auburn preparing to evict the mob, to the FATB troops inching down Mass. Ave. in armored carriers, the sound seemed evidence that their mission was hopeless. They listened to a chant take hold, and swell into something close to thunder:

"AWE-SOME! AWE-SOME! AWE-SOME!"

"Awe-some!" Darlene chanted. "Awe-some, awe-some!" The crowd's roar scared her. At the same time, she found it exciting. Dr. Trefethen had made it happen, she knew. Poor Dr. Trefethen . . .

An angry-looking man ran down the stairs. A mad lady and three soldiers followed him. "Where are they?" the man demanded.

"Who?" Darlene asked.

"You know!" the man shouted. "Where's Barclay Piston?"

Darlene pointed.

"As you can hear, we have quite a situation," Barclay told the camera. "We have a mob outside this building that seems—I'm not sure what . . . my executive producer wants my attention."

"General Raffenelli," Marvin called from the door, "has arrived."

"Repeat what you just said," Earnest told Helen.

They stood in the truck's overfurnished salon. The TV set was on. General Raffenelli had just arrived. The crew in the conference room had taken cover, because the general was about to shoot down the door.

Helen said, "Grace has been kidnapped."

Earnest sat. "Helen," he said.

"I know," she said.

"By whom?" he asked.

The TV spewed machine-gun fire.

Helen burst into tears. "Hoodlums," she gasped.

"Helen," Earnest said, more forcefully.

"We can get her back," Helen said between sobs. "The people who did it—I caught one of them. And I'll use him—to find a way to get her back . . . "

Earnest thought for a moment. "Where," he asked, "is the hoodlum you caught?"

"Brian's room. Brian won't let the boy in Grace's room."

"Helen. Get a grip. And explain."

The rest room door wasn't fitted with the industrial locks that had bedeviled Raffenelli on the roof. He knew it from a forceful shake of the doorknob. To Gwathmey he said, "Show the world why you're a black belt, Colonel."

She did it with a single kick. The door flew open.

Raffenelli nodded at Barclay and the cameraman. They followed him in.

News of the rest room's emptiness spread quickly from Plympton Street to Mass. Ave. and Mt. Auburn. It spread through the Square, the city, the world; leaving in its wake outrage and delirium, for this was overload. The day's events had become too much to grasp.

Not so for Darlene, however. As far as she was concerned, she had a sound grasp of the latest news item.

What she saw on her monitor made her clap.

The warehouse door rattled up. The truck rumbled out. Three vans followed. The warehouse door rattled down.

In the salon, Earnest poured drinks. He gave Helen hers. They saluted each other, and drank.

"It could be worse," Earnest remarked.

"Yes," Helen agreed.

"If anyone can get her back, you can, dear."

Helen nodded.

"But I still don't understand why they took the badge."

Helen sighed. "I told you," she said. "They didn't know you'd made it one of the icons. To them, it was just—something like—memorabilia. Think about that, Earnest. They'd left the only home they ever knew. Memorabilia means a lot."

Earnest studied Helen carefully. He murmured, "That's what it was. Of course." He took another pull at his drink.

"She was devastated," Helen said. "Convinced she'd ruined everything. Particularly after she realized that the waiter had pocketed it. She and Brian, they both were so frightened."

"Yes. But they convinced you they could retrieve it?"

Helen pressed a tissue to her eyes. "They were desperate to make things right. Before you returned from Barclay. And I felt—it was important to let them redeem themselves. With Fladgate and the others with them . . . I didn't think they'd have any problem."

"I see," Earnest said. He rubbed his face tiredly. "Fladgate walked back. He's okay?"

"In one of the vans, with a concussion. He'll be fine. Despite the savagery of the attack."

Earnest raised furry eyebrows. He thought a moment; and asked, "You're sure you got all the Polaroids?"

"Oh, yes," Helen said crisply. "All three of them."

"The badge itself, you're positive Brian destroyed it?"

Helen nodded. "Brian cannot lie," she pointed out. "Not when threatened with a procedure."

"And you're equally sure Grace doesn't know where we're going tonight?"

"She doesn't. She has no idea, Earnest. None."

"In that case we should make it." Earnest stared at the TV set. Mary McMurtry was on now, defending the FATB in its moment of ignominy. "Unless Grace, for some reason, tells somebody about our ties to Martha."

"She'd rather kill herself," Helen said. "She doesn't want to lose Brian. Or us, either, you know that." Helen stared at the floor. "We'll get her back," she muttered.

Earnest gazed at Mary's tight face on the television. "I know we will," he murmured.

They looked at each other.

The truck skirted the Harvard Square traffic meltdown, and roared through the night.

Toby dreamed he was voyaging to the stars.

His ship churned steadily along. The powerful engine throbbed through the walls and the floor, through the undergirding of his bunk, through all the metal fixtures of his dimly lit cabin. The sound lulled Toby. It helped him rest.

He needed more than rest, though. He'd just endured a harrowing ordeal. But—what was it?

A lock clicked. A door opened. Bright light shone through. Blurry beings stood there—doctors, perhaps—members of the crew? Members of a noble and clever tribe . . .

The female said, "He won't think until morning."

The male said, "I'll talk with him then."

"He'll be confused," the female said.

"Yes," the male said thoughtfully. "We'll see."

Dimness returned as the door closed. The lock clicked; Toby pondered what he'd heard. Gradually he became aware that this wasn't his ship. Those beings weren't his crew.

It's obvious, he thought with sudden clarity and panic, the two sensations twisting into the phantasmic rush of a nightmare. I've been abducted, he realized—by aliens.

The idea woke Toby up. He discovered he couldn't move.

The CNN anchorwoman said, "In a night filled with horrifying surprises, one surprise dwarfs the others: Earnest Trefethen's claim that he has placed seven additional nuclear bombs under the West Antarctic Ice Sheet. Since he appears to have exploded four nuclear bombs in Antarctica already, the claim must be taken seriously. Soon we will ask a panel of scientific experts to evaluate the consequences of more explosions, particularly with regard to the now-paramount question of ice sheet stability.

"But before we turn to that subject, we'll address some of the more mystifying comments Trefethen made on tonight's *Barclay Piston Show*. They relate to the alleged additional bombs. Trefethen asserted that these bombs are 'watching television.' He said they're engaged in that activity, surely unique in the history of nuclear weapons, because they're 'looking for something.'" The anchorwoman paused. For an instant, her composure cracked. Worry flashed from her eyes. She frowned and took a careful breath. "They're looking, he claimed, for 'two faces of the Beast.' He said 'the Beast' will show those faces on TV through two particular images—one 'primitive,' one 'scientific.'" In a manner suggesting disbelief, the anchorwoman shook her head. She added, "Trefethen also declared, 'The bombs must remain integrated with the datasphere. If there is any hint of disconnection, they will explode.'"

"I'm having trouble believing any of this," Dan said.

"I don't believe it," Selma said flatly.

"Believe it," Grace muttered.

The three sat on a moldering sofa in a sixth-floor Somerville loft, watching the news. Since their arrival forty minutes before, via the car Grace had stolen from the man whose fire escape they'd visited, they each had tried, in different ways, to avoid nervous collapse. Television was proving to be of questionable help in that endeavor. Strange things were happening, Dan and Selma had learned, all over the world.

That those things were connected with the girl sitting between them, closely connected with this beautiful and somber child in a fancy dress with vomit on it, seemed ridiculous. But the whole day had been so confusing already; what with murder, gunpoint kidnappings, death-defying stunts, and multiple more murders. Unable to think clearly about those events, Dan and Selma were even less prepared to absorb the TV's dire reports.

Nonetheless, they were trying. The TV image expanded to include a grave-faced man sitting beside the anchorwoman. She said, "Here to offer comments is Zack Zinman, CNN's senior media analyst. Zack—what exactly is the 'datasphere'?"

"That's easy, Chantelle," Zinman said. "The datasphere is the totality of the planet's information."

"It's not limited to information carried by satellites?"

Zinman chuckled. "No," he said. "It's information in computers, in fiber-optic lines, in newspapers and magazines, in television and radio, in libraries—and on the sides of cereal boxes, on the menu you look at at lunch. All media are part of the datasphere—because all media, of course, mediate information."

"I see. But Trefethen mentioned satellites for a reason, didn't he?"

"Well yes, Chantelle. Satellites are just about the only way to get information to Antarctica. Unless of course you physically carry it there. Oh, I suppose ham radio could do it . . . "

Chantelle said, "Let me ask you something else. The idea of nuclear bombs 'watching' TV—could that have any basis in reality?"

"In a way, sure. We saw Trefethen make telephone calls to bombs in Antarctica. Giving them television signal isn't much different. In both cases, it's a question of sending streams of digitized data via satellite. The bombs need dish receivers, and computers to decode the data, that's all. Of course, for a bomb to be able to thoroughly analyze video data—to, so to speak, 'look for something'—that would require powerful computers."

"Can such computers function in the extreme conditions of remote Antarctica?"

Zinman smiled uneasily. "They function in space," he said. "That is, in the extreme conditions that satellites deal with. So, yes. Properly protected, computers could function . . . "

Dan turned to Grace. "When do they hit?" he asked.

"Huh?" Grace said. She hadn't been listening. Her thoughts weren't in the here and now. They mostly concerned the truck, its flight through the night with her parents, her brother, her life.

"Tidal waves," Selma said. "A few minutes ago, the news lady said people are stampeding because of . . . "

"Yeah," Grace said. "No tidal waves." She gestured dismissively at the TV set. "The tidal wave stuff is just panic. Exactly the way Father planned it."

Dan and Selma exchanged glances. Selma said, "What else did Father plan? Besides exploding the continent of Antarctica?"

Grace sighed. Her manner suggested she didn't know how to reply. Selma was getting tired of that.

The purple party boots lay in a heap by the battered coffee table. Dan had rescued them from the sidewalk during their departure from Magazine Street. "The least we can do," he'd said, referring to Toby's thwarted attempt to take them away.

Those boots are all I have left, Selma thought. The apartment had been totalled. It held so much death, she wanted never to go back there again. She stared at the telephone sitting on the coffee table. FATBOY's looking for us, she thought for the fiftieth time. Probably with orders to shoot on sight. Why don't we do the right thing, and turn ourselves in?

Because, she reminded herself, we're destroyed with shock.

Chantelle and the media expert wound up their discussion of the connections between computers, satellites, and the datasphere. CNN then launched into another replay of Ross Shelf's crack-up.

They watched titanic fractures zoom and boom through ice. Once again, hushed voices intoned, "The size of France," "A potential rise of a hundred and seventy feet," "If we're lucky, a slow inward creep."

Dan said, "Now it's the incontinent of Antarctica."

"Ha," Grace said tonelessly.

Dan stood, went to the loft's kitchen area, and opened the refrigerator. "Jeremy doesn't eat a lot," he observed.

"Yeah he does," Selma said. "Take-out. Gallons of it." She stared at her tightly clenched hands. "He doesn't cook, though."

"Looks that way," Dan said, eying the refrigerator's skeletal provisions. He extracted a jar of peanut butter. "My parents have to be worried," he remarked. "They live on an island that doesn't get much higher than twenty feet. They'll be swamped, right?"

Grace's gray eyes flickered at him and then back to the TV, the one object she could watch without seeing anything. It was a convenient blur in which to lose herself. "They'll have time to get off," she said. "Father's only exploded four bombs. That's not enough to kill the ice sheet. The WAIS is bigger than you think." Her voice thinned. "It's really huge. Also, winter's coming to Antarctica. The ocean freezes there in winter, so Ross Shelf, what's left of it, isn't going anywhere soon."

Dan sniffed peanut butter. "No Great Flood?"

Grace said, "The soonest it can start is seven months off."

"What they're saying on TV makes it seem like it's already happening," Selma pointed out.

Grace nodded. "Father wants people to think that. He wants a major media spasm. So the reality sinks in."

Dan found a spoon. "Seems like it's sinking in," he said, glancing at the TV. The image had switched to refugees fleeing the coasts of Holland. "People are flipping out."

"Hysteria," Grace said. "Just hysteria."

Selma lit a cigarette. "That's all?" she murmured. "Grace, I don't get it. What's the point of any of this?"

"When it sinks in that Father can do it—that he unquestionably has the power to do it—things go to a different level."

Dan swallowed peanut butter. He asked, "He makes demands?"

"No," Grace said. "This isn't blackmail. He doesn't want anything except attention. And people pay attention when you control their coastlines. When you threaten to redraw the map."

Dan and Selma considered that idea. "He has a real need to make people pay attention," Selma commented.

Grace nodded. "To make them watch," she said.

"To watch?" Dan said.

Grace gestured tiredly at the TV. "Father's staging a show. A giant, unforgettable show."

"Ah," Selma said. "First he's boobytrapping the datasphere. Now Father's in show business. Grace, what was that stuff the news people were talking about? Supposedly, the bombs are watching TV? Looking for 'the Beast'?"

Dan choked on peanut butter. "Jesus!" he gasped, turning to the sink. He filled a glass with water, swallowed some, and yelled, "*What are they looking for?*"

Grace stared at him. Dan swallowed more water. "The bombs," he hissed. "What are they looking for, Grace?"

"Guess," she replied, eyes vacantly drinking in TV.

"Oh my God," Selma whispered. "Do not reproduce? In any form whatsoever? Is that why . . . ?"

Dan blurted, "'Use it to filter the media streams!' Is that it? The bombs are looking for the rabbit? And if they see it, it's ka-boom or something?"

"Tell us!" Selma bellowed.

Grace stared gloomily at the TV. "I was wondering," she said, "when you'd figure it out."

Toby lay paralyzed on the bunk, brain seething. The truck's vibration seemed akin to his mental state. His mind resembled the truck in several ways, he realized. It was mysterious, it held secret compartments, and the part that could think, the part that was trying to understand this, was locked in a very small room.

A nightlight by the corridor door provided the only illumination. Toby couldn't move his body. But he could roll his eyes. He saw built-in metal cabinets and drawers; a small armchair; and bookshelves full of books. Whose books? The titles shimmied, too dim to read. His head leaned on a cushion. Embroidery decorated the fabric. He registered letters, curling beyond his nose.

The letters spelled: "BRIAN IS MY."

BRIAN IS MY . . . What? Toby thought. What is my Brian?

He wished he could move.

The lock clicked in the corridor door. He closed his eyes. His eyelids brightened; someone had turned on a light. The door swung shut. He heard rustles of movement, sounds of breathing. Two people, he guessed. The "aliens"—Drs. Scarf and Trefethen?

Something poked his shoulder, shifting him a few inches. Hands moved his head with the self-assured brusqueness of a medical professional, and touched his eyelids. Toby imagined being deeply unconscious. The eyelids must have given that impression, because Dr. Helen Scarf's voice said, "He's out."

"You're going to keep him out?" Brian's voice asked.

"What do you think?" Helen asked huskily.

Brian said, "I'm surprised you didn't . . . "

Didn't do what? Toby wondered.

"We need him," Helen said. "Because of his friends."

"His brother, Mother. One of them is his brother."

"Whoever they are. They might still be with Grace."

Toby listened to several seconds of tense silence.

"I think Father believes me," Helen whispered.

"It's hard to tell," Brian whispered.

"I'm worried he'll find out that Grace knows where we're going. He'll be so furious with me for having told you."

"Actually, Martha sort of told us. At the restaurant. She said, 'We'll talk Sunday, at my place.'"

"Good," Helen said. "If it's a problem, I'll blame it on her." Their breathing grew tenser. "Why, Brian? Why did you do it? I'm protecting you," she said softly. "The least you can do is give an explanation."

"Mother," Brian said just as softly. "Father's insane."

"He's not!" Helen exclaimed under her breath.

"And you are too."

Toby heard an astonished gasp. Helen then whispered, "How dare you?" Ten seconds crawled by. She said, "The world's been thinking that for under an hour. And already you agree."

"We've known a while, Mother. Ever since Father killed those people. Since the 'tragedy.'" Brian's voice sounded empty now.

"Who? What are you talking about?"

"The team in Antarctica. He murdered them."

"He did not do any such thing!"

"You weren't there, Mother. We were."

"Do you have evidence? Did you see him do it? How did he do it—he created that crevasse, I suppose?"

"Fladgate planted dynamite. We heard a small explosion. It happened two minutes after we passed over the area—Father or Fladgate set it off by radio, just in time for the other traxes to fall through. When the ice bridge went down."

"As I thought. You have no proof."

"Those people knew where we'd been. They knew what we'd done. Father didn't want witnesses—it's completely obvious."

"This," Helen asked, voice heavy with shock, "is why you betrayed us? Because you misunderstood the accident?"

"It wasn't an accident."

"Stress did this to you. It made you hallucinate."

"You're the one hallucinating. You and Martha. You're in so far, you don't even know what's going on."

"Why didn't you tell me you've been dreaming these things?" Toby heard desperation creep into the voice, and wondered if he was the one dreaming these things.

"We didn't have the guts," Brian quavered. "To make a couple of psychotics even crazier."

Silence fell between them. Neither seemed to breathe.

Brian said, with a catch in his voice, "Grace is lucky she got kidnapped."

Helen rasped something that could have been a laugh. A tortured laugh. She said, "But she wasn't kidnapped."

"What?"

"She left us, Brian. Of her own will."

"No." The word came out with an audible tremble.

"She did it because Father and I are insane, I suppose."

"You're making this up. To punish me!"

"Keep your voice down."

"She wouldn't leave me. You're lying, Mother!"

Helen seemed to sniffle. "My poor babies," she moaned. "No, honey. I'm not making it up. She really did—leave us."

Brian started crying. One of them moved clumsily. Brian, Toby thought. He heard a door open, not the corridor door, a side door. Another door opened. Then he heard Helen crying. She seemed to follow Brian. Wracking sobs echoed from the next room. Wherever it was that they'd gone. Great, huge, profound sobs.

Toby opened his eyes. From the corners, he saw a metal bathroom. Through it, in a room that looked much like this room, he glimpsed heaving shoulders. Helen Scarf's shoulders. Was she comforting Brian? Toby suspected she was. Trying to, anyway.

But Brian sounded beyond comfort. Way beyond. Toby rolled his eyes, to scope out the new view from his immobile head. The embroidered cushion lay fully revealed now. The legend stitched in it read:

> BRIAN IS MY
> BOY-TWIN
> AND I LOVE HIM SO!

How terrible, Toby thought. He wondered if Grace had a similar pillow. It struck him as highly likely.

Dan paced around Jeremy's loft. Selma sat on the couch, trying to ignore the TV. Grace, slumped on the couch with chin pressed to chest, was slipping further and further into an uncommunicative funk.

"Okay," Dan said. "I think I get it. Part of it, anyway. The bombs are watching television. And the reason they're watching is because they're looking for something. That something—'the *Beast*'—is the rabbit." He stopped moving, widened his eyes, and sneered. "But you and Brian don't want the bombs to find it. If you did, why make the big deal about filtering it from the media streams? From the programming that goes through satellites and stuff, I guess. You'd use some kind of digital process that cancels the image out, or changes the way it looks, right? So, this must mean that if the bombs see the rabbit—if they see that particular image—they explode. Which means that the rabbit is . . . a kind of high-tech trigger. That's the rabbit's purpose? And it's why your father calls it 'the Beast'?"

"Low-tech," Grace mumbled. "The rabbit is a low-tech trigger."

"Yeah?" Selma said skeptically.

"Yeah," Grace said. "It is. In more ways than one."

Dan said, "The bombs have computers looking for it. If that isn't high-tech, what is?"

Grace said, "Think about how easy it is to use. It's a simple image. All Father has to do is toss it in the media streams. A newspaper photo, a Net graphic, a background visual in some TV program—it's like, fire and forget. Father leaves everything else to the global information system. The datasphere does the rest. Free delivery to the bombs."

Dan frowned. He said, "But it has to be unique, doesn't it? The rabbit has to be the only image of its kind anywhere. At least, the only image of its kind floating around the datasphere. Because if it weren't, you'd risk a random set-off. Wouldn't you?"

Grace said, "Of course. But the reason it's unique isn't high-tech. The opposite. It's a children's drawing."

"I thought so!" Selma exclaimed.

Grace ignored her. She said, "They have other triggers. Things the bombs are looking for, on TV. They're more high-tech than the rabbit. The rabbit, it's backup. It's a last resort. If they're on the run or something, and don't have time to use the high-tech system. The rabbit's so simple. Fire and forget."

"But why?" Selma said. "Why call it 'the Beast'?"

"Because the rabbit's an icon. It's more than a trigger, see. If Father just needed a trigger, all he'd have to do is make a phone call. Send E-mail. Fax. Page. Whatever . . . "

"An icon," Dan said reflectively. "The rabbit's the 'primitive' face? What's the 'scientific' one?"

"You don't want to know," Grace replied.

Dan rubbed his face. "That pin isn't like a billboard," he muttered. "It's tiny. Even if the bombs have megacomputers, how are they supposed to see the rabbit? Against the background of global TV?"

Grace said, "Pattern recognition software. Anything that resembles the rabbit, even remotely, goes into a special processor. The processor enhances the image—taking into account lighting conditions, angles, all kinds of possible distortions. It's powerful software. So powerful that, theoretically, if the bombs get even a brief glimpse, they'll make a match in nanoseconds."

Selma shivered. She said, "Low-tech, huh? I still don't get it. What's the point?"

"I told you," Grace replied. "Father's staging a show. The rabbit's a prop. It's part of his show."

Selma asked, "How does it end, this show?"

"That I can't tell you," Grace said. "Nobody knows how it'll end. Not even Father." She took a roll of lozenges from her purse. "Excuse me. Have to take one of these. For my ulcers."

"Gutzyme," Selma said, reading the roll's label. "All right, Grace. If the rabbit's a trigger, and it can be filtered from the 'media streams,' the 'datasphere,' whatever you call it—why don't we phone FAT-BOY? And blow the whistle?"

Grace took a deep breath, and said, "Because it won't work. There is only one thing we can try to do. And that's save Brian."

Dan stared at her. He said, "What about Toby?"

Grace gave him a businesslike glance. "Toby too," she said.

"How?" Dan said.

"We get another car," Grace said. "We drive to where they're going. And then, I play my parents against each other."

"Brilliant," Selma remarked. "Why didn't I think of it?"

"Where are they going?" Dan asked.

"I'm not telling you that," Grace said. "Yet."

"Grace," Selma growled in a menacing tone Dan hadn't heard her use before, "do you know how many times, over the last two hours, I've stopped myself from picking up a phone and calling the cops?"

Grace said, "Actually, I'm amazed you haven't."

"I'm doing it!" Selma declared. "I'm sick of sitting around waiting for Jeremy to show up. All he'd do is call the cops—it doesn't take a genius to know that that's what we have to do! And don't get the gun. It was cute at first. It isn't now."

"Take it," Grace said. "I hate guns." She pulled it from her purse and thrust it at Selma.

Selma glared at her. Then, grimacing, she took the gun.

"But you're not calling the cops," Grace said authoritatively.

"Why not?" Selma demanded.

"Three reasons," Grace replied. "First, I'll describe what FATBOY will do to you if they interrogate you, using techniques to get things from your brain you don't know are there. Second, the filter won't work. It's Brian's idea. Like most of his ideas, it's full of holes."

"That's a pity," Dan said. "How come?"

Grace said, "Too many satellites. The geostationaries alone—lots of those with Antarctic footprints. Then you have low earth orbiters with shifting footprints. Various countries and corporations control them. Who's going to administer filtration?"

"They have reasons to cooperate," Selma said.

Grace nodded. "But the information industry is gigantic. How could they filter every media stream?" She shrugged. "Complicating it is the fact that many satellites aren't remote-programmable. To get some kind of filter working, I mean. You can't just press buttons. You'd have to shut them down. Almost all of them."

"What's wrong with that?" Dan asked.

"The bombs explode," Selma said. "They hate reception interruption. Just like the rest of us, they're completely hooked on the data-sphere. Right, Grace?"

"Speak for yourself," she said. "I wouldn't mind never seeing TV again."

"So is Brian stupid?" Dan demanded.

"No," Grace said sullenly. "He's in denial. And he'd like to make Father look stupid. But he can't. Father's too smart."

"The world's fucked," Dan said. "That's what you're saying?"

"Uh-huh." With mournful certitude, Grace sighed. "It is."

Selma lit another cigarette. To Dan she said, "What if she's lying? What if Brian's a genius? And we can, like, do the heroism thing? Squish the Beast? Save the world?"

Grace flicked a fingernail at specks on her dress. "I hate to say this," she remarked, studying air in the middle distance. "You know how in movies, something big is about to explode? Something like a nuclear core, or a missile launch? And a gong is counting down with loud, emergency clangs—Ten! Nine! Eight! Seven . . . "

"Yeah?" Dan said.

"That's what the world is. Now that Father's wired it . . ." Grace peeled off another Gutzyme and popped it in her mouth. "He's made it a self-destruct machine," she continued, sucking ravenously on the lozenge. "There is no way to stop it. No way at all. Which means it will explode in our faces. While billions watch."

Selma muttered, "You're trying to scare us."

"The truth is scary," Grace remarked.

Dan said, "The third reason not to call the cops?"

"Third," Grace said. "How fond of Toby are you?"

"What a personal question," Dan muttered.

Selma said, "At the moment, I could wring his neck. Why?"

"He'll die," Grace said. "If you don't help me."

"How come?" Dan said.

Grace said, "My parents won't let him go. And it's not safe to be around them. They'll die too, of course."

"Why?" Selma asked.

"You can't do what they're doing, and live very long," Grace replied. "Basically, my family is a suicide pact."

Dan's neck hairs rose. He said, "I guess that's clear. Uh—they're a self-destruct machine?"

"You have no idea how bad it is." Quietly, Grace began to weep.

Toby lay in the truck's loud roar, his mind squirming. Helen had medicated him an hour before. She'd come in with vials and needles; Brian had quieted by then, probably because she'd medicated him as well. The doors were locked. Toby felt helpless, very alone, and terribly sick.

The slow-motion war in his head seemed like psychedelic crash. Major drugs had to be responsible; a ghastly cocktail, given to him hours ago, at the Clinic. The effects were fading. That clued Toby in to their magnitude. Earlier, some kind of buffer, probably an opiate, had screened out the pain. Now it was coming through. His eyes seemed swollen to the size of oranges, his right temple felt crushed, and his brain was saturated with flavors that not only hadn't mixed well—they were leaving new, more toxic aftertastes even as they dissipated.

He remained paralyzed, too. This, he kept thinking, is worse than hell.

The bathroom door clicked. It opened. Toby stared through the blurriness, wanting to shout.

Then he saw who was entering. The sight felt like balm on his poisoned mind. She looked so sexy in that snug little dress. In that chic, head-gripping cap. Makeup rendered her face more adult, almost too perfect; lipstick glowed on her big, hot lips. The pale eyes shone.

How can Grace be here? Toby wondered. She came back? They found her? Brian must be so happy . . .

She sat on the edge of the bunk, her ass touching Toby's leg, her face downcast, giving him the perfect profile. After a few moments, she murmured, "I'm sorry. I'm so sorry."

Huh, Toby thought.

"Do you forgive me?" she asked in the throaty voice he'd heard too few times, but knew so well. A voice subtly different from her brother's. Richer. Softer.

Yes, Toby thought. I forgive you.

She leaned over, and looked directly at him. Or almost directly; from the luminous eyes a pleading energy poured forth. It seemed to graze his cheekbone, and hit the bunk. She licked her lips and said, "Please, Brian. Forgive me."

What? Toby thought.

"I love you," she said. "I was bad, I know it. I shouldn't have run away. And left you here. Poor Brian—all alone."

I'm not him, Toby thought. He wanted to tell her he wasn't, but he couldn't even open his mouth. He wished he could, to kiss her . . . God, how he wanted to kiss her. And hold her.

However, Grace was looking a little weird. She grabbed him by the shoulders and exclaimed, "You know I love you!"

Her stare seemed to miss his face by an inch.

"Brian, talk to me!" she exclaimed. Toby realized what she was addressing. Not him. She was talking to the embroidered cushion next to his head. "Please!" she gasped at it.

Suddenly, Toby knew who she was. No, he thought.

"If you don't forgive me," she said to the cushion, "I'll get upset. Really, really upset!"

Shit, Toby thought.

"I'll do something," the beautiful and terrifying mouth snarled. "Something that'll prove I love you!"

Go away, Toby thought. But the strong body scrambled on him, sinking fingers into his arms, gasping incoherently, crazily at the cushion, at the brother who wasn't there—who wasn't there because his sister wasn't there, and he wanted her back very, very badly—so badly, he'll do anything, Toby realized. Even this.

The crazy boy in the dress slapped his face.

Jesus, Toby thought. Powerful hands rolled him over. They gripped his pajamas, and ripped them.

"I'll show you!" the boy shouted. He slapped Toby's butt, and howled, "Grace left you, didn't she—but now, she's back!"

A door opened. Helen Scarf exclaimed, "Stop it!"

Toby listened to frantic breathing.

"We're busy!" Brian yelled. "Can't you see we're busy?"

"Go back to your room," Helen said.

Brian collapsed onto Toby, hugging him. Hugging him desperately, and much too intimately. The sensation horrified Toby. It amazed him, too.

"I miss Brian," Brian moaned into Toby's hair. "Don't I?"

"Yes, honey. Grace misses Brian—very, very much. Now go back to your room. And I'll bring you something nice."

Holy shit, Toby thought. They really are aliens.

Mary McMurtry, director general of the Federal Anti-Terror Bureau, sat in a high-ceilinged room with sweeping views of the Potomac River, National Airport, and various of Washington, D.C.'s historical monuments. It was 11:33 Saturday night. Brilliantly lit bridges partitioned the Potomac into darkling arcs. The airport's blue-latticed runways winked in the distance. As if confected from sugar, edifices dedicated to Thomas Jefferson, Abraham Lincoln, and George Washington rose incandescently from the blacks of their respective parks.

High definition videoscreens provided these vistas. But pinpoints swooping toward National belonged to real-time aircraft, and ribbons of pearl and ruby on the highways to real-time vehicles. The videoscreens had been made as windowlike as possible; to dispel the claustrophobia that otherwise would have enveloped an office buried thirty stories below ground level.

McMurtry wasn't paying attention to her views. A monitor adjacent to the desk displayed General Theodore Raffenelli, face ruddied with stress, sitting in his office at FATB regional headquarters in Boston. He'd just come onscreen. It was his first face-to-face with the DG since the night's disastrous finale.

Hilton Decter, McMurtry's young executive assistant, sat on a leather couch out of range of the teleconference camera. McMurtry had invited him onscreen. Decter had declined. Not only was he occupied with several microcomputers spread across the couch. Raffenelli, he'd pointed out, would have enough trouble dealing with the boss's contemptuous stare. Why subject the man to Decter's?

McMurtry's would more than suffice. The tiny woman's hair, lacquered as always into a kind of Napoleonic hat, put wings on a face that could shatter concrete. To the general she said, "Report."

"Ms. Director General," Raffenelli said, "Trefethen and Scarf continue to elude us. But based on findings from witnesses . . . "

"The witnesses are going to Amarillo?" Decter interrupted. He referred to the Clinic's sister facility in Texas.

Raffenelli heard the question. McMurtry's face told him to answer it. He said, "As we speak. They include a photographer who took pictures of the kidnappings in Harvard Square, and bystanders at incidents involving the man we believe to be Slotsky . . . "

"Any Slotsky leads?" Decter said.

"Not much," replied the general. "A man who lives behind the Swett-Swearingen apartment building saw the man we think is Slotsky fall from the third-floor porch. Agents searched the yard. No sign of Slotsky—trash bins broke his fall. We found blood on the bins, and in the yard. Results of blood ID tests are pending."

"The 'code' Miles Malt tried to sell Agent Whipple? According to Whipple's notes, Malt claimed it's in a pen?" Decter spoke with rapid-fire bluntness. Jacked into the Bureau's Boston datawork, he already knew the answers to his questions. He posed them to remind the general he was under very close scrutiny.

"No trace. But we're looking."

"I'm done with him," Decter said.

Raffenelli's jaw muscles bunched. McMurtry regarded him thoughtfully. "Ted," she said. "Do you have more to tell me?"

"Yes, Ms. Director General. I tender my resignation." Raffenelli swallowed, eyes glistening. "With sorrow, regret, and . . . "

"Shut up," McMurtry said. Swiveling her chair, she gazed at the Potomac's dark arabesque. "Your status is under review, General. My decision regarding it depends largely on one thing." She swiveled back, looking him in the eyes. "Find Trefethen and Scarf. Do it quickly, you'll be all right. If you don't—you're in serious difficulty. Very serious difficulty. Good night." She clicked off. The monitor blanked. To Decter she said, "I was due at the White House half an hour ago."

"Yes," Decter said, accessing a new dataspread on one of his computers. "Analysis, Ms. Director General?"

"Yeah," McMurtry said. She turned her notetaker to "Record."

Decter looked up from the computer. He clasped his hands in his lap, closed his eyes, raised his eyebrows, opened his eyes, and said, eyebrows still raised—eyes cold sapphires below them—"Trefethen has created a bomb. A vast, intricate bomb."

McMurtry exhaled softly. "The nukes?" she said.

"They're part of it. A small one. This bomb, I'm afraid, is bigger than any nuke ever made. Or even conceived."

"Explain, Hilton. What bomb?"

"It consists of the nukes in Antarctica, of Antarctica itself, of the global information system, and, most crucially, of the worldwide media audience Trefethen now commands. But that's not all. In its totality, this . . . this *device* that he's made—Ms. Director General, it's nothing less than the zeitgeist itself. Trefethen has turned the zeitgeist into a ticking doomsday machine."

McMurtry scowled. She said, "That's what the zeitgeist was a couple years ago, Hilton. When the Frenzy hit."

"Quite so," Decter replied. "But there is a difference between then and now. The Frenzy was a confluence of historical forces over which no one person, class, or nation had any control. It was a social combustion, so to speak—that various trends fueled. Mostly, fear fueled it."

"We stamped it out," McMurtry remarked.

"We did," Decter said. "However, the public hasn't gotten over it. Millennarian insecurities, a readiness to buy into notions of Apocalypse, are still widespread."

McMurtry said impatiently, "You sound like you're quoting one of the President's speeches. What are you getting at?"

"We repressed the Frenzy, yes, but the fear that made it happen is still there—in explosively compressed form. That is the warhead of Trefethen's bomb. All he has to do is ignite it."

"Absurd!" McMurtry declared. "You're saying Earnest can take us back to the Frenzy? Just by striking a match?"

"Hold on," Decter said smoothly. "To pursue the bomb metaphor, consider this. How does he detonate his device? He causes a major, possibly rapid, sea level rise."

"We don't know if he can do it," McMurtry said dismissively.

"If anyone can, he can. Let's assume he can."

"All right," McMurtry muttered.

"Keep in mind the potency of flood myths. The Great Flood, Atlantis—they deal with the 'cleansing effects of water.' That is, with the erasure of mankind's sinful ways. This I suspect is Trefethen's objective. He wants to change what he perceives to be our sinful ways. Which amounts to exploding the status quo."

McMurtry stared glumly at the Washington Monument. "We live in explosive times," she said. "You're saying Earnest can make that fact his personal bomb?"

"Exactly what I'm saying. As he so spectacularly demonstrated tonight, he controls a media event of monumental proportions. But more important, and more frightening, he's customized the bomb's detonation system. In a way that will send a message."

McMurtry smiled archly. "'The Beast,' I assume?"

"Of course," Decter said.

"Mumbo-jumbo," McMurtry muttered. "You think he'll get any-where with . . . with media voodoo? How is anyone supposed to know what he means? I doubt even he knows what he . . . ."

"Ms. Director General, I respectfully submit that Trefethen already has told us what he means. Indirectly, but quite cunningly. At the Mif-flin Place dinner party."

"Oh, yes?" McMurtry said, surprised. "How?"

"I and other staff have spoken with all six attendees of that dinner. They called, over the last hour and a half, wanting to speak with you. You've been too busy, of course." Decter joined hands under his chin. "But there is something you should know. They report that Trefethen, at the dinner, alluded to 'the Beast.' He said it consists of 'two evils facing mankind.' One is overpopulation. The other is 'technology in the service of greed.'"

Irritably, McMurtry exhaled. "Earnest has been talking about those things for years."

Decter nodded. "No one listened. So he found a way to make them. And he used the 'retirement party' to launch his campaign."

McMurtry stared at Decter. "I was supposed to attend."

"But you didn't. And Trefethen knew you wouldn't. He knew you'd be occupied with the first Antarctica explosion." Decter studied per-fect creases in his trousers. "Which gave him latitude to be more dar-ing than he otherwise could have been."

"Daring?"

Decter nodded. "I spoke at length with Martha Cliffcloud. She said that at the dinner, Trefethen came close to confessing he was behind the 'eruption.' In retrospect, she said, she should have suspected his involvement. Had you been there—well. We might have interrogated him before he went on Barclay. Cliffcloud feels dreadful about it. So does Senator Molloy."

"But who could have suspected? I'm reeling with shock!"

Decter said impassively, "In their youth, Ms. Director General, both Trefethen and Scarf were quite radical, politically. Radicals of the first water, I believe."

"An unfortunate way to put it." She grunted with exasperation. "Their youth, that was thirty-five years ago. A different era! Why, I was a so-called radical back then. In the late '60s. Hilton, wrap it up. How did Earnest use the dinner party?"

"First, he made comments that deeply spooked the six guests. That laid the groundwork for today's rumors of a cover-up in Antarctica. Which in turn delivered a huge audience for tonight's *Barclay Piston Show*."

McMurtry said, "I'm putting Barclay away. For good. Go on."

"The people at the dinner—Senator Molloy, Ambassador Loring, Reheema Sampson, Lawrence Sforza, Piston, and Cliffcloud—all feel they are in possession of privileged information. They think they know what everyone in the world is wondering. Namely, what the 'two faces of the Beast' are. Naturally, therefore, they'll talk. What they have to say will be widely reported. And in fact, they've told us that media already are hounding them, demanding comments, wanting details. Which serves Trefethen beautifully."

McMurtry tapped a talon-like fingernail on her desk. "How?"

"Because he doesn't have to spell out his message. Others will do it for him. Those six people at the dinner will do it for him. In effect, they're an unwitting echo chamber. Or to put it differently, unwitting apostles."

"This taxes my credulity, Hilton. I don't see it."

"Think biblically, Ms. Director General. A prophet speaks in grand generalities. He doesn't unfurl his vision with fine print. He lets interpreters—apostles, if you will—do the detail work. This is a well-known aspect of prophet psychology."

"Earnest is setting himself up as a prophet?" McMurtry shook her head. "How will he pull that off?"

Decter smiled. "Prophets deal with symbols. With general symbols. Ones which, by virtue of sheer simplicity, lend themselves to deep interpretations. Think of the cross. Of the richness of meaning seen by those who revere that very simple image."

McMurtry reached for the gold crucifix hanging on a fine chain from her neck. "The two-faced Beast," she murmured. "You theorize he has a particular symbol in mind?"

"I do," Decter replied. "The technical term, by the way, is 'condensation symbol.' Such symbols are among the most potent artifacts of human cosmology. The cross, the swastika, national flags—these are things into which humans are fully capable of reading whole world-views."

"That's quite a theory, Hilton."

"With much to back it up," he insisted. "Why else would Trefethen propel the public into a guessing game about the 'face of the Beast'? Why else would he make the assertion that nukes in Antarctica are combing the datasphere, looking, looking, looking for that face? Thereby motivating the public to follow suit? That is, to watch TV— searching for signs of the Beast? Wondering what they are, where they are. And therefore beholding the spectacle of this crisis not only with dread, but intense fascination."

McMurtry sniffed. "People are curious, of course," she said.

"More than curious. They're being conditioned to think that television will reveal the devil. Which, I'm arguing, sets them up for buying into a dangerous symbology. A symbology that Trefethen wants to foist on the gullible, frightened public."

"Do you have any idea what Earnest's symbol might be?"

"No. The actual symbol he plans to use—or symbols, he could use more than one—I've no idea what they are."

"You're making me queasy, Hilton. I don't like it."

"I'm afraid the implications get worse. As it stands now, we have no way to stop Trefethen from causing a Great Flood. A real one, in the physical world—but one which he'll manipulate the public into thinking is the product of his 'Beast.' That is, of his cockamamie notions of mankind's sin. In other words, he is poised to force his radical ideology on a world that's so superstitious, it just might buy it, and go berserk. The Luddies alone . . . "

McMurtry shoved her notetaker across the desk. "Abstractions!" she shouted. "I want *facts*. Let's deal with facts, Hilton. What do I tell the President? If you have something besides elaborate theory, give it to me—bullet-point!"

"First," Decter said inflectionlessly. "The Russians are worried about climate shift. The President should know that we also have reasons to worry. The Northern Hemisphere could plunge into an ice age, or turn to dust in scorching drought, or be flattened by storms far more destructive than any we've ever seen."

"Could," McMurtry said. "The operative word is *could*."

"The fact of the matter is, the Russians are terrified, which is worth bearing in mind. Now, fact number two. The Net message Trefethen said he was sending out. He did send it. However, it's encrypted, and he hasn't provided the decrypt key. But he will."

"Why would he do it that way? Send it out encrypted?"

"To prove his authorship of future messages. It's a technical issue. The salient fact is, the message is long. Very long. Which means it's video."

"Lovely," McMurtry muttered. "In millions of computers around the world. Next fact?"

"He warned against tampering with satellites. Unfortunately, such tampering would be difficult. We neither own nor control them all, to begin with. Then there is the problem of disrupting global telecommunications. That would add to the panic we're seeing, which in my view has reached unacceptable levels. We're getting reports of Luddite unrest across the country. New York City is dealing with a riot situation right now."

McMurtry glanced at her videoscreens. "Washington isn't."

"Washington is a military installation," Decter pointed out. "And has been since we started relocating the blacks."

"What else?"

"Our best chance to resolve this is catching Trefethen and making him defuse the bombs. Until we do that, let us hope quickly, I advise two courses of action. One, we try to rattle him. We drop hints suggesting we have leads on where he's hiding, for example. We also could drop hints that we're close to finding his daughter. That I think would shake him up."

"Maybe. The other course of action?"

"The President must address the nation. Soon. He must attempt to rally public opinion to attitudes of calm and reason. Ms. Director General, I cannot emphasize too strongly that this is more than a contest over coastlines. I believe it to be a contest for world sanity. Social order, the stability of government rule—we could lose it." Decter gestured at the nightime panorama of the federal capital. "If Trefethen puts Washington underwater . . . he won't drown it. He'll blow it sky high."

PART 3
SUNDAY

The New York Times, front page:

SEA LEVEL CRISIS
ROILS WORLD
NUCLEAR BOMBS
DEMOLISH ANTARCTICA'S
ROSS ICE SHELF
"ERUPTION" IN ICE SHEET REVEALED
TO BE WORK OF A BOMB
FOUR EXPLOSIONS AND COUNTING—
SEVEN MORE ON THE WAY?

The Boston Sunday Globe:

NUKES IN ANTARCTICA
SEEK "BEAST"
"TWO FACES": OVERPOPULATION,
HIGH TECHNOLOGY?
Cambridge dinner party provides clues

The Daily News:

MAD PROF TURNS
WORLDWIDE TV
INTO CYBERBOMB!

The Lure Of The Litchfield Hills:

COASTAL INHABITANTS FLEE
WARNING, WARNING, WARNING:
THEY ARE HEADED FOR HIGH GROUND
THIS MEANS US!

Sunday dawned gloriously over the storybook hills of Cheswick, Connecticut. On the knolls and in the valleys, along the undulating banks of the Piscatawny River, around the occasional lake, around the lawns of secluded residences and the confines of Cheswick Village itself, the sun lit the early-spring lime of awakening trees. Of many, many awakening trees, for Cheswick consisted largely of forest.

Located in the northwestern portion of the state, the township had been founded in the mid-1700s to accommodate colonial agricultural ambitions. It remained a patchwork of farms, struggling up hill and down dale, through the nineteenth century. By the early twentieth, however, many of those farms had gone bust, victims of competition from more fertile land to the west. The population shrank. Fields and pastures, painstakingly cleared of forest and rock by ox-driving Yankees, reverted to the woods of pre-European times. The old clapboard farmhouses, many rambling and some stately, witnessed a spectacle that products of human labor always witnessed when the labor quit—nature's relentless reclamation of land.

With the arrival of the 1920s, this state of affairs had progressed to the point where numerous properties of a hundred acres or more lay abandoned, vacant except for the invading trees, and for sale. Prospects didn't look good. At the time a grinding six-hour drive from New York City, Cheswick didn't fit the era's idea of a vacation spot. To the average Manhattan rake it might as well have been over the Continental Divide; somewhere in, say, Wyoming. The dirt roads wending through its hills became mud gullies every spring, glaciers every winter. Why brave such an obstacle course to get to a place where nothing ever happened?

For a segment of New York's cultural set—writers, professors, intellectual types, mostly—that question, it turned out, contained its own answer.

These people led fast and furious lives in places like Greenwich Village. They dined out at different restaurants every night of the week. Over kitchen tables they plotted the smuggling-in of *Ulysses*. Marxism they took seriously, they read *The Masses* and consorted with Mike

Gold; they spelunked the murky realms of Freud and Jung. And they practiced free love, or so they thought, as they flouted the Victorian prudery that had ruled their rather immediate pasts. They edited, they wrote, they talked, talked, talked, the while drinking tubfuls of gin. In short, these people needed a respite from city life. They craved a place where nothing ever happened.

They wanted a locale with "no there there." Cheswick fit the bill, in more ways than one.

The first pioneers numbered two or three households. Relations with the locals posed a bit of a problem; no one understood what these dissolute slickers thought they were doing. Not farming a living, of that the locals were certain. But after a few homesteads had been revitalized, and accounts had been written about the experience, and more New Yorkers had braved the ordeal, a community, a brainy and self-confident bohemia, was established in Cheswick's woody hills. The locals grew used to it. After all, these lunatics meant revenue.

Time passed. The war came, and went. More New Yorkers bought Cheswick getaways. The roads improved, the economy expanded, and gradually the summer/weekend colony changed. In addition to the writers and artists of the first wave, doctors, lawyers, stockbrokers, and the generic rich started acquiring big old houses with lots of land. The price of real estate went up, way up. By the '70s it became hard to buy in Cheswick. Nobody wanted to sell. Everyone wanted to preserve the township's in-the-wild legend; that legend was the point, of course. By the late '90s, finding a large chunk of land had become virtually impossible. Unless the buyer happened to be very rich, and rather lucky.

Thereness had arrived, with gusto, in no-there-there.

So it was that when the sun rose over Cheswick's bright-lime hills that springtime Sunday, bringing day two, the first full day, of the Antarctica Sea Level Crisis, the township's culture already had been conditioned to be wary of city people. To be wary, that is, of people from the restless and populous coast.

And yet—a coastal mob seemed most assuredly on its way.

Catastrophic collapse. Tidal waves. The stealthy slow inward creep, and the Beast, the *Beast*—what did this mean?

It was perfectly obvious what it meant. Like rats deserting a sinking ship, every last desperado in the city was headed for Cheswick's hills, armed to the teeth and ready to use any means, including rape, torture, and murder, to seize high ground. Serbian-style. Maybe even Algerian-style.

Kotzler's in Cheswick Village had sold out of shotguns, indeed of every kind of gun, by seven-thirty in the morning.

Gula Gance, high up on Yank Hill several miles away and surrounded in all directions by dense woods, found this fact appalling. "You mean I need a shotgun?" she screeched over the phone to Floyd Kotzler. A liver-spotted hand fluttered at her throat. Rheumy eyes glared through kitchen windows at green lawns and thirsty gardens. At the age of ninety-four, widowed and alone except for Constance and Harry, who helped keep the place in order, Gula couldn't imagine fighting off refugee hordes. Suppose they wanted sandwiches? Could they expect her to make so many sandwiches? The thought induced a fit of the trembles.

"I don't know, Gula," Floyd said. "That's what people are saying. That they're heading our way lickety-split, scared and miserable and madder than hell."

"Oh, no," Gula moaned. She wasn't up to this.

"We've been lucky so far," Floyd observed. "What with the country gone straight to the devil. Guess our luck's run out."

"They'll trample the garden," Gula said with deadly earnestness. "And they'll devour the vegetable garden. Just eat it raw, worse than deer on a hungry night—it's a good thing nothing's grown yet. I want a shotgun, Floyd. Three of them. One for Harry, one for Constance, and one for me."

"Now, Gula," Floyd said. "A gun like that would knock you right over. And you know it."

"That's what you think, Floyd," Gula said in her high-strung warble. "You're not sold out. How many can you give me?"

"That Constance girl. She's fit to use a gun?"

"No," Gula replied. "She doesn't even know what goes where in the refrigerator." Gula happened to be highly precise about what went where in her refrigerator. She was the same about everything in her house; as a succession of Constances had learned, over the years. "But Harry'll teach her. He'll get 'em today."

"Gula," Floyd grumbled. "I really don't have any more guns. Say, did you hear about the message?"

"What message?"

"The nut who blew up the ice shelf sent a message out on the Net. In code. But he just released the decrepit key."

"What is a decrepit key?" Gula asked.

"Uncodes the code. Don't you watch TV?"

"Floyd," Gula squeaked. "It's eight-fifteen in the morning!"

"Yep," he said. "Gula, I don't know what the key is, either. Some computer thing. Anyway, seems the message is going on TV any minute. Maybe the nut'll explain himself. What the Beast is. Why it's sneaking around on television." Feverishness crept into Floyd's voice as he added, "I'm worried. There's talk—ugly, crazy talk. We're in trouble, dear. This could be it."

"What do you mean?"

"Civil war. Us against the coast. That McMurtry lady—the one who shoots terrorists—she's having a press conference at ten. Don't miss it."

"I'm not watching," Gula said, wrinkles deep with dismay. "Have to go, Floyd. Bye."

Gula hauled herself to her feet, clutching the kitchen table for support. Floyd's call was the latest of many. The phone hadn't stopped all morning, bringing doom, gloom, and the Beast. She was sick of it. Anyhow, she needed to get out to the garden. That's harder and harder to do these days, she thought impatiently.

Old age. A disaster. Everything required so much work. However, she would advance on the weeds. She'd visit upon them the destruction they so richly deserved. Off with their heads!

Gula hobbled across the kitchen to the marble-topped bread table, above which, on the shelf where she kept certain supplies, the citronella oil lived. With slightly vibrating but deft movements she unstoppered the bottle, soaked two cotton balls with the pungent oil, and stuffed them in her ears. Then she smeared more oil over her skinny arms. Where was her hat? She grabbed it from the table, a frayed bamboo coolie hat that, with the citronella, would keep bugs at bay. Through the windows the lawn and trees waggled at her, a beckoning immensity of green. Gula felt keenly the garden's scolding. Like a needful friend, it couldn't be ignored for long. With Harry, and Chucky some days, and a crew of others for the big jobs, she was its life-support machine.

As long as I'm able, she thought with the bleakness of an old lady who knew not how long that might be.

A faint drone penetrated the kitchen. "Dammit," Gula said. She went through the dining room to the door to the porch, the door she mostly used to get outside, although she had five in all. From the porch, she scowled at the sky. There it was, a mile away over the ridge, that infernal helicopter. Martha herself at the controls, no doubt. She always patrolled for a half hour or so when arriving in Cheswick. Why, Gula wondered. To scare her deer? To count her trees?

Martha Cliffcloud she'd always considered a glorified thief. That land of hers, over the ridge beyond Gula's woods—it used to be a state forest, all six and a half square miles of it, until Cliffcloud's billionaire husband, now dead, made a deal with a bunch of crooked Hartford politicians. Sure, he'd given the state thirty miles of land near the coast; marshland mostly, and useless. Sure, he'd moved his laser factories to New Haven, creating jobs, paying taxes. The fact of the matter was that Gula's hundred acres once had abutted a lovely state forest. Now they abutted an oligarch's fortified private domain. A disgrace, in Gula's opinion. Even if Cliffcloud was part Native American.

Gula inspected her outfit, an assortment of shabby and wildly colored gardening clothes, items no longer fit for her evening wardrobe. She asked herself, Do I cut a striking figure?

She did. Harry would get an eyeful today.

The cart waited by the porch steps. On the way with Harry to the Torrington showroom to look at it last year, she'd expected something like a golf cart, a contraption for fat slobs, and had sworn she never in a million years would buy anything so useless and effete. Harry had listened stoically, as was his way with Gula's outbursts. He'd known, she suspected, that she would come to like the cart. In any case, pragmatic man that he was, he knew she shouldn't pay him good money to wheelbarrow her up and down the hill, now that she couldn't make it on her own. That, of course, had been the reason for Gula's fit en route to the showroom. The cart business made her feel helpless. Weak.

Something else bore on the matter. Gula rather enjoyed being wheelbarrowed about by Harry. In fact, she could spend her whole day watching him push her from arbor to orchard to pond.

But if barrowing were all she and Harry ever did, the garden would degenerate to jungle, something Gula would allow literally over her dead body. She got in the low-slung cart and checked the tool bins. All seemed where it should be. The telephone caught her eye; she turned the switch to off. No cart-calls today, the usual gossip and scandal would just distract her, besides which everybody would bend her ear with tales of invasion and flood. And the Beast. And the Net. What was that, some kind of video tennis?

Gula had decided how to deal with this crisis. And she didn't want to talk about it. Because as far as she was concerned, if the Beast did its worst . . . well, life would be that much shorter. No great loss. She had about ten minutes left anyway.

She started the electric motor and headed across the lawn to the hill. Gula kept gardens around the house and the barns, and along the stone wall that bordered the lower lawn out front. But the centerpiece of her existence lay in the downhill sweep of the rock garden behind the house. Wildflowers would bloom there soon. Exotic wildflowers, that she and her late husband had brought back from various parts of the world. In a week or so—too early, by Gula's reckoning; spring had arrived with peculiar aggressiveness this year—they'd cascade over boulders and ledges to the forest-edged field at the bottom.

Huddled before the wheel of her sleek machine, coolie-hat bobbing as she peered anxiously in all directions, Gula knew she presented something of a spectacle descending the hill's lawn lane. Nonetheless, she felt like Cleopatra in her barge. The garden was the Nile flowing around her. Sliding through its mossy shimmer, she made a procession royal, a procession to battle. To epic battle, in a glade at the bottom by the frog pond, where, under dogwoods and surrounded by the first peeps of yellow lady slippers, she would vanquish the enemy. She would slaughter weeds—off with their heads!

Gula caught sight of something in the frog pond.

She stopped the cart and stared. Befuddled, she removed her glasses, polished them, and put them back on. Still she saw what she thought she'd seen. Binoculars were stashed somewhere, to birdwatch if something special appeared. Gula rummaged through a stowbin, snatched up the binoculars, and trained them on the pond.

"I'll be damned," she muttered as the image unblurred, and the objects of her attention turned carnally crisp. She made the cart creep forward, slowly now, to soften the engine's whine. Harry, she recollected, was out in the woods doing maintenance on the water supply. Constance was dusting the study, or running a wash. Gula considered using the cart's telephone. But by the time anyone got here from the village, she might well be a goner, strangled in her fancy cart. If this turned into trouble.

Somehow, though, she thought as she crept down the hill, closer, closer to the shady pond, this doesn't seem like trouble. Two youths, nude; wading in her pond like something out of Rossetti. Exactly like something out of Rossetti, or Parrish. Gula caught sight of a metallic glint by the water. Radio, she thought. Are they listening, she wondered, to something romantic and faunish? That boy, she noticed, is quite some faun. A hunk of faun, slender with rank youth, but nicely muscled. And the girl—her alabaster skin, mighty limbs, and yet mightier jet-black hair, seemed altogether—Amazonian.

Gula nosed down a path that turned from the hill through bushes and trees to the pond. The trespassers hadn't registered her presence. Why would they, besotted as they were in their glimmering glade? My glade, Gula reminded herself. The radio, she discerned, wasn't playing music. It played news. Ugh, Gula thought. Why ruin this with news? She was about to beep her horn, to let them know the law had arrived, when she heard a voice say, "Hold it."

She looked around. An unearthly child, clothed in a stained gown and looking desperate, had stepped from behind a tree.

Gula cleared her throat. She said, "What the hell are you doing with that gun, my dear?"

"Heads up, you two!" the girl shouted at the naked ones. Gula sensed condemnation in the voice. Does this beautiful girl, she wondered, disapprove of nudity? The pond children peered. Abruptly, they started scrambling into clothes.

"What's the matter?" Gula asked the blond gunslinger. "Feeling left out?"

The girl swallowed a sharp reply. She came closer, studying the cart's controls. Studying the phone, Gula realized. "I'm sorry," the girl muttered as she took the receiver. "I can't let you use this."

Gula didn't argue. She watched the tall girl pull on a gigantic circus-style boot. Purple, Gula noted admiringly; those boots equaled anything she had in the attic. They looked a little scuffed. From tramping through her woods? Gula supposed they'd keep the ticks off, at least. The boy ran up barefoot, jeans on, shirt open. Gula inspected the smooth chest, the washboard tummy; the guileless and quite cute face, the tousled brown hair with turquoise in it. He'd make, she decided, a good wheelbarrower. A more than adequate barrower. If he didn't murder her.

He exclaimed to the girl with the gun, "Grace, put it away!"

Distantly, the helicopter droned. The blond with sleepless gray eyes winced at the sky, then moved under a dogwood's shade, gun arm slack now. She called to the girl by the pond—who was struggling with her other boot—"Get out of sight, Selma!"

Gula inquired with interest, "Don't tell me you're on the run from Martha?"

The boy and the girl exchanged nervous glances. "You know her?" the blond asked with a twitch.

Gula nodded. "She's not looking over here," she said. "If that's what's got you so frightened. Why are you, by the way, so frightened?"

Martha swung the chopper into another pass through the valley. The lake at the east end reflected woods, putting a lime iris around the blue-gray center. Knobby hilltops, too rocky to vegetate, protruded from forest. The other flanking hills rose and fell like mounded cushions, upholstered in the sallow green. Her house lay directly below the western ridge, on a plateau that jutted over the valley's oval, four-mile floor. Flat lawns and ocher walls made the plateau an orderly end table in a vast, unruly room. That isn't, Martha reflected, how the ancestors saw this landscape. But then, who knew what those people thought?

She didn't. Sometimes she pretended, even to herself, that she did. Not today, though. Today was full of modern exigency. The trouble with Helen, for instance.

Martha recalled Earnest's tensely spoken words of the night before, when he'd phoned from the truck. Grace was missing. Due to kidnapping or defection, he wasn't sure which. More incredible still, she and Brian had stolen the original of the fertility icon.

Earnest suspected Helen hadn't told the full story. He wasn't even sure that Grace didn't know, from Helen's loose lips, about coming to Cheswick. A troublesome uncertainty. To say the least.

Martha hated the prospect of landing and finding more trouble. She therefore had lingered longer than usual, roaring up and down her secret realm. She thought of it as secret because, on the ground from the outside, no one could see the fairy-tale valley folded in these hills. Arugula Gance, the ancient creature over the ridge, probably could hear her, however. Several residents over there probably were cursing the chopper that very moment.

Fuck 'em, Martha thought. They'd have lots to complain about shortly. The prospect drew her mind to the question of defense.

Many people soon would have cause to complain a good deal. Those people would blame her, and try to take it out of her hide, if Grace squealed. Defense, if Grace squealed, would become crucial very quickly.

Martha pulled the chopper around. The road winding up to the plateau was nearly invisible now, under newly burgeoning trees. Excellent, she thought. Enemies shouldn't know the lay of that road. She pressed buttons, accessing the computer in the control room at the house. She'd checked in already, as always on approach. But she hadn't run a status review.

Data flooded her screen. Firetowers were functional, at optimum power. Almost all sensors—the road's, the perimeter's, the plateau's—were functional. Air surveillance was functional. Martha skipped the wildlife report. Now wasn't the time to look at animal counts. Systems in the house, around it, on the ridge looming over it—all were go.

Finally, the zappers were go. Not only go, but going. That was important, because Martha detested most bugs. Especially gnats, mosquitoes, and flies. Dragonflies she tolerated. Her sensors didn't target them, when they appeared in late summer. She loved bumblebees, she loathed yellow jackets; the sensors discriminated accordingly. Butterflies were welcome, but moths weren't, nor bats. As for birds, Martha adored birds. The sensors ignored them, except bluejays and crows, which had learned not to visit. Mosquitoes, gnats, and flies, however—those pesty bastards didn't get anywhere near the house. They fried when they tried.

And they did, of course, try, particularly as the sun dropped behind the western ridge. At that time of day, an eerily gorgeous light show flickered through the shrubs and lawns on the plateau jutting over

Martha's sunset-reddened valley. She often thought that the system's ability to detect the tiniest of flying creatures, its ability to distinguish between them, and its pinpoint accuracy in hitting them—erasing the hapless things from existence with hair-thin bolts of light—represented the single most useful application of technology she'd ever devised.

All looked very much go. Martha took the chopper into a dive. The plateau grew bigger, its lawns broader, and the ocher octagon sitting there gradually ceased to be something decorative on a small tabletop, at the far end of an enormous and unruly room. As Martha came closer, it revealed its size.

Earnest sat under a parasol in the courtyard garden, watching fountains splash, leaves quiver, and lasers play. With the bug population inactive at this hour of the morning, there wasn't much reason for the lasing. There isn't ever, he considered, a lot of bug activity in this courtyard; not of the flyer-biter variety, at least. Could Martha be so enamored of her apparatus, he wondered, that she'd programmed it to lase imaginary bugs? Now that it had made the courtyard, ha-ha, a no-fly zone?

He would ask Martha if the courtyard firetowers, designed to resemble fashionable sculpture, were zapping away just for the fun of it. Or could they be zapping to maintain readiness? Combat readiness, perhaps?

Earnest wasn't prepared to think about that. The courtyard, octagonal like the single-story edifice enclosing it, measured one hundred feet across. In the center lay a circular mosaic that Martha had lifted from an ancient villa near Florence. Appropriately, it depicted Vesuvius heaving fire to the heavens, in the process entombing Pompeii. Shrubwork ringed the mosaic, emphasizing the concentricity of the design. The house, itself a grand ring of neo-Classical stucco, rose twenty feet to the red-tiled, low-pitched roof. The walls of the eastern segments consisted of French doors on both the interior and the exterior, giving a multi-paneled view from the courtyard of the valley and, in the distance, its lake. Those segments held the public rooms. Public rooms, Earnest thought with a mental snort. They were about as public as the National Reconnaissance Office. He imagined them full of guests, nabobs drifting to and fro with cocktails and canapes. How many could fit? A thousand, easily.

What on earth, he wondered, induced me to get involved with someone capable of such piggery?

Money, of course. He'd never have financed Ecologic on the paltry forty million Uncle Herbert had left him. Those millions had been useful, and quite well spent, especially considering their more-than-filthy source, an Oakland, California styrofoam empire. But that money had amounted to less than a drop in the bucket, considering Ecologic's expense, and the cost of the bombs. The question wasn't why he'd allied himself with Martha's billions. The answer couldn't have been more obvious. What puzzled Earnest was how he'd become so fond of the woman.

The thought prompted unsettling reminders of Helen's malaise. Something had gone extremely wrong with her. Earnest knew the root cause wasn't Grace's disappearance. Helen had been coming apart, in unnerving slow motion, for quite a while.

Pressure had cooked her, he supposed. Helen couldn't take the heat. She simply couldn't handle the brute prerequisite of their work—cold-blooded monstrosity.

Martha, however, could handle it. Her helicopter, flitting about like a giant bug making a mockery of the insecticide system, seemed on the way down, at last. Earnest stood, careful to keep the parasol over his head. An orbiting zoom lens could have this courtyard in its crosshairs. He wasn't risking the chance that his gleaming pate might reach somebody's desk at the National Reconnaissance Office. Commercial satellites posed a threat as well; one celebrities ignored at their peril if they wanted their stinking lifestyles under wraps. Did tabloid orbiters have cameras trained on Martha? Probably not. But a competitor might be looking for dirt. If she or he were to see Earnest, he or she certainly would find it.

The helicopter cast a Jurassic shadow over the courtyard. It descended to Vesuvius's belching cone, grit flying in the downdraft. A firm grip on the parasol, Earnest glanced at his watch: 8:43. McMurtry had scheduled a press conference for 10:00, according to CNN. Earnest anticipated her reaction to the coded video he'd sent out on the Net. He had Net-posted the decrypt key—via anonymous re-mailers, to prevent tracing—at 8:30 sharp. Time enough for Mary to have gotten the video decoded. She and her minions surely were studying it that minute. Along with millions of others.

Earnest hunched under the parasol, deflecting gale-force grit. Mary, he reflected, must be thinking hard right now.

━ ━ ━

Brian crouched behind the iron fence of the deck that ran the circumference of the roof's red-tiled octagon. He was watching Father wait for Martha in the courtyard.

The deck, ten feet wide and oak-planked, looked to be a jogging track. It wasn't noticeable from the ground. Due to the roof's shallow slope, Brian figured the fence appeared ornamental from Father's point of view; an edging of black atop the red tile. He'd found the stairway leading up here by accident. On seeing the track, he'd been tempted to strip and run a few miles, to try to work out his corrosive tension. But Father had ordered him to avoid the sky's scrutiny, its invisible satellites. Brian was disobeying that order at the moment; although he'd kept himself inconspicuous until a minute before, to evade Martha's eagle eye as she approached for a landing. The roof appealed to him. Why not have a track on this mausoleum? Why not run round and round the huge octagon, savoring the unbelievable view? Why not fantasize hurling oneself to the courtyard, to end this misery?

Rage, grief, and shame were consuming Brian's soul, and he didn't know how to stop it. He felt so bad about his madness of last night; his psychotic break, that's what it seemed, when for a time he thought he'd become his sister. And almost did something terrible to Toby. Mother, basket case that she'd become, wasn't any help. The end approached, Brian felt certain. The end of his tormented and now intolerable life. No Grace here. Just a stranger—whose male body, symbolically somehow, had taken her place.

Brian didn't see how he could last much longer. He stared at the 'copter's slowing rotors, feeling ready to explode. The wind in the courtyard quieted. He glimpsed Martha in the cockpit, shutting down controls, gathering her things. Brian wanted to steal the 'copter and plunge it into that disgustingly pretty lake at the far end of the valley. He wanted, fervently, to die.

Helen sat in what the electronic butler called the "Great Hall," watching Earnest stroll, with parasol, to the helicopter. The French doors screening the courtyard stood fifty feet from Martha's noisy black machine. To Helen the distance seemed like miles.

She didn't trust Martha. She didn't enjoy the buddyship the woman had developed with Earnest over the years. Their plans coming to fruition, that buddyship now had achieved apotheosis. Helen felt excluded; particularly since she'd shown herself to be devious, unreliable, and soft.

Martha's house amplified the feeling. Its grandeur appealed to Helen's taste for luxury, but activated her dislike of waste, her sensitivity to the finitude of the planet's resources. Martha seemed to have no qualms about waste. Helen almost admired her for it. And she hated the way Earnest didn't seem bothered at all.

They'd never before visited any of Martha's various establishments. Helen and Earnest always had maintained a careful distance, socially and professionally, from Martha. Security required it. No one could have reason to suspect her role in their work.

However, the relationship had changed. They'd become Martha's secret house guests. Here for an indefinite stay.

Helen found the prospect unbearable. Always the ruler of her surroundings, she was beholden to a billionaire chatelaine. . . .

There Martha stood, under the parasol, talking with Earnest. Helen squeezed her hands. She couldn't think about their discussion, what words Earnest might be using to describe her state of mind. Thinking about it would drive her mad. She tried to focus on the young man in the basement who really had gone mad. She didn't dare use more drugs. Somehow, she'd blanked Toby's brain. From working too fast? How could she have been so reckless, when he might yet provide clues to Grace's retrieval?

Grace haunted Helen's every waking moment, every sleeping one too. She couldn't bear what the loss was doing—this ineradicable burn in her heart. What the loss was doing to Brian . . .

She wondered if the TV she'd left on in Toby's cell was irrigating his mind. Bringing it back to coherence. She hoped so, for she hadn't finished with the scoundrel. She wouldn't, until she'd wrung from him whatever she could.

In the courtyard, Martha sighed. "Doesn't sound like improvement," she remarked. "You're worried, aren't you?"

Earnest nodded. "We need Helen," he said. "And will continue to as long as we need the guards."

"They're barracked in the basement?" Martha asked.

"Yes," Earnest said. He smiled, eyeing the bulge of Martha's midriff. It gave her a Venus quality he found appealing. "This establishment," he remarked, "is satisfactory."

She guffawed. "Admit it, you puritan," she said. "Plutocracy has its points. Have you looked around?"

"A bit," Earnest replied. "There is much I haven't seen."

"Come," Martha said, taking his arm. She led him across the courtyard to a door he hadn't noticed before. So many doors in the endless stucco encirclement, Earnest thought. It could take months to know it well.

Watching from the roof, Brian wondered where Martha was taking Father. Their conspiratorial huddle under the parasol made him curious. He rose from his crouch, and walked to the stairs.

Martha showed Earnest down another flight to the basement, then through a corridor to a massive steel hatch. She opened it with taps of her blunt fingertips on a panel of buttons. Beyond the hatchway lay a roomful of consoles, monitors, and equipment. An enormous oval dais, completely bare and with no apparent connection to the electronics, filled the room's far side. Apart from the dais, the facility resembled the control room of a submarine. Or perhaps that of a small nuclear reactor.

"Can we get CNN down here?" Earnest asked.

Martha laughed her rumbling laugh. "Mary's on at 10:00. So what? Does whatever she'll say affect anything in the slightest?"

Earnest shrugged. "The Net message," he said. "There should be quite a lot of discussion, right now." He crossed to the dais, stepped on it, and walked to the middle. "Do you know," he said loudly, voice echoing in the cavernous, empty space, "what this makes me feel like?"

"I could guess," Martha said. She studied a monitor.

A moment passed. "Look," he called.

Martha turned. He'd dropped his trousers. The sight hit her hard, the way it always did. He looked so sweet. Like a randy, superannuated Boy Scout—defiantly being naughty. "Honey," Martha said, licking her lips. "Honey, you're such a show-off. And I love it."

"Come here," he said. Martha walked over, unfastening her suit. The silk fell to her knees as she knelt. Serenely grinning, Earnest closed his eyes.

Brian, peering through the hatchway, watched them get down to business. They rolled around the stage thing, grunting like . . . like animals. Brian trembled. He felt totally disgusted. Everything about it horrified him, made him crazily sick. But what horrified him the most was the ferocious hard-on in his pants.

Toby lay on a bed in a small, windowless room. The only door out consisted of vertical metal bars. For reasons he didn't understand, a TV was blaring CNN. His last memory, pre-here, featured Helen Scarf. Last night in the truck, she'd given him another injection. It had put him to sleep.

Then he'd woken in this cell. Other than TV shouting from the wall, he heard no sounds. Through the bars he saw a corridor, plain and short, across which another barred door faced his. That cell looked vacant. Toby supposed he could be in some kind of government prison. One with two cells off a single corridor. Did such prisons provide TVs? Did they keep beds in deluxe linen? Did they clothe prisoners in expensive pajamas? Did they have private and rather opulent bathrooms?

Toby doubted it. But he unquestionably was imprisoned. A trip to the bathroom had underscored something else about his circumstances. From the mirror, luridly discolored eyes had looked him over—red, lemon-yellow, and chartreuse stains in the whites, even in the browns.

He'd almost passed out at the sight.

If television time reflected reality in a place like this, he'd been awake since about 6:30. The whirring clank of an electronic lock had roused him. Through gummy eyelashes he'd watched Helen Scarf enter from the corridor, carrying a black case. She'd glanced at him; then hit a wall switch, unleashing CNN. She'd proceeded to unpack medical instruments onto the bedside table. Like fragments of a nightmare, lines from her conversation in the truck with Brian had wafted through Toby's mind:

"He's out."

"Are you going to keep him out?"

"What do you think?"

With no desire to be kept out, Toby had figured she might not bother if he appeared out of it already. So he'd gazed at her, then at the TV, with all the vacancy he could summon.

Scarf had touched him, gently, on the face. He'd kept his eyes unfocused. She stared for what seemed like days. Finally she'd muttered something, grabbed her gear, left the cell, re-locked it, and strode away, leaving Toby in possession of his faculties and at the mercy of the outrageous stories the TV was telling.

In his wildest dreams, he couldn't have made up anything better. If Toby understood correctly, Earnest Trefethen controlled planetary sea level. He'd become, overnight, the most feared human being on earth. Somehow, Toby had the honor of being this man's prisoner. What could be better than that?

Many things, if he was about to die. Trefethen wouldn't hesitate to snuff him. Not if it suited his purposes. He already was responsible for hundreds of deaths in Holland alone, where hordes were stampeding from coasts, trampling everything in their way.

And that was just the beginning. If Trefethen went through with the sea level threat, millions would die. Or so it seemed to Toby. Scientists were arguing about it. Some called the idea of ice sheet collapse an "absurd distortion of the data." But others weren't so sure. Especially the volcanologists. And the glaciovolcanologists,

At any rate, lots of people were taking Trefethen seriously. A consensus seemed to be evolving that the crisis wasn't a question of whether he could raise sea level. It was a question of whether the madman would go ahead and do it.

He seemed prepared to force the biggest human migration in history. The economic impact alone—while no one had even tried to assess it, pundits were finding fresh applications for the term "catastrophic collapse."

This boggled Toby's mind. The world was glued to TV, watching "Frenzy-like unrest," "Luddite rallies," "panic along coastlines," "acute unease" everywhere else, and above all, speculation about the "face of the Beast."

Why were bombs in Antarctica looking for the Beast? No one knew. Maybe an answer to the question didn't exist. Anyway, for Toby, answering it wasn't the crux. That such a question was even being asked struck him as amazing.

Trefethen had done the impossible. He'd smashed the public's indifference to catastrophe—because the Beast was out there, somewhere, on TV. Invisibly gone amok. But preparing to show itself, to flash signs of its identity, at any moment. All over the planet, according to CNN, people were asking what the "primitive" face could be, what the "scientific" face could be. Fringe people were advancing candidates for both insidious guises.

However, mainstreamers were doing the same. Few seemed immune to the name-the-Beast obsession Trefethen had inspired. Joltingly to Toby, CNN said the *Boston Globe* had found "major clues" in accounts of the "notorious dinner party at a Cambridge, Massachusetts restaurant." Trefethen had used the occasion, witnesses claimed, to "categorically identify the 'faces of the Beast.'"

Toby thought he knew what the faces might be. That only deepened his awe. How far would Trefethen go with this makeover of the Antichrist? This apparent campaign to reincarnate the devil—as overpopulation and greed-serving technology?

To Toby's way of thinking, it was about time somebody demonized those threats to survival. Trefethen's tactics seemed a mite drastic, though. Murderously drastic. Inexplicable, too. How could an environmentalist commit such crimes?

The question reminded Toby of other crimes he'd recently witnessed. They'd involved, all of them, a rabbit that the twins didn't want "reproduced."

It seemed improbable to the point of ludicrousness. But could the rabbit be the Beast? The "overpopulation" face, maybe?

At least Trefethen hadn't exploded more bombs. CNN's talking heads thought they knew why. "Satellites linking Antarctica to the datasphere," they'd reported with meaningful solemnity, "are functioning as usual. There has been no interruption of service."

How reassuring, Toby thought. It meant governments and corporations worldwide were bending over. Which underscored the major point Toby's TV was making: This maniac ruled the planet.

But the current focus, the event-of-the-moment around which all talking heads orbited, concerned the Net message Trefethen had sent out last night. CNN soon would air it.

Toby couldn't wait. For the last few minutes he'd listened to a debate about Trefethen's reasons for releasing the message in code, and for waiting until this morning to release the decryption key. Some commentators maintained he was continuing to demonstrate the flair for the dramatic he'd so resoundingly revealed on *Barclay*. Others argued Trefethen was staggering his bombshells for more sinister reasons. The man seemed bent on doing to planetary business-as-usual what he'd done to Ross Shelf—the infliction of maximum fracture. That, no one disputed, he'd accomplished. Business-as-usual most everywhere had ground to a halt.

One aspect of his timing, everyone agreed, made perfect sense. Trefethen pretty much had been obliged to release the statement while still in control of Ecologic's Netlink. Had he released it today—from some anonymous origination-point—what proof, verifiable to all, would there have been that he'd written it?

Impostors and wannabes already were jamming the Net with mindless ravings. Trefethen had anticipated this, evidently. For his code scheme dealt with impostors.

It involved dual-key cryptography. If Trefethen were to release more coded statements, large portions of the public, now in possession of his decryption key, could decode them. However, only Trefethen could code them in the first place. Unless, that is, he supplied the encryption key—which commentators considered unlikely, given his setup.

The technicalities boiled down to something simple. Trefethen's decryption key decoded only his messages, of course. To the messages of others it did nothing whatever. Cranks on the Net could issue statements, coded whichever way they liked and signed Earnest Trefethen. But they would be revealed as frauds when Trefethen's decryption key didn't fit their locks.

Smart, Toby reflected. Everybody can unlock. But only Trefethen, sole possessor of the encryption key, can lock. The point wasn't to stop people from unlocking his messages. From his perspective, the more people decoding them the better. The point was, if he and no one else could lock them up, they were his messages.

So what did he have to say?

Carson O'Doyle, CNN's premier anchor, came onscreen. He looked unwell. "Greetings," he said. "A dispute with the government has delayed our broadcast of Earnest Trefethen's now-decoded message. I am enjoined from commenting on the negotiations, but will say that we reminded FATB officials that the message has been available—decoded—to millions of high-bandwidth Net subscribers since 8:30 this morning. Why not, we and other broadcasters inquired, give the general public access to something the information elite already possesses?" He smiled queasily. "Our argument prevailed. Without further introduction, we bring you his message."

Carson O'Doyle disappeared.

Water and sand took his place. An expansive beach lay below a bright, cheerful sun. In the far background, sedate waves curled ashore, dissolving to fizz behind a gaily striped sun umbrella. Under the umbrella, someone reclined in a canvas chaise longue. No other signs of humans were anywhere visible.

The image pulled in on the umbrella. A lanky bald man occupied the chaise. His black double-breasted suit, pale shirt, and dark tie lent the tableau a somber note. Beyond him, ocean glittered to the horizon.

The image came closer; Earnest Trefethen looked up from a book. His blue eyes reached through the TV screen. "It's nice here," he remarked, seeming to confide the sentiment directly to Toby. "Very nice, here by the shore."

Oh no, Toby thought.

"An appropriate place to have a chat." Trefethen jerked a thumb over his shoulder, at the water. As if responding, a wave hissed across the sand, foaming to nothingness behind the chaise. Trefethen asked, "Are you wondering if I show the ocean to prompt fear?" His eyebrows hoisted. "Perhaps you wonder if the Beast will stride from those waves? Like the Beast in scripture, that comes from the sea?" The eyebrows lowered. "No. That isn't the Beast with which we deal. For the Beast, you see, is you."

Trefethen smiled thinly. "Yes," he murmured. "The Beast is you. And me. It's everyone, really. We all of us harbor it in our hearts. That is the reason, of course, it's our terrible enemy. Our mortal enemy— and the enemy, as well, of Mother Earth."

Sounds like a sermon, Toby thought.

"Something else you may be wondering," Trefethen continued. "Why did I put bombs in Antarctica? Why did I explode them?" Again, the thin smile. "I'll tell you. Mother told me to do it."

Who told him? Toby wondered.

Trefethen declared, "Mother Earth ordered me to do it! Because she has declared war on the Beast. And is at war, therefore, with all of us. With our dark sides, I should say. The sides we have surrendered to evil."

Apoco-frenzies are loving this, Toby thought.

"And what does this mean?" Trefethen inquired, face turning grim. "I should think it's obvious. We are being put to a test. It's a trial, of sorts—which will result in judgment. Whose side, Mother Earth wants to know, are you on?"

Toby pondered the question. Not Trefethen's, he decided.

"You have a choice, you see. You can choose for whom to fight, in this war. And you must choose. This war, that Mother Earth has declared—no one can stay neutral. No one." His face grew yet grimmer. "If you doubt that, just wait." He glanced over his shoulder at the ocean.

Behind him, on the horizon, Toby noticed an odd change. Something was happening to the distant juncture of sky and sea. It had been a flat line. Now it seemed blurred.

"So you must decide," Trefethen declared. "Will you submit to the Beast within?" He stood, eyes suddenly stark. Arms raised, he asked loudly, "Or will you join Mother's crusade?"

Sheesh, Toby thought. Now something was happening to the water behind Trefethen. The tide was going out. But with extreme, unnatural speed. A huge expanse of wet sand, extending to the horizon, glimmered in the sun.

As for the horizon . . . it had become a dark, shuddering ridge. A moving ridge, Toby realized. It was coming at the beach. Coming closer rapidly, and getting bigger.

Uh-oh, he thought, thrilled and horrified at the same time. He watched the tsunami mount higher.

A rumbling roar shook the beach. Trefethen looked at the cataclysmic wave rushing toward him. Then he turned to Toby, to the world, with peculiar nonchalance. "As I said," he shouted, "this is war! And you must choose sides!"

The wave reared higher, a thunderous wall moving at such speed that Trefethen's doom seemed momentary. The entire ocean looked to have been hurled into a great, sky-darkening curl. Watching it, Toby felt fragile. The thing had to be four hundred feet tall. Purple-green hues suggested water's deepest, stoniest textures. The crest began to spill like an endless Niagara.

Trefethen smiled ruefully. The image pulled back and up, way up, highlighting his miniature size compared to the wave. He turned to it. Then, as if in salutation, he extended an arm.

And the wave stopped. It simply froze, midcrash.

The gargantuan curve glinted like jade in absolute silence. Trefethen was a tiny figurine below the overhang. He reseated himself on the tiny chaise under the tiny, laughably flimsy umbrella.

The image started zooming toward him. Or seemed to.

But was it? What's going on? Toby wondered. Trefethen, chaise, and umbrella—were—what? Getting bigger?

They were. Getting impossibly bigger, they were becoming titanic. In tandem, the stilled wave became smaller. Seconds passed as this continued with supernatural rapidity, and suddenly the wave was an ordinary wave, a sedate wave, frozen in place behind the sitting Trefethen.

It unfroze. Breaking, it hissed across sand, expiring in bubbly foam a few inches from the chaise's rear legs.

Clever, Toby thought. He started breathing again.

Trefethen said with jarring calm, "Why, it's enough to get you off the beach." He chuckled dryly. "Now then. Four nuclear explosions, experts allege, have undermined the West Antarctic Ice Sheet. This happens to be true. They did undermine it.

"But my calculations indicate that ice sheet collapse requires at least three more, and possibly as many as six more, explosions. Last night, I announced that I have seven additional bombs in Antarctica. They are looking, I said, for our enemy, the Beast." He leaned forward, arms on his knees, hands clasped. "Since you now know the Beast resides within you—indeed, within all of us—it follows that the bombs are looking at you. Searching you—seeking the Beast's two faces. The primitive face. The scientific face."

Creepy, Toby thought.

"I now wish to address the question of what will happen if the bombs find those faces." Trefethen leaned further forward. "As you may have surmised, it won't be pretty. If the bombs see what they are looking for, they'll explode."

He sat back, hands speculatively splayed. "Thus you wonder: How do we stop this?" The hands closed into fists. "I'll tell you how. We must fight the Beast. Tooth and claw, we must wage battle against it. And quell it." Again he leaned forward. "But how, you now wonder, do we fight it? If it resides within?"

Almost charmingly, Trefethen smiled. "Antarctica will tell you," he said. The smile deepened, and looked sincere. "Antarctica will tell you how to survive this ordeal. How to prove your worth—how to be tested, that is. And of course, be judged." He sighed contentedly. "When will Antarctica tell you? Tonight, at eight o'clock. On international television."

Trefethen stood. Thrusting hands in his trouser pockets, he

seemed the distinguished academic whom, until yesterday, he'd so successfully impersonated. As if referring to a faculty skirmish he added, "I'm sure there will be no problem arranging the airtime. Relevant officials and executives will receive instructions soon. I do hope you'll watch."

Cold bleakness crept through Toby. He wondered if he'd be busy at eight.

37

The first impression Selma got as they followed Gula through the house that kept going back, was of carpets. They mostly were Navajo. Rugs from other tribal traditions, ones she couldn't identify, lay interspersed. Geometrically bold, subtly tinted, and old, they were everywhere—big ones, little ones, runners, a spectacular chief's blanket under the dining room table.

The second thing Selma noticed was the floor itself. Composed of wide-plank wood, it had been painted a sharp, rich red. A gleaming enamel of a red; which possessed an inner tang she knew she'd seen somewhere, but not on a floor, much less on the antique floors of a New England farmhouse. They all seemed to be painted this particular red. It would stifle the rooms, Selma realized, without the rugs floating over it. The Navajo patterns tamed the color. Or rather, the rugs and the red modulated each other. They held each other in check, making a visual hum.

Furniture was the third thing she noticed. A mixture of styles, most of it wouldn't raise eyebrows at an expensive store. But the tables, chairs, wrought-iron fixtures, and endless other artifacts were to kill for, as far as Selma was concerned. They so effortlessly pleased the eye. On them, around them, behind them, she saw more of this woman's affinity for pattern—in upholstery and cushions, in the curtains.

Looking as if she could use a cane, clutching the bag that held the gun she'd confiscated, Gula led them toward a whitewashed archway. They passed a very large room stretching to the left. Selma took it in and entered visual overload.

More carpets floated on the magic red. Wicker armchairs surrounded low tables fashioned from giant brass platters. Along a wall, two sofas sat like patriarchs, dependents arrayed. Cushy armchairs flanked a fireplace at the far end, and other seating arrangements were scattered about; including a collection of exotic stools, as if elves visited from time to time. What stopped Selma cold, though, and Dan too, were the books.

Apart from windows and the fireplace, the walls consisted of floor-to-ceiling shelves packed with books. They didn't seem ornamental. They didn't, for example, present the monotony of leather-bound editions. Quite the opposite; the several thousand hardbacks gave the walls a variegated texture. It had a certain feel. Selma realized these books looked like they'd actually been read.

Dan caught her eye. They registered each other's fatigue, and shared a silent reaction to the establishment. It went something like: *Thanks for inviting us. Where are our rooms?*

"Come along," Gula said with high-pitched impatience. She stood in the archway, a gnarled hand beckoning. Grace passed through a twin archway to the place Gula had chosen for their talk. Selma grabbed Dan's arm and dragged him in.

More cozily, books lined this room too. A sofa and armchairs faced a hearth in which wrought-iron cooking hooks hung archaically. Gula, emitting gasps, sat with effort on a Victorian daybed.

Grace said, "Are you sure no one else is around?"

Gula wheezed, and coughed. The cough became a fit. As it worsened, she gave Grace a needle-sharp succession of outraged glares. "Water," she croaked. No one knew what to do. "Water!" she gasped, glaring now at Dan and Selma. Dan ran out in search of the kitchen he'd glimpsed during their long march back here.

He found it near the door through which they'd entered. The tap water being cool, he dispensed with ice. Anyway, this lady was so unbelievably old, she might keel over any second. He ran back with a glassful, thinking about the way Grace had persuaded her to clear the house of witnesses. Grace wouldn't leave the pond, she'd declared, unless Gula promised to do that. For quite a while, Gula had sat scowling in her cart, eyes flaring. But after a protracted wheezing attack, she'd seized the cart's phone from Grace, and called people. Announcing she didn't want visitors.

Gula now seized the water glass with the same irritable energy. She sipped. Her breathing calmed. As if stepping back from the brink of death, she thrust the glass at Selma; then cleared her throat, fixed beady eyes on Grace, and snapped, "You heard me call Constance. You heard me call Harry. What do you think, you little sourpuss—of course nobody's here! Except for you . . . you . . . I don't know what you are! Criminals, maybe?" She stared searchingly at Dan. And muttered, "Thanks."

"He's used to it," Selma said. "He got water for me, yesterday. When our—uh—adventure started."

"Speak to me," Gula said. "I've an idea the adventure isn't so wonderful. In fact I know it isn't."

"How?" Grace asked.

"The way you look. The way," Gula added with an edge of malice, "you smell!"

"It's not wonderful," Dan said. "The adventure, I mean." He dropped into the sofa, adding, "I have no idea how we smell."

Selma sighed unhappily, and sat in an armchair near Gula. Grace remained standing. "Something has scared you witless," Gula said. "You can tell me about it. I insist you do—especially if it involves that wretched woman."

Dan thought about the back roads they'd driven through the night, listening to the radio's escalating hysteria; to steadily scarier reports that, around midnight, started mentioning him, Selma, and Grace by name. It was clear they'd be caught. How could they outrun FAT-BOY? They couldn't. But every time he or Selma had mentioned this to Grace, she'd painted yet grislier pictures of the surgical techniques that Mother had developed on behalf of law enforcement. When those images dulled in the face of exhaustion, trauma, and the endlessness of their irrational, spiraling route through Connecticut, she'd found other ways to freshen their resolve, and keep them going. The coast, she predicted, soon would be bedlam. Soon, everyone everywhere would be in the thrall of Father's deadly rapture. Neither Dan nor Selma could quite visualize this. But the general idea had convinced them that they didn't have much to lose, sticking with Grace. For they already seemed thoroughly lost.

Dan said to Gula, "Grace will explain."

"You're the mystery, then," Gula said, eyeing her.

"I'm surprised you haven't heard about us," Grace said.

Gula blinked. "Why?" she inquired.

Selma said, "My roommate—Dan's brother—got involved in the crisis. You know about the crisis?"

"The gloom crisis?" Gula asked disbelievingly.

"Uh-huh," Dan affirmed. "That one."

Gula demanded, "What's Martha got to do with that crisis?"

Dan and Selma looked at Grace. She stared into the hearth. After a moment she said, "Do you mind if I turn on the TV?" A fairly modern set sat below a window. The sun pouring through, and the peaceful green outside, made the notion of news distasteful. "It might be simpler," Grace went on, "if we watch the press conference. Simpler to explain things."

"What press conference?" Gula asked.

"FATBOY," Selma said. "Radio news is excited about it. And about tonight's fistfight between Antarctica—and the Beast."

Gula directed a thoughtful stare at Grace. "Go ahead, then. Turn it on."

Brian walked down the never-ending basement corridor, mind in flames. Should he tell Mother? What would happen if he did? She'd die, he felt certain. She'd at least have a breakdown, if she got any inkling Father and Martha were lovers. The shock of it—of them rolling around half-clothed, grunting—wasn't going away. Had he not seen it with his own two eyes, Brian wouldn't have thought such a thing possible. It never had occurred to him, not once, that Father and Mother could be anything but one-hundred-percent faithful. Just like him and Grace.

The revelation that they weren't was suffocating. If Father could cheat, what about . . . ? The idea made Brian see double. It made him feel unreal. How real would he be, what form would life have, if Grace, like Father, could cheat?

No, he thought. She can't do it. Doing it, even thinking of doing it, would make her rot with shame. Just as he would, of course. If he somehow could be so wicked.

On the other hand, Grace had run away. With a good-looking guy. But Grace wouldn't find him attractive—would she? Of course not. However, Brian couldn't help but think that psychiatrists probably spend half their time dealing with the fact that people change, sometimes in unexpected ways, when subjected to new circumstances. It seemed to Brian that shrinks must spend at least half their time telling patients about that reality. In fact they dealt with it full-time, that was all they ever did, obviously. The more he thought about this, the more clear it became. And he couldn't deny that Grace had plunged into new circumstances. Of her own free will, according to Mother. She'd made it happen!

Therefore, Brian reasoned, she might be—changing. In unexpected ways. For instance, she might be getting attached to Dan. Who, reciprocally, might be getting attached to her.

The idea of them getting attached, now that he and she had been so violently detached, filled Brian with the profoundest dread he'd ever experienced. It made everything else seem trivial. What could be worse than Grace and Dan getting attached?

And maybe doing it. Having sex. The very word sent shiny little dots swarming through the air around his head. Brian didn't understand how this possibility could have materialized. And he had no clue whatsoever why he'd reacted that way to seeing Father and Martha. It was so revolting. So impure, polluting, defiling—it shocked him to the core that he'd almost come in his pants.

How could he ease the pressure that was pulping his mind? There seemed only one way. Brian had to learn about this guy who threatened his existence. He had find out about Dan.

The corridor made another wide-angle turn under the octagon. Brian hoped he was close to finishing his tour of the basement facilities. He'd checked out zombie quarters, vacant servant quarters, laundry rooms, kitchen annexes, storage rooms, garages that kept the truck and vans out of sight along with a dozen other vehicles, the hangar to which the hydraulically descending Vesuvius could deliver the helicopter from the courtyard, and the complex that he knew to contain, because Mother had mentioned it in one of her "you-don't-know-this" tellings of secrets, a nuclear reactor. The thing would be powering a Navy submarine if budget cuts hadn't made it so much costly surplus. Martha, ever willing to exploit her ownership of a measurable chunk of the defense industry, had put it to use here. Illegally; but her billions had ways to make the law accommodate her whims. At least, ways to keep them hidden.

Not much more of the basement remained unscouted. Brian neared a secure-looking steel door. Like many of the other secure-looking steel doors, it wasn't locked. He opened it and saw a short corridor with two barred doors facing each other from either side. This has to be it, Brian thought. I've found him.

Toby heard the door open. Damn, he mentally moaned. Somebody would have to come just as the press conference was starting. He lay back in a position suggesting coma, head pillow-propped so he could keep an eye on the TV.

From the bars, Brian's youthful tenor said, "Hello."

Toby put a twitch in his face.

"I don't know if you can hear me, or understand me," Brian continued. "But if some part of you can, I want you to know—I'm sorry about this. Really sorry. And wish I could . . . do something."

Get me out of here, Toby thought. He tried to conceal the fact that the TV was riveting him.

Presumably to add heft, the press conference was being held at the White House, in a big, chandelier-hung room. Any minute McMurtry would come out. Meantime the camera panned the jammed seating area, where every prominent journalist in the world was fidgeting, laptopping, telephoning, faxing, and urgently conferring.

Carson O'Doyle, the CNN anchor, said with a reverential voice-over, "The mood in the East Room is expectant and tense as we wait for Director General McMurtry to make what could be the most important appearance she yet has made before the American public."

"I also want to mention," Brian said, "that your brother Dan— because he took Grace away—is, um, on my mind."

Mine too, Toby thought. So what?

"I wish we could talk about it," Brian said.

Thank God you can't make me, Toby thought.

O'Doyle intoned, "This is the first government response since the decoding of the Net statement earlier today. How will the administration reply to Earnest Trefethen's demand for television time at eight tonight? We soon will know. As you see, the director general is approaching the podium. Live, from the White House, Mary McMurtry speaks to the nation."

"Good morning!" the small, bird-boned woman exclaimed. Toby noted that not a hair was out of place in her tricorne-like coiffure. "I will begin with some announcements," she said. "Then I'll discuss developments. Finally, I'll take a few questions."

"Could you try blinking your eyes?" Brian said.

Toby steadfastly kept his eyes wide open.

"First," McMurtry said. "I'm pleased to announce that the President will address the nation. His speech will be carried live, on all major television networks." She paused, then added with lethal cool, "Tonight, at eight sharp."

Excitement rippled through the East Room. The reaction reminded

Toby of the collective "Yes!" that home-team fans express on hearing inspirational news. The President, it seemed, felt no need to roll over. The President was hanging tough.

"Second!" McMurtry declared. "I speak for the President and the entire administration when I say this—insofar as we are concerned, Earnest Trefethen can go . . . "

"Could you try breathing . . . "

"straight to hell!"

"a little differently?"

Get out! Toby mentally exclaimed.

The East Room audience abandoned all pretense of being impartial stewards of journalistic truth, and rose to an impassioned standing ovation. McMurtry allowed herself a smile. With stately control, she took a sip of water.

"Can't you even blink your eyes?"

Incredible, Toby thought. Brian didn't care about what McMurtry was saying. To him, this brush-off—this complete fuck-you to his father—wasn't even happening.

The East Room applause subsided. Journalists, Toby thought, must hate Trefethen. Considering what he'd done to Barclay Piston.

"Third," McMurtry said. "Telecommunications to and from Antarctica are being monitored." A hand chopped the air with startling savagery. "Every link is being traced!"

Applause rippled. But without heat. Everyone knows, Toby thought, that's an empty claim. The datasphere in general, but the Net especially—laced as both were with myriad, mutating pathways—by definition constituted a smuggler's paradise. Even the NSA's megacomputers could track only a fraction of the traffic.

"Toby!" Brian exclaimed. "I know you're awake!"

"Fourth," McMurtry said quietly. "Let us remind ourselves of something. Let us remember: This is the United States of America. We are the nation that stands up to terror. We are an island of stability, *hard-won* stability, in a world full of barbarism and chaos. Are we going to surrender now?" She paused; then let loose with tremendous bellows, *"Not on your life! We'd rather die!"*

The audience leapt to its feet, roaring approval. Toby had to admire McMurtry for the sheer bravado. At this point, she could say she was leaving for hemorrhoid surgery, and get an ovation. Put a cigar in her mouth, she'd be Winston Churchill. He realized he loved her for it. In fact, his eyes were brimming.

"Wow," Brian murmured. "Toby, you're crying."

"Fifth," McMurtry said as the audience calmed. "I am glad to announce we have made progress tracking down Trefethen."

The audience sat down en masse, and the room filled with the burr of rapidly clicking keyboards. Real news, Toby thought, feeling a bizarre emotion surge through his body. He realized it was hope. He then realized the extent of his physical and mental wreckage. God, he thought. I'm so wasted. And scared.

"Am I getting through?" Brian asked hopefully.

Toby wanted to yell, Can't you hear what she's saying?

But Brian said, voice soft with concern, "That's right. Just let go. If you let the sadness out, you'll be able to think. And maybe even talk. You'd like to talk—right, Toby?"

I'll garrote him, Toby thought. Just like the heroic flying Louise will garrote his father. If he doesn't get away from here, I'll tear him from limb to limb.

"For the moment," McMurtry was saying, "I cannot disclose the details of what we have learned concerning Trefethen's location. Absolutely no further information on the subject is available at this time, to ensure that he and his allies have no opportunity to escape swift, and most certainly terrible, justice."

Uh-oh, Toby thought.

McMurtry snapped her fingers. An aide wheeled a big videoscreen to the podium.

"Do you miss Dan?" Brian asked soulfully. "We have something in common, you know. See, Mother thinks my sister might be with Dan. And here you are, his brother—with me!"

Jesus Christ, Toby thought. He just won't shut up.

McMurtry turned to the videoscreen, a control wand in her hand. "However, I'll share one aspect of the investigation. I do this to bring to the public's attention the identity of certain individuals we believe could contribute to our ongoing efforts." She waved the control wand. A grainy close-up of Dan appeared on the video-screen.

"So why don't we talk about it?" Brian said.

Toby cracked. He said, "If you're so obsessed with my brother, shut your mouth and look at the fucking TV."

They studied Dan's face on McMurtry's videoscreen. The eyes blazed fiercely. The mouth appeared to be delivering a shout, or maybe a snarl. Blurriness suggested some kind of violent motion. Altogether, the photo indicated that Dan might be dangerous. He looked like a killer about to strike.

Selma leaned forward. Gula groped for the water glass on the coffee table, brought it unsteadily to her lips, and gulped. Grace turned slightly paler. Dan just closed his eyes.

McMurtry was saying, "This is a digital photograph of Daniel Swett." The diminutive woman with cast-iron hair waved her control wand. On the videoscreen, the image shifted to an even grainier photo, a close-up of a car's back window; through which, despite the graininess, the silhouettes of three people sitting in the rear compartment were clearly visible. On the left, back to the camera, a broad-shouldered man held a telephone to his head. In the middle, back also to the camera, a girl was sitting still. On the right, showing a full profile that made her features evident, Selma leaned across the girl—as if she were about to engage the man on the left in conversation, or perhaps call to his attention the spray can she was extending with her right hand.

"The young woman holding the spray can," McMurtry said, "is Selma Swearingen."

"What on earth?" Gula muttered. She leaned forward, planting arms on vibrating knees.

Dan said to Selma in a scandalized whisper, "You know where that is, right?"

"Yeah," she replied. "Dick's. Outside Dick's."

Help, Gula thought. Gang headquarters? A drug den?

McMurtry waved her wand. The videoscreen shifted to a third photo, of which the first two images turned out to be details. The full picture supported the idea that Dan possessed killer instincts. He clutched a jackiron, which he'd obviously just finished smacking on the head of a stunned-looking man.

McMurtry said crisply, "This shows the commission of two criminal acts. In the foreground, Dan Swett has knocked unconscious Samuel Jenkins, an employee of the Center for the Study of Moral Reasoning.

In the background in the car, Selma Swearingen is spraying mace at the Center's security chief, Charles Fladgate."

"Doris," Selma growled. "Doris took that picture."

Again McMurtry waved her wand. The videoscreen, displaying a series of photos in quick succession, looked as if it had switched to video that was playing in jerky reverse motion. Dan's jackiron hit Jenkins' head. Dan then turned and staggered backward out of the frame. Jenkins, now unscathed, engaged the attention of a uniformed man who stood in front of a white limousine. Fladgate meantime disgorged himself from the car just ahead. The girl in the middle and Selma followed, and the three proceeded to lurch backward down a brick sidewalk. The girl turned. Her face came into view. McMurtry waved the wand; the image sequence stopped with a final photo that revealed the girl to be Grace.

"Doris took a lot of pictures," Dan observed.

McMurtry used the wand to enlarge Grace. Her lovely face filled the screen. "This girl," McMurtry announced, "is Grace Trefethen— the daughter of Earnest Trefethen and Helen Scarf."

A murmur washed through the East Room. Gula also reacted; she dropped her water glass. It fell with a splattering clunk on the rug below the coffee table. She didn't seem to notice. Her eyes turned to Grace, who, with a trace of nervousness, yawned.

McMurtry said with verve, "My reason for bringing these photographs to your attention will soon be apparent." She stabbed the air with the wand. The videoscreen displayed the photos in a rapid forward-moving sequence.

Fladgate and Jenkins jerkily hustled Selma and Grace down the sidewalk. The limo guy, arms waving like a mechanical doll with broken gears, accosted Jenkins. Fladgate meantime seemed to have an epileptic seizure as he pushed Selma and Grace into the car, and shoved in after them.

Dan stalked into the frame, holding the jackiron. He stared at Selma through the car's rear window. She turned, and looked at him; they made eye contact. She then watched him use a hand to simulate the spraying of a can.

"Wow," Grace said softly. "You guys. That's so . . . "

What? Gula wondered. What "so" is it?

Like an aggressive marionette, Dan turned to Jenkins and bonked him. Jenkins collapsed with a series of almost comical shudders. Selma, twitchily resembling someone with Parkinson's, meanwhile extended the mace can toward Fladgate. He proceeded to thrash like a mechanical ape gone haywire. Dan moved to the car in a series of staccato spasms. He leaned through the open front door; the rear window framed the jackiron blurring onto Fladgate's head. Fladgate became still. Grace's head, however, went into a major jerk-fit.

Dan remarked, "The loudest scream I ever heard."

Selma nodded. "I never heard a louder one," she said.

"I was amazed myself," Grace said. She grinned. Dan and Selma, Gula noted, studied her with interest. Gula also found the grin absorbing. There was something naive about it. Something almost bumpkinish, Gula thought. As if Grace, under the hard, controlled, and disturbingly beautiful exterior, was a kind of secret hick. Despite the horrifying circumstances, the thought charmed Gula. It touched her; for it brought to mind a frightened girl who'd moved to New York City from the remote sticks of southern California, so many decades ago.

Both doors wide open, the car pulsed down the street. The acceleration made the doors flap shut. The car reached an intersection, bolted right, and disappeared.

"Never again," Dan said.

"Yeah," Selma said, shivering.

Gula watched them share a memory of something quite terrible.

"I hope," Grace said, "she doesn't show what happened next."

Brian stared balefully through the bars at the TV set. "They did kidnap her!" he exclaimed.

"You dolt," Toby said. "Dan saved Selma. Selma helped him do it. In the process they left with Grace—which, if you ask me, did her a huge favor."

Eyes hard, Brian chewed his lower lip.

McMurtry said, "These photographs document the abduction of Grace Trefethen. It occurred yesterday at 7:13 P.M. in Harvard Square—less than two hours before Earnest Trefethen appeared on the *Barclay Piston Show*, and just a half-mile from the building where the show originated."

"See?" Brian said.

"Quiet," Toby said. He couldn't get a fix on why Brian had come here. Apologizing didn't seem to be his motive. Why, exactly, was Brian here?

"The significance of that act," McMurtry continued, making the videoscreen go blank with a slash of the wand, "isn't, however, a question of criminal conduct. From our standpoint, those two young people are to be congratulated for having performed a valuable service. Had they not abducted Grace Trefethen, Mr. Fladgate would have delivered her to her parents—something that Fladgate's associates were doing that very moment to Grace's twin brother, Brian Trefethen. And, I might add, to Dan Swett's brother, Toby Swett.

"While it is unclear what the precise motivations for these kidnappings were, we have evidence: A, that the Trefethen twins had gotten into serious difficulty with their parents; and B, that the two Swetts, along with Swearingen, somehow became involved. The full ramifications need not concern us. The point is that Grace Trefethen escaped from her parents, and remains at large—we presume in the company of Dan Swett and Selma Swearingen."

"See?" Toby said.

Brian voiced no reply.

McMurtry pointed the wand at the videoscreen. On it appeared a mug-shot-like photo of a man whose high forehead, curly satin-black hair, piercing black eyes, and bulbously noble nose combined to suggest an aristocrat of the Roman Empire; or perhaps a seventeenth-century highway robber. "This individual," McMurtry said with cold gravity, "is a man we know by one name only—Slotsky. The photograph was taken ten years ago; of Eastern European extraction, the man is an exceptionally murderous gangster. He too became embroiled with the Trefethen twins. He is at large, likely interfering with our attempts to resolve the crisis."

McMurtry dipped the wand. Slotsky's face aged, acquired a heavy bandage, and lost the noble nose. "Slotsky recently suffered injuries, of which one result was the mutilation of his face. We think this image conveys his current appearance."

"Huh," Toby said. "So that's him. Bandage."

"The guy who bumped off Miles," Brian muttered.

"Who nearly bumped off Selma, Dan, and me," Toby said.

Brian didn't offer an opinion about that missed opportunity. The boy's attitude was beginning to creep Toby out.

McMurtry said, "In view of the fact that we haven't yet neutralized Trefethen—although, as I mentioned, we plan to do so soon—it is vital that Grace come forward and provide us with whatever intelligence she may have. For the same reason, we must apprehend the man known as Slotsky.

"Accordingly, I hereby invoke powers granted to the FATB under the Federal Anti-Terror Act of 1999. I require:

"That Grace Trefethen report to law enforcement officials immediately. That Dan Swett and Selma Swearingen do the same. That anyone with knowledge of the whereabouts, conditions, and intentions of those three individuals, and/or of Slotsky, do the same.

"Noncompliance will result in the imposition of the maximum penalties provided by all applicable laws. I cannot stress too forcefully the seriousness with which we view this matter."

McMurtry took a sip of water. A dense noise that had been underlying her oration filled the otherwise hushed East Room. It came from thousands of fingers working keyboard buttons.

"Will they turn Grace in?" Brian blurted at Toby.

Toby shrugged. "I doubt it," he said.

In the great hall, Helen watched the McMurtry performance with a mixture of relief and glee. Relief she derived from the fact that the twins hadn't been exposed as traitors to the family; Helen had been very afraid that McMurtry might characterize them as would-be FATB informants. Such a disclosure would have brought ruin. Earnest and Martha couldn't have handled it.

Glee she derived from the fact that Grace wasn't in the Amarillo clinic. She remained "at large." Might Grace decide to return to the family? She did, after all, know their refuge. Conceivably, Grace could even be hiding out somewhere nearby.

Helen felt a motherly intuition that she was nearby. The idea stimulated her dormant intellect. I must find, she thought, locals who make rounds. Utility people, mailmen, police officers; I must find them, and question them.

She considered other means by which she might investigate the area. Possibilities, ones that only would occur to a professional, stormed through her mind.

In the basement control room, McMurtry's fearsome face filled a monitor. She was advising the public to disregard Earnest Trefethen's "fantasy" of ice sheet collapse. Such a scenario, according to "the most knowledgeable experts available," had been concocted by a "diseased and megalomaniacal mind." His "ravings about the Beast" amounted to "stale apocalyptic obsession." Coastline worries should be "dismissed." A sea level rise "cannot happen."

Earnest turned his chair from the monitor to watch Martha make the call. She'd already punched the number. Somewhere in the vast Mantis organization, on the desk of an executive who had been ordered to report to work today, a telephone was ringing.

Martha said, "Hello, Fay. This is Martha."

Earnest imagined Fay's attention coming to a very sharp point.

"I've decided," Martha said, "to launch Libra series B early. I want it launched now." She was referring to phase two of the television advertising campaign unveiling Libra LaserWorks, a new line of home-defense systems. The campaign's storytelling catch centered on a variation of the Mantis orb logo. The LaserWorks version featured an ability to fire potent beams of light; the orb used them to repel would-be burglars, robbers, and intruders, the general gamut of home invader. As with all Mantis products awaiting launch, the ad campaign, and most especially the new version of the orb, had been kept secret under heavy security.

The security surrounding Libra's launch happened to be quite heavy indeed. Apart from the designer, two senior supervisors, Martha, and Earnest, no one anywhere had seen it. To guarantee that no one might chance to see it, only Martha had access to the optical storage bank where, in digital form, the ad campaign reposed. Earnest listened to her supply Fay with an access code.

Access, Earnest mused, and codes. The elaborate digitization making the world turn depended so completely on access and codes.

"Series B," Martha said to Fay. "Yank the ads in the upcoming slots, and plug in series B. When are the first available slots?" She listened, glanced at Earnest, and said, "Ten fifty-seven?"

Earnest nodded.

"Very good," Martha said. "Fay, I'll have to think about the timing of series C. The environment's so volatile, and viewership so saturated, I want to maximize our launch windows. Yes—thank you. You'll hear from me when I've decided. Until then, I'll retain access to C, and the others." Martha listened a moment. Earnest watched her frown.

She was listening to Fay say, "Forgive me if this seems silly, but I should inform you of something."

"Do it," Martha said.

"You received a message with a rather odd—introduction."

"Introduction?" Martha asked. This did seem silly.

"It says that the rest of the message concerns your, and I quote, 'relationship with the Trefethen twins.'"

"How peculiar," Martha said. She glanced at Earnest. He'd reabsorbed himself in that dog-and-pony circus, the McMurtry Show.

"Should I dispose of it?" Fay asked.

"No," Martha replied. "No, send it. I'm curious. Have you read the entire message, by the way?"

"It's an audio message. I haven't listened to the rest—the introduction says, 'Cliffcloud Only.'"

"Send it, Fay." Martha put the phone down, watching the data-in readout. Moments later it signaled the reception of a message. She debated listening to it now, and decided to wait. To Earnest she said, "Ten fifty-seven it is."

"Fine," Earnest said. He consulted his watch. "Thirty-four minutes away. Your people can deliver the ad in time?"

Martha said, "Oh, sure. A squirt. Probably at the broadcasters already."

Earnest stood. He said, "I am most curious about Mary's idea that Grace 'escaped,' and about this Slotsky fellow, and whatever it is that persuaded Mary that she's on to us. So I think I better have a chat with Helen." He rubbed his eyes. "I'm now sure she's withholding information. Critical information."

"Mary is telling tall tales," Martha said.

"What if she's not?" Earnest muttered. He strode to the hatchway and stepped through it.

Martha listened to his footfalls recede in the corridor.

When she heard complete silence, she tapped buttons, and accessed the audio message.

39

Selma couldn't find paper towels in the kitchen. Gula seemed to use cloth towels for clean-ups; green of her, Selma thought. She left the kitchen, went through the dining room hating the clomp of her boots, entered the room off which the big room lay, and stopped short.

A man leaned against a piano between the twin archways to the TV room. He looked about thirty. Dirty-blond hair fell to his shoulders. The soiled denims suggested manual labor. The flesh in them suggested a brick shithouse. His calm face suggested a placid disposition; except the eyes, which, studying Selma, seemed very alert. He put a filthy fingernail to his lips. Then he pointed the finger at his chest and mouthed, "Harry."

Selma took a deep breath. Harry looked all right. He worked for Gula, so he had to be sort of okay. She nodded, clomped past him through an archway to the coffee table, where she kneeled to get at Gula's spilled water.

"Don't worry about it," Gula said. "Just water."

"Selma," Dan said. "Guess what's on TV?"

She looked, and saw the rusty pickup truck they'd borrowed last night. The plate number blazed beneath it. McMurtry's disembodied voice was saying, "Sightings should be reported to local law enforcement officials, or to this toll-free telephone number." An 800 number replaced the plate number.

"Where'd you park?" Gula asked.

"Deep in the woods," Dan replied.

"One of the fire trails," Gula murmured.

The image shifted to Jeremy, seated in a generic television studio. He seemed extremely uncomfortable. McMurtry's voice said, "This is Jeremy O'Toole, owner of the stolen truck and a friend of Swearingen's. Jeremy, do you have something to say to Selma?"

Jeremy bobbed his head, swallowed hard, and quavered, "I'd just like to say, uh, that, like, Selma, why'd you have to run away? You shouldn't have run away. I mean the whole country's freaking and there you go, off to somewhere with that nutcake's kid, what do you think you're doing, anyway? You should come home. And turn yourself in. And give me back my truck. Thank you."

The image shifted to McMurtry at the East Room podium.

"God," Selma muttered. Manically, she wiped the rug.

"Stop that," Gula commanded.

Grace stood. She turned the TV off and said, "Let's talk."

Selma hauled herself up from the floor. Gula leaned back on the daybed. Dan, grimacing, took a furtive sniff of an underarm. Grace retook her chair, face composed with the usual impassivity. Heavily, Selma sat.

"You're in trouble, all right," Gula remarked.

"God damn Toby," Dan said in a low tone. "Damn him."

"I could strangle him," Selma agreed.

"If only he hadn't taken the pin!" Dan exclaimed.

"Uh-huh," Selma said. "If only. But he had to do it. And he's probably wishing he could tell us, 'See, I was right. The world's out of control. It's total doom.'"

"The pin?" Gula said, eyes roaming through the window to her unattended garden.

"Grace will explain," Dan said.

"Never mind," Gula snapped. To Grace she said, "You're one tough cookie. But you're nuts if you think you can do battle with Martha Cliffcloud."

"I've said nothing about Cliffcloud," Grace remarked.

"'I've said nothing,'" Gula mimicked with devastating accuracy, "'about Cliffcloud.' What do think I am—a fool?"

Grace's vacant eyes sought shelter in the hearth.

"Obviously," Gula said, "your fiendish parents are right over that ridge!" She flung an arm at the window above the couch. Dan craned his neck, Selma stood to look; they stared at the mile-distant, densely wooded ridge. Grace meantime studied the hearth's andirons. Fancifully shaped with curling legs and arms, they looked like a pair of dancers.

"You think," Gula went on, "the two boys are there too. And you think you can"—Gula closed her eyes with disbelief—"rescue them!" Opening the eyes, she glanced at Dan and Selma. "And that," she said with conclusionary disgust, "is how you hornswoggled these innocents into joining forces. They thought they'd rescue Dan's brother— Toby."

"You're right, of course," Grace said. "In every respect."

"Harry!" Gula yelled.

Harry lumbered in. Grace, eyes wide, went white with anger. "You promised!" she hissed.

"Oh ho," Gula said calmly. "Now we see fire, do we? It's about time. You're so bottled up, you'll bust something in that body—and wouldn't you like it if we took you to a doctor? Don't worry about Harry. If you can trust me, you can trust him. Harry, meet the renegades. Renegades, meet Harry."

Harry nodded at Grace and said, "Howdy." He glanced at Dan and said, "Hey." He turned to Selma, inclined his head slightly, and murmured, "Hello."

"Hi," Selma said. She mustered a faint smile.

Harry said to Gula, "I listened to everything. First over the intercom in the study, then from the piano out there—crept up like I was stalking pheasant."

"I heard you coming," Gula informed him.

Harry sighed. "Thought I missed the creaks," he said.

Grace muttered, "I'm angry about this."

"Yes, dear," Gula said. "You also pulled a gun on me." She reached for the bag she'd carried in. "Harry, take it."

Harry took the bag, examined the contents, and whistled. "This thing," he said appreciatively, "is mean. Truly mean."

"Have a seat," Gula said. "Grace wants to talk. And that is what we will do."

Grace looked at the ceiling. Here goes, she thought. To get cooperation, I maintain strategy. Just like with Dan and Selma—I scare them to death with the simple truth.

From her purse she extracted the pin. She held it up, face-forward, to give Gula and Harry a look at the rabbit.

"The Beast," Dan said.

"The what?" Harry said incredulously.

"The Beast," Grace said. "That's one name. A long time ago, Brian and I called it 'the badge.' More recently, for unpleasant reasons, we started calling it 'the pin.' Those reasons relate to the fact that my parents have their own name for it. They call it the 'fertility icon.'"

She proceeded to fill them in.

Martha sat at the basement control console, massaging the sides of her close-cropped head. She felt a migraine coming. For the first time in years, she wanted a cigarette. I'd do almost anything, she thought, for even thirty seconds of nicotine.

She'd just finished listening to the audio message. No question about it—she faced disaster. She and Earnest both. A horrific disaster.

Unless she paid up. Suppose I do, she thought with febrile vertigo. The threat won't vanish. We're stuck with it.

Martha had prepared for such an eventuality. She'd reconciled herself to ruin—to glorious, immortal ruin. But she hadn't counted on it happening quite so quickly.

She brooded for several minutes. Then she called one of her off-shore banks. Bypassing the human staff, she did business with an automated transfer utility, and arranged for the movement of an extremely large amount of cash.

Toby's TV had gone to commercial. The press conference, he reflected, could be summed up with a handful of facts. Dan and Selma were loose, maybe with Grace. McMurtry meanwhile seemed confident she could find the "Trefethen terrorists." She also seemed confident the terrorists were talking big but not doing much. Her general drift raised the prospect of Toby's quick liberation; or, possibly, quick incineration. She'd made her desire for "terrible justice" very clear.

Toby said to Brian, "We have to get out. Before the tanks roll in, blasting us to smithereens."

"That's bullshit," Brian said from the bars. "It's an act, claiming they have leads on where we are. They hope they can spook Father into making a mistake. They won't."

"How do you figure that?" Toby asked.

"Easy," Brian replied. "The proof is the big deal they made about Grace. It's because they need her. Without her, they'll never find us, and I think they know it. Anyway—what they don't know is how carefully Martha and my parents set this up."

"Martha?"

"Cliffcloud."

"Holy shit."

"Yeah. That's where we are. At Martha's. It's her country place in Cheswick, Connecticut."

Something Toby had overheard him say last night, in the truck, came back. Brian and Helen had discussed the truck's destination. Apparently, the twins weren't supposed to have known that it was going to "Martha's." Helen was concerned that Earnest might find out Grace knew. But Brian then said that Martha herself—in a lapse of discretion, Toby supposed—had indicated to the twins they'd be staying with her. Hearing that, Helen said, "What a relief. If it's a problem, I'll blame it on Martha."

Toby began to see possibilities for a truce with Brian. Maybe even a pact. The kid didn't seem quite as creepy. Furthermore, both he and

Helen were keeping secrets from Earnest. How shaky might their loyalties be?

At any rate, if FATBOY didn't have a clue about this hideout, Brian would be necessary. Crucial, in fact. Toby said, "I assume you want to get out of here? And find Grace?"

Brian nodded. They heard the outer door open. Brian looked down the corridor. Toby watched his hands tighten on the bars. He then heard him say, "Hello, Mother."

Toby signaled he was reverting to idiot-state. Brian raised his right eyebrow. Meaning, Toby hoped, he'd go along.

Helen appeared. She carried a tray. "What are you doing?" she asked Brian with odd good humor.

"Trying to get him to talk," Brian said in discouraged tones.

"No luck?" Helen asked.

"He has the consciousness of an artichoke," Brian said.

Thank you, Toby thought. Helen handed Brian the tray and fished a cardkey from a pocket of her white lab jacket. "Let's see if I can do something about that," she said determinedly. She unlocked the cell's bars and entered. Toby, gazing at nothing in particular, saw food on the tray Brian carried in. Food, and an array of needles. Brian sent him an apprehensive glance.

"Put it there," Helen said, indicating the bedside table. Brian deposited the tray two feet from Toby's head. Helen took a pair of surgical gloves from the jacket. Her hands, knuckling into the latex, made sharp, rubbery squeals.

Toby thought, I should jump her.

From a speaker none of them had known existed, Earnest's voice blared, "Helen, Brian! I must speak with you! Please join me in the library."

"I guess," Helen said, staring at Toby, "he'll have to wait."

It was so vile. The very idea had provoked two separate coughing fits. First Dan, then Harry, had gone running for water. Still Gula sat trembling, gasping for breath. This could be it, she thought. The last straw before the stroke.

Grace's explanations were providing fresh proof of something Gula knew to be true. A new age, one beyond her comprehension, had dawned. Gula long since had given up trying to understand modernity. Still, she wasn't prepared for Grace's piece de resistance:

"The nukes are watching Martha's commercials."

Nuclear bombs were devotees of the woman's pointless, offensive television *advertisements*.

Since Gula had avoided news lately, she'd learned little, prior to Grace's revelations, about the Beast's sudden stardom; or for that matter about the preposterous idea that bombs could watch TV, period, never mind pay attention to commercials. The morning's phone calls had alerted her to strange goings-on, yes. But she hadn't felt a need to know much about them.

She'd now learned much too much. Worse, she was realizing she might not be able to make it go away. This horrified her. Descriptions of TV-watching bombs meantime put an image in her mind she couldn't get rid of. It concerned the showbiz personality whose hey-day she'd found so appalling. How she'd detested that silly woman with red hair. Yet Gula couldn't stop seeing it—brutish, bald-domed H-bombs, watching *I Love Lucy* with rapt devotion. Down to the last detail, she knew how Herblock would have drawn it.

Throughout Grace's exposition, Dan and Selma had sat still as rocks. Harry, asway in the Shaker rocking chair, had quietly stewed. He grunted, stopped swaying, and said, "The orb is the high-tech face? The greed face?"

"Uh-huh," Grace said. "A version of the orb is."

"Martha's made that obvious for years," Gula declared. "In so many ways, including commercials." Her wrinkles furrowing with disgust, Gula added, "But why does she have *bombs* watching them?"

Chilly silence descended. Breaking it, Harry said, "The whole thing seems foolish. If this is a doomsday plot, what with bombs watching TV, and satellites that can't be turned off else the bombs'll explode, and the icons or whatever are making 'em explode anyway sooner or later—it's pretty damn ornate."

"Yeah?" Grace said. "So?"

"I just can't believe anybody'd go to the trouble," Harry replied. "And I sure as hell don't believe that rabbit's a trigger. What's that you're sucking, girl? Advanced trank?"

"Gutzyme," Selma said. "For her ulcers."

Harry grunted. "Mental ulcers," he muttered. To Grace he said, "You're telling us the Mantis orb also triggers them?"

She nodded. "In a particular ad campaign. It consists of eight separate commercials. The first went on the air early Friday morning— it set off the bomb that caused the eruption. The others, released over time, will set off the seven other bombs. I bet one of them's already . . . "

"Sure," Harry snorted. "And the rabbit sets 'em all off?"

"Right. All at once."

Gula said peevishly, "Why that rabbit? Couldn't it be some other rabbit? Grace, there are many rabbits in the world . . . "

"This rabbit is a unique image," Grace said. "Never reproduced. The possibility another one like it exists is nil."

Harry said, "Gula, I got FATBOY's 800 number memorized. You tell me when to call it."

"Not so fast," Grace said. She held up the rabbit badge. "You don't think this explodes the bombs?"

"Nope," Harry said.

"And you don't think the Mantis commercials explode them?"

"Hell no!" Harry exclaimed, shaking his head. Long dirty-blond hair scrambled across his shoulders. "You have no proof of this," he said. "It's your word that Cliffcloud's involved. That's all. Your word." He glowered at Gula. "Why would a billionaire self-destruct? Why would she involve her company?"

Grace regarded him meditatively. She said, "Martha married that company. She got it from her husband, who's dead now. It means nothing to her. Mantis just means she's a billionaire—and what's a billionaire compared to a god?"

"A god?" Harry said. "Grace, you need sleep. Or something."

"How much you want to bet," Grace said, suddenly riled up, "that if we turn the TV on, they'll soon be talking about another explosion? An explosion that—I'll give you good odds. One that will go off in the next half hour?" Harry smiled scornfully. "And how much you want to bet that Mantis just introduced a new LaserWorks commercial?"

"I'll bet you an hour-long massage," Harry said.

Grace blanched.

"If you think you're going to win, dear," Gula croaked, "I'd take him up on that. Harry's the Leonardo da Vinci of massage."

Dan and Selma studied Harry with new respect.

"Let's make it a gentleman's bet," Grace said. She stood, hand extended. Harry stood and shook it.

"All right," he said. "What're you waiting for, girl? Turn the TV on."

Arthur Cannon peered at the twilit wasteland many thousand feet below. He tried to imagine its sprawl. He couldn't, despite having been through a crash course on the square mileage, the cubic mileage, the tonnage to the nth power. Arthur had crunched those numbers. Their significance remained abstract. The dimensions in question—like those, say, of galaxies—defied imagining. The ice sheet was just too big.

He would be flying over the thing for days to come. After a fashion, he'd get to know it. Not lovingly perhaps. Aside from the possibility of nuclear blasts, he'd be in the company of that redoubtable media phenom, Louise Lemieux.

Louise's howl of fury—"I'll garrote him!"—had endeared her to the hearts of millions. Still circling the globe as video of Ross Shelf's demise continued to replay, those words seemed to have crystallized the moment. They expressed, Arthur's rulers thought, how everyone felt.

Most everyone. Arthur suspected counter-opinions were building. In his gut, he felt an apprehension that agreed with something Trefethen had said. This corrupt, dying world . . . it does need, Arthur had caught himself thinking, a kick in the butt.

Should Trefethen give it? Arthur thought not.

Scant hours before, he'd been in Port Stanley on East Falkland Island researching the Falklands' natural gas boom. Midinterview with the British military commander, a serious fellow obsessed with flood, his communicator had signaled a priority fax from New York.

It contained instructions. A plane was chartered. Louise Lemieux was contracted. Arthur was to drop everything, get on the plane, fly clear across Antarctica to McMurdo Base, and produce Lemieux's reportage—her impassioned, outraged reportage—for the benefit of countless television viewers. Not to mention the benefit of Dracut Productions, Ltd.

"Just the man for the job," Dracut's CEO, Dracut Hornsby, had scrawled in a personal note at the bottom. "Coach her, Art. You have the people skills. Go to it."

The meaning was clear. Hornsby didn't expect gregarious, even-tempered Arthur to coach Louise Lemieux. He expected him to coax her—into coming up with as many variations as possible of the edifying, "I'll garrote him!"

Louise was to be the vengeance cheerleader. Arthur was to be her keeper and trainer. She would devise yet more bloodcurdling vows of punishment; he would egg her on. If Hornsby's business hunch paid off, and Arthur had no reason to think it wouldn't, a new superheroine would mount the tabloid equivalent of Mount Olympus. From that lofty peak, she would generate an avalanche of tie-ins—comics, games, lunch boxes, dolls, a cascade of mindless shit.

Arthur thought it over. The job might be all right. Given the melodrama of the whole crisis, this might even be weirdly fun. He reclined his seat to maximum tilt, pulled out his cigarette case, and examined its trove of sinsemilla-packed joints. Arthur didn't smoke tobacco. But he did smoke pot. High-grade pot was his sole self-indulgence. His only vice.

Why not light up here? For the time being, the plane was his. A new Boeing with lots of room, it held nothing but crew, himself, his equipment, and a quite cute technical staff, asleep at the moment in the back. The plane furthermore had entered a no-man's-land, jurisdictionally speaking. Antarctica's airspace, like the rest of its territory, was governed by guidelines that self-appointed nations had patched together to keep a lid on commercial exploitation. They wanted to preserve Antarctica as an international scientific park. A worthy aim. In dispute, unfortunately, now that the continent's mineral riches had become more evident.

The sinsemilla was hitting. Arthur found himself marveling at the idea of worthy aims. International organizations . . . the UN scarcely had said boo to the North African zealots busy murdering hundreds of thousands of their own people.

A videoscreen dropped from the ceiling just ahead. Arthur wondered what he could get over the West Antarctic Ice Sheet. He'd found plenty while approaching Drake Passage, as the plane passed the southernmost reaches of Argentina; a wide assortment of programming, including extensive crisis reportage. He played with his armrest's remote. The menu came up. Arthur studied it with blissfully drooping eyelids, and dialed.

Sun News was interviewing Reheema Sampson. More on the sinister Cambridge dinner, Arthur thought wearily. He liked Reheema, however. She was good on gay rights. Spectacular, actually.

"I don't get," she complained to the liverish-looking anchor, "why people think we should have realized what Earnest is doing. When he stood up after dinner, he didn't say, you know, 'I'm a terrorist and I nuked the volcano and I have ten more nukes that'll mess the planet.' He didn't say, 'The Beast is a biblical monster hiding in your TV set.' And he didn't say, 'Mother Earth's a bad momma fixing to whack the brats.' What he said—this is what he *said*—he said, 'We know the two evils threatening our future. Overpopulation, technology in the service of greed—they're the enemy. They are the Beast.'"

The anchor said, "I understand he made a final comment similar to his final statement on *Barclay*. Do you recall it?"

Reheema nodded. "Sure. 'Consider the cleansing effects of water.'" She shivered. Lustrous platinum-blond dreadlocks shimmied.

"At the time, you didn't think he meant that as a hint?"

"Are you kidding?" Reheema asked indignantly. "You're suggesting we should have figured he's Noah? Ready to board the ark and set sail while God cleans house?"

"Sources tell us that after the Trefethens left the restaurant, Lawrence Sforza made a startling remark. He said, to you and the other guests, 'Earnest has announced the Great Flood.' If Dr. Sforza said that . . . I should ask, did he say that?"

"Something along those lines. You have to remember, Earnest is a scientist, an expert on Antarctica volcanoes. Myself—I can't speak for Larry or the others—I thought he was talking about natural disaster. Not man-made disaster." She chuckled, her face somehow conveying a combination of hilarity, awe, and terror. "You gotta realize, the idea of Earnest nuking Antarctica—that wasn't thinkable. I mean, no way, totally no way . . ."

"However . . ." The anchor shuffled papers, not bothering to pretend they had anything to do with this interview. He's freaked, Arthur thought. What's the audience, he wondered—a couple billion? I'd be freaked too, he decided. I'd worry that Trefethen has this rigged. That he's using the media to maximum advantage.

"However?" Reheema said.

"Let's move on. Can you tell us what Trefethen thinks he'll accomplish? The 'Beast' business . . . has the man gone insane? Or does he know what he's doing?"

Reheema shrugged. "Maybe both. I'll tell you one thing. In his terms, he probably thinks he's being idealistic. I mention that not because I agree with him. Obviously, I don't. I mention it because it makes him even more dangerous."

"Idealistic? When he's causing untold misery?"

Pensively, Reheema put her chin in a palm. She thought a few moments, then murmured, "He doesn't get off on misery. You know, Earnest has been talking about the Beast, the so-called Beast, for years. No one's listened."

"He's enraged because no one has listened?"

"He's angry, yes. But sad, too." Clearly upset now, Reheema frowned. "And—dare I say this?—for good reason."

"That is what we want to know," the anchor declared. "His 'good reason.' What is it?"

"I'll get in trouble. But I'll say it anyway. His reason, I think, is the biggest cliché around. It's so obvious, what it is. We're poisoning the planet. We're killing the biosphere. And the amazing thing is, we *know* we're doing it. The evidence—come on, the evidence has been plain as day since the early '90s, since before even then . . . "

"There is disagreement about that," the anchor said testily.

"And it's bull," Reheema retorted. "We've known about carbon emissions, we've known about greenhouse, we've known about global warming and climate shift and the whole ball of wax. We've known about ozone depletion screwing the food chain—about the way ultraviolet hardens the shells of the diatoms that krill eat, so bad the diatoms are getting indigestible, which means—hell, nothing in the ocean eats, if the krill don't eat. We know this stuff. And yet—what do we do? The UN passes a toothless carbon cap? That nobody obeys? The UN tells China and the Pacific Rim they can't use ozone-eating chemicals, but what goes on in China? In the entire Pacific Rim? We know what goes on. And what do we do? Almost *zilch*."

Arthur yawned. Are things really that dire? he wondered. Probably, he reflected. But what can we, in fact, do? Stop being the piglets we so enjoy being? Forget it.

"We'll take a break," the anchor said.

The show cut to commercial. Arthur muted the videoscreen. He had no interest in the Mantis orb. Or in Libra LaserWorks, which, since he'd seen this ad before, he knew to be Mantis's novelty of the moment. Drowsily, he watched the egg-shaped orb emit energy waves. Mutating energy waves. It never put out the same patterns twice, according to Mantis hype. A viral ecology in the software generated the thing. Experts claimed it was alive . . .

Arthur realized he hadn't seen this episode before. It's a sequel, he thought. Part two of the LaserWorks campaign?

Like a softball-size UFO, the orb floated through dark gardens. Glowing unpredictably, uniquely. It's evening at a major exurb spread. Acres and acres of lawn and shrubs. All appears well. But wait a second . . . what's coming from the trees? Creeping toward the distant, innocent, unsuspecting mansion? My God—heavily armed thugs. Five of them . . . leathery thongs hanging from the ears . . . trophy-takers, striking again! Obviously the thongs are dried human flesh! Bits of hair . . . maybe an eyeball . . . but we know, of course, the orb will get them. We know it'll unleash a stunning new technology, lasers no doubt, that the rich will rush out and buy. Now it's following the doomed killers across the lawn. And seems ready to make its move . . . it's flaring, shooting multicolored beams of light—our villains freeze! They're terrified. A thong incinerates . . .

Miniature Star Wars, Arthur mused. The arms industry, he dreamily considered, is putting science to unexpected use. Laser weapons, for example. That burglars, not missiles, now were targets, seemed emblematic of a trend. Charming, Arthur thought. The old king, geopolitical ideology, is dead. Long live the new king, personal security.

Blizzards had deposited fresh snow over the last few months. Almost nothing on the ice sheet's highlands possessed the means to notice. Microscopic spores, the only living entities for hundreds of miles in any direction, and thousands in many, didn't have the kind of sentience that paid attention to snow. Or to the blackness of the night, the ferocity of the winds, the intensity of the cold.

But seven machines, buried neck-deep in the ice, did notice snowfall. They noticed when it covered their modular dishes.

The machines originally had been climatological sensors that fed data to satellites. Technologically, they were cousins of those satellites. The designers of both had faced similar problems providing means to cope with cold, and with high-speed bombardment; space trash in one case, ice crystals in the other. The similarities weren't limited to those considerations. They extended to such things as plutonium power packs, precision-tooled servomechanisms, and compact, powerful computers.

The computers of the seven machines in the ice were very powerful. Terafloppingly so, which, as Arthur Cannon might have put it, was inconceivably powerful. They needed that power to do their work. For they'd been assigned a daunting task.

It involved looking. These machines were looking for needles in an electromagnetic haystack.

Neck-deep they were buried, but that didn't quite describe them, due to the periscopic extendability of their necks. Like reverse ostriches, the machines could unbury heads from the Antarctic sand, to regain sight if storms had blinded them. It so happened that when Arthur was meditating about home defense weaponry in his high-flying jet, one of the machines was preening itself, clearing snow from its dish with vigorous head tosses. It therefore missed the first few seconds of LaserWorks' Antarctic visit. However, it caught the rest of the commercial; for it had been programmed to relock quickly, following preenings, on the satellites to which its multiple eyes were dedicated.

Thus the machine's computer, like those of its six distant sisters, caught sight of the commercial's laser-firing orb. That is, it and its sisters isolated the orb from the flood of television signal coming from the sky. The computer proceeded to scan every binary iota of the digitized flow bringing the orb to earth.

Unlike its sisters, which also were scanning, it found something special in the orb's laser-fire. That particular pattern of fire—one of eight different patterns that the orb, during eight different commercials, eventually would spew—was the needle in the haystack for which the computer had been looking.

Actually, it had been looking for two needles. But having found one of them, it no longer was bothering with the other. Without passion it cyberyelped, "Eureka." A nanosecond later, it prepared to send a command to the device that waited more than a mile below, in the caldera of a dormant volcano.

Fourteen minutes and forty-seven seconds would go by, however, and then a fraction of a second more, before it sent the command.

When designing the system, Earnest hadn't worried about the NSA's computers finding a relationship between the LaserWorks ad campaign and nuclear explosions. In fact, he wanted the NSA, and other intelligence agencies as well, to find that relationship. He was counting on it.

But he'd seen no reason to provide too exact a coincidence this early in the game.

Helen and Brian entered the library. They immediately saw it was serious. Father's eyes held a distant, otherworldly focus. Martha appeared to be suffering from severe angina.

The library occupied the octagon's northeast pavilion and thus afforded a view of the lake at the other end of the valley. It contained very few books, perhaps three. However, the seating arrangements featured tasteful viewscreens, which accessed a large collection of digitized text. The room also contained several hundred print periodicals, Martha's one concession to old-style publishing. The magazines and journals, devoted to a range of business and political topics, covered three massive wood tables she'd acquired from a monastery in the Austrian Alps. According to antiquarians, the tables dated to the sixteenth century. They'd originally supported, if the provenance documents were accurate, the labors of a celebrated Gutenberg disciple.

Martha's librarian helicoptered from Manhattan twice a week, along with the rest of the household staff, to deliver fresh periodicals and keep the room in order. Her recent efforts, as well as those of the florists, were evident. The reading material lay displayed in perfect alignment. Gibbous bouquets of rain-forest blooms rose from large crystal vases. From thirteen crystal vases. The fourteenth, contents glistening in a shard-strewn puddle, lay shattered on the parquet floor.

"What is the matter?" Helen said.

"Sit!" Earnest snapped, pointing at an Italianate sofa in the room's middle. Helen and Brian sat. "What were you doing with the prisoner?" Earnest demanded.

Helen replied coolly, "I was about to see if I could make him think, and talk."

"And you, Brian?"

"The same," Brian said.

"You'll be going back there shortly," Earnest declared. "I'm going with you—because I too intend to make him think, and talk."

Not if I can stop it, Helen thought. She said, "How did you find us?"

Martha rumbled, "The house keeps track of where anyone in it is. But you have to . . . "

"Know how to ask it," Earnest said. "Something I now know how to do." He grimaced introspectively. Then, in threatening tones, he said, "I will play a portion of something Martha received this morning. Give it your full attention." He pressed a button on a data-retrieval control panel.

From concealed speakers came a festive babble of voices so vivid, invisible guests seemed to have gathered fifteen feet away. Helen and Brian, recognizing the voices, frowned with surprise. Their eyes then narrowed with shock. As if a phantom Grace had joined them on the sofa, they heard her whisper, "It's desperation." Her voice suggested she was speaking confidentially.

A phantom Brian replied bitterly, but with equal confidentiality, "Like it never was?"

Thirty seconds passed. The background phantoms continued to babble. The real Brian, feeling not real at all, listened to his parents' voices rise and fall with the others. This was becoming quite horrible. He didn't think he could control his rising panic.

From thin air, a phantom Martha remarked, "I bet you kids have better things to do than be cooped up with the likes of us."

Phantom Grace said flatly, "Very funny."

Phantom Martha said, voice pitched lower, "Are you ready?" The question was delivered with almost shocking intimacy. It suggested that Martha had entered the twins' confidential zone, and that entering it brought her closer to whatever had recorded this.

Brian, the phantom one, muttered, "Ready for what?"

Grace sighed with palpable tension, prompting a violent twitch in the real Brian.

"Come on," Martha said, voice pitched even lower. "You're standing on the edge of history and you say for what?"

Grace whispered, "You shouldn't be talking to us."

Brian whispered, "Father's looking, Martha."

Martha whispered, "Relax. We'll talk, Sunday, at my place."

Thirty seconds passed. Brian murmured, "She's excited."

Grace said, fear evident in the voice, "You can't do it. Father will see it." Again, she sighed tensely. "Just mail it."

"Stop talking about it," Brian snapped. "The edge of history," he muttered.

"Ours," Grace said. "We're history."

Earnest pressed a button. The playback stopped. Arms folded across his chest, lips compressed to a bloodless horizontal, eyes darkened to near-cobalt, he gazed at wife and son. "What was it that 'Father will see'?"

Helen glanced at Brian. His knees vibrated; they shook. Suddenly Helen felt as if she were falling headfirst down a very deep well. Brian stammered, "I . . . I don't . . . really know."

"You don't know!" Earnest shouted. "You don't know what it was that Grace urged you to—mail?" Helen forced herself to look at him. "Might it have been," Earnest inquired, "the rabbit badge? The original of the fertility icon?"

Helen had no choice. It was either seize this by the horns, or face extinction. She turned to Brian and smacked a palm across his face with all the force she could deliver.

Brian's head exploded. The room reddened; tectonic slips shuddered through his skull. Rage, siren-like, spiraled through his stomach, his chest. Deep in the welter, in the roaring shock and pain, he wondered if he could do it. If he wanted to do it—confess everything, on the spot.

Mother said poisonously, "How dare you not tell me?"

Brian decided he didn't just want to. He needed to do it. To confess everything to Father, right here, right now.

Then he looked at Mother, and saw her eyes.

In the agonized, desperate gray, something quivered. It seemed a kind of mental substance. A mental energy, that pain had both spiritualized and depraved; somehow, suffering had refined it. Brian thought about this. As he thought, gazing into Mother's eyes, the substance there seemed to spurt. Brian felt it penetrate his mind with the force of a bullet. He shook his head. And knew what he had to do.

He said, "I lied, Mother. I thought I could get away with it, when you didn't probe me. So I lied about everything." He turned to Father and said, "Mother knew nothing. As for me—it's obvious. I deserve to die."

Helen stood, walked to the French doors, and gazed at the far-off lake. She asked slowly, "What does the blackmailer want?"

With a sound that evoked the mixing of concrete, Martha cleared her throat. She said, "One hundred million dollars."

"How did he put it?" Helen asked. "The demand?"

"He has a recording of the entire dinner party," Martha said. She clawed her ebony helmet of hair. "He says he's auctioning it to a group of media bidders. Interest, he claims, is high. The fee for deleting the section you just heard is a hundred million." Martha paused. And added, "Which, of course, I've paid."

"Slotsky," Helen murmured. "It must be the man Mary talked

about—Slotsky." She turned to face Earnest, eyes glittery with tears. "I am sorry our son betrayed us. And I'm sorry Martha made that incredibly stupid . . ." Helen gestured at the still-lingering presence of the phantom voices, "mistake. But whatever this means, Earnest—our work must go on."

Earnest scowled at the broken vase. Seconds passed. With a sudden sigh, he nodded. Shoulders drooping, he said, "Yes. Yes, of course. Where is the icon? The badge, I should say."

Helen said, "Brian? You told me you destroyed it."

Brian evaluated that assertion. He said, "I didn't, Mother. Grace gave it to Fladgate. But then Fladgate . . . I guess Grace has the badge. I'm sure she does."

"Superb," Earnest said. "Grace knows where we are, too. You told her, Martha—'We'll talk, Sunday, at my place.' Just superb."

"Don't rub it in," Martha said.

Helen studied Martha's discomfiture, and savored it.

Earnest remarked, "If Grace hasn't already destroyed us, she easily could. Is that what Mary meant? Has Grace, perhaps, been in touch with her?"

"No," Helen said. She smiled with a self-assurance that both Earnest and Martha found peculiar. Brian, for his part, was beyond noticing such things. "It occurs to me," Helen continued, "that Grace may be somewhere close by. Somewhere in our near vicinity."

"Oh, yes?" Earnest said.

Helen said, "Earlier I was thinking that if she knew where we are, she'd try to contact us." She glanced reprovingly at Martha. "It seems Grace does know. I think she'll be in touch."

Earnest exclaimed, "Grace defected! Why, I have no idea—but she's not out for a joyride! What makes you think she'll be in touch?"

Helen looked at Brian and said, "Because he's here, of course. I'm sure she wants to reassure him that she's all right. And I'm very sure," she added meaningfully, "she'll do nothing that would jeopardize Brian's safety. Any sort of contact with Mary—any contact at all—well, I don't have to spell it out."

Earnest stared at the tangle of flowers on the floor. "There still is the issue of blackmail," he muttered. "Slotsky, if he's who it is. The man didn't provide a name. Just a bank number."

"However, Martha has paid," Helen replied. "For the moment, the blackmailer, whoever it is, has been bought off. When he decides to demand more money—Martha will deal with it, that's all. Given those circumstances, why would he blow our cover? The situation is an indefinite cash cow. Eh, Martha?"

"That was unnecessary," Martha remarked huskily.

Helen ignored her. She said to Earnest, "If we must, we'll evacuate. We're prepared. From the beginning, we've known we might be obliged to take the truck elsewhere."

"Does Toby know anything about Slotsky?" Earnest asked.

"I was trying to determine if he does," Helen said evenly. "When you interrupted."

Martha watched Helen with growing apprehension. It was plain she'd lost her mind. If they were forced to evacuate, it would be due to a major attack; no other kind of attack, given the target they represented, was conceivable. If it came, did Helen think she'd make it out in that flimsy tin can? Her pathetic home-on-wheels would last less than a minute. Attack, if it came, would be swift, thorough, and deadly. A successful evacuation required correspondingly extreme measures.

For various reasons, Helen didn't know about the measures Martha had devised. To those reasons Martha added another.

Earnest said somberly, "Let's pay a visit to Toby."

Helen said, "I should prep some instruments. Surgical items. Getting him to talk could be a job."

"Whatever it takes," Earnest said. "We'll meet you there—in half an hour?"

"That's good," Helen said. She walked out of the room.

Martha caught Earnest's eye. "Don't fret," she said.

He glanced at Brian. "Fret," he said emptily. "My son is a traitor. But I musn't fret. Martha, depending on what's going on with Grace, and Slotsky—we could face assault. At any moment."

"You think I'm not ready?" Martha asked.

Earnest didn't reply.

But I am ready, Martha thought. Maybe it's best, she reflected, that we face sudden assault. Maybe it's best to make it short and brutal. Short and sweet.

Arthur Cannon was dozing when the plane started bucking. His eyes flew open. He groped for the seat belt, thinking they'd hit unusual turbulence.

The pilot came over the intercom. "Something pretty damn strange is happening on the ground," he informed the cabin. "East of us. Maybe a hundred and eighty miles away."

Arthur's window faced west. He looked across the cabin. Through the opposite windows, a glow was seeping.

Groggily, Arthur wondered what it was. Nothing should be down there. Nothing but inconceivable wasteland. He got up and staggered to a seat on the other side.

A giant opalescence, like celestial mother-of-pearl, was rising through the clouds. Arthur gaped at it. Sure, he was stoned. Very stoned, on very good pot. But it didn't look like Antarctica down there. The unearthly glow—it looked like hellfire.

Then he saw sparks shooting through. Small, brilliant sparks. If they're a hundred and eighty miles away, Arthur slowly realized, they can't be so small. Not small at all.

It dawned on him he was watching the upper flares of an eruption. A major eruption. On the surface—or rather, under it—a volcano was blowing its top.

Twenty rows back, he heard frightened murmurs. His techies had wakened. They too were watching the show.

Arthur remembered why they'd been sent to the world's frozen underside. He yelled, "Set up, guys! Set up, and get the uplink going—now!"

42

From the TV in Toby's cell, Carson O'Doyle said urgently, "We have received word of another nuclear explosion in West Antarctica. Like the Friday blast, it has spawned a volcanic eruption. By exclusive arrangement with Dracut Productions, Ltd., we shortly will bring you live video of the event."

Toby didn't find this news promising. For the government's hang-tough policy, or for his personal future.

"CNN's scientific advisory team," O'Doyle went on, "is studying data that scientists in New Zealand and Chile have obtained from seismological sensors. The team's first comments came to my desk moments ago. This eruption, we regret to report, appears several orders of magnitude more powerful than the first one. 'It's a Kraka-toa,' one analyst remarked." O'Doyle winced. "Stay with us. We'll be right back with that exclusive video. It's—astounding."

A beer commercial came on. Lager foamed cheerfully. What would I do, Toby wondered, without this TV set?

The corridor's door unlocked. Toby heard a shuffle of footsteps. It indicated the approach of more than one person.

The needle tray lay on the corridor floor. Toby had been thinking about the needles since Trefethen had summoned Helen. Would they wake him up? Or "keep him out"?

Helen unlocked the bars. She entered briskly, carrying the needle tray and a medical valise. The commercial she muted, not giving it a glance. Toby glimpsed others in the corridor. Without moving his head he couldn't tell who they were.

Two feet away on the bedside table, Helen put down the tray. She sat on the bed, opened her valise, and unpacked implements. From the corridor came a familiar squeal of swinging metal. It was like the sound Toby's bars made, when opening.

Toby craned his neck slightly. He saw Earnest Trefethen close the opposite cell's bars on a scared-looking Brian. Toby then saw Martha Cliffcloud give Trefethen a cardkey. He put it in the lock slot. Huh, thought Toby. Brian in the slammer? A low gasp caused him to shift his attention.

Helen was watching Toby's every eyelash flicker. Her lips curled. She leaned over and stared, face rigid with ill intent, directly into his eyes. Involuntarily, Toby stared back.

They shared an electrified eye-to-eye moment. Transmitting, each to the other, undisguised loathing.

She grabbed a spray device. Toby saw urgency, even panic in the way she gripped it. Her fingers sought a button. The button that would spray paralyzing shit in his face.

Toby snapped his arm back and punched her hard on the chin.

Helen reeled, screaming the mother of all screams. Toby swatted the spray thing from her hands; she toppled from the bed, screaming louder. Suddenly the cell seemed three feet square.

"Psychotic bitch!" Toby bellowed, shrinking the cell yet more.

Trefethen rushed in, hands double-gripping a gun. "Ah!" he exclaimed, blue eyes bulging. "Awake, it seems!"

"Attacked me!" Helen howled. On hands and knees she scuttled to the wall. To the spray device, Toby realized. "Have to sedate him," she gasped as she stood, device double-gripped. Emulating her husband's combat stance, Toby thought. He grabbed a pillow.

Helen lunged with the spray thing. Toby shoved the pillow at her, yelling, "She wants to shut me up!"

Helen snarled, "Earnest, *help me*."

"She's lied to you!" Toby shouted to Trefethen, shaking the pillow as hard as he could at the desperate, deadly woman.

"He nearly killed me!" Helen screamed. She lunged, trying to out-flank the pillow.

Toby shook it at her harder, shouting at Trefethen, "She doesn't want you to know what I know!"

"Helen!" Trefethen exclaimed. "I have him covered!"

"He's dangerous," Helen panted, going into a cougar-like crouch that Toby didn't like. She thought she could get him.

"Bet your ass," Toby blurted through pounding hyperventilation. "I know how you *covered up*."

Beyond Trefethen's fascinated glare, something about the TV caught Toby's eye. For some reason the Disney Channel had come on. Then Toby realized it wasn't the Magic Kingdom, shooting fireworks. It was Krakatoa.

"Helen, get back," Trefethen said.

"Don't listen to him," she hissed, jaw muscles working, hands clutching the spray thing so tightly, she looked like she'd crumple it. "A classic borderline! Capable of clever manipulation!"

"Right," Toby said, brandishing the pillow at her. "I'm so disturbed, I melt bullets with my mind. Dr. Trefethen, believe it—she doesn't *want me to talk!*"

"*To lie!*" she shouted, maddened eyes flicking at her husband.

"His lies interest me," Trefethen said. "Talk," he told Toby.

Toby took a deep breath. "In the truck," he said, "she and Brian checked on me. They thought I was out but I wasn't, and I listened to them. She was afraid you'd discover that Grace knew where you were going. Where the truck was taking you—here, I guess. But then Brian said Cliffcloud had revealed where you were going. To which your wife replied, 'Good. If it's a problem, I'll blame it on Martha.'"

Cliffcloud's tall frame filled the doorway. Her eyes gleamed.

"There's more, lots more," Toby said. "If you want to know it, get her out of here."

"Keep talking," Trefethen said.

"Not with her around. Get her out."

"You're giving orders?" Earnest asked coldly.

Toby considered the question. He took another deep breath, tossed his chin at Helen, and said, "I bet she covered up the fact that the twins tried to give FATBOY the rabbit. How the twins tried to wreck your plans—obviously she covered the whole thing up. Because other-wise, you'd have jailed Brian way before now."

Trefethen said quietly, "Martha, I want you to escort Helen upstairs. Keep an eye on her. Helen, leave that medication here." She stared at her husband, stunned. "Go upstairs," he said.

Face gray, eyes dulling, Helen dropped the sprayer. She moved to the doorway. Martha stepped through to let her out. "Earnest," she said with a catch in her throat. "Look at the TV."

Trefethen looked. The image on the screen seemed to hit him with physical force. It reminded Toby of Jupiter's cloud cover. The center roiled and flickered. Glowing sparks shot through.

Cliffcloud unmuted the set. A deep voice, professionally pitched but unable to disguise the speaker's dread, said, "Captain Baedeker tells me we're forty miles away, and not going closer. It is hard to con-vey the scale of this event. The airplane from which I speak is twenty thousand feet in the air. But as you can see, fiery debris is shooting close to that altitude. I do not know if viewers can hear the plane's vibration as it encounters the turbulence—turbulence the captain tells me comes from the blast. To the people aboard this plane, it feels as if we are trespassing on sacred territory. On damned territory, perhaps. We are circling the habitat of angry gods."

Cliffcloud gave Trefethen a startled glance. He appeared thunder-struck. Toby, although interested in these reactions, kept a closer eye on Helen. Her face a death mask of hate, she was staring at him from the doorway.

The TV voice continued, "What would the eruption look like if clouds weren't obscuring it? I venture to guess we'd glimpse what Dante saw, in his mind's eye, as he penned *The Inferno*. This is Arthur Cannon—reporting live above a raging Antarctic volcano."

"Son of a gun," Trefethen murmured. "I never thought we'd get pictures of one of those. Didn't think they'd blow through the cloud cover."

"Habitat of angry gods," Cliffcloud said. "That's excellent."

Trefethen muttered, "Yes. Well, of course—Martha, take Helen upstairs. Please." Toby noted his ashen pallor. The man's shaken, he realized. He's feeling ill.

Cliffcloud led Helen down the corridor. Toby listened to their foot-steps pass through the outer door and fade. Then he noticed some-thing.

Helen had abandoned more than the sprayer, the needles, and the medical implements. She'd also left the cardkey. It was lying on the bedside table.

Through the purplish vortex of clouds, glowing junk shot skyward. It was like watching something from the planet's early days. Primordial ooze, rotating with the slow spiral of a tropical storm, was spitting fire.

"That must be stopped," Gula said weakly.

"Let's call the 800 number," Harry muttered.

"You didn't listen to me," Grace remarked.

Harry couldn't look at her. This girl now scared him silly. Not only was Antarctica once again exploding. Grace, channel-surfing, had found a new LaserWorks commercial. He and Gula had been startled to see that this episode revealed whose estate the orb's lasers were defending. Martha Cliffcloud's estate. The place over the ridge.

"Listen to me," Grace said, suddenly seeming younger. Like a four-teen-year-old street waif, Harry thought. "Father can set off the bombs whenever he wants," she said in a monotone. "He'll use either the orb or the rabbit. Probably the rabbit, because the commercials could be yanked. But the rabbit will get through. It'll get through even if we give FATBOY the pin—there's no way to filter the nets. There are too many nets."

"To filter them?" Harry said.

"An idea Brian had. To try to stop Father. Stop the rabbit." Grace slumped lower in her chair, looking even younger. Listlessly she con-tinued, "What I'm saying is, if you call the general, he'll strike Martha's right away. Then Father releases the rabbit, and the bombs go off right away. Or almost right away. At least, eventually. The rab-bit, see, is a virus. That's the beauty of it. Father can slip it in the datasphere any way he wants, through a newspaper photograph, through anything, and the datasphere is infected. Terminally infected. Which means the rabbit might hit the bombs quickly—but even if it doesn't, it could take a long, indirect route through the media streams. Replicating as it goes, see. Increasing its chances of getting through."

"An attractive concept," Dan remarked.

Harry said, "What if your father sics the rabbit on the bombs right away anyway? Even if the general doesn't attack?"

"He won't," Grace said. "Can't you see the game he's playing? He wants to play it as long as he can. To do that, he can't waste bombs—every bomb used, he loses leverage. So Father won't explode another bomb for at least a week, maybe longer. Unless the government's even stupider than it's been already. Which I doubt. Now they know he has them by the . . ." She blushed.

"Say it," Harry said. "Balls."

"Grace," Selma said. "What do you propose?"

"I propose," she said, gazing pinkly at Gula, "that you don't call anybody. It would make things worse."

Harry stared at the plasma on TV. "How much worse can they get?" he grumbled.

"Are you some kind of moron?" Grace demanded, color draining from her face. "If the bombs go off, can't you see what will happen? Civil war between coasts and uplands. Everywhere, mass population rush. Panic, chaos, collapse. Military rule for the lucky places where gang terror doesn't take over."

They sat in motionless quiet, contemplating those images.

Gula sputtered, "You mean, if we blow the whistle on Martha, barbarians will lay waste? The sack of Connecticut?"

"You can't begin to imagine it," Grace replied. "You call FATBOY now, it'll get ugly sometime tonight. By tomorrow morning, the 'triumph'—the obliteration of everything over that ridge—will be on page eleven of the newspapers." She jerked a thumb at the TV. "Because you'll have six more of those happening, and people will freak. They'll start running around like rabid coyotes. They will think it's Judgment Day."

Harry felt follicles go on point all over his body. It was as if Grace had shapeshifted, revealing herself to be the smirking Charles Manson. He said to her, "In ten words or less, what does your father want?"

She thought. And said, extending her ten fingers one by one, "To make Antarctica an unforgettable symbol of the planet's rage."

"Its rage about what?" Gula snapped.

"The Beast," Grace said. "Overpopulation. High-tech greed."

Harry shuddered. "Adds up to us being neighbors of a self-destruct machine," he commented. "A billionaire self-destruct . . ."

"That's what I've been trying to tell you!" Grace declared. "They've wired the world to self-destruct. But they're playing a role in it—my parents and Martha, they've wired themselves into the whole thing. You have to get this through your heads—Martha *wants* to be exposed. If she didn't, why would the orb be an icon? Why would Mantis, the ads on TV, be part of the plan?"

"Martha's the Beast," Dan said thoughtfully.

"Half true," Grace said. "Her estate is orb-land. It's the Beast theme park over there. Which means it'll be crushed. If you make that call, it will be blown to bits."

My stupefaction is complete, Gula thought. "Martha wants to be blown to bits?" she asked.

Grace shrugged. "They won't stay if they think FATBOY's coming. They'll run, if they can. They'll run as long as possible. But eventually they'll get it. And they know it."

With varying degrees of incredulity, Grace's audience absorbed what she'd said. Harry said, "So we don't call FATBOY. That'll delay Armageddon by maybe a week. What do you propose we do?"

"Bathe," Grace declared. "Eat. Nap. And try to think."

Gula frowned at the child's presumption. She drew the back of her hand over her eyes; this was so much more than she'd bargained for. Grace's whims required instant fulfillment, of course. Or the sky would fall. She quavered to Harry, "Take these creatures upstairs. And drown them."

Harry lurched to his feet. "Come, kittens," he said.

Grace stood. With a hint of anxiety she said, "I hope I can use a bathroom that's, um, private?"

"Level four containment," Harry replied. "Wear a spacesuit when you take a shower, that's how we deal with microbes like you. Completely sealed off. Completely private."

Dan said to Selma as they followed Harry and Grace out of the room, "I wonder if Toby's heard about the rabid coyotes?"

"Probably he thought of them himself," Selma replied, watching Harry lead Grace to an alcove. They followed the two into it.

The alcove housed a back staircase. Its walls and verticals were painted white, against which the steps, enameled the floor's color, floated redly upward. Selma paused. She put a hand on Dan's shoulder, stopping him. When Harry and Grace reached the second story, she whispered, "She's a genius."

"Grace?"

"Yes. She's convinced us that doing anything that might put her brother in danger will destroy civilization."

"Toby would love it," Dan whispered.

"Especially," Selma pointed out, "considering the predicament he's probably in."

They looked at each other. And shook their heads.

Toby had begun to wonder, shortly after Cliffcloud took Helen away, if he should try to escape. He'd stashed the cardkey in the breast pocket of his pajamas. Might it unlock places besides the cell?

Whether it did or not, the cell bars were wide open. Trefethen sat a few feet away, gun in his lap, attention fixed on the TV. He didn't have a direct view of the bed; Toby sat cross-legged on it to his right and rear. Had he forgotten about the prisoner with tales of traitorous deeds?

He hadn't. Three minutes into their joint occupation of the cell— TV blaring, Brian invisible and silent across the corridor—Earnest had said over his shoulder, "The place is full of security lasers. You'll be burnt toast if you try to get out."

Huh, Toby had thought. Mantis LaserWorks, of course. He'd seen the orb's latest episode hype it not long before.

More time passed. On CNN, reactions escalated. Government spokespeople declined comment, creating a vacuum that analysts rushed to fill. Their voice-overs found ominous significance in the volcano-torn clouds filling the screen. Why were they moving like a whirlpool? Was the eruption creating a cyclone? Were atmospheric physics at play; or did the rotation symbolize something? Could it be taken to mean that Antarctica was circling the drain? The clouds were moving counterclockwise. The analysts deemed this appropriate. Antarctica, the ultimate Down Under, naturally would drain in that direction.

And why did the phrase, "Habitat of angry gods," sound so haunting? Speaking of angry figures on high, would the President go ahead with his speech tonight? Could Trefethen, having counter-punched with such diabolical force, end up bumping him? But how could the President even consider allowing a terrorist to bump him? On the other hand, given the panic of coastal populations everywhere, maybe the President, and other leaders, would find it advisable to allow Trefethen to have his say. Would they cave? The world wanted to know.

Trefethen sat drinking it in, displaying no sign that wife and children were on his agenda. Toby, watching him watch the world react to his latest enormity, discovered something about himself. He realized that the principal item on his own agenda wasn't escape.

Getting out would be nice. And he certainly planned to make use of the cardkey in whatever way he could. But another issue had taken hold of his mind. The evil mastermind, the archdemon of doom, sat right there, his back casually turned toward him.

Why was this guy bashing the planet?

When Toby couldn't take it any longer, he coughed a fake cough, the kind one uses to get attention. Trefethen didn't react. Toby steeled himself, and said, "May I ask a question?"

Eyes staying with the TV, Trefethen said, "Yes."

"Why is a dedicated environmentalist turning the world's coastlines into an ecological nightmare?"

"For the fun of it, of course," Trefethen replied.

Oh, Toby thought. He said, "I realize you have no reason to take me seriously. But I'd like to know—are the bombs looking for the rabbit?"

Trefethen shifted his chair and said, "Right you are. Tell me what you have to say about my wife, and do so quickly."

Amazing himself, Toby said, "No."

The blue eyes seemed to map every square micron of his face. Trefethen said, "I think I'll call Dr. Scarf back. She'd love to get her hands on you. After what you pulled."

"Call her back," Toby replied, amazing himself further. "I'll say I haven't talked about her, or the twins. With great relief, she'll proceed to kill me. And you will learn nothing."

"You think you're being clever?"

"Look, the way I see it, I have nothing to lose. You'll kill me anyway. Sooner or later."

Trefethen frowned. "Do you really believe that?" he asked.

Toby nodded. "I'm also very curious. About what you hope to

accomplish by . . ." He pointed at the TV. "Making the planet have a giant nervous breakdown."

"So I explain myself, eh? In return, you provide information. That's the deal?"

"Uh-huh," Toby said.

"What makes you think your information is valuable?"

"Why is it hard to tell me what you're doing?"

"That doesn't answer my question."

"Yeah. I'll tell you why the information is valuable. It's not just about your charming wife and kids. I have other information as well."

"On what subject?"

"Wouldn't you like to know?"

"This will not get you very far."

"But I'm not going anywhere. As you pointed out when you mentioned burnt toast. I just want to know—why?"

Trefethen's eyes now mapped every cubic angstrom of Toby's brain. "Nice try," he said. "The fact of the matter is, you've given me the information already. It wasn't a surprise, by the way. Cool your feverish curiosity. And talk."

"Slotsky would laugh," Toby remarked.

"Slotsky?"

"Yes," Toby said. "A fascinating man. Do you know him?"

Trefethen's features sharpened. He said, "You know him?"

"Do I know him? It's amazing I got away from the guy. After what I learned about his plans. Not to mention . . ." Toby left it at that.

"You're under the impression that I'm interested in Slotsky?"

I am now, Toby thought. He'd caught Trefethen off-guard. Adept at deception though the man obviously was, he hadn't thought he'd have to use it on a mere nuisance of a prisoner; interest in Slotsky had blazed from his face. Toby said, "Put it this way. You must have seen McMurtry's press conference. So you know FATBOY's interested in Slotsky. It goes way beyond that, though. FATBOY happens to be obsessed with him. And I know why."

"Do you?" Trefethen said.

Toby said, "Did Dr. Scarf tell you about the bugging of the dinner party at Mifflin Place?" Trefethen cleared his throat. Toby sensed he'd hooked him. Emboldened, he said, "Your janitor, Miles Malt, planted the bug. Did you know Malt worked for Slotsky until Slotsky murdered him on the stairs of my apartment building?"

Trefethen said, "Go on."

Toby shook his head. "First, you answer my questions. Then, I reveal all. But it's a two-way street. If you're going to get answers out of me, I'm going to get them out of you."

"Young man, you do not seem to grasp the nature of the circumstances here . . . "

"You don't seem to realize," Toby yelled, "that I don't care!" His head suddenly felt like an industrial espresso machine. Memories of the torture Helen had inflicted steamed through his brain, brewing exceptionally sober awareness of what he faced. He said, "Do you know how many corpses I've seen in the last couple of days? You think I'm stupid—that I'm unaware that if you succeed, you'll murder millions? Don't tell me about circumstances!"

"Please try to calm down."

"Look at me! Look at my eyes! Did somebody put food coloring in my Visine? What happened to my *eyes*? You and your wife—you use people like *lab rats!* When you're done with me, you'll kill me without a second thought—don't think I don't know it, okay?"

Ever so slightly, Trefethen shuddered. Huh, Toby thought. Could the man be feeling a little queasy about this?

"I won't waste time arguing," Trefethen snapped. "Let me make this clear. I am fully prepared to call Dr. Scarf if you don't cooperate."

"I don't think so."

Trefethen stood. "I'm getting her right now."

"I've noticed something about your wife, Dr. Trefethen. She'd rather die than have you lose faith in her."

Trefethen stared at him.

"She isn't capable of making me say what I know," Toby continued. "The consequences worry her more than you think."

"You have no idea of what she's capable of doing."

"Oh yes I do. The monster Roto-rootered my brain. But she won't repeat the procedure so you can hear about the deal she made with Slotsky."

"Repeat what you just said."

"No."

"You're being tiresome."

"Call her down. Then watch an accident, or an outright stabbing, make me die. You'll end up knowing nothing at all."

Trefethen said, "You're implying my wife was involved in the restaurant bugging?"

"I have no more to say," Toby replied. "Until you tell me what you're doing."

Trefethen muttered, "Breathtaking."

Toby noticed the pulse throbbing in Trefethen's temple. The man better sit down, he thought. He said, "Let's pretend this is a seminar, years in the future, on Earnest Trefethen. 'What were his motivations? Why did he do it?' That kind of thing."

Trefethen sat. "I doubt," he said with an exasperated snort, "that you have the conceptual ability for such a review."

"Maybe. Maybe not. I'm a catastrophist. A doomsday nut. So I might have more familiarity with your concepts than you think."

"A doomsday nut. What a thoroughly useless thing to be."

"That's provocative. Why, Professor Trefethen?"

"Stop the seminar bullshit right now!"

"Okay. Why is a doomsday nut useless?"

"Because doom suggests hopelessness, obviously. A resignation to the idea that nothing can be done. It's incredible I'm discussing this subject with the likes of you."

"Then you'll appreciate the fact I feel the same way. But more so. Uh—you really believe in hope?"

The blue eyes conveyed the iciest superciliousness Toby ever had seen. Trefethen asked slowly, "Do you imagine that I have labored and schemed for years and years—out of simple spite?"

"How would I know?" Toby said, taken aback.

"Of course I have hope!" He waved at whatever it was that lay beyond the cell. "This entire enterprise is built around hope!" He leaned forward and said with chilling certitude, "It's built around the recognition that the whiners and complainers who call themselves doomsday nuts are worse than useless. That in fact, they're complicit with the evil that will crash this planet."

"Huh," Toby said. Fighting words, he thought. "Doom-believers do what—create self-fulfilling prophecies? Is that it?"

Trefethen nodded. "The implicit attitude of such a person is that nothing can be done. The attitude takes for granted that action is futile. You get enough people thinking along those lines, of course nothing gets done. How about you? What, as a doom nut, have you accomplished with your miserable life?"

"Not much," Toby said, painfully aware of how much that understated the reality. "What will you accomplish with yours?"

"We're going to make this short and simple," Trefethen announced. "Then you're going to tell me about Slotsky. And if you don't, I will put a bullet between your eyes." He raised the gun, nodded sourly at Toby, sat back, and crossed his legs.

"Fine," Toby said. He had a feeling Trefethen wouldn't kill him when he found out he'd lied about Slotsky. But he might; the conversation accordingly seemed a kind of last meal. Let's make it good, Toby thought. He glanced at the TV and said, "I noticed that when you saw the eruption, you were shaken. The sight appeared to make you ill. Why?"

Trefethen gazed at the gun. "You happen to be right," he remarked. "The sight does make me ill." Abruptly he stood and turned the TV off. "That's better." He sat. "I'll explain something," he went on, voice harder-edged without the background audio. "I don't like what I'm doing. Most of it, I don't enjoy at all. Assaulting Antarctica with nuclear explosions happens to be something that sickens me. Have you any idea why?"

Toby nodded. "You're a scientist. Antarctica is pure. Scientists love purity."

"Not bad," Trefethen said. Toby opened his mouth; Trefethen held up a hand. "How could I commit such atrocities? That is the question that burns in your tiny mind. Tell me. Are you familiar with the historical significance of purification and sacrifice?"

Toby gaped at him. "You're sacrificing Antarctica?"

"It's not that simple," Trefethen replied. "In a way, however—it is."

"So it's a wake-up call," Toby said. "You slaughter Antarctica, you slaughter coasts. That's supposed to wake people up?"

"Ah. You think people are asleep."

"Yeah," Toby said. "I do, as a matter of fact. Everyone seems like they're sleepwalking."

"You have the wrong metaphor," Trefethen said. "The usual cant of a doom nut. Everyone's sleeping—except yourself, of course. No, doom nuts are wide awake." He sighed. "If it isn't the sleep metaphor that underlies the idea that you possess higher consciousness, it's one of the other flabby metaphors. There is a whole list. Psychic numbing.

Anesthesia. Dissociation. Denial. For religious doomers, there's the nightmarish sleep of not having been saved. Religions take narcolepsy very seriously—unbelievers are snoring away as they stagger through life. All of it is absolute rubbish. Because in actual fact, doom nuts are comatose."

"Oh yeah?" Toby said.

"Of course. They think that those who don't share their conception of doom aren't conscious. The sleep metaphor implies diminished or absent consciousness. If people would only wake up, they'd immediately see whatever vision it is that the doomers think is their special knowledge. But those doomers are catching Zs."

"Why?"

"I already told you. By proclaiming hopelessness, doom theory induces passive acceptance. In other words, my fine young napper, it induces sleep."

"All right. What's the right metaphor, then?"

"Enchantment. The metaphor is enchantment. Put that in your pot pipe and smoke it."

The word startled Toby. He said, "Wait a second. Doesn't that imply . . . diminished consciousness?"

"The contrary. Enchantment implies the fusion of consciousness with vision. With purpose. With a meaningful world that excites one, in which one can do things. It's the opposite of diminished consciousness." Trefethen turned to the corridor. "Brian!" he shouted. "Are you listening to this?"

"Yes, Father," Brian called back.

Interesting, Toby thought. Is he trying to re-enchant his disloyal son? Trefethen turned to Toby, cocked an eyebrow, and said, "I must admit, you've quite some nerve."

Toby shrugged. He said, "Given that the world's screwed up, how can enchantment be a better metaphor than sleep?"

Trefethen swallowed biliously. "Because it isn't always a good thing, of course—our current enchantments are taking us to ruin. But that's not because people are asleep. The idea that people are sleeping is a profound analytic mistake. People are conscious of what they're doing, they're wide awake, and they're industrious, they run around working very hard. In other words, they are active—not passive. And this is why we're in such trouble. We have a lot of enchantment out there. A lot of vision, a lot of consciousness. It's poisoning the planet."

"All right. How do you change it?"

"We need a new form of enchantment, obviously. The old ones aren't working. They're killing us."

Toby said, "What are they, the killer enchantments?"

"You're a doom nut and you have no theory about what's gone wrong?" Toby started to say something; Trefethen waved him to silence, and said, "One, the idea that people should reproduce at will. Two, oppressive moralities that legitimize plunder. High-tech, systematic plunder—the first world's God-given right to unjustly apportioned prosperity. The Pacific Rim's adoption of the Singapore model."

"The Beast," Toby said.

Trefethen smiled contemptuously. "You've been watching TV!"

"Does the rabbit stand for fertility or something?"

"Very good."

"What's the other face? The high-tech greed one?"

"You happen to have wormed your way deep inside it."

"No kidding. What do you mean?"

Trefethen looked at his watch.

"So," Toby said. "Here I am. In the belly of the Beast."

Trefethen said, "Start talking about Slotsky."

"I will. But I don't understand . . . if you're liberating people from bad enchantments, isn't that the same as waking them up?"

"You're so naive. Waking up implies becoming rational. It implies an ability to see the truth. I'm not arguing that enchantment is rational. Like everything else about human thinking, it's full of superstition, magical fantasies, even madness. We're stuck with it. There's no getting around it, and anyone who thinks there is, is a fool."

"Ahhh," Toby said. "Enchantment is like myth. It can be great or hateful, but it tells us what life's all about—on some kind of spiritual level?" Curtly, Trefethen nodded. "But how will messing with sea level re-enchant the world in a better way? It seems like you'll just end up killing a lot of people."

"I won't. The planet will."

"The planet will?"

"Yes, you birdbrain. The planet will do it. In the process, I'm hopeful, the human race will experience new enchantments."

"Ohhh," Toby said. "Mother Earth gets in the act. Isn't that a euphemism for being the biggest mass murderer in history?"

"One way of putting it," Trefethen said indifferently. "I'll wrap this up with two points. First, mass murder is committed every day. The world economy, with its political, demographic, and cultural back-wash, regulates megadeath by systematic routine. It's called business-as-usual, and is the chief evil enchantment of our time. Unchecked, it will end up killing us all. Not because it wants to, of course. It's a metastasizing system that welcomes more consumers—it greets every fresh billion with open arms. But like any metastasis, indefinite growth leads to death."

Toby nodded. "I agree," he said.

"Good doomsday nut!" Trefethen exclaimed. "Of course you agree. It's the most banal verity around. And the wonderful thing is, no one has the faintest idea how to stop it."

"Except you, I guess," Toby muttered. "Point number two?"

"Point number two," Trefethen said. "You keep referring to the killer effects of a sea level rise. You think because I am setting off bombs that will trigger it, I will be responsible for those deaths. Con-sider this. Sooner or later, the sea will rise anyway—with or without the stimulus of my bombs. The consequent climate shifts also are coming. And they will kill vast numbers of people. No one knows how, exactly, because climate is unpredictable. But whatever happens won't be fun for humans—we are in a kind of climatic lull, you see. We've been coddled. We think things will stay the way they are for-ever. They won't."

"Because of greenhouse effect?"

"Greenhouse will push it. And greenhouse is something that, unchecked, easily could render us extinct. However, there also is the ten-thousand-year trigger. It's been ten thousand years since the end of the last ice age. We've established it would take about that much time for post-ice-age warming to reach the base of the ice sheet. A col-lapse, you see, could happen without greenhouse. And without bombs. In other words, without any help from humans."

"Could? That means it might not."

"My research shows high probability. There is a lot of basal melt underneath the sheet. Not just from geothermals, either."

Is he telling the truth? Toby wondered. He thought a moment; and said, "At the restaurant you told your guests, 'Civilization has evolved into a self-destruct machine.' What I don't get is, why make it worse? Will that serve re-enchantment?"

Trefethen scowled. He muttered, "What I'm trying to do is break the spell. How does one tell a civilization that doesn't want to hear it, that it's self-destructing? Is there a better way than forcing people into bondage with their TV sets? And demonstrating, irrefutably, that the planet is a doomsday system?"

"Oh. So the solution is to make doomsday actually happen."

"The solution is to teach the human race a lesson we would have learned anyway—the planet is bigger than we are. And therefore cannot be treated with the disrespect we so foolishly have shown it." He frowned at his watch. "That's the re-enchantment. As for my role in making it happen, I am rather like the Wizard of Oz. Everyone thinks I'm the most supreme evil that ever stalked the earth. I am a monster in a Japanese science fiction movie. This amuses me hugely. For you see, what I'm doing is staging a show. Through stagecraft, I've made it appear that I'm raising sea level through a turn of the faucet. It's all in the wrist, so to speak.

"But the faucet already has been turned by something bigger than me, by something with tremendously greater momentum and complexity than the puffs of steam rising over Antarctica. True, the bombs are speeding things up a bit. And true, that will bring death and suffering sooner than otherwise would have happened. This serves a purpose, however. The cataclysm will have a face. An unforgettable face that will live on—as an afterimage, a cosmic afterimage that will influence human destiny. For the better."

A glow had ignited in Trefethen's eyes. My God, Toby thought. He really believes this.

"Furthermore," the man continued, "the time to break the spell is now, not fifty, a hundred years down the road, with billions more people on the planet. Because if they continue to hold sway over an exploding population, our current enchantments will create suffering far beyond what Antarctica can inflict. Breaking the spell now causes short-term pain, yes. But over the long run, it's a net reducer of pain, an *enormous* net reducer. And although it's coincidence, it's perfect of course that we're entering a new millennium. What better time for re-enchantment than when slamming into millennarian suggestibility?"

Toby said, "You seriously think you're the Wizard of Oz?"

"I'm a kind of fraud. Taking credit for geophysical cycles that predate human history by millions of years. Now what the hell do you mean, my wife made a deal with Slotsky?"

Toby felt dizzy. Just when the archdemon had revealed a fascinating doom theory—one which, to Toby's hurtling mind, merited lengthy thought—the archdemon would put a bullet through his brain. "One question," he mumbled.

Trefethen pointed the gun at his forehead.

"Please, one more question—and I swear to God I'll tell you anything you want to know!" Toby's fervor must have made an impression, because Trefethen smiled thinly. Toby stammered, "D-Did you kill those people in Antarctica?"

"What?" Trefethen seemed shocked.

"Did you set off an explosion that sent the ice-crawlers behind you into the crevasse?"

"Of course not. What gave you that abominable idea?"

"In the truck, Brian told Helen you'd bumped off those people because they knew where you'd been, what you'd done. She told Brian that isn't true. I'm just—curious if it is true."

"Helen's right, for once. I could no more have killed . . . look, you cannot say I haven't explained myself. I have, to a degree that astonishes me. Now explain yourself. What is this story about Slotsky and my wife?"

Toby blurted, "Helen covered up the twins' attempt to give the rabbit to FATBOY. She also knew about the bug—I told her everything I saw and heard while serving that dinner. The bug was planted by Malt, who did work for Slotsky, who did kill Malt on my stairs, why I don't know, maybe because Malt screwed up getting the rabbit. Uh—what else?—Malt had fake FATBOY ID—he must have used it to convince the twins that he was an undercover agent investigating you. But he didn't work for FATBOY, Detective Potts proved it, he called FATBOY with the numbers. What else? In the truck, Helen did say, about the question of Grace knowing where you were going, 'I can blame it on Martha.' Uh—what else?"

"The deal between Slotsky and my wife?"

"No such deal. Sorry. I fibbed."

"Worm!" Trefethen snarled. The gun's hole got bigger. Toby imagined the scarlet tunnel through his brain. The curtain coming down, the fade to black. He closed his eyes.

And heard a stupendously loud bang.

Toby opened his eyes. Trefethen had pointed the gun at the TV. Its screen was shattered.

"More brains there than in your skull!" Trefethen shouted. He turned to the door. "Brian!"

"Yes?" Brian quavered.

"Is what this boy said about Mother true?"

"Every word. True."

"You lied upstairs, about her not knowing those things?"

"Yes, Father. To protect her from you. Uh—you didn't kill those people on the Ice?"

"Of course I didn't!" Trefethen glared at Toby, aimed at the TV, and sent five more rounds in it. "Take that, doomsday nut. If anything makes a doomsday nut distraught, it's TV deprivation."

He seized Helen's medical stuff, went through the doorway, slammed the bars shut, locked them, and stomped down the corridor. Toby and Brian listened to the outer door slam.

Toby went to the bars. He and Brian stared at each other. "Wow," Toby said.

Brian burst into tears.

Mary McMurtry threw the headset onto her desk. "Despicable!" she exclaimed.

Hilton Decter agreed. "It came in at eleven. When you were at the press . . . "

"Don't talk about it!" McMurtry checked the time. Twelve-fifteen. Ten minutes back at the office, and now this. Today's spin blown to bits, reduced to neutrinos by the latest Antarctic explosion—and now, of all things, this. She said, "If we pay, I don't suppose there's any guarantee of a trace?"

"Of where the payment goes?" Decter asked. McMurtry nodded. "No. Particularly if we don't notify the Czech authorities immediately. The money could disappear within—really, within seconds. A transfer cascade through several dozen cash havens? It might take weeks to trace. If we could trace at all."

"And I suppose the same holds for tracing the place from which he sent this?"

"We're working on it. So far, it leads to a public datastand in the former Zaire. It's amazing the stand is still working. Prognosis for trace, I fear, is bad."

"A public datastand? Suppose somebody intercepted?"

"The message self-decoded on hitting our data-in. The techies doubt an interceptor could crack it. It's hard code."

"So what do you think?" she said. "Myself, I can't think," she went on before he had a chance to reply. "The President won't take calls. His senior staff won't take calls. They're wetting their big leather chairs over there, the pee's puddling the floor, they're just paralyzed, so what the hell am I supposed to do? What, Hilton? What . . ." she stood and shouted, hair Sphinx-solid astride her head, "*can I do?*"

"First," he said, his phlegmatic disposition rising to the challenge, "you should take a sedative, one with stimulants in it, because if you don't settle down and deal, I too will wet my big leather chair. And then what use will I be?"

McMurtry sat, lips pursed. In one of the video-windows, a fat aircraft swooped toward National Airport. It seemed sure to flop into the Potomac instead. McMurtry found herself hoping it would. Give me, she thought, an emergency I can handle.

"Second," Decter said. "There might be information we can use—in the dinner party recording itself, and in the demand for payment. Analysis will determine if the demand matches voiceprints the Russians have sent. I am quite sure it's Slotsky. But without confirmation, we can't be certain.

"Third. Let's assume it's Slotsky. We cannot ignore his claim he knows Trefethen's location. He had Malt spying on him. He got that recording at the restaurant, and he liaised with the twins—it's quite possible Slotsky knows.

"Now. Fourth. The consequences of not paying. The consequences of the media getting the recording." Decter plucked lint from his cashmere jacket. "An objective person wouldn't infer from the recording that Trefethen, at the restaurant, told his guests he'd detonated a bomb and caused an eruption. But Ms. Director General, we're not dealing with objective people. We are dealing with the wild imaginations of the press. If they get the recording, we are in for a major embarrassment. And more."

"Why?" McMurtry demanded.

"Because we also are dealing with the wild imagination of the public. The media will point out that attendees of the dinner called us to report what Trefethen had told them. Worse, the media will play and replay Trefethen's remarks, drawing attention to his disturbingly suggestive tone of voice. Which, of course, will make 'the Beast,' 'overpopulation,' 'technology in the service of greed,' and 'cleansing water'—all those code phrases—into an even bigger sensation than they already are. They will inflate with an aura of extreme significance.

"We must be careful about this. It will expose us to charges that we spurned the intelligent concern of Lawrence Sforza, Martha Cliff-cloud, and Reheema Sampson.

"But that's not all. Fringe commentators, and now even the mainstream, are attributing to the dinner a kind of religious import. The last supper of Christ, nonsense to that effect. 'Cleansing water,' I'm afraid, is becoming a mantra. And 'the Beast,' thanks to the *Boston Globe* and Reheema Sampson, now has a face. Two faces. Opinion leaders are babbling about it like gnostic mystics. As if profundities have been revealed."

"Pat yourself on the back, Hilton. Your 'unwitting echo chamber' is booming. But so what?"

"If the recording went public, it would expand Trefethen's cult phenom by orders of magnitude. Which of course he'd exploit. For example, and I don't mean to suggest the President will give him television time, but imagine the President does. Suppose Trefethen uses it to promote mass hysteria?"

McMurtry glared at her inch-and-a-half-long nails, and said, "We're already seeing mass hysteria."

"Yes. We are. I therefore recommend immediate payment."

"Fifty million," she whispered. "And he doesn't promise to tell us where Earnest is hiding. We don't even know if Slotsky knows where he's hiding. All we get is the assurance that the media don't get the recording."

"Not quite. We cultivate a relationship. When Slotsky receives the money, he'll know we'll be good for more. I think he makes that clear—how did he put it? 'Prompt payment will encourage my consideration of additional arrangements.'"

"Bastard!" McMurtry spat. She stared directionlessly for a moment, and said, "I can't think. If in your opinion . . . "

"I take it you're authorizing payment."

She nodded. "Have the recording analyzed every way we can. Send it around to secure people in the Bureau, tell them to listen till their implants fall out. We better get our money's worth from this one. We don't, there will be hell. There will be hell."

━ ━ ━

Harry found Gula in the study. The room held a sanatorial gloom. She was stretched out on the antique couch, quilts pulled up to her chin. A fire popped in the wood stove. "Are you all right?" Harry asked.

"Just a chill," Gula replied. "They're eating?"

"Like starving coyotes."

"Don't let them do anything to the refrigerator, Harry."

The dictionary, open on its stand, provided a resting place for Harry's elbows. He clasped his hands, and said, "Yeah."

"Where did you put them?"

"Grace is across from you. Selma's in the old man's room. Dan has one of the back rooms. The downstairs bedrooms—I figured they're too accessible if people drop by."

"Clothes?"

"I took them to the attic and showed them the costume trunk. I think they like the stuff. Especially Selma."

"Do they still intend to nap?"

"They look like they could sleep for days."

"They won't." Gula peered at him. Elbows on the dictionary, fists supporting his chin, he looked like a weary bishop behind a lectern. Or a rustic angel. The dear man, she thought. How could she let him get deeper? "Harry . . . what's really going on?"

"Grace is telling the truth," he replied, "the way she sees it. Which isn't the whole truth."

"Yes. What about the barbarians? The rabid coyotes?"

He moved to the desk, sat with a drawn-out sigh, and muttered, "We're in a mess. There's no good fix." He took off his denim jacket. "Boiling hot," he remarked. "Gula, it's damned-if-we-do and damned-if-we-don't. First, if we don't. If we don't call FATBOY, shit hits the fan anyway, sooner or later. Cliffcloud will be taken out. Bombs probably will go off. Grace, Selma and Dan will get arrested, or worse. And we will too."

"They're not taking me anywhere. But never mind. What if we do make the call?"

"Numerous problems. Numerous. First, who would believe us? Who'd believe Cliffcloud's in cahoots with the terrorists? Who'd believe a bunny sets off doomsday?" Harry grunted. "The only way FATBOY will believe it is handing Grace over lock, stock, barrel, and bunny. Which brings more problems."

"Like what?"

"Cliffcloud has nasty stuff. Nasty defenses—who knows what she's got over there? The fence alone is state-of-the-art. She has sensors on that fence I never even heard of, much less saw."

"Well?" Gula said. "What about it?"

"FATBOY hits her, she could put up a fight. If it escalates—we're too close for comfort. We'd have to watch out for things like stray lasers. Stray bombs, stray whatever. The 'friendly fire' issue? For us, a mile away, that could be real."

"No!" Gula exclaimed, shivering under her quilts.

Harry nodded dolefully.

"Oh, dear," Gula said. "So that's it. The barbarians are coming no matter what. It's not a question of if they're coming, it's when. This is what you're telling me?"

"Yes. Two different kinds are coming. Civilian barbarians. And military barbarians. Tell you the truth, I don't know which'll be worse. But the main point, that you put your finger on—it's a question of when."

"I thought so," Gula said. "That's just what I thought. Harry, you have to get out of here. You can't stay."

"But you will?"

"What do you think?" she croaked. "That I'll leave the garden? Look, I'm not going anywhere. And you know it. So let's not even discuss it. But as for you—at the least, you'd go to jail. You heard that woman. Mary McMurder. She's serious, Harry."

"I know, Gula. Believe me, I know."

Earnest left the suite he and Helen were occupying, walked through the northwest pavilion's music room and dining room, and asked the house to locate Martha. He hadn't wanted to make the inquiry in Helen's presence. Talking with the house wasn't something he thought she should know how to do.

The annoyingly butlerish voice, seeming to speak in his ear, directed him to the library. There he found Martha occupied with an array of glowing holographic configurations. Like kinetic sculpture, they undulated through the air around her. What new toy, Earnest wondered, is she wasting time on now?

It reminded him of the wand system McMurtry had used at the press conference. But unlike that holo setup—which gave television viewers the impression Mary was waving her wand magically through empty air—these holos weren't invisible to video cameras. They were too bright. Furthermore, Martha waved no wand. She instead moved arms and hands, her head, her entire body—nudging, bumping, doing the hully-gully with the sinuously kinetic shapes, which meanwhile improvised their own odd routines.

Martha, Earnest decided, is controlling something. Or interacting with something. More complexly than waving a wand at a hovering videoscreen menu. He said, "Hello?"

She froze. Staring at him, she exclaimed, "A major flaw!"

"You've discovered a major flaw? Are you doing repairs? Are you spot-welding the reactor? What the devil are you doing?"

"I wasn't warned of your approach," she said. She touched a pendulous earring. The holograms vanished. Earnest noticed a black cube on the floor. It had been humming. Now it wasn't. "A training routine," Martha said. "Brushing up, that's all."

"It looked like martial dance."

"That's exactly what it was. How is she?"

"Not well," he said. "Nor am I." He sat on the sofa and pulled a silver-colored object from his suit jacket. "Martha, have a look at this."

She sat beside him and took it. The device resembled an old-fashioned Zippo cigarette lighter. Martha flipped the lid. Under it, secured with a safety catch, a highly polished metal button reflected her face in shiny miniature.

"It's a pager," Earnest said quietly. "It activates a Net release. Of an image that will get wide exposure." He smiled bitterly. "A family portrait. Helen, the twins, myself. We're lined up against a wall. Four soldiers point rifles at us, indicating we face execution. On the wall, above our heads . . . "

"The fertility icon, of course," Martha said. "Why are you showing me this?" She handed him the pager.

"I want you to use it if I'm incapacitated."

Martha frowned. "How bad is she, Earnest?"

"She sedated herself, thank heavens."

"Having made unpleasant revelations?"

He nodded. "She leveled, I think. I'm sure she told me everything. And it's so sad. The situation with the twins, it simply unhinged her. She was terrified, Martha. Afraid we'd spurn her, if we found out what the twins had done. As for them, I'm so shocked. They've been living a paranoid fantasy for months. And I had no idea. None."

"What fantasy?"

"That the accident on the Ice wasn't an accident. That it was murder. Committed by me."

"Oh, honey. You're joking."

"No. How could I have been so blind?"

"Have you talked with Brian?"

"Very briefly. I had to deal with that Toby fellow. He's curious, spunky, insufferable. Led me on a wild goose chase to get an explanation for my motives."

"Tell me."

Earnest briefed her on Toby.

"So then," Martha said reflectively, "you spoke with Helen. She leveled, you think. You feel we're in no immediate danger?"

"With our blackmailer, who knows? But Helen makes a good point about Grace. She isn't in Amarillo. If she were we'd be dead."

"Don't be so sure. That we'd be dead."

"You have extraordinary confidence, Martha."

"If we're attacked, you'll see why. I have a surprise for the attacker." Martha studied his distraught face. "Maybe we should leave now."

"And zoom into deepest Canada?" Earnest said moodily. "Where is it, in Canada?"

"Do you want to know?"

He shook his head. After a moment he said, "I believe Helen is right. I think Grace is somewhere nearby. Trying to come up with a way to contact us, get Brian, and take him away. But you know—I don't want them to abandon us. I want them both to stay." He sighed. "Maybe that's selfish. Maybe we should let Brian go off with Grace, and let them have lives of their own."

"You're shaken," Martha said, taking the hand he was waving.

"They've never had lives of their own. Which must have helped motivate the betrayal. Helen's story about how they tried to give away the badge—it's heartwrenching, it's so pathetic. The poor kids. They obviously felt so desperate. And thinking it over, it's clear how they might have thought I killed the team. When the ice bridge gave way, it sounded like an explosion. The cracking ice, it made a sickening bang." Earnest shook his head. "They never said a word about it. They just held it in. I feel terrible about this."

"Tunnel vision," Martha remarked. "You've been working so hard . . . you simply didn't notice."

"Yes. Yes, I'm a monster."

"Now, now," Martha said chidingly. "You should have a talk with Brian. But he stays in the cell. We don't know how . . . let's face it, how crazy he is. Earnest, I have something upsetting to tell you."

"No surprise," he said. "What?"

"I checked the house log. Brian has been disobedient. He wandered around outdoors, unshielded. Even on the roof."

"Inexcusable," Earnest said.

"It gets worse. He prowled the basement too. And happened to be right outside the control room—when we were going at it."

"Oh no."

"Let's hope," Martha said, "he doesn't tell Helen."

"It would break her. Break her in half."

"You think I'm unaware of that?"

"My God," Earnest muttered. "What has happened? What has happened to my family?"

"That I don't know," Martha said flatly.

"I'm sorry," Earnest said. He didn't meet her irritated stare. "Unfair to you, of course. But I'm just—overwhelmed."

"Get over it, dear. Get over it right now."

Toby ate the delicious dinner, meditating about sleep, enchantment, and his lack of TV; and the fact that Trefethen was across the corridor, talking with Brian in Brian's bathroom. They'd gone in there so he wouldn't hear the conversation, Toby assumed. That he found reasonable. After all, a father-son chat did seem called for. Why should he be privy to it?

He wondered if Helen had poisoned the food he was eating. If she hadn't, the long arm of her vengeance would get him somehow. Maybe by sneaky means. For example, the cardkey. Toby suspected she had left it behind on purpose. Was she hoping he'd try to escape? And become burnt toast?

The idea had stopped him from using the cardkey. Not merely because it might be fatal. Toby had skirmished with death so many times the last couple of days, its shock value was shot. What really bothered him was the prospect of dying without having clarified certain mysteries.

His confrontation with Trefethen had multiplied Toby's curiosity tenfold. Brian meantime hadn't been much help. Earlier, when he had finished with his crying jag following his father's departure, he'd passed out on his bed.

Televisionless years had seemed to go by. Then Trefethen reappeared. He'd wheeled a cart down the corridor, bringing dinner. Toby's tray he'd sent under the bars with almost a kick.

Brian and he now were eating in Brian's 'private dining room.' How odd, Toby thought as he munched succulent asparagus, that they didn't request me as their waiter. A little champagne, gentlemen? Some artificial sweetener, perhaps?

The lamb chops were perfectly rosé. The pilaf was suffused with subtle spice. Toby wondered if Cliffcloud's Connecticut establishment had a chef on the staff. If it did, spaciousness was implied. So why were Trefethen and son cooped up in a bathroom?

Maybe Trefethen simply wanted to talk with his son, and didn't care where they did it. Or when they did it. Or what kinds of television events they missed while they did it.

The destroyed appliance on the wall was driving Toby crazy. He glared at its bullet-riddled screen. "Damn you," he muttered. Without the thing working, he didn't even know the time. But it had to be well past 8:00. Therefore the President had spoken. What, Toby wanted to know, had he said?

Dan groggily carried the stuff from the kitchen through the dining room. Selma followed, equally groggily, and Grace stumbled along behind; both also carried trays. It'll be a miracle, Dan thought, if we don't drop something.

Harry had used unrefined tactics to wake them up and put them to work. They'd gone from deep sleep to dinner duty in less than a minute, it seemed. "Nazi," Dan heard Selma say under her breath. The book-lined room, dark as a cavern and as big, stretched to the left. Dan passed through the archway into the smaller room lined with books.

Gula sat under the glow of an antique stainless steel lamp, wearing a brilliant off-scarlet pantsuit. A cocktail clinked in her hands. She pointed at the hearth and said, "Put it there."

Dan set the tray down before a fire that must have started sizably; it had reduced to a thick bed of glowing coals. Ah, he thought, understanding now why Grace lugged a huge raw steak on her tray. His tray held a carving knife, a carving fork, a carving board, and a bowl of water with a brush in it, along with five sets of salt cellars and midget pepper grinders. A long-handled metal-mesh device leaned against the hearth's side. The steak was going in it, Dan realized, and over the fire.

Grace put the five-pound slab by his tray. Selma deposited plates and silverware on the coffee table. Harry entered, carrying a giant salad bowl. He started giving orders.

"Excuse me," Dan said, holding up a hand. "I can't do anything until I have some coffee. Sorry about that. May I please make some coffee?"

"It's nine o'clock," Gula informed him. "You really want coffee?"

Dan nodded. "What," Grace asked, her voice sleep-deep, "did the President say?"

"That poor man didn't look his best tonight," Gula replied. "He didn't say a whole lot, either. Mostly, after making some very threatening remarks . . ." She and Harry exchanged nervous glances. "Mostly, he announced that your father can have a half hour on TV tomorrow evening. At six o'clock."

Dan, Selma, and Grace absorbed this news with vigorous blinks. Gula stared back, a trace of amusement in the set of her lips. Harry put the salad bowl on the table. "I'll make the damn coffee," he said, voice explosively tense. He stomped out.

"Sit down," Gula said. They sat. "You three," she remarked, "are quite some scarecrows."

They realized she was talking about their clothes.

"Well, then. Have we cleared things up?"

"I think so, Father."

Earnest, reclined in the tub, wasn't sure he'd gotten through to the beautiful boy sitting on the toilet. He remained so pale. Earnest realized he'd never been gifted with insight or even empathy when it came to his children. That he'd always left to Helen. A mistake, he now knew. He said, "I hope we've at least cleared some things up. I want you to know that although I am deeply disappointed—in a state of shock, really—I love you. And care for you more than perhaps you're aware."

"I love you too, Father."

"Being apart from Grace—this is a torment. Please believe me when I say I understand that."

"But that's the thing. You don't."

Brian looked directly at Earnest, who thought, No. Not now.

But Brian did it. He said, "You've never acknowledged we're lovers, Father."

"You're siblings!" Earnest exclaimed. The tub suddenly seemed an excruciatingly awkward place to be.

"Yes. And lovers."

"Well, we cannot go into that now. I have trouble with it. You know I do." He pulled himself from the tub, and stooped to pick up his tray. "You understand why I must keep you confined? That I do so not out of anger?"

"Yes. You do so out of Martha. Father. How long have you and she been lovers?"

"I implored you not to question me about that."

"You implored me not to tell Mother about it. You didn't implore me not to ask a simple question. And don't worry, I won't tell Mother. She'd die if she knew."

Earnest nodded dourly. "Martha and I . . . we have been . . . intimate . . . for several years, Brian. Not on a regular basis. There have been many reasons to keep it discreet, of course. The lengths to which we've gone—you've no idea." Exhaustedly, he yawned. "She means a great deal to me. She has made everything possible, you see. I'd have accomplished nothing without her. But it goes beyond that—I am very fond of her. I know this . . . upsets you."

"You love her?"

"Yes. I love her."

"More than Mother?"

"I cannot lie to you about it! Yes! I love her more than Mother!" Sweating a little, and breathing too hard, Earnest was ready to leave. He strove to find a note on which to do so that wouldn't be clumsy. "But I love Mother. How could I not? She in many ways is the most remarkable human being I've ever known."

"She adores you. She worships you. You're everything to her. But it doesn't matter I guess—we're all going to die soon anyway."

Earnest came very close to flinging the tray at the tub. He instead muttered, "So are a lot of people. Don't think I'm joyous about it. This isn't easy, son. It isn't easy at all."

"Yeah," Brian said. "I know."

In his cell, Toby had heard the raised voice and wondered what it meant. Finally, some sort of external stimulation. But to whom had the man been referring when he'd shouted, "Yes! I love her more than Mother!"

My one clue of the evening, Toby thought. He tried to look at it from every angle. Did Trefethen mean, "I love her more than Mother Earth"? Did he mean, "I love her more than Mother loves her"? Or did he mean, "I love her more than I love Mother"?

Brian's bathroom door opened. Trefethen approached the bars, carrying two trays. He deposited them on the cart, locked Brian's cell, and wheeled the cart away. Toby heard it scrape through the outer door. He then heard the outer door's lock turn. Huh, he thought. First time they've locked that door. Why do it now?

Dan sipped coffee, trying not to dip his lacy cuff in it. The shabby brocades of Selma's dress made her look like a French aristocrat fallen on hard times. As if she'd been run out of her chateau and faced the guillotine. Grace, preoccupied with dark thoughts and wearing a plainer antique getup, could be the peasant lass who'd turned Selma in. As for Dan, he fancied himself the long-lost Dauphin in his powder-blue satin coat with diagonal sashes. The Dauphin after having fled Europe's glittering courts; that accounted for the rips here and there.

The steak sizzled on the fire. Harry, tending it, was being conspicuously silent. Gula sipped at her cocktail. She'd appeared somewhat surprised when "you kids" had declined alcoholic beverages. The idea had made Dan shudder. Coffee was barely making him conscious as it was.

"Where did you get the incredible costumes?" Selma asked, filling what threatened to become a conversational black hole.

"Oh," Gula said. "They accumulated. Parties. Theatricals. Gifts, I suppose—it's hard to remember." Faintly, she smiled. "We used to have a lot of fun here. Years ago."

No kidding, Dan thought. What he'd seen of the house convinced him that people had died of bliss here. The place seemed like an unending psychedelic trip. The things in the studio, upstairs; and the stuff in those back bedrooms. Only a genius, age eight or younger in terms of imagination, could have come up with it all. "You're an artist?" he said to Gula.

She nodded.

"Who made the puppets?" Selma inquired.

"Me," Gula said.

"And the anatomically detailed mobiles?" Dan asked. Two large mobiles, featuring angels with champagne-cork heads, fabulous tin wings, and conical gilt-foil gowns with hilarious genitalia between the legs under them, were suspended from the studio ceiling. Their tiny star-eyes seemed to keep a celestial vigil over all the other exotic inhabitants of the room.

"I made many of the things here," Gula replied. "Not the books, of course. I didn't make those."

"Did you read them?" Dan asked.

Gula laughed dryly. "No," she said.

"Who did?" Dan asked. He had to know.

"My departed husband," Gula said.

"How could anybody read so many books?" Dan demanded. He and Selma had discovered that the books weren't confined to these rooms. The halls of the main staircase were crammed with them too. Everywhere, books and more books.

"There was a time," Gula said, smile fading, "when people did read, you know. Tell me—what do you do?"

"What do I do," Dan said. "I don't know."

"You don't know what you do?"

"I don't do anything," he said. "Except go to school. Uh—I work every now and then." Dan gulped coffee, feeling a complete do-nothing. This woman's competence at so many crafts was overwhelming. "I guess I'm just another aimless white fag," he said. "Who doesn't have a clue."

"Hmmmm," Gula said, studying him beadily. "You're not a dancer then, Mr. Dance Wet?"

"What?" Dan said. "How do you know . . . about . . . ?"

"Why," Gula inquired, "do you have turquoise in your hair?"

"It's called the spinster look," Dan said.

Gula swallowed an incredulous laugh. She turned her attention to Selma. "You?" she asked.

Selma also was confused. Gula knew the nickname some ditzy kid had given Dan. How? Selma said, "I tend bar," wondering why she was talking in the present tense. She used to tend bar. Back in the Middle Ages, before she met Grace. "And," she added meekly, "I sew."

"Really?" Gula said. "Well, that's nice. Sewing is a very good thing to know how to do. I sew too—Madame Swear Engine."

"All right," Dan said. "How'd you find out the nicknames?"

Harry, who'd been watching with neutral avidity, said, "You were on TV again." He turned to Grace. Like he expects her to pipe up with a self-explanation, Dan thought. But Grace looked unwilling to do that. Another black hole loomed. To ward it off, Dan said to Gula, "Did your husband, like, read all day long?"

"Oh, for God's sake," Gula snapped, putting her drink on the table with a sharp clunk. "You make it sound so tedious! This house has been full of books and people who read them and wrote them since 1928! And we used to be very much like you—young and pretty and full of life!"

Grace said, "Can we get down to business now?"

"Steak's ready," Harry announced. "Why don't we eat before we do business?"

"Seems sensible," Gula said. "Newspaper, please."

Harry took newspaper from the fireplace's kindling closet and handed it to Gula. She spread part of it on the carpet below her feet. The rest she handed to Dan. "Put it on the floor," she said, "and pass it on. It catches dropping food. Protects the rug—I hate having 'em cleaned. They don't know how to do it right. I guess nobody wants wine?"

"Not me," Grace said.

"I'll have some," Dan said.

Selma said, "Me, too."

Four feet, the corridor's width, sepa-rated their bars. Toby stared through at his fellow inmate. Brian lay on the floor, an arm thrust into the corridor. Like a boater, Toby thought, skimming water with his hand.

"We're talking ten thousand years," Toby said. "Since the end of the last ice age. Considering this is nature, couldn't it turn out to be eleven thousand years—another whole millennium away? Maybe there's a thousand years to go."

Brian's fingers twirled. "No," he said. "Too much basal decay. The ice sheet's rotting—why don't you believe me?"

"How come nobody else knows about this?"

"The ten-thousand-year-trigger is an old theory. It's been around a while. But nobody's field-tested as thoroughly as we have. With laser drills that probe to the base. Look, it's true."

Toby sighed. He said, "Even if the sheet collapses all on its own, the bombs still make your father guilty as hell. There have been numerous deaths. People probably are dropping like flies from heart attacks . . . "

Brian said, "Condo owners on Miami Beach."

"You think they deserve this?"

"Your bumper sticker should read: "Save the Condo Owners.""

"Right. Now the whales and the sharks get to move into the condos, and eat all the dead floating heart-attack victims, and proceed to live in luxury—that's amusing, isn't it?"

"I think so. You don't?"

Toby wouldn't admit it to Brian, but he did. The idiots with exposed beachfront developments deserved whatever they got. That had been sinking in, slowly, ever since Hurricane Andrew. This line of questioning was heading nowhere. "What's the purification stuff all about?" Toby asked. "And the sacrifice bullshit—Father sacrifices himself in the court of public opinion? Why?"

"Don't call him, 'Father.' No, that's not what he's doing."

"Then what the hell is he doing?"

"I'll tell you. But first, I need to know some things."

"Ah. Ah. The tables are turned. I feel the sting of poetic justice. The hoist of my own petard . . . "

"What's that?"

"I have no idea. Brian, my brain is your data bank. Whatever I know, it's yours—if you'll just answer a few simple questions."

The twirling fingers became a fist. "I want to know about your brother. About Dan. Tell me everything about Dan." Toby watched Brian's knuckles whiten.

"You can't be serious," Dan said. He used his midget grinder to pepper his slices of steak. Rare slices. The way he liked it.

Harry nodded. "They're digging up all they can," he said.

"Our parents must be thrilled," Selma remarked.

Dan said, "I bet mine are screaming at places that rent helicopters.

Which aren't available. They thought they'd be safe on Grand Cayman—that's why they moved there, you know. To live on a guarded island. I guess the joke's on them."

"Have you called them?" Gula asked.

"No," Dan replied. "Everything's been a blur that keeps getting weirder. Anyway, couldn't FATBOY trace it?"

"Yes," Harry said, loading more steak on his plate. "No doubt about it, your parents' phone is tapped. Selma's parents' too."

"If they only could see me now," Selma said as she readjusted her extravagant ruffles. She'd gone upstairs to get the hat. Its skewed feathers made her a roadkill peacock.

Dan said, "They know we're alive, at least."

Selma nodded. She sighed, and said, "Dan, we did go out a lot. During the three nights you were there."

"The kind of clubs they always warned me about," Dan said glumly. "Disease. Predatory older men. Killer youths, spreading contagion. Every single tired stereotype, they believe them all. Selma—who do you think told FATBOY we'd gone out?"

Grace said, "FATBOY has interrogated everybody you know."

"I bet that's true," Harry said.

"Did you have fun dancing?" Gula asked with interest.

"Sure," Dan replied.

"And you got wet," Gula said, "from—sweating?"

"Well, what else . . ." Dan didn't finish the sentence.

"We both did," Selma said, a toss of her feathers camouflaging a wink at Dan. "What's the point if you don't?"

"Yow," Harry said.

Gula drained her drink. With studied casualness she said, "I didn't know homo bars welcome women."

In unison, Dan and Selma said, "Please!"

"I beg your pardon," Gula said huffily. "Times change, I suppose. For example, I never would have thought that either of you is homosexual. But then, the TV program . . . "

"Selma isn't," Dan said.

Harry dropped his fork. "Damn," he said.

"I see," Gula said, now studying Harry.

"It is kind of funny," Grace said in a small voice.

"What is, dear?" Gula said.

"That Selma and Dan are . . ." Grace wrinkled her nose. The gray eyes took on a dreamy quality.

"Poster girl and poster boy?" Selma suggested.

Grace nodded. "I mean, you don't seem like . . . "

"Raving barfly sluts?" Dan said. "That's us. At four on a Monday morning, you know what we'll be doing. Tossing back tequila at a live-sex-act disco." He chewed steak. "No fooling around, Harry. FAT-BOY's really putting up posters of Selma and me?"

Harry said, "CNN did a thing on it. Every queer bar in the entire Northeast. Plastered with 'Dance Wet' and 'Swear Engine.'"

Helplessly, Dan and Selma started to giggle. The blue satin coat shivered and glinted. Dustily, the feathers waggled. Watching them, Grace tried to stop the smile she felt coming. She wanted to stop it. But she couldn't.

Gula watched the grin, the secret-hick grin, spread across Grace's face. She said to herself, Oh, good. At last.

Harry drank in Selma's voluptuously brocaded mirth. He said to himself, Mama Mia.

Grace, watching Selma and Dan continue to giggle, and send each other watery-eyed glances full of hilarity, thought about how much she liked those two. And how fervently she envied them.

Brian's hand drooped, fingertips grazing the floor. "That's a lie," he said.

"Why would I lie about it?" Toby asked wonderingly.

"'They both like dick.' That's—disgusting!"

Toby noted the revulsion in Brian's face. It seemed real. This kid is bizarre, he thought. "What's disgusting?" he said. "Selma is straight. Dan is queer. They both like dick, it's totally simple. So don't worry about Grace. If she's with them, she's safer than—than . . ." Toby couldn't think of an adequate way to put it. "Listen, Brian. If you were the one shacked up with them, yes, unclean thoughts would run through Dan and Selma's minds. They'd be hatching plots to get you naked, and have their way with you, and fuck your brains out . . . "

Brian sat up violently. "They would not!" he yelled.

Uh-oh, Toby thought. "All I meant is, they'd find you irresistible. But Grace isn't having that effect. So don't worry . . . "

"And how could Selma do that?" Brian demanded, breathing raggedly. Panic flooded from his wide gray eyes.

"Do what?" Toby said.

"What you just said!" Brian shouted.

A bad choice of words, Toby concluded. "Well, you know, Brian, what I just said is, like, a two-way street. It isn't only—uh—one person doing it. It's sort of mutual."

"Yuuucckkkk!" Brian howled.

"You're beginning to really puzzle me," Toby remarked.

"And you're being manipulative," Brian said with accusatory venom. "You're trying to break me down, to get answers to your stupid questions! But forget it. All I can say is, Dan better not be trying anything with her. If I find out he is, I'll . . ." Both fists, thrust through the bars, shook at Toby.

"What nerve you have. You little fudgepacker."

"What is a fudgepacker?" Brian asked heatedly.

"I seem to recall that you came close to raping me last night. In the truck—when I was drugged and helpless."

Brian trembled. His face turned a vermillion color.

"You thought," Toby inquired, "I was too drugged to notice? Too gone to feel what you had going under your cute little dress?" Brian gulped. Toby added, "What made you think I wouldn't remember what you did—when you thought you were Grace?"

"Look," Brian stammered. "I am so incredibly sorry."

"Nice to hear."

"Really, I—I don't know. I'm just so—crazy now." The eyes brimmed shinily. "Without my sister, see. I've gone—insane. Really! I don't know what to do! And I'm sorry . . . "

"Okay," Toby said. "Okay, take it easy."

"And I don't understand it," Brian went on. "If Dan would like me . . . why . . . wouldn't he like Grace?"

Toby sighed. "Maybe it's because you're twins. I got news for you, Brian. You and your sister are different people. You're not the same person. And that's why. That's why Dan would get hard just thinking about you. And why he wouldn't with Grace. It's one of those chemical things—you're a boy. She's a girl."

"Yeah," Brian moaned. "I know. But . . . it's more than that."

"How?"

"My sister and I are lovers."

It hit Toby with a crashing shock that didn't confuse him. To his astonishment, it brought vivid clarity. Of course, he thought. Of course. It made perfect sense. He let a minute go by. With every passing second, Brian's shame and bewilderment hit him harder. Toby realized why the kid had done what he'd done in the truck. Brian really did think he and Grace were the same person. Worse, Toby suspected, the twins had been encouraged to think that way. So much so, Brian literally hadn't been himself in the truck. Half of him had been amputated; the near-rape was an attempt to reattach it. Grace he'd replaced with his own body. Himself he'd transferred to Toby's paralyzed body. The twins, together again. It totally blew Toby away.

"Do your parents know?" he asked when he couldn't endure the silence any longer.

Brian nodded tearily. "Mother approves. Father doesn't."

"Uh-huh. But it's convenient for both of them. Right?"

"What d'you mean?"

"Brian—it's obvious. It's a way to keep you at home. A way to keep other people out, and keep you in the plot. Man. It's just—amazing."

"Grace isn't at home," Brian muttered, "anymore."

"Yeah. You poor kid. I feel bad for you. I really do."

"First," Gula said, "I have to know something. The rabbit, Grace. You said it's a unique image. Why is it unique?"

They'd cleared dinner items from the room. Dan drank more coffee. Selma smoked by the hearth, the updraft of which was protecting Gula's lungs. Grace considered the question. "It's a child's drawing," she said.

"That's plain," Gula said. "Who, by the way, was the child?"

"Do we have to talk about it?" Grace asked.

"We're curious about how it's unique," Harry said.

"Father is a math genius," Grace said. "He thinks that the likelihood of another image exactly like it being out there is nil. As for who drew it—Brian and I drew it together. When we were five. It was a present for Father. We told him it's 'a badge of honor.' Anything else you want to know?"

Her face, scared now, uncannily resembled the rabbit she'd co-drawn. Selma wondered if Brian's face did the same when he was scared. She bet it did.

Dan asked, "Why did you start calling it 'the pin'?"

"Because we got sick to our stomachs thinking about what Father was doing with it."

"Perfectly horrid," Gula murmured. "The 'fertility icon' was created by the mastermind's . . . *children.*"

Harry's forehead furrowed. Gula cleared her throat. They looked at each other. Gula nodded, as if saying, Continue.

"We see things this way," Harry said. "We don't know if sending FATBOY the rabbit will stop the bombs. But not giving them a chance to try is madness. Anyone disagree?"

No one said a word.

"However, you've convinced us, Grace," Harry went on. "Blowing the whistle on Cliffcloud is bad for us. And bad for you."

Grace twitched. With relief, Selma thought. She realized she herself was quite relieved too.

"So the solution is this," Harry said. "You write a letter, Grace. One that proves your identity. It explains how the rabbit works. We enclose the badge—excuse me, the pin. Somebody Gula and I know takes it to FATBOY. And we pray they don't screw up."

"Who takes it to FATBOY?" Grace asked.

Gula blinked. "My first choice was Harry. But Harry, fool that he is, refuses to leave. So . . . the friend, oddly enough, is my mailman. He's trustworthy. His name is Frick. He'll be here tomorrow morning; he can pick up your letter and take it to Boston."

"You already talked with him?" Grace asked.

Gula shook her head. "Tomorrow's Monday. He'll be here with the delivery. I'll talk to him then."

"I see," Grace said. "Uh—I also have a plan. It concerns Brian and Toby."

"A plan for getting them?" Dan asked.

"That's right," Grace said. "A plan for getting them."

48

"What do you think?" Toby said. "Did he kill those people in Antarctica? Or was it an accident?"

"Probably an accident," Brian mumbled.

Both now lay on their respective floors. Their conversation had slowed. Brian seemed a bit out of it.

Toby wasn't giving up, however. He said, "Could you really filter the rabbit? From the media streams?"

"You could try."

"What's the Beast's other face, Brian?"

"The orb. Mantis's logo."

"Huh," Toby said. "Technology in the service of greed." He thought about it. "Martha's in deep," he remarked.

"More ways than one."

Toby thought more. "The orb is on TV already."

"Special ads do it. LaserWorks home defense ads."

"Oh. Of course. The current episodes. That's weird."

"Why?" Brian asked.

"Your father called for war on the Beast. That means war on the orb. On Mantis. Which means war on—here." Toby sat up. "It's ironic. The Beast has a defense system to fight the war."

"It's part of the plot," Brian said. "Part of the show."

"Oh, yeah?"

"This house is a demo. A demo of the orb in action. It's in the LaserWorks commercials, this house, by the way. The orb defends it. Get it? The shoot-out here, if there is one, will be an extension of the ad campaign. Which really is an icon campaign."

"Icon campaign?"

"That's what they call the orb and the rabbit. Icons."

"Jesus," Toby said. "This place will be vaporized."

"Part of the show."

"Great. What does Martha get out of it?"

"Eternal infamy. Plus, she gets Father."

"I see. He loves her 'more than Mother.'"

Brian turned on his side. Alertly, he studied Toby.

Toby said, "So—what's the purification stuff?"

Brian thrust a nervous hand through his bars. "Isn't it obvious?" he said.

"It's obvious that it's stupid!" Toby exclaimed. What's a sea level rise going to purify? Not the coasts or the oceans—they'll just get filthier. Much filthier, if oceans absorb urban areas. As for the enchantment bullshit, it'll just piss people off. Make them crazy—people with guns will rule even more brutally than they already do, if coastlines flood. And so, like always, life will go on. More hideously than ever."

Brian said, "You don't want to believe Father is nuts."

"Is he?" Toby said angrily.

In a way that reminded Toby of Earnest, and also brought to mind

Grace, Brian's eyebrows arched. He said, "You're forgetting that sea level's rising anyway. Look—if you want proof he isn't nuts, consider two things."

"Okay," Toby said. "What?"

"First, a madman with eleven nuclear bombs could be blowing up worse places than Antarctica. Antarctica's the remotest place on earth. As far as humans are concerned."

"Not when it melts, it isn't. The other thing?"

"Antarctica is big. Really big. Eleven nuclear explosions shouldn't be able to affect it at all. Even with volcanoes erupting, the ice sheet shouldn't be affected. It's hundreds of thousands of square miles."

"But it is being affected."

"That proves my point. The sheet's about to go. Anybody with insight into the science of this knows a thousand bombs couldn't toss the sheet into the ocean. Unless it's going there already."

"Fine," Toby said. "So it's going there. How will that be a purification of anything?"

"Because Father's given the human race enemies to blame."

"I don't buy it," Toby declared. "For the rest of history, mankind will think of the Beast with fear and loathing? This means that over-population and high-tech greed will disappear?"

"The Beast will be loathed. For a long, long time."

"Why?" Toby demanded.

"People will remember a technologically advanced, greedy, over-populous civilization that wired itself, with extreme ingenuity, into self-destruction."

"Right. The 'afterimage' your father mentioned. This insures a glorious destiny for human beings? I just don't see it."

"Father hopes it'll scare people enough that they won't repeat our mistakes. When water rises, and things fall apart—people will associate the icons with savagery, dark times. Most of all, with the die-off. With the dying." Brian rapped knuckles on his bars. "But Antarctica will be a god. A purity god, washing away the Beast. An unforgettable symbol of the planet's rage."

Exasperated, and chilled, Toby stared at Brian. "How many people does your father think will die?"

"After climate shift?"

Toby nodded.

"A quarter of the global human population. At least a quarter. Maybe half, or more."

Toby suddenly felt quite ill.

"It's amazing, I know. But likely."

"Uh—if it were left alone, how long would the sheet last?"

"Hard to tell," Brian replied. "Ten, twenty years."

"Which means people could be warned. Right?"

"People are warned all the time. But they don't listen."

Toby's stomach convulsed. Unable to hold it down, he retched dinner all over the floor.

"It seems like what I proposed this morning," Gula said.

"With two differences," Grace said. "First, the timing. Second, talking to them from the gate. At six o'clock, Father will be busy with the broadcast. That's the reason for doing it then—he'll be busy. So, I'll be talking with Mother. The key is not dealing with Father. It's dealing with her."

Harry said, "Won't work. She'll send somebody to grab you. Then she'll force you to tell the truth. Your mom's got a talent for that, I hear. She makes people talk."

"Wrong," Grace said. "The gate has a video camera. When Martha answers, she'll get Mother. The two of them will see me holding a phone. Which means they'll see me talking with you. The first thing I'll say is, 'I have allies on the phone—one false move, they call FAT-BOY.' I'll tell them you've already punched the touchtones. One more punch, you get the 800 line. It'll be like having a gun pointed at their heads. I'll give them ten minutes. 'If I don't get Brian and Toby in ten minutes, my friends make the call.' That's what I'll say."

"What if they grab you anyway?" Selma asked.

"Then I'm done for," Grace replied. "But the good thing is, you aren't fingered. They won't know who you are or where you are. So the risk is only to me. Doesn't that make sense?"

"Grace," Dan said, "if they grab you, and your mother's a genius at making people talk, she'll find out where we are."

"Not if I have the gun with me," Grace said. "And use it."

"Wait a second," Harry said.

"Kind of drastic," Dan said.

"Use it on yourself?" Gula quavered.

Grace nodded. In a way that made them speechless.

Harry recovered first. He said, "You'd have to give them more than ten minutes. They'd need fifteen, or twenty, to drive down from that house."

"You're not taking this seriously?" Gula said with alarm.

"I don't know," Harry said. "Grace wants her brother. Dan wants his. Problem is—do we trust Grace to use the gun?"

Selma remarked to Grace, "You're prepared to do anything, huh? To get him back."

Grace said, "If that's not clear by now, what is?"

Toby toweled his floor.

Brian watched. He said, "You're thinking that Father's crime is not warning people. About the ice sheet."

"Uh-huh," Toby said. "I do think that."

"He's warned people all his life. It hasn't done any good. So the question is, if he quit—if he turned off the bombs and committed suicide or something—would the world change its behavior? In other words, would the warning work?"

Toby stood with his vomit-soaked towel. He couldn't figure out what to do with it. He said, "If your father quits now, business-as-usual returns immediately. But that doesn't mean he should get away with this."

"So if you could, you'd stop him?"

Toby glanced at Brian. He sat cross-legged, face upturned, and looked serious. Toby said, "Of course."

"But it's obvious you want to believe in him."

Toby yelled, "Brian, your father is a *monster!*" He threw the towel in a corner, and leaned against his bars. "But I'll give him one thing," he muttered. "At least he's doing something. The man really is doing something . . . "

"I know how to stop him," Brian said quietly.

"You tried once. It didn't work."

"The circumstances are different," Brian said.

"Explain," Toby said.

"We could screw up tomorrow's broadcast. If we interrupted it, and told the public some facts about the icons, we'd screw it up good. Stuff about the orb system, for example."

"That requires getting out of here," Toby remarked.

"Right. Toby, I saw you pocket Mother's cardkey."

"No kidding," Toby said.

● ━ ● ━ ●

Dan and Selma sat in Jeremy's pickup truck. Selma had left her bag there; they'd gone for a walk through Gula's woods to get it. Around them, blackness croaked, burped, and hummed.

"I wonder what Toby's doing right now," Dan said.

Selma said, "He's saying, 'I told you so.' Over and over. To whoever will listen. And even if nobody is."

"You don't think he's entitled?"

"Yeah. But I hate to admit it. Don't you?"

"He might not be alive, Selma."

"So we engrave his tombstone, 'I told you so.'"

"Funny. No, really. It is. Can I have a cigarette?"

Selma gave him one. "He would," she said. "Think it is."

Dan lit the cigarette. They listened to amazingly loud insect violins. "I'm going tomorrow," he said.

"Where?"

"To that gate. Grace isn't going. I am."

"Why?"

"Selma—what else do I have to do?"

"But why not her?"

"She isn't reliable," Dan said. "She's too into her family trip. What if her mother hypnotizes her?"

"And she doesn't use the gun?" Selma said. Dan nodded. "Well—would you? Use it?"

"I don't know." Something scurried through the woods. They both shivered. "In a way, it would be a relief."

"Dan!" Selma exclaimed. "What are you talking about?"

"My future, Selma—is such a blank. I'm such a blank."

"You are not!"

"I am. And that's not all. Way down, I'm more of a pessimist than Toby is. Unlike him, though, I hide it."

"I'm getting upset, Dan. Are you saying something about a virus? Or what?"

Dan didn't reply.

Selma muttered, "What's wrong?"

"Aren't you, deep down, a pessimist?"

"I think Father Trefethen's having a bad influence on everybody."

"I'm a closet pessimist, Selma. You know what's really funny? Toby's a closet optimist. He's a dreamer. That's why he gets so pissed off. His natural tendency—and I'm not kidding—is to hope things will be okay."

"He's a dreamer. I agree on that."

"You have your stuff?" Dan asked.

Selma picked up the bag. She said, "Yeah."

Dan lit the flashlight and opened his door. Selma opened hers. "Careful," Dan said, too late. He heard a squelching noise.

"Shit!" Selma yelled. Dan listened to her angrily pant. She growled, "At least I have these things on." She slammed the door and tromped around into the flash's beam. It revealed freshly dyed party boots. Beyond ankle level, they'd gone from purple to black.

"Not the end of the world," Dan said. "Heh-heh-heh."

His silhouette, satinly iridescent behind the flash, made Selma smile. "I feel like we're a couple of shady refugees," she said. "On the run from the eighteenth century."

They walked down the fire trail, and came to the field below Gula's garden. Lights glowed from her hilltop windows. Dan stopped. He said, "You know, when Gula brought up my hair, I wish I'd had the nerve to tell her something. About the spinster look."

"Yeah? What?"

"That it represents a kind of, well, jealousy, I think."

"Say why. Even though I know what it is."

"I'm someone with no future. She's someone with a past."

"I'm gonna slap you!"

"Selma—think of her memories!"

"Give me a hug, please."

They hugged tightly in the buzzing night.

PART 4
MONDAY

49

The New York Times:

TREFETHEN SPEAKS
AT SIX P.M.
NEO-LUDDITE MOBS
RAMPAGE THROUGH CITY
SENSE OF IMPENDING DOOM IS
WORLDWIDE AND GROWING
SCIENTISTS WARN:
"ICE SHEET IS DETERIORATING"

The Boston Globe:

SIX BOMBS NOW TICK
World Leadership Betrays
Aura Of Impotence
"The Beast": Inspiration for Holy War?

The Daily News:

RAGING
LUDDIES
SCREAM:
SMASH
THE MACHINE!

The Lure Of The Litchfield Hills:

LOAD YOUR GUNS
WARNING, WARNING, WARNING:
RATS ARE DESERTING SHIP
SHERIFF CALLS FOR
"MAXIMUM MEASURES"

From his specially fitted bed, Slotsky surveyed the bumper-to-bumper traffic. It was 8:32 Monday morning. The Mass. Pike, a four-lane, limited-access highway that bisected Massachusetts east to west, was paralyzed. Slotsky had left Boston at 7:00. Now creeping through suburban Framingham, his ambulance was averaging less than twenty miles an hour.

Perfect, he thought as he scoped fellow travelers. Pickups and utilities they'd stuffed to the limit. Worldly goods they'd lashed to roofs. Vacation trailers of every make they'd pressed into evacuation service . . . ahead, a motorboat sat dead in the water. Mattresses, TV sets, and an exercise bike peeked over the gunwales—unenthralled, it seemed to Slotsky, with this outing. The Lincoln towing them was overheating, the scope's thermal read indicated. Slotsky adjusted the audioprobe. Amid desultory honks, quarrels, and idling motors, frightened children howled in his headset.

The scope's view mask, appended to a cantilevered boom, had been designed for use from a seated position. Minor modifications extended its reach to Slotsky's pillow. He liked the thing; it enabled him to surveille the ambulance's environment with exceptional thoroughness. However, the current environment didn't merit such scrutiny. Slotsky slapped the scope. It swung away, looking, to his ill-tempered eye, like a robot snatching the mask off a diver's face. Slotsky imagined the thrash. The frantic bubbles. He found the image cheering.

All told, he reminded himself, I'm not doing badly.

His stay at Dr. Dragan Voisonovich's had been productive and brief. An associate of associates, Dragan was neither too mercenary to pose a threat, nor too scrupulous to resist the kind of remuneration Slotsky could offer. No doubt he by now realized what he might have netted, had he informed the FATB of Slotsky's Saturday night arrival. On the other hand, Dragan had enjoyed watching the transfer of a cool million to his offshore account. That transpired minutes after Slotsky's car crashed into the office wing of his Belmont house. Sure a drunk had veered up his driveway, Dragan found a blood-soaked Slotsky brandishing the tracker; which, supplied with an access code, swiftly displayed enrichment in crisp, glowing numerals.

Slotsky received immediate attention. He'd needed it. Dragan informed him that, had he arrived even fifteen minutes later, nothing—really, nothing—could have been done. He'd lost too much blood. A leg was broken in several places. Ribs had cracked, his skull had concussed, the facial wound was suppurating. On top of the 'dorph overdose, Slotsky's trauma would have finished him.

But Dragan, using skills acquired serving with the Serbian army during its liquidation of Bosnia, brought him back. Dragan furthermore put Slotsky in touch with vendors of hard-to-get merchandise. This led to the acquisition of a vehicle suited to Slotsky's needs.

Certain associates of Dragan's associates, having profited from the Eastern European black market in war materiel, had discovered that opportunities for such commerce existed in North America as well. The reorganization and downsizing of the American armed forces through the mid-'90s had forced huge quantities of hardware into early retirement—and by extension, into the marketplace.

The ambulance provided an exemplary case history. The Pentagon had developed it for the "Doom Project," a multi-billion-dollar program to cope with nuclear attack. At one time a priority, and extremely classified, the Doom Project knew no limits. It hollowed entire mountains to house civilian and military personnel. It constructed underground cities in various parts of the country; it "hardened" transportation and communication systems to endure the withering electromagnetic pulse associated with nuclear explosions. In short, the program expended an enormous amount of effort and ingenuity to assure the survival of those who would carry on after the rest of the population had been incinerated.

Slotsky found it ironic that his doom ambulance, still in service twenty years later, should be immobilized in a panic-driven traffic jam. After all, its raison d'etre was to rush through chaos. Hardened in every conceivable way, resembling an armored cash carrier but bigger, it essentially was a battering ram. The designers had been told that no mob, no rioting faction of the terrified citizenry, could be allowed to impede the salvation of the general or congressman or cabinet secretary it some day might carry.

In 1995, the government mothballed the Doom Project and decommissioned the ambulance fleet. Stripped of firepower—of weapons designed to cut through walls of flesh—the machines were auctioned to the public at bargain prices. Most of them, that is, went that route.

Corrupt depot-keepers sold a few intact. Slotsky had just parted with thirty million dollars to get one of those. Indistinguishable on the outside from its emasculated brethren, the machine not only was intact, but enhanced.

And yet, Slotsky thought, here I am—trapped.

If the traffic didn't clear up, or his men didn't find an alternative route, he wouldn't get to Cheswick, Connecticut until mid-evening. That was unacceptable. Slotsky had business to attend to in Cheswick. Cash flow, thanks to Cliffcloud and the FATB, had been satisfactory so far. But expenses were mounting.

The two hirelings up front, for instance. Ralph and Edward cost ten thousand dollars a day apiece. At that rate, Slotsky thought pettishly, couldn't they devise some way to get off this detestable highway?

He eyed his 'dorph pouch. Should I? he wondered. Of course. He unpeeled a Number 4 and applied it to the shaved spot on his neck. Dragan had told him to avoid the face gash for dose delivery. Interferes with the healing, he'd said. Slotsky thought that a shame. Delivery through the gash came with such . . . force.

But neck application did the trick. A painless leg wriggled in its cast; shattered ribs purred as he heaved out a sigh. Even if obliged to order Edward to career over the raw countryside, Slotsky would get to Cheswick by 6:00.

He felt ninety-five percent sure that Cliffcloud was harboring Trefethen and company there. He'd assayed all the known residences. Cheswick looked the likeliest refuge by far.

Slotsky wanted to confirm that, however. For with confirmation, cash flow would cease to be a problem. Edward and Ralph could stay on staff indefinitely. That appealed to Slotsky. He needed their services. They would help safeguard what he hoped to be a lengthy retirement.

Frick parked the Jeep in the usual spot out front, grabbed Gula's mail, and walked to the porch. He paused at the steps. Somebody had left a pair of purple suede hipboots near the door. The feet were mudcaked. Gee, Frick thought, studying the extravagant things. Did they belong to one of Gula's grandchildren? He couldn't recall her mentioning any were coming.

Harry came through the door. "Morning," he said.

The man looks peaked, Frick thought. He said, "Whose boots?"

"Huh," said Harry, frowning at them. "Mine," he declared. He picked them up.

"Yours?" Frick asked skeptically.

"That's right," Harry said, heading across the lawn to the barns. "Gorgeous, aren't they?"

"Yep," Frick said. He went through the door and into the kitchen. Gula already was buttering toast. She too looked under the weather.

"How are you?" she said, voice strained.

"Fine as can be," Frick replied, putting mail on the table.

"Wish I could say that," Gula muttered.

Frick sat. "What's going on with Harry?"

"What do you mean, what's going on?"

She asked it too sharply. Something has happened here, Frick realized. "Town's in an uproar," he remarked, scratching spots on his tanned dome of a head. "Driving itself to frenzy. Talk of armed patrols and the like. The traffic's pouring in, Gula. Can't get a stool at the cafe. No Vacancy signs everywhere. Kotzler's lot is jammed. I guess the President didn't inspire a lot of confidence last night. Did you watch him?"

"Yes I did," Gula grumbled. She shoved toast across the table, and stood to get coffee.

"You're worried. Can't blame you. But I think we're seeing overreaction. Dr. Klantz over the hill? He told me there's no way that ice'll take a dive. It's too massive—did you hear it's so heavy, it depresses the earth under it?"

"You don't say," Gula said, plunking coffee by the toast.

"Just like the ice that used to cover Scandinavia," Frick went on. "Klantz says Scandinavia's still on the rebound from the weight of it—and it fell off ten thousand years ago. These things take time, Gula. We won't see a flood. Not in our lifetimes."

Gula said, "Thanks for the good cheer."

"You're welcome. What's the matter?"

"I'm about to ask you for a favor. A big one. But I'm afraid I can't . . ." Feebly, she sighed. "Really explain it."

Frick watched her pull on a pair of dishwashing gloves. She took a plastic-wrapped envelope from a shelf. He smiled and said, "A mail delivery?"

"Yes," Gula said, eyes going bleaker. "Out of town. I hardly can bring myself to ask you to do it."

"How far out of town?"

"Far. To Boston."

Frick shook his head. "The roads, Gula. I might get to Boston. But I wouldn't get back. Everybody's leaving there for places like here. Don't you watch the news?"

"This is Martha Cliffcloud," Helen said into the phone. "I'm calling about an ulcer medication, made in Germany, called Gutzyme. Some people pronounce it Gootzyme. Do you carry it?"

"Ma'am—I—uh—don't know. Can you hold?"

"Did you hear me?" Helen barked. "This is Martha Cliffcloud!"

"Yes. You said that. Ms. Cliffcloud, I'm sorry, we're really busy. The store is, like, packed. Lot of people here, ma'am. Can you call back later?"

"Give me the manager. Immediately."

"Okay. Hold on."

Helen gnawed her lip. This was so frustrating. Every pharmacy in the area was full of desperate shoppers. All stores everywhere were completely overrun. That complicated her strategy. She bit her lip harder, and tasted salt.

"Ms. Cliffcloud?" the clerk boy said.

"Yes?"

"The manager's in the parking lot. Some people are fighting out there. It's kind of bad, so . . . "

"Can you please tell me if you have heard the words 'Gutzyme' or 'Gootzyme' in the last day and a half?"

"Can't say as I have," the boy replied.

"Ask the manager to return my call," Helen said. She gave the number Martha had provided. "Please remember whose number it is."

"Sure will."

Helen hung up. She hated impersonating Martha. But given the near-impossibility of getting through, she thought it the most effective way to proceed.

Luckily, she didn't have to mimic Martha's voice. Helen couldn't even have attempted such a thing. Martha, understanding this with unusual tact, had supplied a voice-matrixer that made Helen's voice her own. Thus Helen could speak normally, and not worry about it, as long as she stuck to line four. That was the matrixed line.

Helen stared at the silence around her. The room seemed too big.

But it wasn't so very big; just a nook off the vast music room. Am I too frazzled to do this? she wondered.

No. For Helen was sure that Grace was looking for Gutzyme. She, or someone whose help she'd enlisted, almost certainly was placing a special order for it, if local stores didn't carry it. Helen now knew most local stores didn't. She'd talked with too many people who'd never even heard of the product.

She stared at the phone. The couple dozen closest retailers of anything resembling ulcer medication had promised to call back. Despite shopping conditions, Helen suspected they would call back. With news of a customer asking for Gutzyme.

Helen intended to find that person. She wanted to question her or him. In person.

50

General Raffenelli swallowed a last mouthful of coffee and put the mug down. The sun, blasting over the harbor into his windows, sent unfamiliar shadows through the office. Nothing was in its usual place. Sofas and armchairs sat in the huddles of last night's working groups, covered with files, laptops, half-eaten sandwiches, even articles of clothing. The general and his staff had labored here since Saturday night, straight through, until this morning. The staff he'd sent away for a few hours' rest. He hadn't been able to get any himself. He hadn't even bathed. Liberal applications of cologne failed to suppress the aroma that emanated from his uniform. It possessed complex qualities, this aroma; generated as it was from fury, humiliation, bewilderment, exhaustion, other feelings bruised beyond recognition, and, yes, paranoia.

I am, he'd been telling himself, a paranoid man.

At this point, Raffenelli had no problem admitting that fact. Admitting it, he found, invigorated the pump of his adrenal glands. But it wasn't helping him understand Dr. Curby Cottage. A bearded man wearing an antique Dilbert T-shirt, Cottage was discussing an image on the viewscreen he'd set up in the general's office.

Cottage called the image a "trail chart." It analyzed, if the scientist knew what he was talking about, a mysterious gap in the recording that the DG had obtained of the Trefethen dinner party.

Cottage said, "We lucked out with the bug being in a ceramic bowl full of packets."

"Wonderful," Raffenelli said. "Why?"

"The bowl resonated the vibration vectors," Cottage replied. "The packets, in turn, protected the resonations from noise overlay. That enabled more precise mapping of the acoustical topology, and topological flow. Which in turn permitted extrapolation, both forward and backward, into the gap. Which meant I could project outlines of what happened in the gap—from the event sequence just before it, and the event sequence just after it. You see what I'm saying?"

"No," Raffenelli said. "Did you find voices in the gap?"

"No," Cottage said. He failed to curb a sneer. "This isn't analogue. It's not an erased segment of a tape. If you delete a portion, there's no possibility of voice retrieval. The data don't exist. You can't enhance from something that doesn't exist. But you do have acoustical trails going into the gap and coming out of it. And we have discrimination there. We have trails."

"I see," Raffenelli said, resisting an impulse to seize this man by the neck and squeeze. "The trails tell you what, Cottage?"

Ordinarily, the general considered the proximity of MIT an asset to the Boston Bureau office. But he occasionally found the personalities hard to take. Dr. Cottage's, for example. The man made him feel as smart as a broken pencil sharpener.

Cottage said, "Keep in mind that the twins don't move during the gap. They stay put, all the way. And given that the gap is one minute and forty-seven seconds . . . "

"Wait. How do you know the gap is that long?"

"Periodicity of the AC system's background susurrus. The total recording is almost two hours. The air-conditioning cycles all the way through, in patterns I isolated and timed. That provides a clock. Where the gap begins, the particular cycle was at a certain point; where it ends, the same cycle took up at another point. Thus I could infer the gap's length."

"I see. Please continue."

"Knowing the length made it easier to map trails that go in and come out of the gap. You know when a train blows its horn, the sound of the horn changes as the train passes?" Raffenelli nodded. "It's the same with voices. In a situation like this, where they move through a small room, the effect is subtle. That's why the ceramic bowl came in handy. It picked up Doppler subtleties in the voices' movements. It also picked up wave-interference between the voices, giving more data to reticulate the chart. General, look at the screen."

Raffenelli looked. As before, it made no sense. About a dozen blobs were quivering. Some moved around like amoebas, others didn't; some were defined and energetic, others flaccid and sluggish. Mostly, the blobs seemed to vibrate at each other . . . it dawned on the general that they represented people. The spatial location of the sounds people made as they talked. Cottage pressed a button. In the blobs, names appeared.

"This is pre-gap," he said. "See the twins, side-by-side?" Raffenelli nodded. "They're at the table. The bug's on it, by the way, right under Grace's chin. You see this one approaching?"

Again Raffenelli nodded. A blob was traveling to the twin-blobs. Its nametag read, "Cliffcloud."

Cottage said, "Now we hit the gap." As the Cliffcloud-blob neared the twin-blobs, all blobs suddenly froze. "Imagine it," Cottage went on. "A minute and forty-seven seconds is going by. Something's happening during that period. We don't know what it is. But we do know what happens as we exit the gap." He pressed another button. The blobs started quivering again. Raffenelli watched the Cliffcloud-blob move away from the twin-blobs. "Do you understand?" Cottage asked.

Raffenelli said, "I think so. The gap coincides with Cliffcloud approaching the twins, staying near them, and then leaving. It could mean that the deleter of that portion of the recording didn't want us to know what Cliffcloud and the twins did."

Cottage nodded. "The bug was right there. It had to have picked up anything they said. The deleter probably didn't want you to hear what Cliffcloud and the twins discussed."

"Thank you," Raffenelli said. He pressed an intercom button. Dworkin entered. "Take Dr. Cottage," the general instructed his secretary, "to one of the secure guest rooms."

"What?" Cottage said, scowling.

The general smiled at him. "You're staying with us for a while. Now get the hell out of my office."

As Dworkin dragged the incredulous Cottage through the door, Raffenelli tried to evaluate the significance of what the scientist had found. Several Bureau experts had discovered the gap in the recording. But only Cottage had uncovered Cliffcloud's apparent connection to it. The general wanted to make maximum use of this intelligence. He smelled a lead. A big one.

He considered the possibility that Slotsky might have made the deletion for purposes of shaking down somebody else, somebody besides the Bureau. Somebody rich enough to equal the Bureau's payment. For example, Cliffcloud. Might the bug have picked up something she'd said? Something she would pay to keep out of the Bureau's hands? Might that have been Slotsky's motivation for making the deletion? In other words, did Slotsky have revenue coming his way because of this gap?

Raffenelli called the Bureau's money-tracing department. He asked for a priority investigation into Cliffcloud's recent banking activity. Specifically, he wanted to know if she had sent significant money to Prague.

I should take another sedative, Helen thought. She stared at the phone she'd thrown against the wall. As if wounded, it mewled.

She popped a pill. The girl who'd just called hadn't been helpful. She'd seemed to resent "Martha Cliffcloud's" threats to speak to the man who owned all two thousand two hundred and eighty-eight Family Farmacies, including the one in Pondville, Connecticut that the brat didn't deserve to assistant-manage. Helen never had expected to feel nostalgia for her days at the Clinic. Her career there hadn't done much for her soul. Sometimes she thought the experience had scarred her deeply. Right now, however, she missed the cutting-edge facilities and the control they'd provided. At the Clinic, a snotty Family Farmacy assistant manager wouldn't have given her any trouble whatever.

The phone rang. Helen crossed the room to where she'd hurled it. She picked it up and said, "Hello?"

Silence came over the line. A surprised silence. Helen thought she heard a slight intake of breath. Another nervous drugstore person, she speculated. Some of these people did find Martha Cliffcloud intimidating. "Hello?" she said more loudly. "Are you calling about ulcer remedies?"

An accented and oddly raspy voice said, "I call for Martha, yes? She is there?"

"This is Martha Cliffcloud," Helen said. "Who are you?"

"Yes. Perhaps you will not remember. We met in Florence many years ago—I am Gustave Voltaire? Count Voltaire, you remember?"

"I don't," Helen snapped, "so drop dead!" She hung up, stood, and took the phone into the music room, looking for a weapon. Anything would do. The concert grand attracted her eye. Its raised, heavy-looking lid would do nicely. She put the phone under it, and was about to smash the lid down when she noticed something strange about the phone's button array. Line four's button wasn't depressed. Line two's was. The last call had come in on line two.

Raffenelli punched the audio lab's number with shaking fingers. His mind, his thoughts, seemed to stutter. He couldn't trust himself to be sure about what he thought he'd heard. One of the engineers would have to confirm it. A voice said, "Audio."

"The general here," Raffenelli said. "I'm sending a squirt. It's a recording of a conversation between a woman claiming to be Martha Cliffcloud and a man claiming to be Count Gustave Voltaire. I suspect neither identity is genuine. I want you to ID both voices. Who is this, by the way?"

"Agent Wharton, sir."

"Agent Wharton, I want you to get everyone except yourself out of the lab, and to lock the door before you run the analysis. Do that now. Get 'em all out and lock the door."

"Yes, sir!" As he listened to Wharton put the phone down and move away, Raffenelli congratulated himself for not having given even a hint of who the people behind the voices might be. Bias wouldn't contaminate Wharton's analysis. His analysis would be completely clean; and that, if the general's suspicion proved correct, would count for a lot when he called McMurtry.

He'd break the news coolly. Yes, he thought—coolness. He realized he could be wrong. He easily could be mistaken. But the general doubted it. He knew that voice too well. Count Gustave Voltaire, a name he'd invented on the spot to conceal his identity, had just spoken with Helen Scarf.

Helen took the smashed phone back in the nook. She knew what she should do. She should find Martha and ask if the house logged incoming calls. And if it identified the origin.

She wasn't going to do that, however. Helen couldn't risk the chance that the gentleman with whom she'd exchanged far too many words in her real voice wasn't a count. He probably was some fusty pal of Martha's. But suppose . . . Helen tried not to think about it. She'd come too close to despair already.

Carefully, she put the destroyed phone on the couch. Then she sat herself down and reached for the sedatives. Two pills would suffice. They'd quiet the scream that was struggling to get free of her chest; the one she couldn't allow herself to release. For if she did release it, Helen felt certain she wouldn't stop.

A voice murmured in her ear, "Dr. Scarf?"

"*What?*" Helen cried out, quite alarmed.

"This is the house speaking. Dr. Cliffcloud asked me to inform you when the mailman arrives. He is at the gate now."

Frick sat in his jeep, staring at the intercom grill in the military-style gate. He wondered if the voice was real. With a machine deadness under the stuck-up accent, it kept saying, "Stand by. Someone will be with you soon."

Suddenly the gate shuddered. It heaved open, revealing a blacktop road winding into hilly forest. Martha Cliffcloud's deep voice said from the grill, "Hello?"

"Hello!" Frick called back.

Cliffcloud said, "Would you be so kind as to drive up to the house? I'd like to talk with you."

Everything happens at once, Frick thought. Gula asks him to do the impossible—drive to Boston and back, delivering a mysterious envelope he can't get fingerprints on. Now Cliffcloud wants him to visit. Meantime, the world's gone crazy. "I'm flattered," he said. "But I'm running late. I—er—put your mail in the box. It's secure, as usual. I used the key."

"I insist you come up. Have you ever been up?"

"It's been years," Frick replied.

"Then it's time," Cliffcloud said.

Goodness, Frick thought. Last I was there was with the grandkids. A camping trip. Ten years ago, when this was still a state forest. "All right," he said.

He drove through the gate. The place seemed much as before. The road, repaved with fancy macadam, looked neater. No lines, just the black running through the trees. Every quarter-mile, he passed strange-looking towers. The famous lasers? They did seem electronic. And the cones on top sure as heck looked aimable.

Frick climbed hills and went down them, then around them, then up another one that didn't stop. Eventually he saw it. The wonderful plateau that used to have the visitor's center with such a grand view of the valley and the lake. Cliffcloud had torn down the center to make way for a house, Frick had heard. A shame.

Then he saw the brownish walls, the red-tile roof. It wasn't a house. Awful, he thought. Plain awful. The whole thing was just a damn shame.

At her console in the basement control room, Martha tracked the Jeep approaching the house. She neither knew nor cared what Helen intended to do with Mr. Frick. Helen's campaign to extract information from locals Martha thought quixotic. Desperate measures for a desperate woman.

I gave her the rope, Martha reflected. And very obligingly, Helen has done it. Hanged herself.

Martha listened again to the chat with "Gustave Voltaire." She decided against telling Earnest about it. He might suspect—and Helen certainly would—that Martha had arranged for the recording of Helen's calls to get evidence of a foul-up.

Now that Martha possessed spectacular evidence, she would use it conservatively. The house phone log registered a call, on line two, that had come in at 11:34 and lasted thirty-six seconds. The log furthermore revealed that the phone Helen was using had taken the call. Finally, the log showed that the caller had used Ted Raffenelli's personal phone line.

Those facts, and the fact that line two hadn't been matrixed, were enough. It was all Earnest needed to know.

Martha brooded about the upcoming showdown. Helen, she knew, could do something stupid.

But Martha had planned for that possibility. She'd assigned Helen the nook off the music room for a reason. The music room held potent security hardware.

Only two questions remain, Martha concluded. When will the FATB show up? And when to tell Earnest they're coming?

I'll wait a bit, she decided, before telling Earnest. If he were to know this early in the day that the FATB was targeting Cheswick, he would become upset, and might not be able to focus on the broadcast.

Martha didn't want to undermine Earnest's performance. In every way that she could, she intended to bolster it. She therefore would dispose of the Helen issue with all possible discretion.

Toby dreamed he was voyaging through the stars.

The mighty *Orb* churned steadily along. Deep in its bowels, in the cramped brig, Toby plotted his suicide mission. He and a comrade were planning a breakout. Their goal: the plasma core that powered the ship.

If they made it there, and sabotaged the iconic transducers, they would strike a blow for freedom and decency all over the galaxy. For they would thwart the *Orb*'s evil captain—a brilliant but misguided warrior who tragically had come to believe himself the doom messiah . . .

Dan went into the kitchen knowing he'd find trouble. He'd heard Harry's angry voice, then Gula's. They were arguing about the Grace plan, he had a feeling. Harry and Grace glared at each other across the table. Selma sat by a window. Gula leaned into the refrigerator, a hand planted on one knee. The other hand banged things around in the fridge. Really loudly.

"Good!" Harry boomed. "We have a quorum! Dan, sit down."

Dan sat. He glanced at Selma; she yawned. Like him, she'd just woken up. Grace looked half-awake too. No wonder, Dan thought. The three of them had stayed up half the night wandering around the house, trying not to make any noise that would wake Gula in her front room on the second floor, or Harry in his ground floor front room by the main staircase. It hadn't been hard to be quiet. The other wings went back so far.

Gula, muttering, smashed something deep in the fridge.

Harry said to Dan, "Grace informs me you held a debate deep through the night. About who's the hero going to Cliffcloud's at five. And blows your brains out if somebody grabs you."

We talked about a lot of other things too, Dan thought. For example, the terrible boredom of Grace's existence. Her parents hadn't let her and her brother do much of anything all their lives. Except—this truly had shocked Dan and Selma both—have sex. Of course, the twins had been on several expeditions to Antarctica. Not many people, Grace had made clear, got to do that. Still. They didn't have any friends. They'd never really had fun. All they'd ever had was each other, and a scarier-than-hell Mother and Father.

"Somebody," Dan said, addressing the issue Harry had raised, "has to do it. We can't forget the brother problem." He felt a horrible urge to burst out laughing. At one point he, Grace, and Selma, cracking up on the floor of the book-stuffed study, had egged themselves into near-hysteria repeating over and over, "Oh, brother!"

That had come after the crying period. Which lasted a while.

Gula lunged at the table with cold cuts. She slapped them down, then thrust herself back in the fridge. Drawers slammed. She emerged again, this time with a jar of homemade-looking pickles. Other foodstuffs followed: butter, mustard, lettuce—lots of different lettuces—bread, and even beer. Harry sighed impatiently. He didn't seem to think he should talk while Gula was doing this. Finally he said, "Gula, would you please sit down? It's almost noon! Dan," he added, "there's coffee. On the counter. Get some."

Dan stood and got it. Gula shut the fridge. Breathing hard, she turned to the table and plunked herself on a chair. Dan, sitting, noted the fierceness in her eyes. She looked ready to kill.

"Do we all have," Harry asked no one in particular, but with ironic solicitousness, "enough coffee?" Dan and Selma nodded. Gula furiously rubbed her nose. Grace shrugged. She didn't drink coffee. She couldn't, Dan knew, because of the ulcer that was killing her now that she'd run out of Gutzyme.

"Okay," Harry said. "About the hero mission. Somebody gets to go on that mission. The somebody takes a phone. But the somebody doesn't take the gun. The gun stays here."

"Listen," Grace said in a low tone. "I'm the one who acquired that gun. It belongs to me."

"Let's see your license," Harry replied.

"I have one at home," Grace declared.

"At home? I guess you could ask for it at the gate. 'Excuse me. Can I have my license so I can shoot myself before you drag me up the road?'" Harry looked at Dan. "And you? You're still having delusions of grandeur? About sticking it in your mouth?"

Dan said, "I've had worse things in my mouth. Hey," he continued when Harry looked about to say something nasty, "don't think I think this is funny. I think all of it sucks. Pardon the expression, but it sucks completely. This idea of glorious death? You and Gula are the ones being heroic. I have to say," he went on, leaning over the table to say it directly to Harry's face, "that the most heroic thing is the fact you haven't turned us in. It's so—extreme. Why haven't you? Seriously—isn't hiding us here the same as going to the gate with the gun?"

"Yes," Gula said quietly, surprising everyone. "It is. Harry agrees with you, by the way. He and I both do. Still, you're not going to the damn gate with the damn gun. Harry, tell them."

"Good," Harry said, apparently relieved to have heard this. "Dan, you're going to Cliffcloud's. Grace, you aren't. The reason is, Dan doesn't have a history with your parents. You do—which could get in the way. Don't argue. I don't have the patience."

"I'm not arguing!" Grace said defiantly. "I just think . . . "

"Quiet," Harry said. "Dan, you should go. If you want to. Gula and I don't think it's a great idea. But if you have to do it, do it. You won't need the gun, I'm glad to say. At least, you won't need it on account of Gula and me and whoever else is here."

"What does that mean?" Selma asked.

"It means," Gula said, "that if Dan gets in trouble at Martha's gate, Harry and I are taking a vacation. We'll just leave. But not before we've called FATBOY."

Harry looked at the clock. It read 11:57. "If Dan gets in trouble six hours from now—we'll call FATBOY, and get the hell out."

"Then why can't I have the gun?" Dan asked.

"What kind of idiot are you?" Gula said, organizing food with feverish skill. "What could you do?"

"Defend myself?" Dan said.

"Against the lasers?" Gula asked sarcastically. "Look—the only reason the gun idea came up is the problem of Martha and them retaliating against us. That problem we've solved. Dan, you'd just put yourself in more danger with the silly gun. All right? Who wants lunch?"

— ● ● ●

Hilton Decter said, "The case is open-and-shut. Raffenelli has a voice match. Furthermore, on Saturday, Cliffcloud sent one hundred million to Prague. The question is, how do we proceed?"

Mary McMurtry said, "We get custody. Preferably, alive."

"A trial would prolong Trefethen's notoriety," Decter said. "His celebrity, I should say, distasteful though the word is. There is another issue, too. Anything short of an overwhelming, all-out assault could give him time to explode bombs—however it is he does it. Which is the problem. Not knowing how he does it, we must assume he could explode all of them. With the latest assessments of the fragility of the ice sheet . . . "

"Yes," McMurtry said. "The timetable?"

Decter checked the time: 12:14 P.M. "If the President green-lights now, it's feasible. Aircraft can reach Cheswick in minutes. Ground troops will take longer. But Raffenelli's right about hovercraft getting there on the Piscatawny. A river route will avoid evacuation traffic, and put forces in place by six o'clock. Raffenelli also is right about satellite surveillance. We can keep an eye on Cliffcloud's estate. If they leave, we'll know, and will be able to track them. Local authorities are poised to swoop the moment we send word." He frowned at notes on a microcomputer. "However, I take serious issue with the point Raffenelli makes about the broadcast."

"The audience will break records," McMurtry said. "It will surpass anything a pope's ever gotten, anything soccer's ever gotten—four-fifths of the planet will be watching. What better time to announce victory?"

"What concerns me is the possibility that Trefethen could get his message on the air."

"That's easy. We tell the broadcasters to turn him off. We let him say three words, and cut in. No one will expect it. The audience, at fever pitch, expecting the worst, will be intact. Then we save the day with maximum drama."

"Broadcast turn-off might not be achievable," Decter said.

"Hilton, if this crisis has accomplished anything, it's strengthened our hand with the media. They will do what we tell them to do. About that there's no question."

"Trefethen could dump his message on the Net," Decter pointed out. "Like the first message, the one he sent from Ecologic. If he does that, the toothpaste squirts. We can't interdict something that's been Netted."

"Don't be tedious," McMurtry said. "If Earnest gets his message out, what of it? He'll be in custody. Defanged."

Decter ran a hand through thinning hair. "Luddite passions are building," he said. "We're seeing extreme destructiveness, extreme general unrest. Directly attributable to Earnest Trefethen."

"So we crush it," McMurtry said. She smacked a palm on her desk. "Like that, Hilton. We've done it before, we'll do it again—and over-all, our position improves. You see a public gone mad. I see a public grateful for order. At whatever cost."

"If water is rising . . . "

McMurtry shouted, "Did you hear me? *We'll crush it!*"

"Very well, Ms. Director General."

"Place the call to the President. Get Raffenelli too."

"Raffenelli's on hold as we speak."

"Tell him it's go," McMurtry said. "We hit at six sharp."

"Shouldn't the President be told? Before we green-light?"

"The President has acquired a new habit." McMurtry smiled scorn-fully. "He listens to me."

Martha and Earnest strode through the music room and entered the nook off it. Helen stood by a table covered with instruments. She gestured at the man lying on a sofa; the elderly side of middle-aged, he was lanky, plainly dressed, balding. Although his eyes were open, he seemed in a nonconscious state. "His name is Abe Frick," Helen said with alarmingly icy confidence. "He has told me where Grace is. I've spoken with Fladgate. He, the men, and I are leaving to get her right now."

Earnest checked the time. It was 3:03, he noted. "No you're not," he said.

"Yes," Helen said, "I am."

Earnest sat down in an armchair adjacent to the couch. He gestured irritably at other chairs and said, "Helen, Martha. Please sit."

Martha sat. Helen remained standing. She said, "Did you hear me, Earnest? I have found Grace."

"I asked you to have a seat," Earnest replied. He glanced at Abe Frick. "This man cannot understand, or remember, or be made to remember what we are saying?"

"Of course not, on all three counts," Helen said. "He's leaving with me. By the time his Jeep reaches the gate, he'll be under the impression he came up here to see the view. The view he showed his grandchildren when this was a public park. That image happens to reside quite permanently in his mind; I had no trouble giving it some spin. I do not intend to sit, Earnest. I intend to leave very shortly. What is your problem?"

He said, "First I want to know what Grace's circumstances are. And how it is that this man knows them."

Helen stalked to the table, picked up an envelope, and gave it to her husband. As he pulled out two sheaves of paper, a round object fell in his lap. He examined it. "My badge of honor," he murmured. "Martha, look." She frowned at the rabbit. Earnest scanned the two pieces of paper. That Helen had managed to extract these items from Mr. Frick seemed nothing short of miraculous.

"Well, Helen," Martha said. "How smart you were to ask me to have the house watch for the mailman."

"The mailman?" Earnest said.

"That's right," Helen said. "The mailman in a town like this knows everyone. It's standard investigatory procedure. In a tightly knit community, talk to people who make rounds. I hoped hypnotizing Mr. Frick would provide indirect evidence of someone hiding something unusual. Something anxiety-provoking. Namely, obviously, Grace. Instead I found direct evidence. A piece of luck in more ways than one—I'd considered staging emergencies here. Plumbing, electrical, telephone. Anything to interrogate people who make rounds. But as you see, that proved unnecessary."

"Good for Grace," Earnest said, finishing his scan of the letter. "This could have been a serious problem. If the FATB had put their minds to it, they might have been able to stop the icon. But the most interesting thing is Grace's unwillingness to turn us in. She doesn't give any indication where we are. That's encouraging—eh, Helen?"

"Yes," she said. "I think so. Earnest, don't complicate matters. Don't get angry. Grace, clearly, is confused."

"Clearly," Earnest said. "Why doesn't the envelope have an address on it? It doesn't have postage, either."

"Frick was going to drive to Boston and drop it off with Raffenelli.

He's very close with the woman whose house it is; it was a favor for her. He himself, by the way, knows nothing about us."

"What woman?" Martha said.

"Somebody named Arugula Gance," Helen said impatiently.

"Oh, yes," Martha said. "Over the ridge."

"She has a handyman named Harry," Helen said. "So you see, Earnest, the target is soft. If you'll excuse me, I'm going now."

Earnest raised a hand. "There is another issue we must discuss. The house notified Martha of a problem with the phone system. It concerns a broken telephone. She called it to my attention. We looked into the matter, and were going over the logs when you summoned us here. A call came in on line two at 11:34. You took it. The conversation lasted thirty-six seconds. Have you anything to say about this?"

Helen's eyelashes fluttered. "There was no conversation," she said. "Line two isn't matrixed, of course."

"No conversation? Why did the call last thirty-six seconds?"

"Because I wanted to see who was calling," Helen replied. "I've been dealing with dozens of store clerks. It seemed conceivable one of them might have had that number. So I suppose," she continued, every blood vessel in her body pumping with frantic force, "thirty-six seconds was how long I—listened."

"Is that why you destroyed the telephone?" Martha asked.

Helen said evenly, "Dealing with clerks has been frustrating. I lost my temper. And killed the phone."

Earnest said, "The call came from Raffenelli's office."

Helen thought she'd faint. Somehow she managed to stay standing. "Really?" she said, knitting her brow. "It's a good thing I didn't say anything." The room spun slowly. "Have you finished with this grilling?" she said.

"Did Ted ask about your health?" Earnest inquired. "What did you discuss during the thirty-six seconds?"

Helen shouted, "I told you, I didn't say a word!" Earnest and Martha exchanged wary glances. They don't know, Helen thought with feverish relief; the phone system, she now was sure, hadn't recorded the call. "The man didn't identify himself," Helen continued. "I thought I recognized the voice, but couldn't place it. He asked for Martha. I listened, hoping the voice would come to me. It didn't. I hung up. There is nothing to worry about."

"I can't prove you wrong," Earnest muttered. "But Helen, it's uncanny how this could have . . . effloresced!" He stood, shouting, "Hours from the most important event of our lives!"

Soothingly Helen said, "Then let me take care of Grace. You don't need the worry. You must focus, Earnest."

Veins throbbed in his temples. He said quietly, "Fladgate will take care of Grace. Not now, however. He and the men are too recognizable. They'll do it when no one will be on the roads. When everybody is at home. Watching me."

"There is no time to lose," Helen said with conviction; a profound conviction, one she regretted she couldn't reveal to her husband. The end had come, Helen realized. Raffenelli had to have them in his crosshairs. The implications evaded her just now. But the end most certainly had come. She turned to the music room and bellowed, "Fladgate!"

Like a large and obedient hound, Fladgate trotted into the music room from the great hall. His four men followed. Earnest noted the bulky jackets. Weapons resided in them. "Don't be childish," he said.

Martha whistled tunelessly. A holocontrol menu appeared near her right arm.

Helen stared at the glowing panel floating midair. "You better not try to stop me," she said.

Earnest said, "Helen, I'm sorry. I am confining you."

"Fladgate won't allow it," she said.

Martha said, "Then Fladgate will die."

"Fladgate will obey me," Earnest said. "You will so direct him, Helen. You will do that now."

"No," Helen said. "Men, protect me."

Fladgate and company drew weapons with startling swiftness. Martha's hand scuttled across the holo panel. "I'll give you a demonstration," she said to Helen. "Of what could happen."

"Don't be a fool!" Helen snapped. "They're prepared to use force. Do you want blood in your house?"

Martha said calmly, "The system has a nice feature, Helen. It's called the 'disarm function.' Sensors already have targeted the weapons. Are you sure you want to play this game?"

Helen sneered. "Martial Martha," she said bitterly. "So at home with destruction . . ."

"Hellish Helen," Martha replied. "The psyche of manipulation . . ." Martha flicked a finger at the panel.

From half a dozen places around the music room, laser beams sizzled at the concert grand. It exploded. The force threw Helen to the floor. Earnest staggered back

The zombies dropped to defensive crouches, weapons trained on the fiery piano. Martha, unperturbed, continued to play the holocontrols. Lasers flashed at the weapons. Their barrels glowed, then cracked. A hand brushed a laser beam. The hand boiled; its owner screamed.

"Stand back!" Helen shouted. The men froze. The one who'd lost a hand collapsed, writhing with pain. Helen rushed to him. "No," she moaned, kneeling to examine the wound. The other men gaped. They seemed in shock. Helen started sobbing.

"Tell them to obey Earnest," Martha said. "Do it now."

An unbearably loud siren wailed through the rooms. Martha gestured at the holocontrols. The siren stopped. In the sudden quiet, the piano crackled. The smoke thickened.

"I told you," Martha said, "to do it now."

53

Toby was taking a bath when he heard a ruckus in the corridor. Brian shouted loudly. A woman, it sounded like Helen, was screaming. Toby jumped out of the tub, pulled on pajama pants, and burst into his cell.

"Not with her!" Brian yelled. Helen stood in Brian's cell, looking crazed. Brian, in the corridor, clutched Toby's bars. Earnest scowled at Brian, then at Helen, face starker than Toby'd yet seen it. Martha stood by, glowering.

"All right!" Earnest bellowed. He slammed Brian's bars on his wife. Martha used the cardkey; the lock turned. She turned to Toby's bars and unlocked them. Brian dove in as if jumping from the path of an oncoming train.

Helen screamed, "How *can you do this!*"

"Let's go," Earnest snapped. Martha locked Toby's cell. Hastily, they left. The outer door slammed. Its lock turned.

Brian stared wild-eyed at Toby, then bolted into the bathroom. Toby went to his bars. Helen's features looked messed up. At first Toby thought she'd been beaten. Then he realized why her face was contorted. The muscles were out of control; an incontinence, Toby thought, of rage. Unnerved, he spun around, entered the bathroom, and closed the door.

Brian sat on the floor, back to the wall, arms clutching drawn-up knees. He wet his lips and started shivering uncontrollably. "Something really bad has happened," he muttered.

Toby stared at his bath. Continuing with it seemed not a good idea. He sat on the toilet instead.

Harry went to the garage barn, got in his '64 Oldsmobile, and tore down the drive. Shopping was his mission. Whatever they faced, they'd require supplies. He didn't have much time to get to Kotzler's, buy stuff, and return to Gula's. It was closing on 5:00 already.

He sped along the hilly road thinking about the way Gula had come to her senses. She must have added things up, Harry concluded, while banging things around in the fridge. He'd argued with her all morning about the senselessness of staying. She'd yammered back about the stupidity of letting someone go to Cliffcloud's with a gun. The two points of view hadn't appeared destined to find a match. But suddenly they did, when she agreed, finally, to taking a vacation. If the need arose.

The need had arisen, Harry was sure. He doubted prospects would improve with Dan's trip to the gate. But maybe a miracle would happen. Maybe Grace's analysis of parent dynamics was on the mark. With the father busy, unavailable to play hard-ass, maybe the mother would relent. And release her son along with Dan's brother.

Then what? Harry wondered. Grace had spoken vaguely of setting off with Brian. To where? And what about the other three, where would they go? Harry expected they all would end up finding attractive reasons to extend their stay with Gula. For how long though? The whole situation was just a mess.

Harry consulted his list. Coffee, butter, bread, lettuce, Gutzyme, if he could find it . . . no wonder Grace had been milk-pale. His thoughts drifted to Selma. Prime womanhood, in Harry's opinion. It was almost unbearable, keeping up a front of indifference.

Gula'd seen through it, he knew. Gula saw through everything. But Selma—Harry didn't think she knew how he felt. If only things could be different, and he didn't have reasons to stay detached. If only he didn't see awful fates in store.

The bathroom made them claustrophobic. Toby was conscious of Brian's sweat. The close quarters had another effect as well; Toby couldn't stop thinking about the boy's resemblance to his sister. That in turn brought flashbacks to the episode in the truck, when Brian had replicated Grace so exactingly. Except, of course, for crucial aspects. To Toby the irony seemed cosmic. Why did he have to be drinking in these body scents? Why couldn't they be Grace's?

"I can't take it," Brian said, breaking a long silence.

"Don't tell me you have to use the toilet."

Brian smiled faintly. "No. I'm dying to find out what Mother did. For Father to lock her up—it had to be terrible."

"So go out and ask her. I'm curious too."

"Why don't you ask her?"

"Because her eyes would turn me to stone."

Brian hiccuped. Toby realized it was a laugh he'd swallowed. "You should be thankful for something," Toby said. "That it's you in here and not your sister."

Brian gave him a quizzical glance. "Why?"

"I don't want to raise a touchy subject. But your idea that Dan might be messing around with Grace?"

Brian nodded gravely.

"It's so unfair, that he's with her, and not even thinking of messing. I'll tell you, if she were in here, I couldn't control myself. I'd have a heart attack. It would just be—gruesome."

"You have a crush on her," Brian said. Toby, staring gloomily at himself in the mirror, nodded. The discoloration in his eyes seemed to be fading. "I knew that," Brian remarked.

"You read such thoughts? If they concern your lover?"

"You don't remember," Brian said.

Toby turned to him. "Remember?"

"At the Clinic." Toby thought about it. He remembered, and looked away. Both he and Brian had been strapped down naked. "Wanda" had asked leading questions on the subject of Grace. Which had caused . . . Toby blushed. Brian mumbled, "Sorry."

"That bitch!" Toby exclaimed under his breath. He dropped with a thump on the toilet. Ugly memories scalded his mind.

"She's pretty bad," Brian said. He sighed. "But . . . at least I'm not Grace. So I guess you won't have a heart attack or anything. I guess you're . . . okay."

"Huh?" Toby said. He looked at Brian. The kid was sitting against the tub, elbows on the rim. His hands dangled; his legs, stretched out and crossed at the ankles, pressed perfect thighs through the pants. Toby watched Brian's eyebrows rise. They seemed friendly. And the eyes had a glow. They almost looked—Toby couldn't figure it out. "What did you just say?" he asked.

"Nothing," Brian said.

"Something about me being okay? Because you're not Grace?"

Brian nodded. He watched an expression of astonishment, mingled with unease, settle on Toby's face. The sight amused him. He didn't know why. The expression was—it just was so funny.

Toby watched Brian's grin widen. The kid's taking in my discomfort, he realized. My acute discomfort with "being okay"—because it's a boy in here, not the delectable sister he resembles uncannily. "What's the matter?" Brian inquired. He swallowed, but the grin returned. He's like a farmboy, Toby thought. That grin—hayseed-simple. Does Grace grin like that?

He felt sudden certainty that she did. And that when she did, guys keeled over. Just fell helpless with lust to the ground . . . "Brian!" Toby said severely. "You're flirting!"

The grin vanished. "I have to get out of here," Brian said. He stood and exited.

Toby heard Helen shout, "What was that? About *flirting?*"

Brian barged back in, closed the door, and stood with his back to it, breathing deeply. "*Brian!*" Helen screamed.

"Now we've done it," Brian said.

Nightmare, Toby thought. He realized he was shirtless. Then he realized he wasn't wearing underwear. Just the pajama bottoms; moist and clingy, due to his swift exit from the tub.

After a moment he said, "Brian. Let's stay cool. We're partners, remember. With a mission. All right?"

Slotsky surveyed the packed parking lot. It seemed a cross between midtown Manhattan and a backwoods survivalist camp. The scope, on automatic scan for weapons, so far had counted seven shotguns and six hunting rifles. The weapons appeared evenly distributed between people wearing expensive clothing and people in more rustic attire. Weekend types, Slotsky judged, versus full-timers. A long line composed of both elements waited to be allowed entry to a store by the name of Kotzler's.

Deluxe autos competed for space with junk heaps. Three limousines idled. Worried folk clustered here and there, discussing, the audioprobe revealed, New York City's untenability, the hopeless highways, self-defense techniques, and television's rapidly approaching rendezvous with Earnest Trefethen. A point of agreement on which all had settled was the importance of rushing home, making drinks, and preparing to watch. Slotsky found this tedious. He very much wanted to be off. However, the men had invoked the clause of their contract that stipulated a right to periodic meals. They'd ambled down the street to some kind of take-out cafe.

Slotsky supposed they shouldn't go into action hungry. He himself felt no need for food. The Number 12 on his face was providing adequate nourishment. Only a third of it covered the wound; the rest leached into his cheek, to reduce interference with healing. Some interference Slotsky was willing to risk. The effects were simply so marvelous. But like all marvelous things, they should be enjoyed with moderation. Slotsky believed that firmly. He watched an old tub of a car block traffic as the disgusted driver took stock of the line to Kotzler's. Something lying in the back caught Slotsky's eye. He zoomed the scope at it; and promptly quivered on his specially fitted bed.

Fifteen seconds of enhancement left no doubt. They were hip length. They were purple suede. Small yellow lightning bolts, exquisitely stitched, electrified the purple. The heels didn't gleam blackly, for they were encrusted with mud; Slotsky's liver writhed anyway. Bells seemed to clang. Orange fog crept.

Another fifteen seconds passed as he composed himself. Into the comm unit he said, "Ralph, deal with the food. Edward, I need you immediately."

Edward soon approached from the rear. Slotsky made his earplug say, "You see the antique Oldsmobile? The driver has pale, shoulder-length hair."

"Yuh," Edward replied.

"Tag the car," Slotsky said. He watched Edward walk toward the Oldsmobile, a hand thrust into his voluminous khaki jacket. The hand came out; the arm fell as Edward suddenly turned, seeming to remember something that startled him. His hand touched the car's right tailfin. Slotsky ran a test. The tag was functional. "It's good," he said. Edward, gazing at the picturesque Piscatawny flowing below the village, wandered off.

Harry tired of the dirty looks from people who were tired of the bottleneck he was making. He'd been hoping somebody would pull out of the lot and give him a space. It didn't seem likely. He had never seen such a crowd. Many of the people he knew, many were complete strangers. Not surprising, Harry thought. A lot of Cheswick came up from the city and didn't budge from their farms.

These here looked to have arrived in a state of distress. Evacuation fever was getting serious; as if to hammer that home, a military ambulance dominated the lot. Harry, during his days in the service, had heard about this particular type. Fully rigged, the things were fearsome. The army had auctioned off a bunch following the liquidation of the doomsday plan. Typical, Harry thought. A doomsday plan might be useful now.

He debated leaving the car on the street, going through Kotzler's' back door, grabbing stuff, and telling Floyd he'd settle up later. Floyd wouldn't mind. He and Gula were buddies.

But it was 5:05. Harry needed fifteen minutes just to get back. Intensely pissed-off, he headed out of town.

Forty miles downstream from Cheswick, bulky machines roared upriver, shattering the Piscatawny's sylvan calm. General Raffenelli stood at the lead hovercraft's exterior helm. He could have piloted from the interior cockpit, shielded from wind and spray. But he liked the unfettered view, the fecund scents of spring.

Ahead, water glowed greenly in the afternoon sun, soon to convulse under powerful rotors. He savored the leafy banks, the trees drooping as if to sip, or genuflect. His binoculars magnified awe on the faces of occasional canoers; who, foreseeing capsizement, paddled vigorously for shore. The general was leaving quite a wake behind him. Its concatenation with the nine following wakes had created minor flash-flood conditions for over a hundred miles. Raffenelli thought that appropriate. Trefethen had made himself a Neptune warrior. But now, spurred by forces of justice, water lashed back.

Each hovercraft, with the exception of the general's, carried thirty highly trained shock troops armed with state-of-the-art electronics. The weapons could see in the dark. They could hear a mouse breathe from fifty feet, and smell cigarette smoke from several hundred; they could target birds from a thousand yards. But these forces were only part of the picture spiraling toward Cheswick. Helicopter carriers, circling far beyond the horizon, held another two hundred soldiers. Fixed-wing aircraft also circled, propeller-powered to give the slowness that was an asset when dealing with civil unrest. The five planes could unleash cruise missiles, smart bombs, and devastating curtains of gunfire, if Cliffcloud were foolish enough to resist. On top of that, were the general to go all-out, he could summon Air Force fighter-bombers. He had ten in the air. Ready to go.

Raffenelli was leading the operation from the ground, or rather at the moment from a river, because he wanted the superior control facilities the command hover offered. An AWACS jet could have provided those facilities, but would have had difficulty landing on Cliffcloud's estate. A command 'copter also could have provided facilities, but not to the degree the hovercraft did. This hover went beyond cutting-edge. On its glowing screens Raffenelli would see the exact locations and movements of every individual soldier, vehicle, and weapon under his command. He could talk to each of those entities. They, in turn, vehicles and weapons included, could talk to him. Beyond those considerations, Raffenelli harbored a mistrust of helicopters. His recent experience with one still rankled.

This campaign, he was confident, would have a different outcome from that of the rooftop penetration of Ecologic Foundation. The forces he'd marshaled amounted to overkill, of course. That was the point. Trefethen's defeat would serve as an object lesson. Terrorists everywhere would think twice, thrice, any number of times, before engaging the wrath of law enforcement.

Raffenelli saw only two possible barriers to complete success. The President had ordered that Trefethen be given an opportunity to surrender. Senior advisers, McMurtry among them, had pointed out that instead of going peacefully, Trefethen might respond by detonating more bombs. He also might use the military technology that Cliffcloud had been allowed to install—for what she'd termed "research purposes."

Either response would lead to Trefethen's quick annihilation, of course. Suppose, however, he didn't care?

The President, on the other hand, was sure that Cliffcloud couldn't be a party to that kind of suicide decision. It was on her account, at bottom, that he wasn't permitting pre-emptive strike. He thought she'd end up talking sense to Trefethen, when push came to shove. Why would she want to die—with all her billions? The President couldn't conceive of it. He knew the woman personally. She'd been a guest in the private White House quarters, where they'd developed a certain rapport. In any case, she was a major contributor.

Raffenelli espied a garden coming up portside. Through it a pair of tractors moved. They stopped moving. He raised his binoculars and saw, astride the machines, an elderly couple. They returned his scrutiny through their own binoculars, birding glasses no doubt. A fine way to pass one's retirement, the general thought. Gardening by a picture-perfect river on his-and-her tractors. He waved. Uncertainly, the couple waved back.

Raffenelli returned to navigation. The garden seemed high enough to escape flash flood. But if it didn't, that was just too bad. Everyone had to be prepared for collateral damage. In today's world, collaterals were a fact of life.

As the ambulance departed Cheswick Village, Slotsky meditated on goals, and strategy. That the boots were here, the very ones he'd seen encasing Selma Swearingen's memorable feet, he took to be evidence that Trefethen indeed was hiding *chez* Cliffcloud.

His original plan involved driving to Cliffcloud's estate, where, brazen tactician that he was, he had been prepared to ring the bell and have a chat with the answerer; after having determined, of course, that the gate didn't possess a means to destroy him. He'd intended to improvise from that point forward. With hopes of eliciting a response from Cliffcloud, gunfire for example, that would suggest Trefethen's presence.

The plan now was obsolete. Instead of going to Cliffcloud's estate, Slotsky was homing in on the tag that Edward had attached to the

Oldsmobile. He suspected this would lead him to Grace. If it did, he would question her, and establish beyond doubt, he was hopeful, the location of her father. There would be another bonus as well, a large one. Slotsky wanted to know how the code worked. How the still-mysterious icon worked. The image of a rabbit—not in a pen, but on a pin—that Miles had failed to obtain from Brian.

Slotsky had developed theories about this icon. Theories about its relationship to the Beast's face.

He scoped the charmingly wooded hills through which he wended. The tracker chimed. A glance at its display screen indicated that the Oldsmobile, some miles ahead, had come to a halt. Excellent, Slotsky thought. What bliss to plunge into Grace's nest and have his way. That, however, could be just the beginning. If Slotsky's fortune continued to wax, more bonuses awaited. The boots, of course. And, not least, Selma herself. She of the ineffable feet.

It was 5:16. Forty-four minutes to go, before everyone near and far sat down for not-to-be-missed television. Slotsky decided to make his visit coincide roughly, so to speak, with it.

Why not? His quarry surely would be finding their TV a major distraction.

55

Harry thought he'd have a seizure. It made no sense at all. Why did the girl have to do this? "Selma," he said. "Please don't. Losing one of you would be bad. Losing both—it's crazy!"

They stood in the garage barn. Dan and Selma, clad in jumpsuits from Gula's costume trunk, were donning rather goofy helmets. Harry, Gula, and Grace watched. The ancient Vespa motorbike already was idling.

Selma appreciated Harry's concern. He'd seemed so macho, most of the time, during their brief acquaintance. But every now and then she'd seen other qualities slip through. Attractive qualities, which might have made him of more than passing interest if they weren't dealing with sudden death.

"What can you do," Harry demanded, his face an avalanche of woe, "that Dan can't do by himself?"

"Provide moral support," Selma replied. "Who's driving, Dan?"

"Me," Dan said. "You drive coming back."

"Let's hope it's in a car," Grace muttered. She too was having a hard time with this farewell. It galled her that the others thought her incapable of performing the mission. If she hadn't shown decisiveness at several junctures, no one would be sallying forth now. Plus, she shared Harry's worry. Dan and Selma looked cool in the jumpsuits and circa-1955 helmets. But coolness wouldn't count for much if they died. Impulsively, she decided to kiss them. It wasn't easy with the helmets. The visors needed prying, the things were so rusty.

"Let us," Dan said after he and Selma had received pecks, "mount our engine." They clambered onto it. Selma hugged Dan's waist, her hipboots giving the Vespa a Jetsonesque flair. She'd been looking all over for the things. Minutes before, with Harry's return, she finally found them in his car.

"You have the map?" Gula asked anxiously. "The phone?"

Selma nodded. They'd gone over the routine so many times. It would take twenty to twenty-five minutes, at Vespa speed, to arrive at the gate. If they succeeded in springing the boys, they'd call the news in, and Harry would meet them down the road. If they didn't succeed, the plateless Vespa wouldn't finger Gula's house. Gula, Harry, and Grace would have time to get out.

Visors squeaked down. The Vespa putt-putted from the barn. Dan headed to the drive; he and Selma turned to wave. Gula, Grace, and a scowling Harry waved back.

With an asthmatically swelling putt-putt, they set off.

Slotsky, pulled over in a meadow a mile away, didn't detect the departure. He wouldn't for a while to come. Dan and Selma were taking the road's opposite direction.

Earnest briefed Fladgate in the courtyard. Martha stood by listening, as did Fladgate's three able-bodied men. Frick, in a wheelchair and still unconscious, awaited the revival spray that Helen, with considerable reluctance, had provided.

"I want you to keep it simple," Earnest said. "No violence unless you get in trouble. All we need is Grace. Get her, and return safely. Is this understood?"

Fladgate nodded. Martha had given directions. They would need fifteen minutes to drive to the gate, and another fifteen on meandering public roads to reach the Gance house. With the broadcast starting in half an hour, Earnest expected light traffic. But he wanted to minimize the chance that someone might recognize Fladgate and the others. They were to wear sunglasses and hats throughout the operation.

Martha said, "If anything comes up, call me. I'm your contact. Do you have any problem with that?"

"No, ma'am," Fladgate said stolidly. "Not if Dr. Scarf approves."

"You know she does," Earnest said. At laser-point, threatened with more boiled flesh, Helen had transferred authority to him. Fortunately, Earnest thought, she wasn't in a position to countermand that order. He was quite aware that her state of mind had evolved to the point of wanting to countermand everything here.

But Helen lacked access to her zombified henchmen. "Be on your way," Earnest said. "Good luck."

Fladgate headed to the garage elevator. His men followed, one wheeling Frick. "Come," Martha said, taking Earnest by the hand. "Let's get you settled."

They walked to the stairwell to the control room.

"Brian!" Helen's voice slammed through the bathroom's closed door. "What are you *doing?* With that *piece of trash?*"

Toby felt less nervous about the possible overture from Brian. For a moment, he'd worried. Maybe it came from being imprisoned. In jail, heterosexuals mutated, he'd heard. Due to the company of beautiful boys? Who, in steamy bathrooms, bizarrely became gorgeous girls? Something like that. Toby didn't want to pursue the line of thought. He found it disturbing.

Helen's presence across the corridor he found more disturbing. The woman's shrill invective sickened him. She didn't occupy high ground, in Toby's opinion.

Brian sat on the tub's rim, elbows on knees, face in hands. Through the hands he said, "I hate to tell you. But I'm starting to think this is sort of—funny."

"Funny?" Toby said.

"Yeah. It really surprises me." He uncovered his face, clasped his hands between his knees, and added, "It started when I saw Father and Martha having sex."

"Yeah?" Toby said. "You burst out laughing?"

"I thought I'd drop dead. I thought if Father could be unfaithful, Grace could too—which made me want to die. Then things got worse. Mother and Father had the confrontation over us trying to give FAT-BOY the pin. Father put me down here. Then you—you had that scene with Mother, and the one with Father. Then last night, we talked. And then today Father puts Mother, who's psychotic, in that cell."

"High comedy," Toby remarked. "Side-splitting."

"Yeah. But see—I thought my parents were like gods. All-powerful. All-knowing. About most things anyway."

"Now you realize they're frauds?" Toby said. "Doctor and Doctor Wizard of Oz?"

Brian nodded. He said, "In some ways, they're pathetic."

"This is funny?"

"It's a relief. To know they're not gods. It's like they can't control me any more. Like I feel . . . "

"Free?"

Brian nodded with gusto. "That's it. Free."

Toby stuck out his hand. "Congratulations, kid."

Brian extended his hand to make the shake. Too eagerly; he slipped, and fell in Toby's undrained bath. Water splashed loudly. It slopped everywhere.

"Now! What! Are! You! DOING!"

Toby extended his hand again. Water cascaded as he pulled Brian out. They started laughing.

"*Brian!*"

They laughed harder. Brian hugged Toby. Toby hugged back; within two seconds he realized it had to stop. He detached himself, heart pounding, and sat on the toilet. "Sorry," he said, "but—could you go out for a minute? I—um—have to take a pee."

"Damn!" Brian blurted. Toby glanced at the wet jeans and saw Brian's reason for agitation. An excellent reason. It wouldn't bear Mother's scrutiny, Toby supposed. Beet-red, Brian turned to the tub. "Give me a second," he muttered.

Toby whispered, "For crying out loud—Brian, it's okay. Let's get focused. Let's face the fact we'll probably be *killed.*"

"That's what I'm doing," Brian mumbled. He shot Toby a burning glance. "I'm realizing a lot of things. It's making death even worse. I haven't, like, you know . . . I haven't really lived."

Earnest and Martha went over the controls one last time. A media server accessed the audiovisual material Earnest had spent months preparing. Each segment was coded, cued, and ready to go. Earnest intended to play it—edit, splice, arrange it—much like a pianist improvising themes on a keyboard.

He would improvise the broadcast in all senses of the term. When he talked, he'd do it without a script. When he accessed recordings, he'd do it without, so to speak, a score. And during those portions when he'd do both at the same time, it would come purely off the top of his head.

The approach held pitfalls. But Earnest wanted a rough, unrefined texture. The message didn't need to be slick. On the contrary, slickness would detract from its power.

Martha asked, "Should the monitors show what you're doing as you do it? Or show what's appearing out there? Should different monitors show both?"

The question concerned the way they'd set up the feed to the broadcast pool in New York. To avoid a trace to the house, Earnest's performance would enter the Net in digitized packets. Each carrying a few seconds' worth, the packets would travel to New York via a series of anonymous reroutings. No packet would take quite the same route as any of the others; armed with navigational agents, they would flit randomly through the Net's oceanic vastness. Docking codes would reassemble them when they reached New York, back-to-front, front-to-back, in exactly the same sequence Earnest had generated in the studio.

Reroutings of this complexity took time. Thus there would be some lag between what Earnest sent out, and its broadcast.

"Both," he said. Seeing a few minutes of lag on the monitors wouldn't confuse him. "Martha, tend to our departure."

"Have you made up your mind about Helen? Does she come with us? Or not?"

"I'll think about it after the broadcast."

Martha decided to break some news. She said, "I wasn't going to mention this until later. But maybe it's best you know now."

Earnest turned to her. "Yes?"

"I got a call from security people on the coast."

"Security people?"

"Informants, Earnest. A convoy of FATB hovercraft left New London an hour and a half ago. It's coming up the Piscatawny."

"Good lord," Earnest said. "How long have you known?"

"Twenty minutes."

"Why didn't you tell me?" The shock in his eyes kindled; it became anger. "Will they get here before Fladgate returns?"

"Possibly."

Earnest rose to his feet, hands trembling. "Martha, you should have told me. This changes everything. If we don't leave immediately—they'll destroy us! Even if they don't, they'll stop the broadcast. And apprehend Grace!"

Martha grunted. She said, "How many times do I have to tell you they cannot destroy us? This isn't the orb for nothing. This house," she continued, voice rising, "doesn't embody what it embodies *for nothing*. All along we've planned it this way. Yet you continue to have no faith!"

Earnest sat down, his face a picture of dumbfoundment. "Yes. Well. We didn't plan on the house—doing its thing—while we're in it. We were supposed to be in Canada!"

"We're going there," Martha growled. "When you finish the broadcast."

"They won't let me *start it!*"

Martha shoved her nose within inches of Earnest's. "Get a grip. The broadcast can play out on the Net. Billions won't see it live, but millions will—which will be *just fine*." Conviction leapt from her face. "Maybe I should have told you on Grace's account. Maybe we should have sent Fladgate twenty minutes ago. The simple truth is, I didn't want to upset you."

"Then why tell me now?"

Martha said, "I realized you'd be even more upset if the FATB surprises you. Midbroadcast." She smiled. Before he could draw back, she kissed him, square on the lips. "I'm going to check defenses," she whispered. "As for you, darling. Knock 'em dead."

Martha tore herself from his searching gaze, left the studio, and went down the basement corridor to her control room. She mounted the circular arena on which she and Earnest had disported themselves the day before, with, unbeknownst to them, Brian watching. In the arena's center, Martha clapped her hands.

A meticulously detailed hologram materialized around her. Martha studied indicator arrays in the fake sky above. No sign, so far, of enemies come near. She admired the lake at the far end of the valley; the illusion that she towered over it was beautiful. Like a phantom giantess she walked through her hills, fingertips brushing trees on the tops. The plateau, the octagonal palace on it, receded behind her as she approached the end of the drive, its intersection with the public road at the Lilliputian gate. Two minuscule cars, much smaller than tinker toys, sped gateward. They held Helen's guards and Frick.

Well, they didn't. Out on the road, far from this virtual landscape, a real sedan and a real Jeep held guards and Frick.

Martha had programmed the gate to activate in response to Fladgate's voice. But the idea of playing Venus-ex-machina appealed to her. She squatted, immersing herself in an escarpment of hills. The cars came within four inches of the public road. That corresponded to four hundred feet. She waited until Fladgate's was an inch away, and whispered, like a goddess issuing an edict from the heavens, "Gate, open." The tiny gate opened. The lead car slowed a bit; Martha imagined Fladgate's befuddlement. He seemed to recover. The cars zipped out. They sped along the road until they passed from the holo-empire into what Martha was fond of calling "the real world," and disappeared.

56

The Vespa did twenty-nine miles an hour uphill. Downhill, it went as fast as Dan dared. Selma was so glad she'd insisted on coming. The engine's buzz, the bulky helmets, made it hard to talk. But who needed talk? The dizzying downswoops, the blue sky, the dense woods, Dan's lean waist in her arms—it was thrilling.

Actually, it went well beyond thrill. They were off to challenge the Beast. Clueless about what would happen.

A car approached, windshield spastic with sky and trees. As it flashed by, Selma glimpsed hatted, sunglassed men. A posse, she thought. "We go right!" she yelled. The upcoming fork, according to the map taped to her thigh, wasn't far from the gate. They whizzed downhill to the right, much too fast. After a mile more they saw the fence. Dusky green, it blended with the trees, and appeared remarkably sturdy.

Huge, solid, industrial, the gate came up on the left. Towers rose from anchoring pillars. This reminds me, Selma thought, of a military installation.

They dismounted and pulled off helmets. Selma unstrapped the telephone from the Vespa's tail. She punched Gula's number.

Harry answered immediately. "We're here," Selma said.

"Anybody around?" Harry asked.

"Nobody," Selma replied. "Just the megagate."

Dan said, "Let's do it."

Into the phone Selma said, "We're doing it." Dan checked out an intercom system set in one of the pillars. Selma watched him press a button.

Here goes, Harry thought. He sat at the kitchen table with Gula and Grace. "They're ringing the buzzer," he said. The clock read 5:47. "Any reply?" he asked the phone.

Moments went by. "No," Selma's throaty voice told him.

Martha studied the holo-enlargement of the gate's exterior. Featureless figurines indicated two people. Not Raffenelli, Martha concluded. If it were he ringing her bell, the holosystem would be registering a somewhat bigger entourage. She waded through hills, stepped off the arena, and went to the console. The gate monitor displayed a young couple wearing antique jumpsuits. An old motorbike stood nearby. The girl held a phone; they both looked nervous. Very nervous. Martha suddenly recognized them—Grace's confederates, of course. What did they think they were doing? She activated the intercom and said, "Yes?"

Dan Swett declared, voice cracking, "We've come to collect Toby and Brian! If you don't put them in a car and let them out—like, *right away* . . . " He pointed resolutely at Selma Swearingen's phone. "Our allies, who are listening to this, have FATBOY on another line. If you don't release Toby and Brian, they'll tell FATBOY where you are. We're not kidding."

Martha considered the ultimatum. She found it touching. Have the "allies," she wondered, considered the fact that these emissaries can be forced to talk?

They must have, Martha thought. Grace must have told them. Had the allies dealt with the problem by leaving the Gance house for some other location?

If so, Fladgate's mission would fail. Martha didn't care if it failed. Retrieving Grace wasn't one of her priorities. However, Earnest felt differently about the matter.

Martha realized what she had to do.

Dan decided he was speaking with insufficient conviction. He shouted into the intercom, "I'm giving you twenty minutes!"

Selma heard something overhead. She looked up. Atop the towers rising from the pillars, dull-red lights were blinking. Conical things moved . . . they seemed to be aiming. "Dan," she said. "I think we're in trou . . . "

From the conical caps, something hot flashed to the asphalt. Something very hot—the asphalt smoked. Lasers, Selma thought. Dan sent her an appalled glance. They could see the beams now, two of them, faintly blue—coming down at different angles from the towers. The beams moved, inscribing arcs in the asphalt. They were drawing a circle, Selma realized, around her and Dan.

Why? To tell them they shouldn't try anything? Like leave, for example?

If that was the goal, the lasers had achieved it. They both were paralyzed. The gate heaved open. A road snaked up through woods. In Selma's hand the phone snapped, "What's happening?"

From the intercom the deep female voice said, "Get on the bike and drive up the road. Do it now. Is this clear?"

"*Damn,*" the phone exclaimed. "Selma—talk to me!"

The beams scorched the circle deeper into the pavement. Unquestionably they were lethal. One flick, Selma thought, will cut us in half. Flames flickered along the melting asphalt. Oily smoke billowed— they stood, literally, in a burning ring of fire. Selma thought she'd pass out. She closed her eyes, gagging on the fumes. And heard Dan shout, "Yes! It's very clear!"

The towers stopped firing. "Get on the bike," the intercom ordered. "Come up the paved road, you will stick to the paved road—all the way to the house. Quickly, now. Do it quickly."

From the phone Harry yelled, "Hey! Answer!"

Selma decided this wasn't a good time to talk. Dan stepped over molten asphalt, and got on the Vespa. She joined him.

"Trouble," Harry told Grace and Gula. "The connection went bad—it fuzzed out. But then I heard Cliffcloud telling 'em . . ." He gulped. "To go up the road."

Gula rapped knuckles on the table. "Call the general," she said.

Grace looked out a window, fighting tears. She saw something turn in the drive. It looked like an armored truck. Above the windshield "AMBULANCE" was reverse-painted in large red letters.

"Who the hell," Harry said, "is in that?"

Slotsky scoped the kitchen windows. People sat at a table. Sun glare obscured the faces; but one of them suggested Grace. He watched her stand and leave the room. "Edward," he said into the comm unit. "Ring the doorbell and ask for a glass of water. Make an assessment, and report."

Grace poked through things in Harry's room. She didn't like the look of the ambulance outside. She liked even less the stentorian voice that was demanding from Harry "a glass of water."

Where had he hidden the gun? My gun, Grace thought desperately. He had to hide it, of course—where? She thrust her hand into the one place she was sure he wouldn't have put it, under the pillow. The hand felt cold steel. Grace grabbed it, left the room, went down the hallway, and paused at the entry to the dining room.

Around the corner, out of sight, Harry was saying, "Why don't you leave, mister? We're not here to entertain people who lie about wanting water . . ." Grace heard a smashing noise.

She turned the corner. Harry twitched on the floor. The man standing over him was pulling a snub rifle.

Grace aimed and fired.

The man dropped, dead as a rock. Grace rushed over. She looked in the kitchen and saw Gula, terrified, holding the phone to her head. Grace couldn't tell which scared her more, the dead thug or what the phone was telling her. "Come on," Grace hissed. She grabbed the guy's rifle.

Harry, gasping, got to his feet. He stared at the ambulance. To Gula he snapped, "Let's go."

"Wait," Grace said, pointing through the front window. A car was turning in from the road. As if checking out the ambulance, it slowed. The men in it . . . hats? Sunglasses . . . that was enough, Grace just knew. "Zombies!" she yelled.

A snapping noise made them jump. From the ambulance's roof, a hatch popped open. Something awful—something that moved quickly—rose from it, burping. The burps sounded dangerous. A machine gun, Grace realized.

The car veered behind the lawn's wall, rear end shredding.

The Vespa putt-putted through woods. Selma, helmetless, held the phone between shoulder and head. "Now it's zombies!" Gula was exclaiming into the phone. She sounded to Selma like she was hurrying somewhere as fast as she could. "The ambulance, it just creamed them! Bye!"

Selma debated relaying this news to Dan. Later, she thought, staring at the laser tower coming up ahead.

Slotsky was elated. Edward was down, but his audiolink, fully functional, had picked up Grace Trefethen's voice.

Casualties Slotsky always regretted. However, expenses had just diminished by ten thousand per day, at the precise moment he'd become certain of success. The synchronicity pleased him.

Audiosweep of Edward's surroundings confirmed the scope's visual data. Grace, along with "Harry" and "Gula"—panicked voices had uttered those names—were retreating. A lot of good that will do them, Slotsky thought. Through the comm unit he told Ralph, "Make a pass by the car."

"Damn," Harry muttered, staring at the phone. "Every single emergency number—busy."

He, Gula, and Grace crouched in the dark cellar, not far from doors that opened on the vegetable garden. Last year's onions half-filled a bin that would conceal them if anyone descended from the first floor. Unable to understand his persistent bad luck with busy signals, Harry shook the phone. Broken? he wondered.

Grace said, "Things probably are getting wild. Father predicted it. He expected people to go nuts around now."

"Why?" Harry asked sharply. "Because of what he's saying?"

Grace shook her head. "He isn't on yet. Because he's allowed to say anything at all."

"'To go nuts,'" Gula muttered. "You just killed somebody!"

"Be glad that I did," Grace retorted. She didn't have a feel for the rifle she'd confiscated. But she'd informed Harry it was hers, not his. He, she'd made clear, would rely on the handgun; which, thanks to her, he was still alive to use. She said, "Can we call Dan and Selma? I doubt we'll get through to anybody who can help . . . "

The phone rang loudly, making them jump. "Selma?" Harry said.

"Hi!" Selma yelled into Harry's ear. The Vespa's engine sounded strained. Struggling with a hill, Harry thought.

"Still going up the road?" he said, keeping his voice as even as he could.

"Yeah," Selma said, eyeing the tower they were approaching. Lights on it blinked. Worse, it had started to talk. In a weirdly formal voice it was saying, "Move along more quickly. Please move along more quickly."

Uphill, they couldn't. As for the downhill parts, Dan had lost his daredevil streak. Selma wasn't complaining. "How bad is it?" she asked.

"We're hiding, but I won't say where," Harry replied. "The goons in the ambulance might have a scanner."

The goon does indeed, Slotsky thought as he scoped the bullet-riddled car. Three corpses and a missing driver. Fladgate, Slotsky judged. He'd be in charge of an errand like this one.

Slotsky checked the tracker. While picking up the phone dialogue, it was achieving its primary goal, finding the location in the house from which Harry was speaking. The first floor, Slotsky noted, or the cellar. Probably the cellar. A shame Selma wasn't cowering there. Slotsky said to Ralph, "Drive around the house. A complete circuit, slowly. I want to eliminate the missing man."

The ambulance backed through the lower lawn, then headed up the driveway. Slotsky listened to Selma and Harry exchange commiserations. Both parties strove for equanimity, and very nearly achieved it. Slotsky found that admirable. Ah well, he thought as he covered his gash with a fresh patch. Commiserate, my friends, while you can.

He checked the time: 5:56. Slotsky tuned a monitor to CNN.

The convoy made the hills tremble. General Raffenelli, helmeted now, continued to lead from external controls. The higher he climbed from the river, the narrower the roads became; at this point, their width barely exceeded that of the hovers. The downdrafts thrashed the underbrush, sending violent surges of debris into the woods. Fortunately, traffic was sparse. The few oncoming vehicles Raffenelli encountered needed no persuasion to get out of the way. The lucky ones U-turned and fled. The unlucky, subjected to thunderous grit storms in the roadside scrub, weathered the equivalent of a very bad winter.

Raffenelli studied electronic charts. His armada was closing in. To the helmet's mike he said, "Has Trefethen come on?"

Colonel Samaraweera, in the cabin directing communications, replied, "No, sir."

"Alert me if he does."

Dan and Selma coasted down another hill. The road curved to the left, putting the sun's slant on their backs, and bringing into view the plateau Harry had mentioned. A mile and a half distant, it jutted high over the valley, the full length of which they could see for the first time. A lake glittered at the far end. On the plateau they glimpsed ocher walls. "Nice," Selma remarked. With helmets off—they hadn't bothered wearing them after the action at the gate—it was easier to talk. "Looks like a public park."

Down the road, another laser tower stood at the ready, lights blinking. They neared it. In the fussy tones they were finding quite creepy, it said what the other towers had said:

"Move along more quickly. Please move along."

Dan said, "Do they seem like butlers in a horror movie? The kind who carry torches and mutter, 'Follow me, Master'?"

To Selma the towers seemed exactly like that. She was about to say so when the tower's lights stopped blinking. Mistrustful of the thing, Dan slowed. They stared at it. Suddenly the lights started blinking again, but faster; quite a bit faster, as if the approaching Vespa had done something to offend it. Selma moaned, "I think it heard what you just said. And wasn't amused."

The tower said, "Halt. Do not move."

The ambulance completed a circuit of the house. The main wing faced the road. From its rear, a second wing projected to a downsloping hill. A third wing, parallel to the main one but set back, stretched from the second one toward a neatly fenced enclosure. A vegetable garden, Slotsky judged. The scope and Ralph's roving eyes had combed various gardens around this house, to no avail. They hadn't found Fladgate. Slotsky considered the possibility he'd taken refuge in the woods. He also might have fled down the hill. Slotsky scoped it, noting the boulders and ledges of a steep rock garden. He saw no Fladgate.

He'd made progress, however. Near the conjunction of the house's rear wings, an earthen ramp led to a diagonally inclined cellar door. Harry hid not far from it, the tracker had established. Slotsky told Ralph, "Go back to the cellar entrance."

As they approached it, the scope alerted Slotsky to movement in a shed adjoining the vegetable garden. The wooden structure's door was ajar. Slotsky magnified it. He beheld, in the dark interior, several centimeters of a muzzle's tip. From the ambulance's rooftop machine gun he sent a bullet through the door.

Fladgate staggered out, disgorging guts from his sundered midriff. He collapsed on the lawn. Slotsky said, "Make sure . . . "

He didn't need to complete the order. Ralph drove over the body. A crunch jostled Slotsky's specially fitted bed. "Turn to the cellar door," he ordered. The ambulance swung around. Slotsky scoped the door. Anyone bolting out would face a trap. The machine gun would lay down a pattern of fire to make that clear.

"Go in the house, Ralph," he said. "Go to the cellar and flush our friends through that door. The girl is what I need—don't hurt her. The other two, kill." He watched Ralph leave the cab, walk past the cellar entrance, and approach the second wing's rear door. It proved locked. Ralph opened it with a bullet.

Selma's eyes widened. "Harry," she said to the phone, "stop talking to me and concentrate on—on whatever you can do." She turned the phone off. The tower above them, blinking too fast, once again said, "Do not move."

"Bad, huh?" Dan said.

"Somebody just shot into the house."

Dan looked away. The lake, pink-orange in dropping sun, was pretty. The entire valley had filled with pinkish haze. "We're all gonna die," he remarked. "Like cornered rats."

The tower said, "Do not move."

Selma said, "I wish Igor would shut up."

Dan studied blinking lights on the plateau. "This place is on red alert . . . hey." He pointed. "What's that?"

Selma squinted at delicate beams of light shooting around the plateau. "Who knows?" she said.

The tower said, "That is the prototype of the Mantis insect-control system. We call it 'Secticide Plus.' The system targets all flying insects, but can discriminate . . . "

Ralph found the door behind a Navajo weaving.

He gazed at steps descending to earthy darkness. He didn't like it. Loudly he called, "Exit from the door to the garden!"

No one replied. Moments passed. Ralph heard an elderly "Ka-choo!" It came from the area to his left. He crept down, stopping at a point beyond which walls wouldn't shield him. His rifle's readout showed a thermal source to the left. He peered. And heard another, even feebler "Ka-choo!"

It came from a different area. What's she doing? Ralph wondered. He scanned right for thermal sources. A trace of something. The girl, he suspected. He wouldn't get a comprehensive read without going further down.

Ralph jumped to the bottom, raking the area to his left with a sustained automatic burst. He dodged behind a wall. Something moved. He whirled.

Four feet away, the girl pointed a rifle at him. Edward's rifle. "Drop your gun," she said.

Ralph studied her. She didn't know how to use the weapon. That was clear from its indicator lights. Ralph lowered his gun, and said, "Relax."

"Get on the floor," a male voice said behind him.

Ralph lunged for the wall. He heard a bang. His head's backside felt a savage kiss. The bullet barged through his brain.

Slotsky listened to Ralph crash to the floor, gasping his last. The audio-link conveyed those distressing sounds. It then conveyed sounds of scurrying. Grace shrieked, "Gula!"

"I'm all right," came a faint reply. "He shot up a bunch of fire-wood." A pause. "Use it for kindling, I suppose."

Kindling, Slotsky thought, reaching for the patch pouch. He would find a use for some kindling. The people in the cellar had begun to seriously annoy him. So much so, he plucked his sole Number 30 from the pouch. While unpeeling it, he activated the voice-control system with a series of verbal codes. The ambulance, not his dead men, would be listening from here on out.

Slotsky couldn't drive the vehicle by voice-control. A shame, considering the circumstances. However, he could give directions to the roof gun. The Number 30 he placed squarely on his gash. The sting rallied him. Everything came into extremely sharp focus.

He noticed something on the monitor. Waves. Large, celestial waves. Ah, thought Slotsky. The broadcast begins.

Raffenelli's helmet said, "General, it's starting." Puzzlement colored Samaraweera's voice as he added, "It's showing waves. Big waves. And the soundtrack is—I suppose you could say it's peaceful, sir."

"Take the helm," Raffenelli ordered. He went into the cabin, nodded at the nine men tending their luminous stations, and sat before a monitor tuned to CNN. Just as Samaraweera had said, the screen showed large waves. Large, sparkling, and somehow very pure-looking waves. A soothing melody played.

The waves became more heavenly. Earnest Trefethen's voice intoned, "Consider the cleansing effects of water." The image shifted to the interior of a vast high-Gothic cathedral. It pulled into the dim baptistery, where, attended by hooded clergy and to the accompaniment of organ fugues, an infant received the baptismal dunk.

"Consider," Trefethen's voice continued with hypnotic conviction, "how important water always has been, for the many ways we maintain . . . "

The voice trailed off. The image shifted to the Ganges River, along which pilgrim hordes performed ancient rituals. This is foolish, Raffenelli thought. Why, then, did he feel so riveted?

Trefethen suddenly appeared on the monitor, eyebrows raised.

Samaraweera said, "General, we've arrived."

"Yes," Raffenelli observed, seeing a large gate on the hovercraft's scopescreen.

From the monitor Trefethen said calmly, "I've been informed I have visitors. They probably will terminate this broadcast. However, it will continue on the Net, from the Mantis Corporation's home page . . . "

Trefethen disappeared. A hard-faced Mary McMurtry filled the monitor. She said, "I am pleased to announce that the FATB has located Earnest Trefethen. Heavily armed forces surround him. He has no chance of escape. Dr. Trefethen, I assume you are watching me speak. The President has directed me to grant you five minutes to surrender. If you do not, we are prepared to destroy you and those who harbor you. We await your reply."

McMurtry disappeared. A stunned Carson O'Doyle came onscreen. The CNN anchor said haltingly, "It appears the saga of Earnest Trefethen is reaching a dramatic . . . "

Raffenelli's priority phone issued its ululating whistle. He picked up the receiver. The dour voice said, "Ted, it's me."

"Yes, Mr. President."

"I've spoken with Cliffcloud. I believe she will try to wake up Trefethen. If you must attack, do it in stages. Give them a chance to reconsider—I don't want needless slaughter. And remember, I've authorized coverage. Make it look good, will you?"

"Of course, sir. Of course."

58

In the studio, Earnest watched Martha reconfigure the broadcast. No longer would it go to the now useless television pool in New York. It would flood omnidirectionally through the Net—to anyone with the desire and the bandwidth to pick it up.

"I spoke with the President," Martha said tersely as she worked the console. "He thinks you're coming to your senses."

"Wonderful!" Earnest snapped. He pulled the Zippo pager from his trousers, flipped its lid, and undid the safety catch.

"Don't jump the gun," Martha said. "This isn't over yet. We've just started."

"We'll see," Earnest muttered. He was thinking of Grace. Of Helen, Brian. It's the end, he reflected. We've come to the end.

Bitterly, he rethought the broadcast. It would be his last shot. The content, he decided, should reflect that reality.

He had to compress his message. Instead of putting out seven broadcasts over a week or more, he now had—what? Ten minutes?

Raffenelli stood at the gate intercom, keeping an uneasy eye on blinking laser mounts atop the pillars. In the pavement, under gusting dust and twigs, he noted fresh burn marks. The lasers had inscribed a large circle.

The roar of the hovercrafts stretching down the road made it hard to think, never mind decipher asphalt runes. It was one thing to be at the helm, moving. It was another to be on the ground in this deafening thrash of grit. He checked his watch: 6:13. The general strode to his hover's boarding ramp, a gangway extruding through the windstorm to the pavement. He climbed it, grit scouring his goggles, invading his uniform. Cliffcloud had better answer her phone, he thought angrily. Standing by a gate getting sandblasted wasn't the general's idea of conducting negotiations. Nor was it his idea of displaying military might.

Martha finished the hookup. Earnest sat in the studio armchair, ready to go.

"Five seconds," Martha said, ignoring ringing phones down the corridor. Raffenelli, no doubt. Or the President again.

Earnest stared at the camera. Its light went on. He smiled and said, "Back again." Glorious waves filled a monitor. Earnest voice-overed, "Consider the cleansing effects of water . . . "

━ ━ ━

From his ambulance bed, in thrall to the Number 30, Slotsky watched, via Net, Trefethen's inventory of the holy properties of water. Holy water, Slotsky mused. Sonorous chants, heard long ago in vaulted, incense-filled places, welled through his mind. Charming, Slotsky reflected. It really was quite lovely.

Trefethen conducted a survey of the Nile's sacred status in Egyptian antiquity. Then he drifted to mistier realms. He spoke of Atlantis, and of flood, of a flood that had effaced a fabled civilization. A Great Flood.

"What was it," Trefethen said, "that prompted the Atlantean waters to rise? And what gave rise to the waters from which Noah saved man and animal alike? As in all stories of flood—they are legion, every culture has passed them down—it concerned water's marvelous power to cleanse. To cleanse vileness and sin from a corrupt, debased mankind . . . "

Of course, Slotsky thought. He found this transfixing.

But he wasn't forgetting his cellar companions. The tracker continued to monitor their phone. They hadn't moved.

Earnest initiated what he called the "filthy flood" sequence. A series of fast-cut images, it featured the Mississippi and Missouri rivers in states of rage, spilling limitless brown stains; it moved on to a typhoon's obliteration of Bangladesh, then to a tsunami's crushing crest. Earnest played with the mix. He interspersed details of classic flood depictions, drawn from the iconographical legacies of Noah, Atlantis, Gilgamesh, Krakatoa. He intensified the pace, the density of texture. Bridges snapped, seawalls sundered, whole shorelines caved as vignettes of apocalypse flashed subliminally. Into the sound track he worked a theme of wrath. The flood cacophonies acquired deific inflections. As if succumbing to a cosmic loss of temper, rampaging waters cursed, muttered, and howled.

The command hover's gun drew a bead on the tower rising from the gate's right pillar. The hover behind targeted the tower rising from the left pillar. The general, watching via scope from the internal cockpit, said, "Fire."

Short bursts snapped off the caps, and the lights under them. "Maneuver to bring to bear on the gate," Raffenelli told his mike. The hovers realigned, allowing a third craft to pull up. Three guns trained on the gate. "Fire," the general said.

The gate's inch-thick steel was no match for uranium-clad shells pounding in at the rate of 180 per second. Nor were the pillars. Thoroughly chewed, the structure toppled. Its laser towers crashed into the woods.

Raffenelli scoped the drive. A quarter mile up, the road turned out of view. At the bend stood another tower, a taller one than the gate's. The light under the cap blinked. As the general studied it, the blinking stopped. A good sign? he wondered. Likely, he concluded. Into the mike he said, "Forward."

Seven hovercraft passed over the gate's smoldering remains before the general joined the cavalcade. With overall command of the operation, he couldn't, he'd decided, risk taking the lead.

Branches scraped plate armor. As if in a frenzy of remonstrance, trees pummeled the machines rushing up Cliffcloud's immaculate blacktop drive.

Martha stood goddess-like athwart the road, legs piercing the flanks of hills. She watched a line of yellow toys scurry toward her. At this level of resolution, the hologram rendered the landscape on a scale of five feet to a hundred; the hovercrafts accordingly were just over eighteen inches long, eleven wide. Martha allowed the lead hover to come within six feet of the tower. Then she sank to her knees, thrusting her face over crest-top trees. She tunneled her right arm through the hill to the road, where her hand surfaced like a demon bursting from the underworld. The middle finger flicked the hover's floatskirt.

From the tower, a brilliant blue beam flashed through the floatskirt. The hover shuddered, and slowed. The following hover hit it, bounced, and swerved into the woods. The next few hovers likewise crunched; the others, including the puce-colored command hover, stopped moving. Martha studied the pile-up. The lead hover reddened. She imagined an engine fire, the seared undercarriage.

The blue beam her middle finger had activated—second only to her index finger's pink beams in terms of power—had to have melted the hovercraft's rotors. Martha wondered if the crew could get out. The holosystem's sensors, reading the scene from the tower, probably wouldn't achieve sufficient resolution to tell her. They'd pick up an explosion, however. So far, to Martha's relief, that hadn't happened. She didn't want to escalate quickly.

The command hover lurched backward. En masse, the entire line inched back. Martha wondered what data Raffenelli was getting from the front. She stood, thinking she should scan his comm links.

The lead hover shuddered. Martha watched it flare into a yellow-orange ball.

The data flooding Raffenelli's command screen told the story. So did his scopescreen. The high-definition monitor displayed an enormous fireball up the road. Bright orange, it expanded. Raffenelli watched it scorch trees. Smoke blotted the sky.

Thirty-seven men, Raffenelli thought numbly. Thirty soldiers and seven crew, reduced to cinders.

He'd almost lost the next hover as well. If he hadn't given the command to move back, it would've gone up too, no question.

This was catastrophe. On top of lost lives and equipment, the hovers were blocked. Raffenelli doubted they could get over that flaming hulk. Or around it, the forest was so dense. And on fire.

The monitor formerly tuned to CNN, now receiving Trefethen via Net, caught the general's fury-dazed eye. The crowning insult, he thought.

Images of hellish water—various examples of the destructive onslaught of flood—were transmuting into bizarre images of heavenly waves. "So we see," Trefethen voice-overed with maddening serenity, "filth can lead to salvation. This is another ancient theme—the dark night of the soul delivers, paradoxically, bliss. How, you may wonder, might we make darkness bliss?"

A hurricane's spiral appeared, then faded to an aerial video of the cloud whorl surrounding yesterday's Antarctic eruption. Lightning bolts—Trefethen had added those, the general noted—gave the whorl a godly corona. "I'll tell you," the voice-over continued, "something strange, but true, about making darkness bliss. Sometimes it helps to give darkness free rein. Sometimes our wickedness is so complete, darkness is the only solution. How can this be? It's elementary—and has to do with the gods. It has to do with making them angrier. For the angrier the gods become, the swifter their retribution—and thus the swifter our cleansing, our entry to the glories of heavenly bliss . . . "

As Raffenelli watched, the rotating clouds acquired a demeanor. A prophet-like face took form in them. Majestically, it stared. The eyes erupted glowing volcanic waste. The mouth opened, and declared with supernatural authority:

"Cast your filth into the sea!"

The image shifted to Trefethen. His own demeanor now held a serely majestic quality. Madness, Raffenelli thought. The man was beyond insane; that fact flooded from the burn in his eyes. "Cast your filth," he said slowly, "into the sea." He smiled. Raffenelli felt nauseous. He reached to turn off the monitor, but paused, hand in midair, to find out what the psychopath could possibly say next. With growing disbelief, the general heard:

"In the name of Antarctica, I instruct you to sink all ships at sea. All ships in port too, any ship, every ship, sink them—sink them now. First sink the fuel tankers, they are the filthiest, then sink the rest, do not stop until you have sunk them all.

"In the name of Antarctica, I instruct you to fly all aircraft into the sea. Any aircraft, all aircraft, crash them into the sea. Start with airliners, they are the filthiest, they carry the destroyers, those who brought us to this pass. Then fly the rest, all of them, into the . . . "

Raffenelli turned it off and sat back, trembling. Incredible, he thought. The man's inciting Luddies to *insurrection* . . .

His crew gaped at him. They'd been watching the monitor before which he sat, he realized. His having turned it off now made him the object of their attention.

The priority phone ululated. Into it he barked, "Raffenelli!"

McMurtry said, "Take him out. Wipe that place off the map."

Toby opened the bathroom door and went into the cell. Brian followed.

Helen stood behind her bars, gazing vacantly at the corridor. On her TV, Carson O'Doyle was discussing the peculiar fact that Trefethen's broadcast now was flooding the Net from the Mantis Corporation's home page. Without making eye contact, Helen said in a monotone, "They're attacking. It's your fault, Toby."

He didn't reply.

"If you hadn't blundered into our lives," she continued with the same flat voice, "none of this would have happened."

Toby put an arm through his bars. He found the cardkey slot, and slipped the card in. The bars clicked open.

Helen's eyes focused. "What are you doing?" she murmured.

Toby and Brian moved down the corridor to the outer door. Toby tried the cardkey. It worked again.

"Wait!" Helen exclaimed. "Brian! Don't leave me!"

Brian turned to her and said, "Mother, drop dead."

"Grace is nearby!" Helen said desperately.

Brian shivered. "Where?" he said.

"Very nearby. I was going to get her. Father stopped me."

Brian gasped. "Why?" he exclaimed.

Toby said impatiently, "Let's go."

"Just a second," Brian snapped. "Why did he stop you?"

In near-hysteria, Helen babbled about "Father and Martha." Toby meantime realized what Carson O'Doyle was saying:

"We are seeing the most nerve-wracking moment thus far. Trefethen, under attack as I speak, nonetheless continues the broadcast by different means. This raises a ghastly possibility. Will he, facing annihilation, explode his remaining bombs in Antarctica?"

Toby seized Brian's arm and pulled him down the corridor.

Helen shouted, "Let me out! I'll help you find Grace!"

Brian shook Toby loose, yelling, "Give me a second!"

Furious, Toby lunged into the hallway he'd never seen.

It was long and plain, and it did feel underground. At irregular intervals, closed doors indicated rooms or closets on both sides. Toby eyed a cart ten feet away. Against the wall, it looked abandoned. Trays with dirty dishes sat on it. A black medical case also sat on it. Needles, too. And Helen's sprayer.

Three strides took Toby to the sprayer. He grabbed the thing and spun around, finger finding the button. Back to the jail corridor he went. Going down it, he saw Helen's face pressed to the bars, saying, "I promise, I'll help you *find her.*"

Toby put the nozzle to the bars and blasted her in the eyes.

Brian whirled angrily, shouting, *"Hey!"*

Toby raised a fist. Brian backed off. They watched as paralysis stilled the outraged shock on Helen's face. It was as if the spray had laminated that emotional instant; preserving it.

Helen crumpled to the floor.

Toby grabbed Brian by his shirtfront. "Didn't you hear," he shouted, "what the fucking TV *said?*"

Martha towered from the valley, head higher than her highest hills. The horizon, a perfect circle around her, was domed with clear sky. She studied floating indicator arrays. They tracked warplanes in holding patterns beyond visual reach, beyond even her visual reach. Ten fighter-bombers, Martha noted, had just broken formation. They were coming at her.

Nice, she thought. She glanced at a monitor on the hologram's periphery. Earnest was doing tsunamis now. Computer-generated, but realer-looking than documentary video, a titanic wave rushed toward a city with a handsome volcano in its far outskirts. Mount Fuji. The fake wave would hit a fake Tokyo.

Hurry up, Martha thought. Earnest, she felt, was hogging. It was time to turn the broadcast over to her. Time for the hologram to take its rightful place in the drama that millions of Net people so attentively were watching. Time for the orb's domain to shed its disguise, and reveal itself for what it was.

The Net audience would see a holo-simulation of that event. But unlike Earnest's wave, the event itself would be real.

They ran down a hallway identical to the last one. They careened through another wide turn into yet another hallway; down it they ran. The trip seemed endless. Toby hadn't known the house was so big. This was like doing laps around the Pentagon.

He wondered if Cliffcloud called the place "the Octagon." Brian had told him that these hallways followed the octagonal format of the building above it. Why not call it "the Orbagon"?

Toby felt as if one of his dreams had taken over. He in flapping pajamas, Brian in clothes soaked to the skin, they were running through a spaceship. They were racing around engineering in the mighty *Orb*.

"Martha must be preoccupied," Brian panted.

As you predicted, Toby thought. Last night, Brian had speculated about Martha's activities during the broadcast. He'd theorized that he and Toby might make it to the TV studio unfried if she were busy helping his father.

It seemed probable, however, that she was busy doing something else right now. Firing up the *Orb*'s death rays, maybe?

Brian slowed as they neared the next turn. He caught Toby's arm, slowing him too. "Almost there," he said as quietly as his heart rate allowed. They reached the turn. Brian pressed himself to the wall and took a quick look at the next stretch of hallway. He muttered, "Sure you want to try this?"

"Maniac!" Toby retorted softly. "*Yes.*"

"What if Father's doing the right thing?"

"Then let history condemn us." Toby looked around the turn. He saw a steel hatch, ajar, beyond which sky-blue brightness filled a large room. "That's the studio?" he whispered.

"Martha's control room. She's probably in there."

"Where's the studio?"

"Other end of the hallway."

"Then we should have come from the other direction. To avoid going by the control room. Will she see us?"

"Don't know. We could run back around . . . "

"Forget it. Let's go." They moved ahead quietly, eyes fastened on the hatchway. Toby got a direct glimpse in, and froze.

Like the jolly green giant, Cliffcloud towered over a pastoral landscape. But she didn't just tower. She was a giant doing exercises, or something, over the landscape. The vividly realistic landscape of hills and dales; which wasn't solid, her legs glided through the hills like a ghost. "Holy shit," Toby breathed.

It was Brian's turn to do the dragging-along. He grabbed Toby's arm; they snuck by the hatch toward an open door, not far down. As they approached they heard a familiar voice.

Toby peered through. Trefethen sat in an armchair, playing a control board, talking into a microphone, and watching a monitor. A huge wave filled the screen. It was about to crash into a metropolis. Trefethen pressed a button. The wave froze; he turned to a camera. He pressed another button. A light on the camera blinked. To the camera Trefethen said with disagreeable conviction, "Fear, sometimes, is a very good thing." Toby edged in. "Sometimes, fear is what teaches the . . . "

Toby came closer, sprayer raised.

Trefethen heard him. He whipped around, jaw dropping, his right hand darting to the console; toward what Toby, absorbing every detail of the man's movements, thought was a Zippo cigarette lighter with the lid flipped open.

Toby sprayed Trefethen's face. On it, fury laminated. Trefethen's hand froze two inches from the Zippo.

What is the thing? Toby wondered.

Trefethen slid from his chair to the floor.

Here goes, Toby thought. Now I do it.

He sat in Trefethen's chair, expecting lasers to boil him alive any second. A glance over his shoulder showed Brian securing the door with a manual bolt. Good, Toby thought. He'd take any protection at all. Even something so simple as a bolted door.

Toby looked into the camera. Knowing he had to get them out as clearly as he could, he marshaled the facts he'd learned from Brian the night before.

Slotsky gazed with perplexity at his monitor. Toby Swett appeared to have gassed Earnest Trefethen. Not content to stop there, Swett now seemed determined to make a statement.

The young man with discolored eyes said, "I will explain how Trefethen explodes his bombs. Authorities, listen carefully. You might be able to prevent further explosions."

I should have killed him, Slotsky thought. Days ago.

Swett cleared his throat. "Trefethen has two separate systems. Both involve specific televisable images, which are the two faces of the Beast; he calls them icons. The high-tech one is the Mantis orb. It's the orb . . .

. . . in the LaserWorks ad campaign that does it."

Martha frowned at the ten silver specks approaching from the southeast sky. Something nagged at her.

The monitor's faint audio hadn't penetrated her absorption with objects in the air. Suddenly, it did. She turned to look. Toby Swett, not Earnest, was speaking.

He said, "I repeat, the orb is the high-tech greed-face. It explodes the bombs—but only in LaserWorks commercials. Don't allow any new LaserWorks commercials on the air."

Martha jumped from the holo-arena and rushed to a console. She took a handgun from a drawer. Swett meantime continued, "More important—this is really important—don't yank the current Laser-Works commercials. Keep them playing. Those commercials tell the

bombs they're connected to the datasphere. In other words, if you
yank the current ads, taking all LaserWorks orbs off the air, the
bombs will think you're trying to limit what they see. And they'll
explode . . . "

Martha scurried through the hallway door. She ran to the studio,
her heart sinking—its door was closed. Months before, Earnest had
asked her to install a deadbolt on the other side of it. He'd had images
of the FATB storming the house as he delivered a final broadcast. The
deadbolt was to have been a last-ditch defense.

That it had become. The door wouldn't open. Martha didn't even
consider shooting her way in. She knew she couldn't succeed.

She charged back to the control room. From the monitor Swett was
saying, "The second trigger system involves the other face of the
Beast, the low-tech icon." Martha dove for the console's master controls. "Of the two systems, it's the more dangerous, because the icon
involved is . . . "

Martha slapped a switch, pulling the plug on the studio, cutting
Swett off. She grabbed a phone. Back into the hologram she plunged.

The silver specks had come much nearer. If they fired missiles, she
would have less than thirty seconds to respond. Bombs would give her
more time . . . no sign, as of yet, of missiles.

Martha called the studio.

After three rings, someone answered.

"Brian?" Martha shouted.

"Yeah," he replied.

"If you harm Earnest, you'll regret it. I'll cut your dicks off. Understand?"

Brian said, "Martha, fuck off."

The hover's situation screen dis-
played the planes' approach. A minute and ten seconds, General Raffenelli noted, to bomb impact. This would be sweet to behold.

"General," Samaraweera said nervously. "The netcast—it's resumed,
sir."

Raffenelli's stare at the situation screen didn't waver. He said, "Swett's telling us about the second icon?"

"No. He's offscreen. You should take a look at this, sir."

Raffenelli looked. Martha Cliffcloud, a colossus Martha Cliffcloud, strode through hills.

The sun dropped behind the ridge looming over the plateau. The valley darkened in the shadow; the lake silvered and grayed. But the eastern sky, still sun-flooded, shone a lustrous blue.

Above Dan and Selma, the tower guarding them said, "Do not . . ." Midorder, the voice fell silent. Then, as if expressing pique, the tower emitted a high-pitched whine.

They looked at the cap. Its light no longer blinked. Dan glanced at the plateau. Secticide Plus had stopped hunting bugs. The other plateau lights also had extinguished.

Selma pointed at the eastern sky. "Do you see something?"

Dan looked. He thought he made out tiny silver dots. They seemed to float in the air. But no, he soon realized. They were approaching the valley. "That's it," he said. "That's an attack."

Selma said to the phone, "Harry, we see planes coming. Dan thinks it's an attack."

Martha's head poked into the sky. Her feet, two miles below, were planted in the patch of murk that was her valley. She studied the silver aircraft approaching from the east.

As if making the first move in a slow-moving martial dance, she stepped forward, turned, and swept her godly arm heavenward. Then, slowly, she brought it down. A flat palm neared the gnatlike planes. With a deliberate, ceremonial wave, she passed the palm through them.

The tower's whine intensified, and climbed to a scream. Something ferocious flew from it; the force hurled Selma and Dan to the ground. The air seemed to fry.

On their backs, breath knocked out, they saw a bright pink energy beam sizzling from the tower's cap into the eastern sky. Dan glanced wildly at the house. More pink beams zapped from it. Pink beams were zapping from the ridge above it, too. He looked back at the sky.

Like strands of a spider web, the beams extended tautly toward the distant silver specks. And into them; the specks exploded.

Fireballs swelled. Against the sky's blue, they resembled flowers budding vivid blooms. In magenta, gray, orange, and black.

Raffenelli glared at Cliffcloud's virtual battleground, jaw muscles bunched. Through his helmet mike he spoke with his Air Force liaison. "Scramble everything you've got," he said. "I do mean everything." The general slammed down the phone. He then radioed his prop-plane squadron. To Jeannette Gwathmey, squadron commander, he said, "Fire them. Fire them all."

The squadron went on point. Hatches in the plane's bellies opened. Cruise missiles dropped, ignited, and sped away. Each carrying eight hundred pounds of enhanced plastic explosive, they targeted the east pavilion of the octagon. They would turn it, the plateau under it, into an avalanche of dust.

In the ambulance, Slotsky watched, enthralled.

The holoscape through which Cliffcloud moved had a way of changing scale. Slotsky supposed she was keeping a grip on details that variously sized big pictures, as it were, could give her. She herself remained the same size, Slotsky had been telling himself. Her body was the only "real" element in the spectacle. But the shifting scales gave the illusion that she too changed dimensions. Sometimes she seemed a giantess on a par with figments of myth. Other times she seemed twice that big. Then there were occasions, such as the swatting of the fighter-bombers, where she grew far too big, impossibly big—so big as to be in danger of slipping from the planet's curvature itself.

When, Slotsky kept asking the monitor. When will you get to the essence of the matter? And show her shoes? Her feet?

Slotsky prayed for boots. For hyperboots. With hyperheels.

On the studio floor, Trefethen stirred, facial fury perfectly preserved. Monitors displayed the ongoing netcast of Brobdingnagian Martha.

Toby flipped shut the Zippo. Brian, who'd never seen it before, suspected it activated the rabbit. Toby wasn't going to fool with what looked like an undone safety catch under the lid. He didn't want to touch anything there. Not the shiny button, or the apparatus around it.

He wondered how he could destroy the thing. Its weight suggested the steel jacket was strong. Maybe very strong. In fact, apart from the button mechanism, this Zippo seemed indestructible.

The button he probably could smash. But would that activate the device? And maybe the rabbit?

On the studio's monitor, Martha raised her arms, saluting the heavens. The heavens rushed earthward, expanding the horizon. In tandem, Martha soared skyward, becoming once again a supergiant.

Slivers of silver—cruise missiles—sped toward her.

She rotated her immensity, extending her palm. It closed on the slivers. They disappeared into a gargantuan fist.

The studio's lights dimmed. Toby, watching Cliffcloud's fist snatch the silverish things from the air, broke into a sweat.

From various points near Cliffcloud's feet, brilliant pink beams zoomed high, high in the sky. They hit the fist.

She opened the fist. Exploding stars dropped from it.

Selma cowered. Dan cowered. The tower above them was screaming, towers all over were screaming, sweeping the eastern sky with horrible pink beams. Seconds passed. The screaming stopped.

More seconds passed. Selma sat up. Dan heaved himself to his knees. Far away in the sky, they saw explosions ripen. The sound rumbled in like thunder.

I'm using too much power, Martha thought.

The hologram had flickered. Now it was back to normal. But how long would it, and the reactor providing the juice, last?

She shrank herself rapidly. The valley reared up around her. Through its hills she strode to the plateau. She enlarged it, and gazed at the red-tiled octagon sitting on the sward of lawn.

An automated camera tracked her. Anything to which she paid attention, it did the same.

Let them get a good look now, Martha thought, imagining her countless viewers. They might not have another chance.

●─●─●

On the situation screen, General Raffenelli assessed indications that Cliffcloud's defenses were fading.

He wanted to finish this. He didn't care what it took. Neither did McMurtry, nor the President. They just wanted it finished, regardless of the cost.

Raffenelli called Air Force liaison. "Hit her with everything you've got," he said. "Including the 'copter carriers—but bring those in low. Very low."

An earthen ramp, suitable for the passage of wheelbarrows and small tractors, rose from the cellar floor to the diagonally tilted metal doors to the garden. Harry crouched beneath the doors, peering through the doors' middle crack at the ambulance outside. It stood twenty-five feet away. Harry had been studying it for several minutes. He'd seen no sign of people within.

From the ramp's bottom, Grace whispered, "Maybe it only held two men. And we got them both."

"Time to find out," Harry said. "Grace, Gula—get back." With a hoe, he lifted one of the doors, and propped it one-quarter open. No response from the ambulance. With an underhand toss, he lobbed a fat onion at the windshield.

The onion hadn't traveled four feet when the ambulance's roof-gun popped up and erased it from the air. The gun didn't stop firing. It sent a fusillade into the grass, chewing a raw line just beyond the cellar doors. Pulverized sod hit Harry's face.

He grabbed the hoe. The door slammed down.

Slotsky scoped the cellar doors, the ravaged lawn. They won't try that again, he thought. However, they might leave by the interior stairs.

It was time to move.

He keyed his bed's controls. Portions of the bed detached and swung away. It then folded, putting him in a sitting position. He secured himself with straps. Falling off, what with his leg in a cast, wouldn't do. The control board swiveled over his lap. All functions, he saw, were go. Sensors, power, ambulation—this bed, now a chair, not only could roll. If necessary it could crawl, and even climb stairs, for it boasted the latest in robotics.

Slotsky wanted to test those capabilities. "Open rear doors," he said. The rear doors opened. A ramp slid to the lawn. Slotsky rolled down it, clutching weapons, his nerve kit, and his tracker. The rear doors slammed shut.

From Ralph's audiolink, the tracker relayed a feverish discussion between Grace and Harry. They didn't know how many more "goons" the ambulance held, or if other goons had entered the house. And they still didn't know how to use their commandeered guns. Small wonder, thought Slotsky as he rolled to the house's open back door. Like the guns he toted, the electronics of those guns were state of the art.

The chair's claws gripped the door frame. Without difficulty, they hauled Slotsky into the house. It was a squeeze, but doable, for the chair had been designed, of course, to get through doorways. If necessary it actually could narrow itself.

Slotsky rolled through the house to the cellar stairs. There he paused. His mind felt so clear, more clear perhaps than it ever had felt. But he wanted to think this through.

A logistical problem confronted him. How to get down the stairs safely? Safe from the handgun which the cellar-people did know how to use?

He meditated about various drugs at his disposal. From the nerve kit he extracted an aerosol grenade.

61

Martha watched the holo-sky's indicators. An armada was circling Cheswick. Raffenelli had brought in the Air Force.

Something of that magnitude Martha couldn't shoot down. At least not with lasers. More quickly than she would have liked, she confronted the necessity of using her ace in the hole. The weapon that would put a resounding end to this engagement.

Through hills to the plateau she strode. She made it grow. Lawn and octagon broadened. She snapped her fingers. In the lawn, not far from the house, a small circular cap lifted, and flipped.

◆ ━ ━ ━

Toby concluded he had to do something about the Zippo. On the floor, Trefethen stirred again. His face was losing the fury mask; any minute, it seemed, he'd revive. Toby was perfectly willing to give him another dose of the spray. On the other hand, he wanted to talk with the man before destruction rained down, ending this. He still had unanswered questions.

But how could he get replies without risking the possibility that Trefethen would find a way to take control of the Zippo?

"We shouldn't bang it," he told Brian. "We might set it off." Toby considered a beaker of ice water on the console. A drinking glass sat there too. "We could try drowning it," he said.

"I bet it's waterproof," Brian replied.

"It is," Trefethen said from the floor. "Give it to me. If you don't, Martha will make things unpleasant for you. You'll wish you'd never been born."

Toby held up the sprayer. "Don't move," he said.

Inch by inch, the wheelchair descended the cellar stairs. Clawed limbs sought braceholds in the walls, on ledges, and on steps. When finding them, it tested them. When proving them secure, other claws detached from previously found holds keeping the chair in place, and started the process anew.

Slotsky, tilted forward but tightly strapped, meanwhile used every electronic means at his disposal to chart the location of his prey. The tracker analyzed the cellar's ambient sounds—the hum of a water heater, the throb of a bank of freezers. It also analyzed the whine of the chair's servomechanisms, the periodic thumps of claws slamming into place. The tracker then filtered those sounds; making itself more sensitive to such things as the scuff of a foot on the earthen floor, rustles of clothing, sounds of breathing and whispers. Slotsky's gun also listened. It scanned for thermal sources, read air movements, and sniffed them. These data Slotsky wasn't getting from the gun's display. He'd jacked the gun into the tracker, which did a far better job of organizing such information. On its screen, a diagram of the cellar, or actually of the cellars, glowed. Grace, Gula, and Harry, he saw, were crouching to the left of the stairs' bottom. Behind the hulking furnace.

Sophisticated though his electronics were, Slotsky had at his disposal another, more potent asset—his 'dorph-saturated brain. It gave him a rich understanding of this damp, dark, subterranean world. He fancied he could taste the soil itself. And analyze, with preternatural sensitivity, the constituent minerals, the trace metals, even the chemical composition of the spirits of those who had lived here, and had died here . . . so many souls, he was learning, had lived here. And had died here. He knew everything about them. Everything about their slow-moving, season-driven world . . . he could taste those lives. Just as he could taste their deaths.

Their deaths. Do Gula and Harry know, he wondered, that I can taste theirs?

Slotsky was certain they knew. For he could taste their terror.

He halted the chair's advance before reaching the point beyond which walls wouldn't protect him. In his tilted lap, from which if he wasn't careful things easily could tumble, he readied the aerosol grenade.

Its effects would spare him Edward and Ralph's fate. The grenade didn't scatter bits of metal; it released a gas which induced brief paralysis, an effect lasting minutes. During that time, those affected would lose the ability to move. But they wouldn't lose the ability to see, hear, feel, and think. Slotsky liked this aspect of the drug. He wanted his prospective victims to see, hear, feel, and think, vividly, as he had his way.

He considered issues of timing. How long, after a robot arm threw the grenade furnaceward, would his chair need to get to the bottom of the stairs? A number of minutes, he suspected. However, the grenade's gas wouldn't keep his friends immobilized for more than ten minutes. That posed a problem.

Slotsky instructed the chair to analyze the feasibility of a rapid roll. The machine was sturdy. It could take a tumble and right itself, if necessary.

The control panel informed him roll-analysis was under way. He would get an answer shortly. Slotsky didn't mind the wait. Nobody here was going anywhere fast.

"You're kidding," Dan said.

"No," Grace whispered desperately through the phone. "Some kind of robot. A machine—slowly coming down the stairs!" Dan heard a distant, echoing *thump*. "Metal arms or something," Grace went on, her whisper fainter. "It's like it can grab walls . . . to come down carefully . . . God I'm so scared."

"Uh," Dan said, "yeah. Try to stay cool. I mean, if you can. I guess there's—um, is there any other way out?"

"There is, but the ambulance is right outside—running. Harry opened the door and it shot up the lawn. Right where we'd have to go. It just like—blew up the whole lawn."

"God," Dan said.

"What's happening with you?"

"We're freaking. The laser towers are blinking again. We think they're waiting for another attack."

"Hold on," Grace said. Dan heard her whisper with Harry.

Harry took the phone. "There's a trail out of there," he said. "Over the western ridge. It leads to the rear of Gula's property. If they level Cliffcloud, the electronic fence that blocks the trail might lose power. So you might be able to get over it. But if you do, Dan—watch out for the ambulance. The thing is dangerous. It's set to shoot at anything approaching it. Automatically."

Toby said to Trefethen, "I guess we just wait to die."

Trefethen was sitting now, on the floor; Toby stood by with the sprayer, making sure he stayed there. Brian, in a corner as far away as possible, played with a length of electrical cord.

"Which means we might as well talk," Toby continued. He held up the Zippo. "Admit it. This sets the rabbit loose. Which explodes the bombs. Dr. Trefethen—why? Haven't you done enough?"

Trefethen muttered, "Not nearly enough." Barrenly, he smiled. "At least the orb is iconified. You helped with that." He looked at Brian. "With my son's assistance."

Toby said, "We helped iconify? How?"

"You told the world about the orb. You were the first to do it. I'm sure Martha's annoyed—you stole her thunder."

Toby glanced at the Net-tuned monitor. Cliffcloud stalked through hills like an Armageddon dinosaur. No fireworks, at the moment. But Toby knew they'd come soon. "Martha has plenty of thunder," he said. "What are you talking about?"

Trefethen moved to stand up. Toby thrust the sprayer at his face. "Damn you!" Trefethen shouted. He blinked angrily at the nozzle; and settled back on the floor, temples throbbing.

"Tell us what you mean," Toby said. "If you don't—I'll spray you." Voice rising to a shout, he added, "Which I should do anyway, you're a fucking menace! So *say it!*"

Trefethen rolled his eyes. "The whole point of my plan," he said with quiet contempt, "is to install three unforgettable images in the consciousness of the human race. Afterimages, if you will. One is the orb. Another is the rabbit. The third is Antarctica—Antarctica, the planet's last pure spot, gone ragingly amok. Now if by this time you can't fill in the dotted lines, you're very stupid." He sent Brian an inquisitive stare.

Toby wondered to whom he was talking.

"But since you do seem stupid," the man continued, returning his attention to Toby, "I'll point out the obvious. My campaign has ground to a halt. I'd planned on at least seven separate broadcasts, and had hoped for more. As it is, all I've managed are the Barclay appearance, the Net message, and today's . . ." he gestured dismissively at the inoperable camera, "fiasco." He sighed with regret. "The result is, the icons aren't installed. The orb has been rammed down throats, that much is accomplished, and you did help do it—I was listening, you know. I was conscious during your blurtings to the camera."

Toby hadn't realized that. He nodded anyway.

"But because we knew the FATB was coming," Trefethen went on, "and because time therefore was short, the orb was installed clumsily. Oh, I patched together some Antarctica iconography—but very clumsily." He cast a frown at the monitor on which Cliffcloud ruled her realm. "It continues to be done clumsily. Much worse, though, the fertility icon hasn't been installed at all. And won't be. The fertility icon is a fizzle. Even if I manage to explode the bombs, it's a fizzle, the public knows nothing about it. It's just an idea. That doesn't make an icon." He stared at his son. "Brian, do you wish the fertility icon to meet that fate?"

Toby decided Trefethen wasn't explaining himself for his, Toby's, benefit. He was doing it to sway Brian.

Brian swallowed, and declared, "Grace and I feel like *we're* the damn fertility icon. And we don't love the fate you planned!"

"Can't you think beyond *yourself*?" Trefethen snarled. More quickly than Toby had thought possible, he leapt to his feet. A fist came at Toby's face. Toby ducked; the tall man's arms seized him, bear-hugging him, immobilizing his arms and the sprayer. Toby tried to break loose. Trefethen squeezed with shocking strength, forcing out his breath. Christ, Toby thought, he'll kill me . . .

Trefethen suddenly gasped and let go. Toby staggered away. He turned—Brian was tightening electrical cord around his father's neck. Trefethen's hands tried in vain to get under it. My God, Toby thought, Brian's garroting him—the man grunted, eyes popping at the ceiling.

"Don't kill him!" Toby yelled.

Brian threw him to the floor.

The camera crashed down with him. Trefethen lay there, panting reedily. The sound serrated sudden silence.

"Don't try that again!" Brian shouted.

Trefethen rolled over. He gasped, "So much for family solidarity!" His eyes, shining like blue marbles, glared at Toby.

Slotsky donned his gas mask and gave the command.

The robot arm tossed the grenade. The tracker's screen showed it landing where Slotsky wanted it—on top of the furnace. He listened to the hiss.

Harry jumped up and groped the furnace's top. He didn't know what the object was doing—if it would explode, for example—but whatever the hissing thing's purpose, he wanted it away, he wanted to throw it to the cellar's far end. In the extreme dimness he couldn't see it . . . his hand brushed metal. He grabbed it. Gas streamed between his fingers. No, he thought. He jerked his arm back to make the throw.

But somehow, Harry couldn't do that. Gagging, he turned, fell against the furnace, and slid down it. His ass hit the floor, then his shoulder crashed. The device rolled from his hand, hissing. Harry now couldn't move at all. He noticed Gula and Grace couldn't either. Like him, they had slumped to the floor.

But like him, they were conscious. That he could tell from something in their eyes, something radiating through the near-total darkness. Harry realized it was fear. Helpless, they stared at each other. Gula, Harry blurrily perceived, had a handkerchief to her nose.

Then they heard bangs. The machine on the stairs was moving again. But faster than before. Loudly, it lurched with rapid, thumping bumps to the bottom.

The chair landed upright, as Slotsky had hoped. He inventoried spillage. He still had two guns, the tracker, and other items of an elec-

tronic nature, but—no nerve kit. He pulled the flashlight from its slot
and probed. The kit was nowhere visible. Slotsky cursed the bad illumination. Ah well, he thought. I shan't toy with their nerves. At least,
not by means the kit would have provided.

He would toy with nerves by other means. "Hello, duckies!" he
called to the furnace. "Are you ready for me?" He rolled through the
darkness, flashlight picking out the most direct route. The chair
could have muddled through on its own. But Slotsky didn't want to
waste time. He wanted to impress upon Grace the desirability of
telling all, of revealing to him every last thing she knew. The next
few minutes, he was sure, would teach the girl the importance of
candor.

Indicators counted enemies in the
tranquil fake sky. Five FATB gunships, prop-powered, carrying
cruise missiles, heavy machine guns, smart bombs. Ten FATB helicopter troop transports, carrying heavily equipped soldiers. Four
squadrons of Air Force fighter-bombers, carrying ordnance too
massive and lethal to contemplate. Finally, a Boeing 777 AWACS
controller.

Overkill, Martha thought. Just what she wanted.

The aircraft had assumed attack formation moments before, and
were on the way. Martha calculated she had three minutes before missiles would be difficult to stop.

Time to call it quits. She turned to the hip-level plateau, extended
an arm across it, pointed a finger at the small round hole in the lawn,
and said, "Launch."

Gasses vented from the hole. Tiny flames flickered forth; Martha
watched the nosecone rise. An inch of fuselage appeared, then the
entire missile was out, lifting faster, faster from the plateau. A petite
missile, Martha thought fondly. A few inches tall here. Twenty-five
feet out there.

Dan and Selma watched it climb. The fiery tail seemed doomsday-bright. "Let's run!" Selma yelled, clutching Dan's arm.

They bolted from the tower and tore into the woods, hoping Igor wouldn't notice and fry them.

The tower's sensors did notice their flight. But the tower didn't care. Dan and Selma headed to a big rock outcrop. Under it they dove.

"What's she doing?" General Raffenelli growled.

Colonel Samaraweera didn't hazard a guess. As they stared at the command hover's situation screen, where the launch was charting, both men felt a slippery sensation of fear.

Earnest stared at the studio monitor. Is the missile, he wondered, Martha's secret weapon? That she so steadfastly had been assuring him would save their hides?

The phone rang. Earnest glanced at pinch-faced Toby. He crawled to the phone, picked it up, and said, "What is that thing?"

"Darling," Martha said, "the power will go out in forty-three seconds. Don't be alarmed. We're leaving soon. Very soon."

"Yes?" Earnest said. "How?"

"The escape plane is EMP-protected, dear. Nothing else is, for a hundred miles in any direction. They won't be able to follow us, you see. They won't know what hit them."

The demon jammed pincers under another fingernail and yanked it off. Harry, still paralyzed, didn't flinch. But Grace saw the pain blazing from his eyes.

It was such a hideous scene. The man had set his flash on a woodpile, to spotlight this torture. Worse, blue-green light radiated from his wheelchair and miscellaneous equipment, from their fancy electronic displays. The man's masked, hideously patched-over face, the shadows, and Harry—and poor Gula watching—they'd all become ghouls in hell.

Grace discovered she could move her fingers. Maybe, she thought with faint hope, she'd recover. And make a dive for the handgun. The rifle was useless, she still didn't know how to . . .

The world outside exploded.

And the lights went out.

━ ━ ━

It was as if someone had unzipped the sky, revealing the primordial Big Bang. Revealing that it was continuing, very brightly, to bang away.

Dan and Selma, from their refuge beneath the outcrop, saw everything turn white. God had flashed his strobe. All over, color drained.

Then came the noise. It was indescribable. Then came the wind. Like a hand running across velvet cloth, turning the nap, an invisible force ran across the forest, bending every tree in the same direction.

General Raffenelli couldn't tolerate the buzz of alarm and confusion. He shouted at the hover's jet-black cabin, "Shut up!"

Power was out. Instrumentation had cut, and the rotors too. With a series of undignified blasts that sounded much like flatulence, the command hovercraft settled to the ground.

The general stormed to the external bridge. He saw something astounding. The entire hover lineup, every flotation skirt flaccid, was settling to the pavement.

Somehow, the missile's explosion had turned them all off at precisely the same moment. Raffenelli suddenly realized why. Oh no, he thought. Oh God, please no. Not EMP.

From the cockpits of dozens of aircraft, pilots watched the ground rotate at them. In the 'copters' holds, troops clutched brain-dead weapons. There was nothing any of them could do. Except listen to the wind whistle across wings and rotors, and stare, terrified, at unresponsive controls, at instrument panels on which not a single light glowed.

Slotsky desperately worked his controls. How could this have happened? It wasn't just the chair that had gone dead. His guns, the tracker, every last electronic item—dead.

The implications sank in. His needle-nose pliers acquired new significance. Slotsky leaned forward, groping for Harry's head—where was the man? The pliers he was obliged to poke, quickly and with maximum force, through an eyeball into the brain . . .

Something moved. Breathing raspily. Getting up. Slotsky swore. He couldn't see a thing in this dark. Whichever one it was tottered around, slowly. And now was picking up something. What? He heard a woody rasp. It sounded like . . . perhaps a stick of firewood. Slotsky flailed with the pliers. He slashed empty air.

The breathing grew raspier. Surely not the old woman? How could she have recovered? Slotsky recalled the kerchief she'd held to her face; he flailed again. Again he met air. He heard the woman shuffle, feebly, behind him. He turned, pliers jabbing. Just air, just air—he couldn't reach. He couldn't turn far enough, the heavy cast wouldn't let him . . .

Something smashed his shoulder. And then, very violently, his head . . . Slotsky blacked out.

Despite the crashes they'd heard, despite the burning woods they could glimpse, Dan and Selma ventured from the outcrop's overhang to take a look. After all, other than the distant crackling of the fires, everything now was so incredibly—silent.

"What do you think happened?" Selma said.

"I don't . . ." Words died in Dan's throat as he looked down the valley. There seemed to have been any number of crashes. Flaming wreckage dotted the landscape.

Selma whispered, "They shot down the Air Force?"

Luminescent strips filled the basement corridor with sickly green. Martha, carrying her gun, walked to the studio door. She banged it. "Open up!" she called. "It's all over, kids. You couldn't be safer. I mean it—you're safe from me. You're safe from FATBOY. You're completely safe—Earnest, open the door."

Martha heard a scuffle inside, and shouts. She fired the gun into the ceiling. The scuffling stopped. A click came from the door, the sound of the deadbolt's slide. The door opened.

Earnest exited the pitch-black room, looking ruffled. "You're okay?" Martha asked.

He nodded. "The little shit tried to spray me. Again."

"Ah," Martha said. "The bad little shit. Shall I shoot him?"

"If he doesn't surrender the pager—yes."

"The pager," Martha said. She looked at Earnest pityingly.

He noticed this. "Tell me what you've done," he said.

"You saw the missile go up?"

Earnest nodded.

"At thirty thousand feet, it detonated a specialty nuke. One designed to flash an exceptionally powerful electromagnetic pulse. Not much else, however. It was clean."

"EMP . . ." Earnest said. "How extensive are the effects?"

"The radius is about a hundred miles. This is ground zero. Nothing electrical within a hundred miles of us is working. It's all dead. Dead, dead, dead. Except, possibly, whatever '80s-vintage military equipment might still be in service."

Earnest thought about it. "Impressive," he murmured.

"And except for our escape plane," Martha continued. "It's under a lead shield. Ready to go."

"So," Earnest said. "The pager?"

"Dead."

"You could have *told* me . . ." Earnest turned furiously to the studio. "Toby!" he shouted. "Come out and be shot!"

"Calm down," Martha said.

Earnest slammed a fist into a palm. "At *spraypoint*," he bellowed, "that *nonentity* kept me from using the *pager!* I could . . . "

"Earnest, we're alive," Martha said in no-nonsense tones. "We will go on. Which means you can use another pager. It's wonderful you weren't forced to use that one—we *haven't finished*." She jabbed a finger in his chest. "We haven't finished with the Net, my dear. The netcasts have only begun."

Earnest thought further. "How do you lift a slab of lead without power?"

"The hoist engine is under the shield. It's battery-powered." Martha couldn't contain herself; she smiled. "So, my precious. I meant everything I said about being prepared. About our escape."

Earnest muttered, "I'm somewhat shocked that you exploded a nuclear device over populated territory."

From the dark studio came an incredulous snort.

"The explosion was clean," Martha said briskly. "Furthermore, it cleared our coast. Shall we?"

"Brian!" Earnest called. "Let's go!"

From the studio's blackness came, "No, Father. I'm staying. And finding Grace."

"Will you?" Earnest shouted.

"Yes! I *will!*"

Trefethen's shoulders drooped. "All right," he muttered. "All right, stay. Martha, I'm collecting Helen."

Martha shook her head. "She isn't coming with us."

"I can't simply leave her here."

"Yes you can. And will."

"Martha, she's locked up. It's inhumane."

Again Martha shook her head. "The cells lock electronically," she remarked. "When the power cut, they opened. Helen is free now. Free to leave. But not with us."

"I'm bringing her. I'm sorry."

"But you have no choice. The plane, dear—is a two-seater."

Earnest understood. She'd planned it this way all along. From the very beginning.

Martha put a hand to his face. Caressing it, she said, "You have much to be happy for."

He was speechless. Shock had gutted him.

Martha drew closer, and kissed him. She said, "Earnest, we will continue our work . . . "

Down the hallway, a voice said, "No you won't." Helen walked through the dimness. Both hands clutched hypodermic needles.

"There you are," Martha murmured.

Earnest said, "Helen . . . we must talk."

"Must we?" Helen said softly. She came closer.

"Keep back," Martha said.

Helen rushed at her, arms upraised, needles glinting. She howled, "Deceitful, *thieving* . . . "

Martha shot her in the face.

Helen thudded to the floor. Mechanically, Earnest walked backward, hands on his eyes. He couldn't see it. He couldn't.

Brian sped from the studio. He saw the body, the blood. "*Mother!*" he wailed ear-shatteringly. Sobbing, he threw himself on her.

63

The disaster's dimensions seeped through General Raffenelli's mind. Why did the troops not possess

even one nonelectronic weapon? Why did everything under his command depend so completely on electrical connections? Nothing
worked. Guns, the rest of the ordnance, the hovers, the helicopters,
the planes, the communications systems, everything—all dead as a
doornail, which meant . . . it was unbearable.

I'm reduced, the general thought, to the Stone Age. Hands and feet,
that's what we've got. Nothing else—hands and feet. And whatever
crude weapons we can fashion. Sticks, for example. And stones.
Sticks and stones.

It seemed so profound. As Harry regained use of his body, he realized
the silence came from something beyond the fact that an outrageously
loud explosion had split apart the aboveground world; this wasn't just
an aftermath quiet. For example, the freezers had stopped rattling.
The water heater had stopped humming. And the wheelchair wasn't
making so much as a click.

Gula, still holding the handkerchief to her face, crawled upstairs.
Soon she returned, preceded by the flicker of a kerosene lamp. Grace
sat up; the lamp's shadow-throwing advance aided her revival. The
man in the wheelchair moaned. Harry got on his feet. He checked the
chair and the weapons. All of it, out. A theory took form in his mind.
The very idea shook him. But that wasn't the only reason he felt shaky.
"Gula," he said. "If you hadn't put the kerchief over your face, and
hadn't had the wherewithal to save me, this man here . . . I don't
know. I think I'd be dead."

"The moment I smelled gas," Gula said. "I knew it was funny.
Harry—what's happened? Nothing's working upstairs. Nothing."

"Mind if I take that?" Harry said. Gula gave him the lamp. She and
Grace watched him cross to the far side of the cellar.

Harry put his face to the crack in the door to the garden. Through it
he saw lights. He heard the motor running. Hairs rose all over his
body.

Luminescent strips gave it the same green gloom. But unlike the basement hallway complex, the tunnel stretched in a single straight line.
Martha led purposefully. Earnest followed, his gait less certain.

"We'll rest a few days," Martha said. "The place is quite peaceful.
It's way north. Nobody around." She glanced over her shoulder.

Instead of the attentiveness she'd hoped for, she saw brooding vacancy in Earnest's face. "But then," she continued, eyes again fixed on the door at the tunnel's far end, "we'll resume our work. Until we've finished, dear. We've only just begun."

"Yes," Earnest said wearily. "Yes, I'm sure that's true."

They kept walking up the road. The sky was fading. Downvalley, in the ridge's deepening shadow, fires burned brighter. Selma said, "I wonder why nobody's come. No rescue people. No planes . . . it's like this place is forgotten. The forgotten valley."

Dan said, "Maybe because the power is out? Maybe it's out all over." He looked at the dark plateau looming over them. "There's no lights anywhere."

"Strange," Selma said.

"Yeah. It is."

In the deserted zombie quarters, they shed pajamas and jeans, and helped themselves to ill-fitting but fresh clothes. Toby tried to think of things to say. Nothing came to mind.

They took the stairs to the courtyard. Toby expected something on a grand scale. But he wasn't prepared for the opulence.

"Wow," he said, taking in the banks of French doors, the great rooms behind them, the valley vistas coming through exterior French doors . . . vistas spotted with fire.

"Martha," Brian murmured. "She really did it."

"The orb has struck," Toby said.

Brian grunted. "You iconified it," he remarked.

"I did not."

"Think of the Net audience. Sooner or later, it'll go on TV too, you know. All those people—seeing you finger the orb."

Behind them, a ragged voice yelled, "Hello!"

They almost jumped out of their skins. Whirling, they saw a man sitting on the courtyard's central mosaic. He waved. A thick bandage enveloped his hand.

"One of Mother's zombies," Brian said.

The man shouted, "Have you seen Dr. Scarf?"

Brian and Toby looked at each other. They indeed had seen her. But what to tell this guy?

Brian pointed to the stairwell whence they'd come. Then he headed for one of the French doors. Toby followed.

Harry pushed the wheelchair through the cellar, and partway up the ramp to the garden doors. The contraption was heavy. Likewise its occupant. Wheeling them made Harry grunt.

He reached the doors, turned, and said to Grace and Gula, "Stand back. I don't know how this will work out." He rapped Slotsky on the goose egg Gula had inflicted. "Ready, my man?"

Slotsky sputtered incomprehensibly. He hadn't adjusted, it seemed, to this turn of events. Harry walked around him and flung open both doors.

The ambulance loomed outside, engine running, lights bright in the falling dusk. Its roof hatch popped open. The gun rose, aiming at Harry.

Harry resumed his position behind the chair. Slowly he pushed it up the ramp.

The gun unleashed a volley into the ramp's top edge, then pulverized the lawn it already had savaged.

Harry rapped the goose egg again. "You'll be the first to get it," he informed Slotsky.

Slotsky produced more sputters. Harry pushed him further up the ramp; the gun fired another volley. His mangled fingers burning, Harry wondered if this was worth it. He said to his prisoner, "Think hard. Think very hard, about turning off that gun."

Brian and Toby wandered through the dim great hall. Its stillness, the quietude of the lawn outside, the hillside fires flickering distantly—how very ominous, Toby thought.

He followed Brian through a French door. In the lawn a hundred yards away, a big hole emitted bright light.

Brian stared at it. He sat on the grass, with the expectancy of one who will witness. Toby settled down beside him.

The road had steepened considerably. Dan and Selma kept walking up it. Selma said through uneven breath, "We'll never find the trail Harry mentioned."

"Ever rock-climbed?" Dan said.

"No."

"If we don't find it, you will. We'll have to climb over the ridge."

The plateau, a dark mass above them, suddenly roared. They flinched, sure it would get them after all.

On a tail of fire, something ejected from the plateau's top. Like a fighter catapulting from an aircraft carrier, it hurtled into the valley's bowl of air, and dipped. Then it pulled up, performed an incredibly tight banking turn, and roared over the west ridge.

Somebody's quick getaway, Dan thought.

Harry heard it. Then he saw it. A rocket-like aircraft, coming low from the east. He was about to abandon the wheelchair and retreat to the cellar when, from the corner of his eye, he saw the ambulance gun swerve skyward.

It started firing.

The plane zoomed overhead, really low, with a force that shook ground, house, and trees alike. The ambulance stopped firing. The plane's roar didn't stop.

Huh, Harry thought. The gun missed. Who, he wondered, is rocketing out of here?

In the plane, Earnest's lap filled with arterial blood. One of his arms was gone. And Martha's head was gone.

We're gone, he thought. Did he regret it? He didn't know.

But he was conscious, as the great spaces outside the plane smeared into silver murk, of an object in the breast pocket of his shirt. An object very close to his fading heart.

It was a badge. His children had made it. Years ago.

The plane ignited. The fireball cartwheeled a long arc over runnels of ridge and hill; it made a comet-like blaze above the valley through which the Piscatawny meandered.

Amid the river's coolly flowing waters, much to the shock of fish, fowl, and deer, it came to an explosive halt.

Grace lay down on the cellar floor. In beams and in the ground, the shock wave vibrated. Not knowing how she knew it, she knew it; she knew whose end the vibrations signaled. The floor's earthy tang acquired the scent of something very sad.

Raffenelli wasn't accustomed to addressing a crowd without electronic amplification of his voice. The same inexperience afflicted his officers. But somehow they had assembled the troops in a semi-orderly fashion. Lined up on the road, well ahead of the raging forest fire, regiments, of a kind, were ready to move.

"Men!" he hollered down the incline, holding high the stave Samaraweera had fashioned from a branch. "Present arms!"

Into smoky air, a forest of wooden staves bristled.

The general bellowed, "Forward!"

He turned on his heel and headed up the road, swinging the stave in time to his marching feet. To his rear, not quite synchronized with his beat, he heard the stamp of hundreds of boots. It's like leading a barbarian legion, he thought. A poor one. Too poor for horses. Or even swords.

Harry said loudly, "Let's try it again!"

Up the cellar ramp he pushed the wheelchair. The ambulance's roof hatch popped open. The gun rose, and aimed.

Slotsky sat straighter. He seemed a good deal more alert now. Harry suspected the plane's explosion had something to do with that. Harry pushed the man closer, closer to the gun. It shot a line in the ground six inches from Slotsky's advancing cast. Shattering earth plastered him.

Slotsky sat straighter still, and snapped, "Fire system off!"

The gun sank. The hatch slammed shut.

"Thank you," Harry said. He went to the cab door, opened it, got in, and studied the vehicle's weapon-control panel.

"Mr. President," Mary McMurtry said into her phone, "it's still a black hole. We have no data whatever. We simply don't have any idea . . . "

"Why haven't you sent reconnaissance?"

"Command and control for a very large area isn't functional. If you'll permit the expression, it's fried. We're trying, believe me. Are you aware New York City is down?"

"It's down?"

"Power cascades, sir. Feedback burn-outs. A big chunk of the seaboard, extending from Massachusetts to New Jersey, is completely blacked out. And I'm afraid that the—ah—riot situation is bad now. Very bad. New York is out of control. There seems to be quite a situation at the, er . . . "

"Talk to me!"

"At the docks, sir."

Grace helped Harry push the chair to the head of the rock garden. Gula followed. Slotsky, gazing at the hill's precipitous slope, understood his fate. "I can make all three of you," he said, the voice seeming to come as much from the filthy patchwork as from the mouth, "very rich."

Harry turned the chair around, to permit a final eye-to-eye. Slotsky saw the faces of his captors, and knew he had no hope. The old woman said, "Well, ducky. Any last words?"

"A request," Slotsky said.

"Hah!" the elderly creature exclaimed. "What?"

"Do it with your feet," Slotsky said.

They glanced at each other. Puzzled, they shrugged. But then they each hoisted a foot and shoved, sending him on his way.

Slotsky's straps held firm as the chair tumbled, side-over-side, to the field at the bottom.

They stood silently a moment, staring at the distant metal heap. Feeling a little guilty, Grace thought. Gula said, "Let's get bandages on those fingers, Harry."

"The ambulance has supplies," he said.

Its lights glowed in the gathering gloom. "I don't understand it," Gula remarked. "Everything else is out. All the flashlights in the house. I even checked a battery radio I know was working—it's gone too. So why is that thing running?"

"It's a doomsday ambulance," Harry said. "The huge explosion? I think it was a nuke that wiped out everything electrical."

Gula sniffed. "When will power come back?" she asked.

"It won't. The wires are fried. Fried for good. They'll have to rewire, Gula. But that ambulance there . . . it's designed to survive EMP. An '80s kind of thing. A Reagan leftover, you could say."

"Gosh," Grace said admiringly. "A real antique."

Harry said, "After we fix my fingers—what say we go for a drive?"

They finally reached the top. The house, dark and huge, resembled a deserted, possibly haunted, corporate headquarters. Acres of lawn surrounded it. Several hundred feet from them in the lawn's middle, a large cavity glowed brightly. It was the only artificial illumination anywhere in sight.

"Like the old *X-Files*," Dan said. "Can't you hear the theme music? Those eerie strains of mystery, regret, and longing?"

"Stop it," Selma said, shivering.

"Well," Dan said. "Should we approach—the light?"

"I dunno," Selma replied. "Why not?" she then said. "We've approached everything else. Haven't we?"

"We have," Dan said.

"Then let us," Selma quavered, "approach the *light*."

"People," Brian said.

He and Toby hadn't moved. They still sat in the grass, at the spot from which they'd witnessed the rocket plane eject from its underground nest. The rocket plane which, they inferred from the boom that had echoed over the ridge, no longer was flying.

To Toby, the bright hole suggested a high-tech grave. Maybe the orb's grave. He looked where Brian was pointing. Two figures approached the launch pit's penumbra of light. One of them had a big head of hair. The other one . . . "Huh," Toby said.

He jumped to his feet and ran at them, yelling, "Hey! Hey! Hey!"

Brian stood. He watched the strangers get a load of Toby coming at them, shouting, waving his arms. Then they shouted too, and ran toward him. The three converged in a screaming hug.

Brian sat back down. The valley's blaze backlit the excitement. Looks like *Lord of the Flies*, he thought. The distant amphitheater of fire—against it, their joy seemed pagan.

━━● ● ●━━

Saplings and scrub clogged the old fire trail. The ambulance pushed through without any trouble. This thing, Harry thought, could roll through rain forest. Grace sat in the middle. Gula had the end spot. They weren't conversing a lot. Harry reckoned they all felt funny about pushing Slotsky down the hill. He did, he knew. Especially after having seen, when they'd passed the wheelchair on their way to the woods, a weakly flapping arm.

The fence came into view. Harry got out and inspected sensor components. They looked dead all right. He got back in and asked Grace and Gula to step out for a moment. When they'd done that, he revved the engine, and rammed the fence.

The ambulance tore through. Harry got out again to inspect damage. Dents in the chrome, solid chrome, bumper. That was it.

Toby made introductions.

"Hi," Brian said, face blank.

"Hi," Selma said.

"Hey," Dan said. They all shook hands.

Selma said, "Why do I feel like I already know you?"

Brian didn't smile. "She's okay?" he asked.

"We hope," Dan said. Nervously he added, "Let's find out."

"How?" Brian demanded.

"Harry told me about a trail," Dan replied. "It goes over the ridge." Chummily, he slapped Brian on the shoulder. "Have to say. Knowing Grace is—it's been a trip."

"Really?" Brian said.

"We went through a lot the last few days."

"Like what?" Brian asked suspiciously.

Selma said, "Numerous near-death experiences. And we had talks. Lots of talks, last night. She told us about you. She was—um, really worried. That's obvious I guess."

Toby said, "Brian wants to know if . . . "

Brian gave Toby an incredulous stare. Screwing up his face, he yelled, "*Shut up!*"

Edgy silence dropped. Dan shot a look at Toby. Almost telepathically, they shared a thought.

Selma said, "We should go find her. Gula and Harry too."

"Who are they?" Toby asked.

"Our saviors," Selma said. "We've been staying at Gula's house.

Come on. We should go." She looked at the valley's fires, and shuddered. "Before they try to bomb again."

"Grace is there?" Brian asked.

Selma nodded.

Brian said, "I saw a trail. From the roof." He moved across the lawn. "It's this way." He broke into a loping run.

The others trotted after him.

First contact was spooky.

They'd climbed a well-tended maintenance trail to the top of the ridge. There, beyond a laser emplacement, its well-tendedness ended. However, the trail had preceded Martha's reign. Choked but followable, it went down the ridge's other side.

Along it they were hiking, through darker and darker dusk, when they saw headlights flickering toward them. They plunged into the woods and hid.

As a hefty vehicle rolled by, Dan and Selma were thankful they'd taken cover. What they'd heard from Harry didn't make them anxious to encounter an ambulance. Instrumentation filled the cab with sinister luminescence. To Selma it looked like a death machine.

Then she glimpsed a familiar face behind the wheel. Selma crashed from the woods onto the trail.

In Kotzler's parking lot, torchlight lit a restive crowd. Men on horseback clip-clopped around the edges. A stout woman was raving about holy water from the back of a pickup. Some people listened. Most whispered worriedly to each other.

The power blackout, and the lack of word of any kind from the outside world, had bred virulent rumors in Cheswick Village. People were talking about Apocalypse at the Cliffcloud estate. What really had happened? No one knew. But that hadn't stopped speculation. Passed from one excitable mouth to the next, it quickly took on the patina of swearable fact.

Aliens had landed. They'd invaded from secret bases in Antarctica, and the government was covering it up. Numerous saucers had crashed. One had flamed like a comet into the river.

Others told different stories. The saucers hadn't crashed; hovercrafts sighted on the Piscatawny had been abducted. Glowing beams had sucked them to the sky, where medical experiments were in progress. The same fate had befallen outlying homes. Whole farms had been sucked up, barns and trees and all. The aliens wanted to preserve them for future study; and the worst thing was, they had to do it fast, because mile-high tidal waves soon would come rushing. Just like Trefethen said.

To those who could cover distance in a practical manner—which was to say, those with access to a horse—the situation boiled down to one difficult issue. Did they dare reconnoiter the scene of the abomination, to bring back word of how bad it was? Or did they hightail it out of Cheswick in hopes of escaping the terrible destiny that surely was in store for the village itself?

However the equestrians decided, one thing was obvious. They would ride armed, heavily armed. Monsters were stalking the land.

The ambulance passed Slotsky once again—he writhed as they went by—and headed up the hill to the house.

Harry continued to drive. Selma, sitting mutely beside him, watched satellite-delivered TV news on the dashboard monitor. The others occupied the rear, where another monitor played.

The twins, entwined in a corner, discussed recent history with feverish whispers that Toby, Dan, and Gula couldn't understand. It was as if they had a secret language. Toby and Dan, in a more subdued fashion, also traded stories. Gula was content to keep her thoughts to herself. What the monitor had to say didn't cheer her. Tremendous power cascades had blacked out much of the East Coast, it seemed. The rest of the world knew very little about what was going in Cheswick, Connecticut, and far beyond.

At the house, Gula lit candles. She and Harry then had a conference, following which they put the others to work collecting things they would need. Blankets, clothing, and food were the priority items. So was liquor. If Gula was obliged to be a refugee she was damned if she'd do it sober.

Harry had convinced them all that they had to get away from here as fast as possible.

But once out on the road, they began to learn about panic. All the houses were dark; not a lightbulb burned. That they'd expected. What they didn't understand was why everybody seemed to be hiding. Or why they were so hostile. The ambulance hadn't traveled a mile when somebody started shooting.

Harry kept going. Bullets couldn't penetrate the walls, luckily. Probably not even the glass, he guessed. Something glowed up ahead. They rounded a curve and saw it—a bonfire on the road, composed of tires. "Jesus," Selma said. She'd remained Harry's cab companion.

A volley of bullets hit the windshield. The glass cracked. Harry backed up, did a U-turn, and sped in the other direction, wondering why they'd flipped out. He knew the folks who lived back there. They were decent people. What the hell had gone wrong?

Soon he discovered the entire area was crazed: bonfires on the roads, especially at intersections; shadowy horsemen coming from woods, guns blazing; surging mini-mobs running from homes, pounding the ambulance with fists.

Harry developed an explanation. Naturally the ambulance would inspire fear. It was the only working motor technology for who knew how many miles? The fact it worked was unearthly. People had to be wondering why it and nothing else was able to move.

In time, the dashboard monitor provided another explanation. Trefethen's broadcast and netcast, according to gradually more detailed reports, had unhinged people everywhere. Unrest raged all over the world. In most places, it was "extremely serious." More to the point, reports were trickling in that things had become especially bad on the blacked-out East Coast of the United States.

"Rabid coyotes," Harry said to Selma.

He headed for the most unpopulated region he could think of. Unfortunately, it took them back toward Gula's. That by itself wasn't bad. In fact it was a comfort. The trouble was, it also took them back near Cliffcloud's.

"Where are we?" Gula asked as Dan helped her down from the rear doors. The woods around them, lit by the nearly full moon, seemed primeval. "Ah," Gula then said. "I know. Harry—you drove around in circles."

"Did you get dizzy?" he asked solemnly. They exchanged pensive stares. He took Gula aside. In a low tone he asked her, "You have any idea what the nuts out there would do to the twins? If they discovered who they are?"

Gula turned to her new friends, the most lynchable people in the world now that the masterminds were dead. She said, "Why don't we have a moon picnic?"

They laid out blankets in the clearing where Harry had delivered them, deep in a grove of towering pines. Moonlight floured the bark on the trunks, the soft beds of needles on the ground, the geometries of the blankets' Navajo designs. Gula mixed drinks. "Just bourbon and water, I'm afraid. Didn't think to bring anything else."

Now supplied with Gutzyme by Brian, Grace accepted a drink. They all accepted drinks. Selma unpacked snacks and paper plates. Nothing fancy, by Gula's standards. Sliced ham, pickles, the last remaining bread, and mustard. Gula didn't do the newspaper food-catching routine. Maybe because she didn't have any newspaper.

But that's not it, Dan thought. He wondered if others were sharing his thoughts. The blankets, he noticed, were arranged in pairs. His and Toby's were side-by-side. The twins shared overlapping ones. Selma's and Harry's blankets weren't far apart. Gula's, occupying a somewhat solitary position, headed the layout.

Toby raised his glass. "To the future!" he proclaimed.

The others looked at him guardedly. "The future?" Selma said.

Nobody seemed eager to pursue the subject. Dan raised his glass and said, "I, for one, propose a moment of silence. Out of respect for . . ." He closed his eyes. "All those beaches."

"What's come over you, Toby?" Selma asked after a few moments had passed.

"Things will be okay," he replied. "In the long run," he added as faces turned stony. "In a few hundred years, maybe."

"Maybe," Selma said. "We won't be around to find out."

They munched and drank in silence. High overhead, a jet plane thundered. "That's military," Brian said. "By tomorrow, we'll be hearing lots of those." He shivered. "When they find us, they'll . . . "

"They'll do what?" Gula said.

"Put it this way," Grace said quietly. "Even if they don't kill us, life will be over."

"Over?" Selma said. "Really over?"

Grace didn't reply. In the sky, another plane thundered.

"She means," Brian said, "that tonight is it. It's what we have."

Probably right, Gula thought. The idea dismayed her. It made her impatient too. "I have an idea," she murmured. "Let's tell each other about the most . . ." She grimaced at the moon. "The most exciting time we ever had. It doesn't have to be glamorous. Just the most exciting time. Whatever it was."

"Sounds good," Dan said. "Who goes first?"

"Me," Gula said, passing the bottle. When it had made the circle, and they'd settled back, she launched in.

"I was young, barely past twenty, from a tiny town on the coast of Southern California. I was pretty. Men liked to look at me, and they did. I'd just moved to Manhattan—to make my life happen without my mother getting involved in whatever it would be, whatever my life would be, in that great big booming city. I was an artist. I'd gone to school for it, at Berkeley, that was rare then for a woman, you know. So I thought I was prepared for this big move—and let me tell you it was a very big move, across the whole damn country that my grand-mother, I'll mention, crossed in a covered wagon. Geography, you see, was different then. Now there's no geography, just fax machines. But never mind."

She told of the oddballs she met in Greenwich Village, and how crazy and foolish and brilliant they were, and how dazzled she was, and scared. But for some reason they liked her, and soon she was in the thick of it, and met the man who would become her first husband. He was the art director of a legendary magazine; a captivating and theatrical man, who enjoyed grand moments.

On their honeymoon at Lake George in upstate New York, a storm was brewing when he decided they should go canoeing. Gula was so in love, it seemed a great idea. They paddled away from the clubhouse in a sumptuous birchbark, and in due course exchanged kisses far out on the water. The storm clouds drew nearer. They glimpsed distant lightning bolts. But instead of paddling back, a course of action Gula advised, her husband wanted to linger on the lake and savor the majestic approach of the elements.

The storm swept in. Suddenly, bolts crashed not far away. The gaps between them and their thunder became shorter and shorter. Gula, terrified, watched her newlywed stand up in the canoe, which wob-bled. He raised his arms—raised them high to the heavens! She shrank back—watching the idiot commune with nature!

But she realized, beholding him act like such an fool, that she didn't care. Because she loved him. It was enough, watching the lightning smash into the lake, to know that she truly loved him.

Later, of course, she scolded him . . .

As she told the story, Gula watched the three couples—three couples they slowly were becoming, even if only one sat together—exchange subtle glances of curiosity, wonderment, and lust. Not surprising, Gula thought. In fact she'd expected it. What could be more natural if tonight was all they had?

Dan related the next account of maximum excitement. The story made his listeners blush. Most especially, Gula noted, Brian.

"It happened when I first set eyes on you," Harry said. "I was leaning against the piano. You were walking over the red floor, over the carpets, in these ridiculous purple boots."

"I hated the sound they made," Selma said. "Clomp, clomp."

"It was beautiful," Harry said. "I couldn't believe my eyes." He kissed her. The blanket around her shoulders slipped off.

Selma hoped the others couldn't see them. She didn't think they could, she and Harry had walked away through the trees to a fairly dark place. Then she realized she didn't care.

They kissed. They took their shirts off, and kissed some more, shyly touching each other. They were very shy about this, both of them, for different reasons. The moon made their skin glow. "You're sure it's okay?" Dan said.

"Yeah," Brian said. "We talked about it."

"You're lovers."

"Uh-huh. We love each other. But."

"But?"

"Life is short," Brian said. He watched Dan pull something from his jeans pocket. "What?"

"Supplies." Their blankets they'd spread out deep in the grove. Dan tossed the little box on one. "Always carry them," Dan said. "Never leave home without 'em."

"Supplies?"

"Don't you know," Dan asked, "about safe sex?"

Brian thought about it. "Why bother?" he said.

"Why not?" Dan replied. He watched the boy hop one-legged out of his jeans. Dan had wanted to go for a walk through the moonlight, and take it slow. But Brian didn't look like he could wait. He didn't look like that at all.

"We continue our coverage of events on the eastern seaboard. From Los Angeles, I'm Jorge Cossette."

A man with wiry black hair, Cossette gazed somberly from the monitor at Toby and Grace. The ambulance's video supplies had proved ample enough to run a hookup to the campfire they'd made. Toby poured bourbon for both of them. He wondered if Grace's silence had anything to do with the walk Brian was taking with Dan. Gula had retired to the ambulance; Toby wished she'd stayed a while longer. To provide some spark to this nonconversation.

"The good news," Cossette continued, "is that no Antarctic explosions have occurred following the apparent destruction of Earnest Trefethen. The bad news, however, remains as earlier reported—a massive power failure has blacked out much of the East Coast, providing cover for what preliminary accounts suggest is the worst civil unrest in this country's history.

"From New Jersey to Massachusetts, authorities are trying to cope with near-total darkness as hysterical mobs inflict unguessable damage on their locales, their neighbors, and themselves. We have reports of violent attacks on transportation facilities, particularly ones involving airplanes and ships. According to eyewitnesses broadcasting from scattered civil defense bunkers in the New York City area, the situation there has worsened in the last half hour. These sources tell us that Kennedy, LaGuardia, and Newark airports resemble, on a grand scale, the terrifying evacuation of American personnel from that embassy rooftop in Saigon, twenty-seven years ago. 'Hoodlums are swarming the runways,' one witness said, 'shooting at planes and passengers, preventing departures.'

"Before we bring you live reports of the New York situation, we once again will air the extraordinary hijacking of Trefethen's netcast—which authorities hope has provided a way to neutralize the remaining bombs in Antarctica. A young man named Toby Swett, apparently Trefethen's prisoner, somehow managed to free himself, render Trefethen unconscious, and tell the world how to stop the doomsday countdown we so helplessly have been watching.

"As already mentioned, the rest of the netcast isn't available for TV broadcast, due to national security considerations.

"Here, then, is Toby Swett . . . "

Toby said, "Sounds like they won't show your father's message. Or Martha's Air Force shootdown."

"'National security,'" Grace said with a trace of sarcasm. "But Father and Martha are on the Net . . . God. Look at this . . . "

The screen displayed her father in a freezeframe, sitting still in a chair. The image unfroze. Trefethen whirled to face someone approaching from his rear. Toby lunged into the frame, sprayer extended, eyes scarily offcolor. Trefethen recoiled as the sprayer neared him. His face rigidified; he slid out of view.

Toby took the chair. As if addressing himself and Grace by the campfire, he said, "I will explain how Trefethen explodes his bombs . . . "

Grace and he listened to the orb explication.

"Your father was smart," Toby said. "To make the orb a signal that tells the bombs they're connected to the datasphere. It means the government can't yank Mantis ads without risking explosions. Which means it can't make the orb disappear. The orb will linger for a while."

"It'll linger forever," Grace murmured. She regarded him thoughtfully. And said, "You did it. You iconified the orb."

Toby sipped bourbon. "You and Brian make it sound like a sacred ceremony," he said. "Like a coronation."

The corners of Grace's mouth turned up. "Well it is like that," she said. "The coronation of a new god . . . an evil god, that Antarctica will battle, and vanquish. Anyway, at least tonight, you're the one telling people about the orb. Don't you see why that's important? It's helping the afterimage."

Toby watched the fire. "The afterimage is missing the rabbit," he remarked. "So what do you call it? The demi-afterimage?"

Grace said nothing.

Toby found it difficult to look at her. Her skin, her eyes, her hair, the perfect junctures of her body—everything about the girl made his mouth go dry. She made his brain go dry. He muttered, "All I did was explain how it works."

Grace tossed a pine cone on the fire. Embers sparked. The cone popped. "So here we are," she said. "Stuck with each other."

"Does that piss you off?" he said.

"It's a novel experience," she said. "But then, everything lately is . . . tell me. What'd he do?"

"Brian?"

She nodded.

"Practically raped me," Toby replied.

"You're kidding," she said.

"He was very freaked. Obsessed with you, and with the fact Dan rescued you—he had ideas about Dan. Oddly enough, though . . . "

Grace said flatly, "I've known about this for years. He looks at boys. But always denied it."

"Now he's got one."

Grace said, "Me too."

Toby sat up. Grace, staring at the monitor, was blushing.

He leaned over, and kissed her ear. She shuddered. But she reached for him and they fell on the blanket, clutching, kissing clumsily. Toby's mind, his entire body, roiled with confusion . . . he couldn't tell if she liked this. He disengaged, stood, and blurted, "Want to go for a walk?"

She stared at him. Then she grinned the grin. The same one her brother had grinned in the basement cell's bathroom. Toby felt faint.

"Okay," she said, standing up. She brushed pine needles from the dress, and said casually, "I'd like to hear about what you did to Mother and Father."

They strolled away from the fire. Toby took her hand. "Let's talk about something else," he said. "About your and Brian's obsession with the afterimage."

"What about it?"

"It's like you want it to become real. To succeed."

"I do."

"Why?"

"Because Father was right, of course. He was right about everything. Overpopulation and the misuse of technology are making civilization a self-destruct machine."

"You think the afterimage will stop that?"

"By the time Antarctica gets done with us? Sure."

"Then why did you want to sabotage your father?"

"I didn't. Brian did. I just wanted . . . to have a life."

"A life," Toby said.

"Uh-huh. You have any idea what it's like being raised by boomers from hell? Parents who are always, always right? We got really, really sick of it. But we . . . didn't quite know what to do."

"What to do," Toby said. "Yeah, that's it. What to do . . . "

They walked on through the trees.

━ ━ ━

Gula lay in the ambulance, blankets wrapped tightly to ward off the chill. As the eldest she rated these luxury quarters. Little lamps provided light. What seemed to be parts of a bed had been lying around. Harry had assembled them into a bunk. It was comfortable enough.

But Gula couldn't sleep. She studied a strange device that dangled from a swingable boom. Something like a diver's mask was appended to it.

She got up and inspected the thing. Buttons surrounded it. Grimacing, Gula pressed one. The mask's inside glowed green. She peered. I'll be damned, she thought.

The grove's moonlit beauty put a catch in her throat. It came through so vividly, in such a subtle palette.

Gula discovered the mask could fly her around out there. The device almost did this on its own. It had its own curiosity, an ability to zip through trees like a magical sprite.

She glimpsed something. So did the device. It magnified a scene in progress. This contraption, Gula thought indignantly—a mechanical peeping Tom!

Scandalized, she pressed buttons, and flew wonderfully through the grove, through silvered half-tones and shadows. Between the trunks of great towering pines . . .

Eventually she tired. She lay down, folded hands on her chest, and composed herself for sleep, a smile warming her face. I've had a good life, she thought. She wished the same for her friends in the grove.

Who could say? A miracle might happen.

PART 5

TUESDAY

67

The New York Times, national on-line edition:

FATB:
TREFETHEN IS DEAD
BOMBS DON'T EXPLODE,
BUT CITIES WORLDWIDE BURN
POWERLESS NEW YORK
THUNDERS WITH
VIOLENT UNREST
NETCAST HIJACKED; ROLE OF MANTIS
"ORB" REVEALED

The Boston Globe:
> not published due to blackout.

The Daily News:
> not published due to blackout.

The Lure of the Litchfield Hills:
> not published due to blackout.

Toby dreamed they were canoeing to Magazine Beach.

It was another beautiful day. The canals, calmly crisscrossing the neighborhood, reflected the sky's dense blue.

He and Grace led. Harry and Selma paddled behind them, Dan and Brian took up the rear. Their sumptuous birchbarks glided along. No noise marred the tranquility, not even a breeze ruffled the water, which was very clear. You could see the street's lane divider, twenty feet under, and the tops of parked cars. Toby wondered if they worked. Like submarines?

They reached Number 94. The building's third floor poked stalwartly from the surface. At its rear, the porch sat in the water like a marina's dock. Toby drew up alongside. He and Grace clambered onto the tarpaper. She tied the canoe to the rail, then swung it perpendicular so the others could come aboard.

In the kitchen, Toby found great food set out on the table. The place was immaculate—gondoliering housekeepers must have visited, he supposed. As he looked it over, feeling very hungry, Gula walked in. So that's why, Toby thought. She's the one who'd made lunch.

"Toby!" Dan called from the porch. Dan sounded worried. Toby went out and followed the point of his arm.

A speedboat, a speck in the distance, was roaring down Magazine. The thing was loud. It came closer and got louder. Christ, Toby thought. The man at the wheel blared something from a megaphone. Why was he so excited?

Toby recognized the squat form. The filthy bandage. Over the boat's intolerable noise, Slotsky megaphoned, "Wake up! Wake up!"

The wrong metaphor, Toby thought. I'm enchanted now. Why should I wake up?

"Wake up!" Slotsky shouted. "WAKE UP!"

Toby woke with a start. In pale dawn light, a soldier stood over him, yelling, "Wake up!"

Grace trembled next to him, clutching his arm. More soldiers walked through the grove. A helicopter hovered just above the trees, thundering the dream's speedboat noise.

"Couple fags," somebody grunted. Toby saw Dan and Brian getting hustled away. They stumbled along naked, blankets wrapped awkwardly. Toby realized he and Grace weren't wearing anything either. Then he saw Selma and Harry staggering half-dressed through the grove, guns in their backs.

"Wake up and get up," the soldier said. He jabbed Toby with his rifle. "Party's over."

Grace snarled, "Eat shit and die!"

The soldier put the muzzle to her head.

"Come on," Toby whispered.

The soldier marched them to the ambulance. Dan, Brian, Selma, and Harry sat on the ground, blanket-draped. An officer jumped from the ambulance's open rear doors. He started talking with soldiers standing guard. Stupefied, Toby and the others listened.

Gula was dead. She'd passed away during the night. "A smile on her face," the officer remarked. "Peaceful."

They couldn't take this. One by one, they started to cry.

The truck drove up the Cliffcloud road. Through cracks in the canvas enclosure came the stench of smoke and fuel. They glimpsed incinerated forest, hovercrafts bulldozed off the pavement. Metal fragments caught in trees. Everywhere, crews working.

They drove straight through the great hall into the courtyard. The French doors were smashed, furniture lay shoved helter-skelter. A lot of trucks had driven in, it seemed. The truck stopped. Soldiers hustled them out.

A sleek helicopter stood on the Vesuvius mosaic. Toby noticed a television crew to one side. Perky Smith, the investigative journalist, held a microphone under the immediately recognizable hairdo of Mary McMurtry. General Theodore Raffenelli stood by with a youngish, slickly dressed man.

Soldiers led them into the house, through a room which harbored a charred grand piano. In a nearby alcove a uniformed woman issued drab-colored clothes. Prison garb, it seemed. Shoving the stuff at them, eyeing their bare skin, she said, "You had your fun."

They dressed. Led back to the courtyard, they were told to sit by the mosaic. Off to one side, diesel-powered generators were roaring. Men in spacesuits came through doors. Grace whispered to Toby, "Radiation suits. They're dealing with the reactor."

"No talking," a guard said.

The TV crew had gone somewhere. Through French doors and gaps where French doors used to be, Toby watched a crew of carpenters constructing a platform on the lawn. A big one, like a reviewing stand. Giant helicopters cruised through the valley, hoist cables dangling. They were hauling wreckage.

A soldier materialized with a chair. The youngish man who'd been with Raffenelli came out of the house, approached with a briefcase, and sat. He said, "I'm Hilton Decter, Director General McMurtry's executive assistant." To Toby he extended a hand. "Congratulations, my man. You did a great service yesterday, telling us about the orb."

Toby shook hands with him.

"The director general asked me to brief you." Decter smiled guardedly. "The country, you might be interested to know, is a mess. A terrible mess. Worse than you imagine." He studied them. "I know, after what you've been through, you can imagine lots. But trust me. It's worse than you think. Much."

"Bombs went off?" Grace said.

Decter shook his head. "No. Mercifully, no further explosions have occurred. But your father did a number, young lady. Half the population thinks its Judgment Day." He opened the briefcase and took out a folder. Brow furrowed, he examined its contents. "A real number," he murmured. "Mantis is gone. Offices worldwide, they're stormed, trashed, demolished. We've got troops outside the factories. They're shooting on sight. In Holland . . . a mob immolated Mantis employees. Literally burnt them up, dozens of them, as if they were witches. People think the orb's the devil, I'm afraid. The Antichrist himself."

Toby and Grace exchanged startled glances.

"And it's just diabolical," Decter continued, "that we have to keep Mantis ads on the air to stop the bombs from going off." He sent Toby a pensive glance. "Trefethen planned it that way? So the orb would stay in the public mind?"

Toby said, "Seems like. What other reason would he have?"

Decter scowled at a small spot on his jacket sleeve. He tossed his folder to the grass and declared, "Two priorities. First, we need to know about the second icon."

"No problem," Toby said. "The rabbit."

"The rabbit?"

Toby nodded. "The fertility icon. A rabbit."

"Video format, I assume?" Decter inquired. "Like the orb?"

"I'm sure," Toby replied. "That it is, I mean, it's . . . "

Decter held up a hand. "We're in a state of video-sanitation," he remarked. "The measures we've taken are extremely comprehensive. We make dead certain we control all video content." He laughed. "Things will stay that way a while. A long while."

"Good," Toby said. "You should . . . "

Decter said, "Hold on. We'll get to it. Let's talk about something else a moment. Priority two, I'm afraid, can't wait." He pointed at the folder. "That's the outline of a script. It's still taking shape. But I can tell you this—if you're willing to play the roles I've assigned, we're prepared to be lenient."

Selma lit a cigarette she'd bummed from one of the guards. She had intended to save it. But now seemed as good a time as any to light up. "Lenient?" she said.

Decter looked at her, eyes impenetrable. "You've all violated various laws," he said. "We could make quite a case if we wanted to. But you see, we don't."

Harry said, "Tell us what you want."

Decter stared at the twins. "Mostly we need you two. But each of you can contribute." He glanced at the folder. "Our story is, you were up here the last few days. Watching everything, helplessly. Against your will."

"All of us?" Harry said. "Up here?"

"Do you want to cooperate?" Decter asked.

"Sure," Harry said.

"Then listen," Decter said. "Next," he went on, "and this concerns the twins especially—your father was a giant fraud." He eyeballed the twins. "You're with me?" he said.

Brian said, "More than you know."

Decter smiled. "All right. Good. So your father was a fraud. He made up the Antarctica stuff. From A to Z, he fabricated the notion that the ice sheet can collapse. Our story is that in actuality, the sheet's unmovable. The broadcast therefore was a scam. A con game, to panic the public. You're going to tell the public how completely he lied about it. You're going to say he was deceitful, manipulative, and full of shit. Any problem?"

The twins shrugged.

"Great," Decter said. "This will unfold over—I'm not sure, probably months, I foresee a major, intricate operation. Bigger than you realize, you don't know how important this is. Now. As to today, what we do first. You saw Perky Smith?"

They nodded. In the sky, a distant speck caught Toby's eye. A helicopter.

"Perky's here to tell the public that Martians haven't landed," Decter said. "A lot of people, you'd be amazed, they think the strangest things." He paused, scanning his audience. "It's nice she's here, because we can kick off the campaign right away. You won't say much. Just the fact you're alive, here in fraud headquarters, is enough. All you need do is look terrorized and pure-hearted and pretty and glad to be alive. Can you do it?"

"Yes," Dan said.

"Wait," Toby said. "What if the ice sheet goes?"

Philosophically, Decter spread hands through the air. "If it goes, it goes. But this is nature. Things take time. We might have ten, thirty, even a hundred years before it goes. Our scientists think five, minimum."

"Good," Toby said. "It means there's time to warn peo . . . "

"No!" Decter shouted vehemently. "No, no, *no!*"

His audience recoiled. Decter inhaled deeply. "Warning people, Toby, can come later. Much later. What we do first is convince the world that Trefethen lied. That's the crux. It's the only way we can stop the panic. Stop the riots, the sinking of the ships, people crashing their damn airplanes—we have to stop it right now. Which means not a shred of an indication that anything Trefethen alleged is true. Is that clear? I'll rephrase. Is that very, very, very, *very* clear?"

"Yes," Toby said. "How many ships have sunk?"

"Let's not get into it. Are you ready for the camera?"

All nodded. Decter pulled out a phone, punched buttons, and said, "Send her out." He took another deep breath, and said to Toby, "After she does the spot, you and the twins go to the technical staff. They'll grill you about the icon. They're anxious to start on that."

"Don't blame them," Toby said, watching the helicopter come closer. Something dangled from it at the end of a cable. A wheelchair, Toby saw. To Decter he said, "Is that Slotsky up there?"

Decter squinted skyward. "You bet," he said. On his smooth face, a cold smile settled. "I got word we found him fifteen minutes ago. It's super." He cast an appraising glance at his charges. "The public will like it. We caught every last fugitive."

68

The wheelchair descended to the mosaic in a gale of downdraft. Soldiers disconnected the cable; the helicopter zipped off. Decter ambled over to make an inspection of his newest prisoner. Men in white smocks strode across the courtyard. Orderlies followed, carrying medical kits. Slotsky's arrival was causing a stir.

To Toby, seated thirty feet away, the man looked almost, but not quite, dead. His eyes were closed. The cast on his leg had crumbled.

Bruises and welts exacerbated the horror of his facial disfigurement, of the stained patches covering it; he couldn't have been a ghastlier portrait of monstrosity.

Perky Smith emerged from the house with General Raffenelli and Mary McMurtry. Camerapeople and techies trailed, toting equipment. "Congratulations, Hilton!" Perky called. "You've got Slotsky!"

Decter was staring at the rank patchwork on Slotsky's face. "Take a look," he said to Perky as she came closer. "He's picture-perfect. A triple-mint villain."

"I have to agree," Perky said. She glanced at the other prisoners. Selma's battered boots caught her eye. "They're cute, too," she murmured. "Triple-mint victims." To McMurtry she said, "We keep it simple, Ms. Director General?"

"Keep it quick," McMurtry replied. "The President's arriving in a matter of hours."

The TV crew set up for satellite feed. "Do you want a rehearsal?" Decter asked Perky.

She said, "No. I want it raw—this will go out live."

"This too?" General Raffenelli said.

"It's the first glimpse of the abused kids," Perky replied. "The networks will announce a special report. This one, I guarantee, they'll rebroadcast all week. Look at them, General. It's priceless." She said to a woman with the crew, "Make the call, Felicia." Then she turned to Toby and said, "How's my cast doing?"

Toby regarded her with confusion.

"Doing great," Perky observed. "Let's see—stand up, all of you." The cast stood. "Look miserable. You've been through hell. You've been prisoners here."

"Some of us were," Dan said.

"Cooperation," Decter said remindingly.

"Just look like a prisoner," Perky said. "And except for brief, preferably monosyllabic replies to my questions, keep your mouth shut. Can you manage it, Dan?"

"Yeah," he said.

"Felicia?" Perky said.

Felicia listened to her headset. "Forty seconds," she said.

"General Raffenelli, Ms. Director General?" Perky said. They joined her before the camera. A makeup man retouched their faces.

"Ten seconds," Felicia called.

"Stand by," Perky ordered.

"On air," Felicia said.

With glorious poise, Perky informed the camera, "This is Perky Smith reporting live from Beast headquarters, from terror central here in Cheswick, Connecticut. We continue with the first look at the evil that General Theodore Raffenelli has uncovered in the palatial estate of none other than the billionaire Martha Cliffcloud. General—you're feeling triumphant?"

"Perky," Raffenelli replied, "I've said to you before, but I'll say it again—this is a special moment. We all, of course, feel triumphant. The nightmare is over."

"Have you recovered from the assault? Earlier, you spoke of hand-to-hand combat through these hills."

"It was grueling, Perky," said the general. "But we did it."

Perky turned to McMurtry and said, "I'm overcome, thinking of how grateful the world is for what you accomplished here." Her eyes moistened. "The operation went smoothly?"

"Without a hitch," McMurtry declared.

"I understand you found a prison under this house."

McMurtry nodded. Felicia signaled the cameraman. He pulled back to include the freshly liberated prisoners. To the camera Perky said, "Whom did the general discover in the prison? Well here they are—faces the public will recognize. The Trefethen twins, Toby Swett, Dan Swett, Selma Swearingen, and . . . who are you, sir?"

"Harry Stein."

"How do you feel, Harry?"

"Glad to be alive."

Perky turned to Selma. "Selma Swearingen. We've heard about you. But you haven't been going out to nightclubs, have you?"

"Uh," Selma said. "No."

"You've been suffering at the hands of the Trefethen terrorists!" Out of camera view, but in Selma's line of sight, Smith moved a hand suggestively. "What was it like?"

"Horrible," Selma muttered.

Perky moved on. "Here's Dan Swett! Hello, Dan. You look like you could use some sleep."

Dan said, "I didn't get much last night."

"You were trembling with terror. Weren't you?"

"I trembled," Dan said expressionlessly. "All over."

"And here are the abused children!" Perky exclaimed. "The twins themselves! Are you holding up, you poor things?"

The twins nodded.

"Grace, Brian, how does it feel—to have a father who could spin such fantasies? With such diabolical deceit?"

Simultaneously, Grace and Brian shrugged.

"Speechless," Perky observed. "But who can give voice to the unspeakable?" She turned to Toby and said, "Last but not least—Toby Swett! Toby, Toby, Toby—do you have any idea what a hero you are? Do you have even the faintest idea?"

Toby cleared his throat.

"Toby, what did they do to your eyes?"

"I'm not sure," he said.

Perky said, "Let's pull in." The camera came closer. Unenthused about being an exhibit for this awful woman, but wanting, somehow, to cooperate, Toby rolled his eyes; and saw, as he rolled, that a commotion had developed around the wheelchair.

"Looks to me like they tortured you, Toby. Did they?"

Toby nodded. The doctors were doing something to Slotsky.

"Tell us about it. The world wants to know."

"Helen Scarf Roto-rootered my brain," he said. "Uh—Perky—I think Slotsky is having a fit."

"Thank you, Toby, for introducing our next attraction." To the camera she said, "Not only do we have victims here. We also have a fiend." Felicia directed the camera to Slotsky. "None other than the notorious gangster, Slotsky! Toby, how do you feel about Slotsky?"

"Well, he tried to kill me. He tried to kill all of us."

"Really?" Perky said. "Come. Let's take a look."

The entire group moved to the wheelchair. A doctor held an oxygen mask over the bandages; Slotsky's breath was labored. Toby saw his eyelashes flicker. Something lit behind them; he began breathing more deeply. His eyes flitted over the assembly of former quarry and victims. And settled on Selma.

On her boots, Selma realized.

Slotsky seemed to choke.

"The drama escalates," Perky confided to the camera.

Slotsky's eyes bulged. Selma sidled behind Harry.

Perky said, "What's wrong with him? Guilt, maybe?"

"I doubt it," Toby said. He couldn't see the man now. The doctors were removing his jacket and shirt.

Perky peered at the patient. With a gesture she directed the cameraman to come in for a close-up. "Let the world decide," she said. "Does

Slotsky, in this moment of humiliation, feel remorse? He looks upset to me—Doctor, what's that under his shirt?" She peered closer. The camera peered with her. "Some kind of ID? It's a plastic pouch . . . with something in it. General, you should have a look at this."

Raffenelli looked, and said, "It's a photo of Toby Swett."

"*What?*" Toby yelled. He sent Grace an electrified glance, and bellowed, "Turn off the camera!"

No one seemed to hear him. Smith, her cameraman, Raffenelli, McMurtry, Decter, and the doctors now barricaded the wheelchair. Toby pushed through soldiers standing by.

The soldiers seized him. "Let go!" Toby yelled.

"The oddest thing!" Perky exclaimed. "In a pouch hanging from his neck, Slotsky carries a photograph—of his victim! Can we get a closeup of that?"

"*No!*" Toby shouted.

Perky turned to him. She said sweetly, "Toby, it's a photo of *you*. Of course that infuriates you . . . why don't you tell us about it?" She gestured at the soldiers.

They let Toby go. He jammed himself between doctors to get a look. His blood froze as he saw it.

From Slotsky's hairy neck, a clear plastic pouch dangled. It held the fourth Polaroid—the one Helen Scarf hadn't found. The one showing the rabbit so clearly against his white shirt.

The camera was drinking it in.

Toby slapped both his hands on the pouch.

Perky cried, "Restrain yourself!"

Toby shouted, "It's the low-tech icon! The rabbit, the fertility icon, the *Beast's other face!* The primitive face—the one meaning overpopulation!"

"Cut the camera," Decter said. Horrified silence descended.

The camera cut. Horrified silence continued. Decter barked at Toby, "It's not video!"

It is now, Toby thought.

Decter pulled out his telephone. Toby pressed the pouch harder into Slotsky's chest. He didn't trust the camera.

Someone touched his shoulder. Keeping his hands on the pouch, he turned. Gray eyes blazed into him. "You did it," Grace whispered. "You iconified. Again."

Toby noticed that Decter, Raffenelli, and McMurtry were staring at him. He stared back. Yeah, he thought. I did do it.

He discovered he was glad.

Decter made a phone call. Nervously, Raffenelli watched. McMurtry, face frozen, continued to stare at Toby. It's like she got hit with Helen's spray, Toby thought. He said to her, "How could you allow this to happen?"

McMurtry whispered, "What has happened?"

Toby became aware of his hands. He still had them on Slotsky's chest. They were vibrating. Because the chest was vibrating. The man was breathing oddly . . . his chest vibrated harder.

Slotsky, Toby realized, was laughing.

EPILOGUE

The icon came flying from space.

It penetrated the upper atmosphere, it dove further through howling wind and cloud. Then it hit the ice sheet.

The ice sheet didn't care. Vast, unfeeling, mute, it had been lying there, accumulating, for hundreds of thousands of years.

But on several of the higher plateaus, instruments detected the icon. The instruments decoded. They processed. And in less than a millisecond of thorough cross-checking, they came to life.

Commands, cable-borne, flashed vertically through the ice. Deep the commands went, to mountains that rose from the rock below. To volcanoes.

Millennia before, these volcanoes had erupted in open air. Now they slept in the sheet's stillness; the command flew down their cones, to the places where the devices were waiting.

The devices exploded.

On the surface, ice shuddered.

Miles below, rock vaporized, ice vaporized, to global diameters of several thousand feet. Beyond that, rock and ice melted more hundreds of feet, and the shapes of the explosions began to change; for the rock, as the blasts enlarged, yielded less willingly than did the ice.

These infernos—liquid rock, boiling water, and steam, cubic miles of it—looked for somewhere to go.

At the surface, gigantic domes slowly rose. In the domes fissures appeared, from which vapor streamed.

Below, the explosions nudged fault lines in the continental crust.

The faults slipped, releasing more energy, earthquakes. In all directions for hundreds of miles, the ice sheet shivered, its adhesion to the earth undone.

The volcanoes' subterranean magma chutes filled, and erupted. Lava smashed into the infernos, into the places where moments before, mountains had towered in the ocean of ice.

The domes on the surface disintegrated. Fiery cauldrons, miles deep, miles wide, crammed vapor into the sky.

Gravity took hold.

The ice sheet, shuddering, commenced a mammoth slide into the sea.